PHARAOH'S GOLD

ALSO FROM ALCON PUBLISHING
AND TITAN BOOKS

SubOrbital 7 by John Shirley
Vertical by Cody Goodfellow

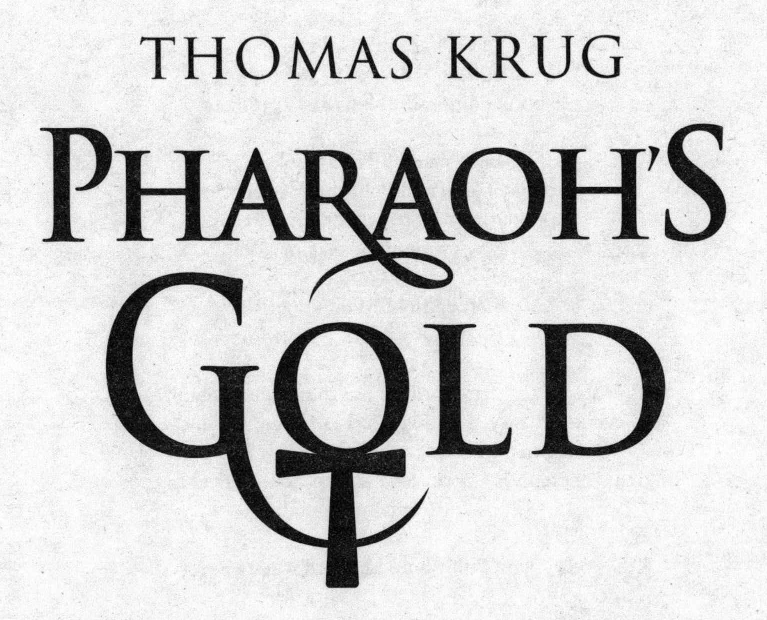

A NOVEL OF ANCIENT EGYPT

TITAN BOOKS

Pharaoh's Gold
Print edition ISBN: 9781803366203
E-book edition ISBN: 9781803366210

Published by Titan Books
A division of Titan Publishing Group Ltd
144 Southwark Street, London SE1 0UP
www.titanbooks.com

First edition: March 2024
10 9 8 7 6 5 4 3 2 1

This is a work of fiction. All of the characters, organizations, and events portrayed in this novel are either products of the author's imagination or are used fictitiously. Any resemblance to actual persons, living or dead (except for satirical purposes), is entirely coincidental.

Typeset by Charlie Mann.
Map illustration by Cheryl Bowman.

A CIP catalogue record for this title is available from the British Library.

Printed and bound CPI Group (UK) Ltd, Croydon, CR0 4YY.

Once night had fallen, an army of field mice swarmed
through the Assyrians' camp and chewed up
their quivers,bowstrings, and even the handles
of their shields, so that the next day,
the enemy found themselves
deprived of their weapons and defenseless.

—Herodotus, *Histories* 2.141

DRAMATIS PERSONAE

THE DESERT MICE

Pisaqar – *The Captain*
Tariq – *The Redhead*
Qorobar – *The Axe Man*
Ermun – *The Priest*
Kalab – *The Acolyte*
Amani – *The Thief*
Nawidemaq – *The Medicine Man*
Yesbokhe – *The Archer*
Pakheme – *The Good One*
Apis – *The Beast of Burden*
Nibamon – *The Foreman*
Eleazar – *The Traitor*

THE KUSHITE LORDS OF EGYPT

Pharaoh Shabaku – *King of Egypt*
Shebitku – *Crown Prince*
Taharqa – *General of the Army*

THE HOUSE OF SAIS

Senanmuht – *Saite Nobleman, Advisor to General Taharqa*
Khaemon – *Saite Nobleman*

THE KINGDOM OF JUDAH

Hezekiah – *King of Judah*
Isaiah – *Advisor*

EGYPT

Senet – *Sister to Nibamon*
Rukhmire – *Guardian of the Valley, Senet's Husband*
Sabef – *Gangster*
Pepy-Nakht – *The Boatmaster*

ASSYRIA

Sennacherib – *King of Assyria*
Ashurizkadain – *The Flayer of Caleb*
Nimrud – *Office*

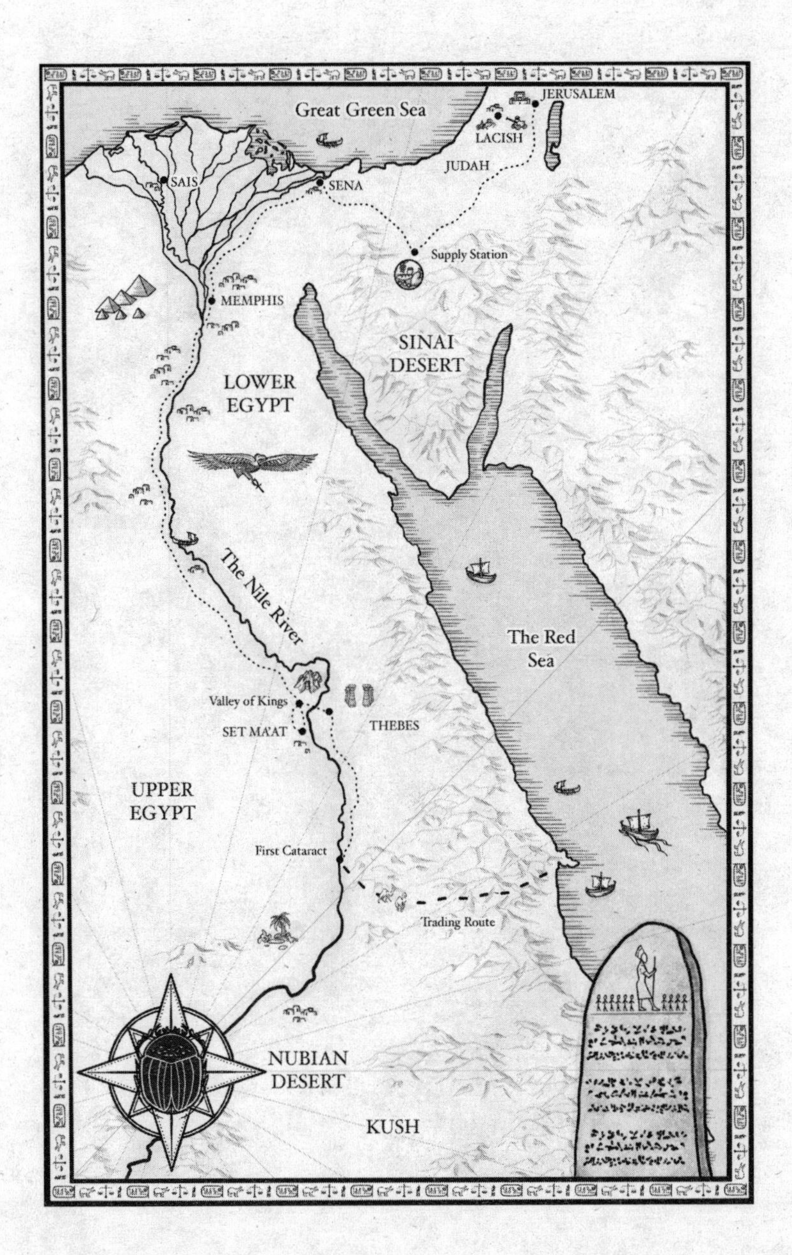
Great Green Sea
JERUSALEM
LACISH
JUDAH
SAIS
SENA
Supply Station
MEMPHIS
SINAI DESERT
LOWER EGYPT
The Nile River
The Red Sea
Valley of Kings
SET MA'AT
THEBES
UPPER EGYPT
First Cataract
Trading Route
NUBIAN DESERT
KUSH

THE GNAWING MICE

THE CART LURCHED and squealed as its wheel snagged on yet another jutting rock. "My apologies," Eleazar winced at his passengers, though he heard no complaint from the clustered amphorae. The tall clay jugs rattled before resuming their quiet. He squinted at the climbing Judean road, or what little he could make out in the light of the quarter moon. What he saw was rocks. The whole country was made up of rocks, big and small, every one of them jagged sharp. He expected it wouldn't be much longer before his pilfered cart simply disintegrated from Judah's onslaught.

He caught scent of his destination before he sighted it. The breeze carried the sweet aroma of burning olive wood over the hills—and the uniquely hideous stench of a besieging army. The latter was almost enough to make him retch, no matter how many times he'd smelled it before.

As he rounded a bend, the Assyrian camp came into view. The *enemy* camp, he remembered with a quickening heart. The flickering orange light of dying campfires outlined its palisades, just enough illumination to make out the shapes of the rotting heads dangling by their ringlets from the archers' perches. *Slain hostages*, Eleazar thought, or perhaps merely some unfortunates who hadn't reached the city before it shut its gates to the enemy. A statement of intent, either way, for the Judean heads hung within sight of Jerusalem's walls. Little doubt they'd been ritually decapitated as their countrymen looked on in horror.

No, my *countrymen*, he reminded himself. As if to accentuate the point, a sentry shouted from the wall, announcing the approach of a mysterious cart. There was no turning back now.

"Halt there!"

Eleazar yanked the reins until the ass lurched to a reluctant stop. Behind him, the amphorae rattled.

Forcing himself not to panic, he waved at the sentry atop the gate, fully cognizant of the arrowhead trained on his clenched grin. Surely the hollow noise had given him away. He was going to end the night spread-eagled between two stakes, skinless and howling.

"Who is your master?" demanded the sentry.

He replied in perfect Akkadian. "Sennacherib, the great king, the mighty king, king without rival, righteous shepherd, lover of justice, neck stock that bends the insubmiss—"

"Where did you come from?" the sentry interrupted, with a suppressed cough.

"From Lacish. Have you not heard of our king's victory there? He sends water and loaves to aid your siege. I am the first in a great procession."

He could practically hear the sentry running his tongue over his chapped lips. "A procession?" He turned and said to someone else, "Sennacherib has sent us water! Hilti, bring the quartermaster!"

After a brief exchange, the crossbar was lifted, and the gate ground open. Eleazar coaxed the laggard animal across the bridge and into the dim camp. A second soldier watched him pass with yellowed eyes before heaving the gate shut behind him.

"Greetings," nodded Eleazar, "and to you as well. It is good to meet two new friends at the end of my long travels."

"You have a queer way of speaking, friend," said the first sentry as he got off his ladder. The two of them loped up with their spears on their shoulders, alternating their wary gazes between driver and cart.

"Forgive my weariness. Lacish is far away."

The jaundiced one rapped his spear shaft on the stopper of one amphora. Eleazar just managed not to flinch. "Water, you say? This jar sounds empty."

Eleazar forced out a laugh. "These Judean potters do such shoddy work. Why, I would be blessed if just a few of these vessels survived the journey." He thought quickly. "Come, you both look thirsty. Let us water ourselves before your officers arrive to take it all. A few gulps would not be missed."

They exchanged a glance. "Hilti is taking his time," commented one.

"The bean counter must still be wrapped up in his bedroll." They turned their mischievous faces on him. "Very well. Quickly!"

Eleazar hopped off the cart with a loud grunt and stomped around to the tailgate, flanked by the eager-faced soldiers. He made a great show of heaving one amphora to the edge of the flatbed. "Here, lend me your hands so we can lower this to the ground without smashing it." The soldiers put down their spears. They braced their legs and began to lift the amphora together.

"This one barely weighs a thing!" protested the jaundiced one.

Eleazar cried, "Be careful, by Amun!"

"What?!"

At Eleazar's last word, the cart came alive. Dark figures sprang up from the concealed space in the center of the cart bed, the tops of the false jugs still teetering on their heads. The soldiers gaped in astonishment with the empty amphora in their arms. The intruders raised longbows, and with a staccato of *thwack*ing strings, drove half a dozen arrows into the Assyrians' bodies. They crashed to the ground writhing. One of the figures leaped down and silenced their groans with deft slices across their throats.

Eleazar lay prone as his nine passengers wordlessly dismounted. He felt a nudge in his ribs and found an ebon-skinned hand offered to him. Shakily, he allowed himself to be pulled standing.

The Kushite nudged his bearded chin at the dead. "Conceal the bodies."

A lumbering giant of a man dragged the limp corpses into the wall's shadow, just as the sound of footsteps presaged company. From amid the tents, a quartet of Assyrians approached, three of them spearmen wearing the typical funnel helmets and scale armor, the last swathed in a long robe with a clay tablet cradled in his elbow.

Eleazar glanced around in rising panic, only to realize he was alone. The Kushites had vanished.

"Ashur keeps vigil," greeted the clerk, stifling a yawn.

Bewildered as he was, Eleazar knew the response by rote. "He punishes the wicked."

One of the soldiers slowed his pace. "Where are Ea and Saris?"

"Ah … they … have begun unloading the water." Had the Kushites all simply gone off without him? Trying not to show his swelling anxiety, he flicked his gaze to the rows of conical tents a good stone's throw away. He might be able to make that sprint. He wouldn't elude capture for long, though. One shout was all it would take to awaken the camp around him.

The soldiers didn't fail to see through the sham. They halted, dropping their spears to the ready. One grabbed the oblivious clerk's robe to stop him. "They would not leave their posts," he asserted. "What have you done?"

The Kushites spared Eleazar from devising another sorry lie. Their arrows hurtled out of the shadows, the well-aimed shots piercing the Assyrians' necks. The enemies toppled with fine sprays of blood. A cluster of mercenaries descended on their shuddering forms, stabbed them into stillness, and then dragged them off. The Kushite girl slunk in and swiftly gathered up the fallen spears and helmets. Eleazar was left to contemplate the bloodstained dirt where living men had just stood.

He was still trying to adjust when the Kushites returned. The mercenaries—the Desert Mice, they called themselves—wore a motley assortment of Assyrian garb, none correctly. The smiling redheaded one, Tariq, had somehow managed to get his scales on backward. He seemed to have given his helmet to the big angry one, Qorobar, who was still bare-chested. The girl, Amani, hadn't bothered to disguise herself at all. She still wore her mouse-skin vest. Neither had Nawidemaq, the medicine man, whose chalked skin made him so distinctly foreign that Eleazar was somewhat amazed they'd brought him at all. The pair of priests—Ermun, the elder, and Kalab, his acolyte—at least wore complete sets of armor, though the crescent swords slung at their belts gave them away. Eleazar felt another nudge. Yesbokhe, the scout, held the dead scribe's clay tablet beneath his nose.

Eleazar took it. He added sheepishly, "It will not make sense without the hat."

Yesbokhe merely shook his head, where the scribe's pointed cap teetered precariously.

Pakheme patted his arm. "Don't worry about the costumes too much, Eleazar. They don't have to make sense." He grinned reassuringly. "They just need to give the Assyrians pause."

"He *is* an Assyrian," Amani muttered. "The sooner we finish our business with him here, the better."

"He is a friend to Egypt," Pisaqar said, calm and firm. The mercenary captain stepped into the midst of their cluster. "He has done his part without complaint. Now we must do the same." He pointed at the camp. "To it, all of you."

The mercenaries needed no further encouragement. They darted off in singles and pairs, their drawn blades glinting in the moonlight, a last brief glimpse before they all vanished into the sleeping camp. Eleazar almost shuddered at the thought of the mayhem they were about to inflict on the army he had once served.

Only Pisaqar remained. "You know the rest, Eleazar?"

"I know it."

"We are still counting on you. As are your people." To the east lay the gleaming walls of Jerusalem. The Judeans didn't know it yet, but their hour of deliverance had arrived—borne by the hands of nine Kushites and one nationless transplant.

"I will not fail," promised Eleazar.

The mercenary gave a shallow nod, and with a glint of plundered armor, he vanished into the night.

There was no art to strangling a man.

Tariq hauled on the bowstring, its twisted cord biting deep into his palms. His victim kicked furiously, with strength enough to briefly propel their joined bodies into the air. The Assyrian's full weight came down on him and drove the back of his head into the rocky soil. Silver sparkled at the edges of his vision, but he gritted his teeth and cinched the string even tighter.

That was the trick, really, not that it could be called a trick in full honesty. Persistence. And brute strength. And wanting it more.

That bothered Tariq. The fact that he'd done this any number of times, and he'd never found an easier way. Choking the life out of someone was always exhausting and ugly and sickening. He felt nauseous as the enemy soldier grasped at his face, his sweat-coated palms running over his cheeks and brows with slick noises. It sounded loud, the rasps too. He was sure the man's tentmates would come out to investigate any instant.

He knew he'd won when the Assyrian quit driving his heels into his shins. The strength had gone out of him. The man made a last sluggish effort to worm his body free, but Tariq wrapped his legs around him and held him fast until his muscles went slack. Only then did the redheaded mercenary let the cord go.

He let himself pant there for a bit, too tired to roll the

drooling corpse off. When his wits came back, he cast about for a place to dispose of the body. There—a circle of stones. A well. Huffing, he dragged his burden along the quiet rows of tents. He raised a cringeworthy racket. His sandals flung jagged pebbles in all directions, plinking against the leather tents lining the way. The Assyrians could be forgiven for sleeping through that—months in the Judean hills would have inured them to the sound of crunching stone—but the sound of dead weight scraping on gravel? He was somewhat amazed the dead man himself didn't stir.

Coming to the well, he pushed the body to a sitting position and heaved it up onto the low wall. He unwound the cord from its neck, then added it to the bag with the other bowstrings he'd already collected. "Sorry for the trouble, friend," he said. A gentle push sent the Assyrian toppling backward—only to land almost immediately with a dull smack, legs still dangling over the side.

Tariq grumbled to himself as he peeked into the well. The whole shaft had been filled up with rocks. "Shitting *shit*."

"What'd you say to me?" whispered Amani.

He recoiled, followed by her amused gaze. "Fuck! Where'd you sneak in from?"

She held up a fistful of bowstrings. "I was working. I haven't had to kill anyone yet, either."

"Alright. But *did* you?"

"Maybe. Yes. Why'd you go through all the trouble of hiding this one?" She pointed to the protruding feet.

"He was coming out for a piss or something. Bumped into me. I can't exactly lay him down with his tentmates again, can I?"

"So instead, you thought you'd just stuff him down a well."

"That was my plan, except this one's all filled up with rocks. Judeans must have done it to every well outside their city. Clever of them."

"How'd you figure that?"

"Because these Assyrians are all dying of thirst."

"Hmm." She nodded. "Anyway. What do you want to do about this?"

"Well, I'm not pulling him back out, that's for certain." After a good deal of cursing, Tariq succeeded in shunting the dead Assyrian's stiffening limbs below the lip of the well. He tossed some fistfuls of dirt on top as a passing attempt at concealment. "Good enough," he pronounced.

"Now if we're finished wasting time, we have a lot more bowstrings to steal."

Qorobar and Pakheme squatted in the shadows, doing their best to ignore the sounds coming from the latrine—to say nothing of the smell. No, not even a smell. A *flavor*. Even holding his nose tight, Qorobar could feel the tang of fermented Assyrian sewage smearing itself onto his tongue.

Pakheme elbowed him lightly as the grunting in the walled latrine approached its crescendo. His grimace and lifted brows said it all. *Is that shitting or fucking?*

Qorobar lifted his free hand, equally appalled. On the other side of the wall, the noise ceased. A few moments later, an Assyrian stumbled out, pulling up his trousers. Another trailed behind. They stole wary glances around before slinking off in opposite directions.

The pair of Kushites rose from their hiding place.

"Balls of Amun," said Qorobar. "Imagine having a go over a shit trench."

"Ah, young love," Pakheme chuckled. He pointed his sword at a domed tent that loomed above the rest. "Shall we?"

"For fuck's sake, let's." Qorobar's sack rustled as he hoisted it over one shoulder.

They crept along the rows of tents, pausing at the odd noise—a hacking cough, a feverish groan. As they approached the great tent, they spotted a soldier stationed at the entrance.

He had his helmet tipped back on his head in order to doze with his brow against his spear, awakening every so often to scratch furiously at his balls. He must have been crawling with lice, just as all these Assyrian bastards were. Qorobar could feel the little pests skittering around the lining of his stolen helmet, which was bad enough, but he could only imagine the misery of wearing a full set of armor infested with the damn things.

Occupied as he was, the soldier didn't fail to note their approach. His bronze helmet glinted in the moonlight as he straightened it. Qorobar willed himself not to reach for his axe as the soldier spoke to them. He didn't know Akkadian, but the tone had that universal chummy quality of one soldier bitching to another. Both Qorobar and Pakheme played along. They chuckled heartily, closing the distance.

The Assyrian spoke again, this time in the interrogative. Qorobar made a grunt that he hoped sounded affirmative. Pakheme faked a laugh.

Now the soldier had grown suspicious. He lifted the butt of his spear out of the dirt, repeating his question.

Pakheme answered. In one expert motion, he unslung and drew his bow. The soldier gasped. He reached for the shield leaning against a tent pole, but too late. The arrow split his skull with a crack. The Assyrian went rigid and toppled over, wrists coiled like a dead insect.

"Nice shot," muttered Qorobar.

"He didn't feel it," Pakheme said by way of agreement. Qorobar put an end to the man's convulsions with a stroke of his axe. Then he put down his lumpy sack and shoved the fallen helmet inside, adding to his growing collection. Pakheme blew out his cheeks disapprovingly, at which Qorobar merely rolled his eyes. *Bring proof of your deeds*, Pisaqar had instructed them. What was he supposed to do, cut off their pricks like the old pharaohs used to? A man deserved a little more dignity in death than that, even if he was only a sandal-licking Assyrian.

They rolled the dead man out of sight. Deed done, they readied themselves at the tent flap. Inside, Qorobar could hear someone grunting in rhythm with the sigh of hay. Downright rude, interrupting a fellow's stroke, but a tent of this size could only mean officer's quarters. That changed things. Some impoliteness was in order.

Pakheme drew his sword while Qorobar hefted his axe. They exchanged nods, then swept through the flap.

No one was there to meet them. Just a dingy corridor lined with curtained stalls, the smell of sex and shame. Pakheme nudged one curtain aside with the point of his sword and recoiled with a silent hiss. A naked woman lay curled on the filthy straw, staring listlessly at her bound wrists. She didn't seem to care about the fat lice slinking in and out of her curls. The only hint of awareness was the way she drew her knees in tighter against her chest as she felt their eyes on her.

Pakheme closed the curtain, his expression grim. He jutted his chin toward another closed stall, where the grunts were coming from. He whispered into Qorobar's ear, "Don't let her see it."

Qorobar stomped up to the noisy stall and rapped on the crosspiece. Inside, a man snarled what must have been a strong oath. Dispensing with politeness, Qorobar barreled through the curtain and hooked his axe handle under the indisposed client's jaw. The Assyrian warbled as he dragged him out kicking and, unfortunately for him, prematurely. Pakheme shut the curtain again to spare the cringing girl the sight of her rapist's end. Qorobar didn't see it either, but he did feel the man's muscles go taut all at once as Pakheme opened him up. The earthy smell of entrails was added to the general awfulness. Pakheme didn't draw out the suffering, though—just let the man feel the pain long enough to understand he was being punished, then ended his odious life with a thrust to the heart.

Qorobar let the corpse drop. "No helmet on this one," he lamented.

"Take his prick."

"Not interested." He settled for chopping off the right hand. Holding the severed appendage gingerly by the small finger, he made for the exit.

"What about the women?"

"I don't know. What about them?"

"We can't just leave them."

"We have to. There's a job to do, Pakheme. There's no time to be pulling strays along behind us."

"Think about what the Assyrians will do to them after tonight."

Qorobar was about to retort when he saw that the first stall was open again. The woman there had come out as far as her lead line would let her. Her dark eyes were fixed on him. She whispered something—in Akkadian, Babylonian, Median, they all sounded the same to his ears. But he understood her open palms. She was pleading with him.

He heard cloth ripping and whirled, axe coming up. Pakheme had torn a curtain off its pole and held it out to the second girl, his eyes averted. She took it and wrapped it shakily around herself, which was when Qorobar noticed Pakheme had already sliced her bonds. The other stall curtains were sliding open one by one. Just like that, they'd added half a dozen souls to their little escape plan.

"Pakheme, this is a mistake. This isn't part of Pisaqar's plan."

"Pisaqar taught me I must always do what's right. Not sometimes, not at my own convenience." Pakheme went along the rows, sawing the women's wrists free. "Always. Come, help them."

Qorobar grumbled. There was a glow of pride that warmed his heart, no doubt of that—but mostly, he felt worry and consternation. Cursed foreign lands just like this one were pocked with the unmarked graves of Egyptians who'd died doing the right thing.

☥

The horns of Yesbokhe's bow clicked against the stones. He stopped dead and clung to the masonry, sucking air between his teeth. He watched the parapet, but no sentry appeared.

For a moment he was back in Siwa, hanging beneath Kasaqa's window as she reassured her father that the strange, quiet boy had not been back. He wondered what she would think to see her husband now.

He rolled his shoulders to adjust the position of his slung bow. With a deep breath, he felt for the next handhold and continued his ascent.

The Assyrians had constructed the watchtower on a hill that surmounted their siege camp, which was nestled in a narrow valley with either end walled up. They had built it higher than they needed—a signal of their dominance over this approach to the city—although for a climber of Yesbokhe's skill, the height was little obstacle. The porous stones sucked the moisture from his fingertips as he climbed, improving his grip, as if the Judean rocks were eager to undermine their occupiers.

Nearing the parapet, Yesbokhe paused once more. Just above him, he could hear a pair of men conversing in low voices. Two sentries, same as previous nights. Yesbokhe maneuvered into a comfortable position and let one arm dangle. His hand tingled as the blood flowed back in. Flexing his fingers, he switched grips, glancing over one shoulder as he did so.

Far below, the Israelite bobbed into view. Eleazar labored up the steps cut into the hill, a brace of waterskins slung over his shoulders. The sentries' conversation quickened. Yesbokhe heard wood creak, then heavy steps as one of the soldiers descended a ladder. The remaining Assyrian called down to the visitor, apparently asking his business. Eleazar indicated his burden in reply. If he noticed Yesbokhe curled in the shadows near the apex of the tower, he gave no sign.

Yesbokhe drew his knife. He took a steadying breath. He rapped the blade on stone. The sentry's follow-up question cut off, and he peeked over the edge. With a hard grunt, the scout lunged upward and delivered a rapid jab to the Assyrian's neck. The bronze blade punched into his windpipe with an audible click. The man's eyes bulged, and he fell out of view. Yesbokhe clambered up and over the parapet. He dropped onto the twisting Assyrian, who gargled horribly through the hole in his neck as the Kushite's knee pressed the air from his lungs. Yesbokhe kept one hand over his mouth until the twitching stopped.

He supposed that Kasaqa would not be terribly pleased to witness him in this moment.

Shaking the blood from his hands, he took stock of his new position. A low fireplace cast the tower top in a dull orange glow, providing some warmth while preserving night vision. There were several urns, all stuffed with arrows. From this vantage, he could draw a line to any point on the palisades. He scanned the perches and noted approvingly that all were vacant. The Mice had done excellent work.

Below, Eleazar was speaking to the now lone sentry, who was happily emptying a waterskin down his gullet. It would have been the ideal moment to strike, but the Israelite's sword remained sheathed. The moment stretched until, with some annoyance, Yesbokhe unslung his bow. Close to the tower as they were, the angle of the shot was not ideal. Yesbokhe had to sit backward on the edge and lean far over, aiming straight down. The arrow, when it came, went right down the sentry's collar. Heart-shot, the man plummeted. Eleazar was left standing alone, shoulders drooped and staring glumly at one who he once would have called a comrade. He looked up at Yesbokhe, nodded—an apology, the scout surmised—and started back down the steps in search of other former comrades to betray.

Yesbokhe watched him. He found that he pitied the poor fellow.

With morning near, there was little time to spare. He drew an arrow from the urn, wadded its point in fabric cut from the slain Assyrian's tunic, and held it in the fireplace until it caught light. With a snap of a bowstring, he sent his arrow arcing high into the air. A few moments later, he followed up with another.

From the walls of distant Jerusalem, a torch waved.

Eleazar was alarmed to discover that the horse pens were nearly all vacant. The remaining horses—four in all—peeked curiously over their gates, roused by noises in the camp that only their keen ears could detect. Like their Assyrian masters, the beasts were in a parlous state, at least judging by their dull hides. He suspected the other horses had wound up in the Assyrians' kitchen pots.

The lone groom was still squinting at the tablet Eleazar had handed him, trying to make something of the jagged text stamped into the moist clay. "What did you claim this said?"

It said exactly nothing. The fact that the groom hadn't picked up on the gibberish told Eleazar that he was merely pretending he knew how to read. "It orders you to make ready the horses."

"Who orders this? To what end?"

Eleazar found that his well-rehearsed answer no longer applied. The Kushites had been certain there were enough horses to seat them all. Their escape was in jeopardy. Casting about for a solution, Eleazar spotted a roofed enclosure with a bulky object sitting beneath, draped with cloth.

He tamped down a rush of relief before telling the groom, "The Tartan has demanded you prepare his chariot. Why must you dare to question his reasons?"

"The Tartan orders this in writing?" the groom said doubtfully. "The *bedridden* Tartan."

Eleazar smothered an upswell of sickly panic. "He does indeed. If you, a simple groom, opt the route of disobedience, I am content to inform him thus."

The groom mulled this over, but didn't take long. He passed the tablet back. "Stay here."

Eleazar relaxed his grip on the dagger hidden up the sleeve of his stolen robe—but he didn't let go. He knew, just as surely as the groom, the penalty for insubordination. And awful as that might have been, it was a stern spanking compared to the punishment Assyria reserved for traitors. The dagger was more for him than any of his one-time comrades.

The groom limped to the enclosure. With a flourish, he pulled off the cloth drape. A huge war chariot sat unveiled, its polished wood gleaming in the moonlight. Its wheels were easily the height of a man, and their studded rims and hook-bladed hubcaps made them weapons in themselves. More blades bristled beneath the bronze cab like diabolical coulters—an affectation, surely, because Eleazar couldn't imagine anyone surviving the crushing hooves of the horses that preceded it. The cab itself, plated in bronze, had ample space for an equal number of men, and quivers enough for seemingly hundreds of arrows. It was a wondrous, horrible machine, which Eleazar didn't have the faintest clue how to operate. Did the Kushites?

He kept throwing nervous glances to the east as the groom led the horses, one at a time, to their yokes. The constellation that the Kushites named "the Lion" gradually cleared the blackened walls of Jerusalem. Their god Ra would soon come charging up behind it on his own chariot, bringing the dawn sun with him. It was nearly time.

"Look at the things these people can build," Ermun whispered, marveling at the massive siege engine. To humble Jerusalem, the Assyrians had built a terrible machine. Its slab-like sides were made of thick cedar planks paneled with wicker. Inside, an iron-shod battering ram hung on taut chains. Above it perched a domed siege tower tall enough to surmount Jerusalem's walls. From the tower's square windows, archers would be able to sweep the battlements of defenders while the gate was smashed open.

The artisans who had built the siege engine weren't difficult to find. They had laid out their sleeping mats inside it. It didn't take much campaigning to understand the luxury a solid shelter represented, and Ermun had been on far too many marches in his forty years. He knew well that any roof was preferable to a tent. Understanding bred empathy. He didn't relish the thought of killing these men. Yet these engineers, when they were finished with Jerusalem, might one day set themselves against the walls of Egypt's cities. This, he would not allow.

He positioned himself at the siege engine's open rear while his acolyte scaled the tower, using the wicker covers as hand and footholds. Kalab had balanced a smoking pan on one shoulder. The embers cast a red glow over his handsome features. He was grimacing with the effort of climbing one-handed. Nearing the siege tower's dome, he gripped the edge of a tiny square window and tipped the embers inside. A good number of them missed the window and tumbled down the side of the ram in a shower of orange sparks. Kalab propelled himself off his precarious perch and landed, catlike, swiping at the embers that had caught on his stolen armor.

Meanwhile, wisps of smoke began to spiral from the windows. Deep inside the tower, a flame burst into life. It spread quickly, gobbling through the wicker and cedarwood beams. By the time the engineers woke up, the front half of their siege engine was enveloped in fire. Alarmed cries competed to be heard above the crackling flames. In bleary panic, the men pushed for the exit.

The first one hopped to the ground and barely staggered two steps before Ermun's *khopesh* lopped his head from his shoulders. The one following tried to stop, his eyes round as he tried to comprehend the nightmare he'd awoken to, but the desperate men behind pushed him straight into Kalab's reach.

The acolyte cleaved his crescent blade deep into the man's collarbone, killing him amid a welter of crimson.

Ermun and Kalab had four decades of swordsmanship between them. The engineers died quickly and cleanly, as far as blades went. The last of them found himself trapped inside the burning tower, unable to decide which manner of death he preferred. Kalab ended the cowering man's dilemma with an arrow through both lungs, sparing him a long agony.

"Sekhmet," intoned Ermun as they faced the towering pyre, "forgive us the things we do for Egypt."

Kalab shook the gore from his khopesh. "The Lioness watches. You see?" He pointed the blade to the east, where the lion constellation had just begun to peek over the hills. Just in time, and exactly as Pisaqar had intended. The fact that they'd managed to kill the siege-masters and fire their engines simultaneously was merely a fortunate coincidence. On the far side of the camp, where the Kushites had first infiltrated, drums had begun to beat.

"Taharqa has come," Ermun told his acolyte. An enemy trumpet blew the alarm. The pair readied their swords and strode off, making straight for the trumpet as more added their notes to the cacophony. The Assyrians were mustering for battle.

The predawn air vibrated, thickened by the beating of war drums. Flint struck, sparks shot, fires caught and sprang alight. The flames danced, the Kushites too, their ululating battle whoops rising as they hopped in place, twirling their bows above their heads, arrows jangling in their quivers. With men such as these, Taharqa thought, how could war be anything but splendid?

"Sekhmet!" bellowed the general, lifting his arms to the Lion in the sky. "Witness my glory!" His archers howled their delight. "For the God-King! Spears, forward!"

All down the line, men echoed their general's call. The ranks of spearmen bulged as those nearest Taharqa began to advance. These, though, were no Kushites, but sons of the old nobility from the Lower and Upper Nile—families whom the great Pharaoh Piye had brought to compliance in decades past. Now, Pharaoh Shabaku had given them a chance to demonstrate their loyalty to the remade Egypt.

Their enthusiasm, Taharqa judged, was somewhat lacking.

Four hundred men he had brought to end the siege of Jerusalem. Yesterday, he had thought that enough to finish the wasted Assyrians. But the way those spears wavered...

If not for the drums, he imagined he might hear their leatherbound shields creak, twisting in anxious hands. The chattering of their bared teeth was lost in the din.

Angrily, Taharqa chased away his dismal thoughts. The sacrifices had been made. The plan was sound. Pisaqar and his famous mercenaries had been at work in that camp for hours. Victory was promised. All that remained was for Taharqa to grasp it.

A servant hurried forward and bowed, holding out a longbow. Taharqa took it. He nocked an arrow, which the servant lit with a torch. He drew the bow, and with a *thwack* of string, his arrow ascended into the night. His elite archers dipped their own arrows into the bonfires. There came a chorus of snaps and hisses, and flights of burning shafts arced over the marching Egyptian spearmen. Before the first volley had begun to descend, the next was airborne. Shouting with glee, the Kushite archers made the sky itself into a fiery river, which emptied without remit into the enemy stronghold.

If Pisaqar had done as he promised, victory was but a scrape away.

☥

The camp was a scene of bedlam. Men tumbled through the flaps of their smoldering tents, shunting on lousy armor. With practice born of ceaseless drill, they whisked spears from weapon racks, only to find their tips snapped off. Squads of archers frantically rifled through their satchels for spare strings, their useless bows lying in the dirt. Shouting junior officers charged into tents whose occupants had failed to rouse, then reappeared in a furor, adding their alarmed shouts to the din. Their men had gone west. They would awaken in Duat, the next world.

No one spared much thought for the pair of dark-skinned passersby. Tariq did his best to keep Amani's mouse-skin vest in sight as they threaded through the confused swarm, not that she was making it easy for him. She kept darting away at a crouch every time something caught her interest, then would return to the sound of screams, her blackstone knife dripping. Tariq flung coiled gumtree branches in their wake, caltrops from the plains of Kush whose thumb-sized thorns could pierce a sandal with ease. Assyrians collapsed as they blundered over them, clutching their soles and yelping.

He and Amani wasted little time. They headed for the prize: a bearded officer and his trumpeter, furiously attempting to rally their soldiers. The officer's gaze fell on the Kushites as they approached. The set of his shoulders spoke of relief. Finally, he must have thought, soldiers who moved with purpose! He raised his sword to greet them—

—just as Tariq caved his helmet in. The trumpeter stopped blowing and turned in surprise. Amani had already reached him. Her knife sliced the backs of his heels, and Kalab's sword smote his neck mid-fall. Tariq grabbed the fallen trumpet and tucked it under his armpit before sweeping on after Amani, having barely broken stride. They left behind a scene of milling confusion. He scattered some more gum thorns to hamper any soldiers who tried to follow.

The horizon was just lightening to purple as Ra's chariot drew near. The mayhem had scarcely begun. Across the camp, the trumpets were falling silent as the Desert Mice found them. Officers struggled to restore order, but there was little distinguishing their shouts from the uproar. Whenever Amani spotted one, she twirled her sling and cracked his skull with a whistling stone. Tariq, finding no officers near to hand, sliced through taut bowstrings wherever he saw them.

But the Assyrians were drilled professionals, and they could not miss the tattoo of war drums outside their main gate. Nor could they misplace the source of the flaming arrows falling among them, in quantities that only Kushite archers could provide. General Taharqa had come.

"Mitzrayim!"

The Assyrians were all taking up the same word. Tariq didn't know much Akkadian, apart from a few choice obscenities, but he recognized their name for Egypt.

Although the nighttime raid had caught the Assyrians badly off guard, open battle was something they understood. The news of the Egyptian attack didn't throw them into a panic, but instead focused their minds. In moments, the milling soldiers all pivoted on their heels and hurried for the gate to meet the attack. If it mattered to them that a not-insignificant number lacked usable shields or spears or bows, rising battle fever simply boiled their trepidation away. Their bellowing nearly drowned out Taharqa's drums.

A pitched battle soon raged in the purple dawn. The palisades were burning. Through newly formed gaps, Tariq could see lines of Egyptian spearmen pressing through the open gate. They overcame the first sparse defenders, only to encounter a mass of Assyrian infantry that swelled with each passing moment. A cascade of Kushite arrows fell into the growing press, sowing carnage. The Assyrians could only reply with scattered volleys. The Desert Mice had done their work well.

With the enemy fully engaged, now was time to escape. Tariq and Amani wordlessly pushed on through the emptying camp, headed toward a large blaze near the sally gate—and beyond it, the battered walls of Jerusalem.

It wasn't long before they bumped into company. Friendly company, gods be thanked. Qorobar's bulk was unmistakable, and Tariq recognized Pakheme from the way he moved. The gaggle trailing after them was a bit of a mystery.

"Green balls of Osiris, I almost killed you," snapped Qorobar, lowering his axe as Tariq's whistle faded.

"Well, you'd have tried your best, anyway," said Tariq, trading grins with Pakheme. He clapped his friend on the back.

Amani jutted her chin at the cluster of barefoot women and girls, all wrapped in threadbare fabric. "Who're they?"

Pakheme's expression turned bleak. "Judeans. We're rescuing them."

"Like fuck you are," said Amani. "There isn't time."

"It's not your decision to make," said Pakheme.

"Neither was it yours!"

"We need to leave. Now," snarled Qorobar. They followed his eyes. A group of Assyrians had taken notice. They were approaching at the double with lowered spears.

The Kushites ran. The Judean women scrambled after them, but they were in poor condition and struggling. Tariq and Pakheme stopped as often as they dared in order to loose arrows at their pursuers. Their shots forced the Assyrians to take cover behind their shields, punching through the rigid planks, but their efforts amounted to little. The starving women's shambling pace ensured that any ground they gained was soon lost as the Assyrians resumed the chase.

Pakheme's good heart, Tariq thought, was going to get everyone killed.

"There they are!" Qorobar yelled as they broke into a clearing. There were workshops and what looked to have been a battering ram, all ablaze. The air stank of charred meat.

"Where'd we get that thing from?" Tariq asked, baffled. The traitor, Eleazar, stood in the cab of an enormous chariot, grasping the reins of four rather scrawny chargers. Tariq had seen plenty of chariots before, especially the two-man machines Egyptian nobles preferred. But this monstrosity—bristling with pointy things—had the footprint of a large wagon and seemed capable of holding half a dozen soldiers. It might have even been an acceptable substitute for their planned horseback escape, if not for Pakheme's bloody conscience.

The other mercenaries had already filtered in from around the camp. Yesbokhe, with longbow in hand and several quivers of filched Assyrian arrows. Ermun and Kalab, their priestly robes swapped for lice-ridden Assyrian scales, their khopeshes bloody from a night's work. Nawidemaq, whose swarthy skin still carried hints of the chalk paste he hadn't quite scrubbed off, his strutting gait like that of an over-tall heron.

Pisaqar hurried to meet them. The captain was clutching at a long scratch across the chest of his stolen armor, and his teeth were bloody. Clearly, he'd killed someone important, judging by the jeweled dagger pommel protruding from his belt.

He beckoned to the newcomers. "There is space enough for all of us if—" He stopped to take it all in—their expressions, their breathlessness, the women following. He immediately understood that the situation had changed drastically.

"Put them onto the chariot," he said, pointing to the women.

As they brought the women forward, Eleazar studied them and let out a foreign oath. The women fixed their eyes on him, astonished to hear their own language from one who looked wholly Assyrian. They exchanged rapid words with him as he pulled them onto the chariot, though whatever they learned only seemed to add to their hopeless confusion. Had they been freed by Kushites, or Egyptians? Was this charioteer an Israelite, or an Assyrian?

The last woman clambered aboard the chariot, which creaked under its passengers' combined weight. Even if there had been room for any of the Kushites, Tariq doubted those malnourished horses could pull them.

"What about us?" asked Amani.

"We run."

Assyrians appeared from the tents just as the last of the Judeans was being pushed onto the chariot. A storm of arrows forced them to duck behind their shields. One shot slithered through a gap in a shield and left its owner writhing with an arrow driven beneath his cheekbone, a feat only Yesbokhe could have managed. Even then, the Assyrians kept up their advance.

"Go, Eleazar!" roared Pisaqar.

The Assyrian traitor held up the reins in confusion. "I have never driven a chariot!"

"It's the same thing as driving a cart!" yelled Tariq.

Eleazar was apoplectic. "No! It is not the same! You mad Kushites!"

"Best learn quickly!" said Pisaqar.

Eleazar looked ready to argue more, but Pisaqar gave him no choice. He lashed one of the lead horses with the flat of his blade. The team pulled the rattling chariot through the sappers' gate, leaving skittering rocks in its wake as its studded wheels tore them from the dirt. Waggling madly on its overburdened axle, the chariot disappeared amid the screams of its helpless passengers, Eleazar's included.

Tariq's bowstring was hot against his joints as he let fly his last few arrows in quick succession. More Assyrians fell, but reinforcements were pouring in, drawn to the flames and the noise. Judging by the lack of it on the far side of camp, Taharqa's assault had been emphatically repelled.

Had the plan gone off, the Desert Mice would have been halfway to the gates of Jerusalem already—but now everything was coming undone.

Pisaqar grabbed Tariq's arm. "Leave now!"

The other Kushites were sprinting for the sally gate, their quivers empty, casting off their various articles of pilfered Assyrian dress to distinguish themselves from the enemy. Tariq slung his bow and went after them. Qorobar and Pakheme were straining to haul the gate shut, but gave up and joined Tariq and Pisaqar as they hurtled past. Hot pain shot up Tariq's leg. He stumbled, his foot suddenly numbed, but Pakheme grabbed him under the armpit.

"Cover your head!" he huffed as they resumed running. The Assyrians were throwing rocks at them.

Yellow dawn had begun to creep over the city walls. The gatehouse was scarcely recognizable, it was so blackened with soot. Evidently the Assyrians had set great fires at its foundation in an attempt to undermine it. Slumped at or near the gate were no less than three siege engines, all reduced to charred wrecks. In the midst of them sat Eleazar in his chariot. He was shaking his fists at the barred gate and gesticulating to the bronze-clad horde flooding out from the siege camp, bent on grinding the Kushite wrongdoers against the walls of the city they'd tried to save.

"They're going to let us die," Tariq uttered in disbelief.

With a boom, the Judeans opened their gate. A great indignant cry went up from the Assyrian ranks as their enemy revealed themselves at last. A herd of squat horses appeared. The riders' crazed assortment of armor mocked Assyrian uniformity. With baying asses in tow, the Judean cavalry rode onto the valley road, making for their Kushite allies, who flapped and shouted to differentiate themselves as such. It worked. Sling stones whirred over Tariq's head and thudded against enemy shields. Archers rose from the battlements and let loose at the limits of their range. The barrage was a mere gust of wind compared to the Egyptian storm the Assyrians had weathered earlier in the night, but they were caught in the open and unable to reply. Their ranks convulsed, caught between the urges to retreat or pursue.

Tariq waved his arms at an approaching Judean horse. The soldier atop it—a swarthy fellow with a mane of black ringlets protruding from his helmet—swept in as close as he dared before dropping the reins of the donkey he was towing. The Judean fled. Pakheme thrust Tariq ahead of him and turned toward the encroaching Assyrians, reaching for his quiver. Tariq grabbed the reins, then clambered onto the donkey's back. To his dismay, the young animal tottered under his weight. It'd barely be able to carry him, much less two full-grown men.

He tried to wave down another Judean rider, but they were fully occupied with evading the advancing clusters of spearmen.

"Pakheme, I can run! Take the donkey!" Tariq swung his swelling leg back over the ass's neck, but the Assyrians had closed in. Pakheme turned to run, only to take a spear in the side. He spun halfway around and fell to one knee, mouth hanging open in shock. Tariq watched in horror as his friend fought to rise again. He never managed it. A second Assyrian strode up. With a tremendous slash, he opened Pakheme's body. Then the Assyrians closed around him, their swords falling and coming up red.

Tariq hauled on the reins and thrashed the donkey toward the gatehouse. He could barely see it through his tears. "No, no, no, no..." He could still see Pakheme's wet pink guts coiled around his knees. He knew he always would. "Not like that, no no..."

The next he knew, he was surrounded by roaring men. Strong arms closed around him and dragged him to the ground. He screamed, eyes shut. He didn't want to see them rip the intestines from his belly.

Someone slapped his cheek. "It is us, Tariq. You are safe."

That persuaded him to quiet down. He cracked his eyelids and saw golden sunlight dappling through the branches of an olive grove. Walls. Soldiers. Horses. A gate, barred shut.

Pisaqar gripped his arms. "You are in Jerusalem."

Qorobar shoved him aside and clasped Tariq's head in his enormous hands. "Tariq, why is Pakheme not with you? Where is he?"

Tariq took a shuddering breath. "Gone."

Qorobar went very still, his broad face etched with disbelief. Then his mouth twisted into a snarl. "You lie." His fingertips dug into Tariq's hair, gripping so tight that he could hear his skull creaking. "*You lie!*" he bellowed. "*Where is he?*"

"He's dead!" Tariq cried. Through the agony, he was dimly aware of the others surrounding them as they tried to pull Qorobar off him. Their fingernails dug furrows in his arms, but he didn't seem to feel the wounds.

Pisaqar lurched away. When he returned, he pressed the curve of Qorobar's own axe against his neck. "Let him go! Let him go, or by Set, I will put an end to you!" Around them, the Judean defenders' exultant cheers had gone quiet, leaving only Qorobar's heaving sobs.

At last, the pressure relented. Qorobar lumbered off to sag against the sealed gate. The howls of his anguish reminded Tariq of a mortally wounded animal. In that awful moment, Tariq thought that killing the man would have been the kinder thing.

His friends lifted him to his feet, their faces somber. A crowd had gathered around the Kushites, curious to gaze on these black-skinned Egyptians who'd come to save them. Among them was Eleazar, his blue Assyrian tunic damp with blood, and at his side, an older man with a long white beard, decked in voluminous robes of multicolored wool. He murmured something into Eleazar's ear before turning away. He walked toward the hill that dominated the city, and the tiered white temple surmounting it, gleaming anew in the morning sun.

"In King Hezekiah's name, Isaiah thanks you for delivering Jerusalem from evil."

THE DUPLICITOUS PEACE

"WE OUGHT TO make a habit of this," said Kalab.

Tariq cracked his eyes, then shut them again and settled deeper into his cushioned couch. "Compelling argument."

Middling and pastoral as the Judeans may have been, they weren't stingy about their luxuries. The idea, Kalab had gathered, was not to flaunt it. Glory belonged to the gods alone. Not that he quite understood that himself; he'd grown up in the shadow of gargantuan temple complexes, their sides etched with the triumphs of Egypt's great men. Still—he was of the priestly class. He appreciated the Judean sentiment.

The acolyte shifted slightly and repositioned the pillow behind his back. His weight caused the bowl to skid beneath his feet, squeaking on the mosaic floor and sloshing an appreciable amount of warm water onto the servant girl's lap. With a gasp, she rose and fled, holding her wet skirt away from her body.

"Oh stop, it's just a bit of water," he called after her, though he knew she wouldn't understand a word.

"What'd you do now?" said Tariq.

Kalab raised his eyebrows at Yesbokhe. "Look. Tariq's speaking in sentences again."

The scout, as usual, made no remark. He lifted his grail amiably and resumed watching a second girl rinse his feet, apparently just as bemused by the local custom as they all were.

Tariq shook his head. His red braids wagged. "Only because I'm finished watching how you torture the women."

"I'm not torturing them, I'm neglecting them."

"Is it truly that big a difference?"

"As someone who knows how to read: yes. Yes, it is." Kalab regretted the barb the moment it left his mouth, but Tariq fortunately chose not to respond. Relieved to be rid of the topic, Kalab turned to Nawidemaq and asked, "What do the gods have to say this afternoon, medicine man?"

Nawidemaq didn't look up from the trinkets spread in an arc between his stuck-out legs. No servant girl for him, despite the vinegary foot odor that permeated the palace room allotted them. Nawidemaq had no time for such trifling things as basic hygiene. He was always busy with his little bag of gods. Bits of them, in any event. An ivory toe, a knot of copper rods, a seashell amulet, a clay eyeball—scraps of local divinities filched from seemingly every corner of the world.

"In Jerusalem, there is only one god," Nawidemaq piped.

"I have it on good authority that they had a collection of gods to rival yours, up until recently," said Tariq.

"No. Only one. He does not speak to foreigners. Other gods are quiet. Bad sign." Apparently deciding the conversation was over, Nawidemaq returned to his whispered—and one-way—consultations.

"That's so vague, the man may as well have not said anything at all," whined Kalab.

"You're in fine form today," snapped Tariq. "Mistreating everybody, friends and strangers alike."

"Are you still stewing over the spilled bowl? It was an accident."

"Not just the bowl. Everything you've just said! We've all been through enough without you flinging shit about! These women, most of all."

Kalab leaned down for a better look at the girl who was now dabbing Tariq's feet dry. She noticed his scrutiny and hid behind her black curls. "I could use some fun, now that you mention it. Do they have whores in this prudish city, you think?"

"I don't bother with brothels," shrugged Tariq. "I'm good with girls. You, on the other hand…"

Now it was Kalab's turn to be indignant. "That is simply false. You remember how it was with Amani before."

Tariq made a scoffing sound. "You're in the right. I do remember. She thought even less of your whoring than I do."

Nawidemaq said, unbidden, "In eastern lands, priests do not…" He searched for a word, and finding none, made an obscene motion. "Not allowed. Gods do not like."

Kalab frowned. "Being a priest is a *job*. You say the words, you make the offerings. I don't see what fucking people in brothels has to do with it."

Tariq pressed his hands together in thanks as his servant girl rose. She offered a fleeting smile and left with her bowl. "Pakheme would have been able to tell you. He was good."

"Are you saying I'm not?"

"I'm starting to doubt it," admitted Tariq. He turned toward the door at the instant Amani came through it. She looked almost instinctively to Kalab first, but her face pinched in self-reproach, and she said to Tariq instead, "The Assyrians are gone."

They all jumped up at once.

"They lifted the siege!" the redhead exclaimed. "We beat the bastards!"

Kalab exchanged a hug with Yesbokhe, then a more reluctant one with Tariq. Amani folded her arms to ward off the acolyte's approach. Pretending he hadn't noticed the slight, he announced, "We'll need to finish all this wine straight away.

There won't be much to go around once Taharqa brings his whole damned army through the gate."

"I can't think of a worse priest," said Tariq, this time without the bite. "Amun gives us victory, and the first thing you can think of is getting drunk. Let's find a lamb to sacrifice. We'll eat it after."

Amani's whistle cut through their banter. "If you idiots would let me get a fucking word in, that's the second piece of news. Taharqa is leaving too."

"Without us," Kalab said in growing dismay.

"Did his runner tell you that?" asked Tariq.

The thief shook her head. "He didn't send us one."

Yesbokhe broke the stretching silence by repeating the medicine man's prognosis. "Bad sign."

Pisaqar stood with poise that was altogether forced. Inauspicious as this day had proven, he'd never seen much advantage in displaying anything but ready capability. It was projection of strength that had won him his first plaudits as a soldier of Khemet, elevated him to the ranks of the *medjay*, and finally to the pharaoh's court itself, teaching his deadly trade to the sons of greater men than he. None of his achievements had come by way of bluster. He was a proven artisan of his craft.

Yet I failed.

The ruined city before him was hardly his fault, but it seemed appropriate testament to the futility of his supposed accomplishment. Foiled at Jerusalem, the foul Assyrians had chosen to spend their wrath on poor Lacish instead. They had pulled down the walls and cast them down the hill, leaving the city itself naked before their fury. Pillars of black smoke rose from the crumbled piles of bricks and combined into a great pillar so high that the gods themselves could have choked on ash. As for the people of Lacish, King Sennacherib flaunted the punishment he'd inflicted on them. He'd executed every man and piled their corpses against the sundered gatehouse, leaving an opening just large enough for their women, children, and aged to pass through into captivity. If Pisaqar squinted, he could just make out the heads of the city elders spiked above the gate.

It was an ominous backdrop to the peace negotiations. Pisaqar had always taught his students to bargain from a position of strength. The Assyrian king, Sennacherib, also knew that lesson well. And in case the awful fate of Lacish hadn't made his ascendancy clear, he'd arrayed the balance of his army on the plain before it. This was his main force, the one that had smashed Crown Prince Shebitku's vanguard at Eltekeh and fanned out across the breadth of Judah, pillaging—he had heard it claimed—no less than two score towns and villages.

But not Jerusalem.

In truth, Sennacherib's show of strength was merely that. Jerusalem had been the capstone to his entire campaign, the glittering prize, and the Assyrian king had failed to grasp it. The force he'd entrusted with its capture—deprived first of water, then its bows, engineers, siege engines, trumpets, and officers—had finally been forced to break their siege. Now, Taharqa had brought the full weight of Pharaoh Shabaku's army to Judah to fight a battle that Sennacherib could not afford to lose.

Pisaqar would have gladly reminded the general of all this—except his former student hadn't sought out his counsel. In fact, he'd been omitted. Left behind at Jerusalem in the apparent hope that he would simply stay there.

Pisaqar had not obliged. He'd followed. Now he stood anonymous amid the tense ranks of Taharqa's great army. He couldn't help but shudder at the thought of Taharqa—headstrong, irascible Taharqa, with his bellicose tongue and his ever rapid glare—attempting to broker peace with another young man who was every bit as volatile.

Murdered Lacish would attest to that.

The mercenary captain waited beneath the shrouded sun, breathing shallowly of the corpse-tainted air. He prayed.

When King Sennacherib and General Taharqa finally emerged, they were hand in hand. The two men could hardly have been starker opposites. Taharqa was bare-chested with a leopard-skin cloak, a golden skull cap, and a pleated kilt. He was an imposing giant of a man, his body swollen to encompass his vast pride.

Sennacherib, in turn, looked every bit the part of a warrior king. He moved with grace, untroubled by the weight of the armored bands encircling his chest. He held his head at a regal tilt to display a square-cut beard that was at odds with Taharqa's shaven jaw.

The men did have one physical trait in common: their lips were blood-smeared from the ritual oath they had just sworn. Together, they lifted their arms to display their bleeding palms. The sea plain thundered with their armies' acclaim. Men bellowed. Spear shafts thudded against shields. Drums pounded. Pipes bleated.

There would be peace after all. Pakheme's sacrifice had not been for nothing.

Pisaqar roared just like all the rest.

When the noise faded, the two great men bid each other farewell and parted ways, each to rejoin his army. As Taharqa drew near, he raised his fists once more. No mere armistice, this, but victory. The ranks surged forward joyously. Pisaqar found himself carried along in the swell of bodies as the soldiers rushed to surround their general. They chanted his name and reached out to him. Basking in the moment, Taharqa grasped the hands of his men. He followed the path his guards beat through the crowd and made straight for his tent, where his lieutenants would be waiting on him. As would Hezekiah, the king of Judah, who must have been anxious to hear what peace Egypt had secured for his diminutive nation.

"I know you!" a soldier exclaimed to Pisaqar. "You're the mercenary! The one who beat the Assyrians at Jerusalem!" He didn't give him a chance to demur. Beckoning, he started to push through the mass, shouting, "Let this one through! Pisaqar is here!"

Pisaqar's small gratification quickly wilted as the men around took up the call. "Pisaqar! The savior of Jerusalem! Pisaqar!"

"Oh no," he muttered, but he no longer had a choice. Eager pairs of hands pushed him onward through the parting crowd. Through the ocean of bobbing heads, Pisaqar caught glimpses of his former student. Taharqa's grin began to sour as he heard another name chanted alongside his. When Taharqa spotted him, his eyes smoldered. His moment of glory had been polluted.

Pisaqar dearly wished he'd stayed in Jerusalem.

Far too late.

He and Taharqa were suddenly face-to-face. Taharqa's broad grin remained so convincingly fixed that Pisaqar could almost persuade himself he was imagining the seething hatred in those eyes. But he wasn't. Taharqa could have no man better than him. He had been that way since he was a small child, and however well he'd learned to conceal that yawning need for acclaim, it had never lessened.

That glass smile frightened Pisaqar. He lowered his gaze and bowed deep.

"Rise, my friend," Taharqa said after a moment, with every impression of sincerity. When Pisaqar straightened, there was no more murder in the general's stare. It was the only reason Pisaqar didn't recoil as Taharqa enfolded him into a generous embrace. Into his ear, Taharqa whispered, "What a privilege it is to be your equal."

Despite the heat, Pisaqar went cold with dread. "Never, Taharqa. I am your servant. The triumph is yours alone."

"Such is the way of *ma'at*," Taharqa agreed with a cheerful clap on the back. *Ma'at*—the Divine Order, in which every man knew his place and strove to fulfill it. A philosophy Pisaqar treasured. Taharqa had always been happy to pretend he felt the same. "Walk with me, Pisaqar."

As they resumed their path through the cheering crowd, Pisaqar dared to ask, "Would you tell me of the peace terms?"

"It's important that my servants be informed, so that they

may provide me with their welcome counsel," beamed Taharqa. "Sennacherib returns to Assyria."

Pisaqar ignored the slight, though it bit. "He is abandoning his campaign?"

"Indeed. I and the king have sworn oaths before the gods: that so long as he lives, there will be no more war between Assyria and Egypt. Not only have I thwarted invasion, Teacher, but I have safeguarded our country for many years to come."

Pisaqar was stunned by the good news. For decades, Assyria had nibbled at the lands between their borders. Babylon and Media were cowed, Lydia subjugated. A mere twenty years past, the Kingdom of Israel had still existed. That was gone—pinned beneath the Assyrian yoke, leaving only its neighbor Judah as a buffer between the two great powers. Assyrian expansionism would eventually goad its mighty armies across the Sinai and into Egypt itself; this supposition was taken for fact in the pharaoh's court. It was the reason Egypt had answered Hezekiah's plea for aid. A preemptive war.

And Egypt had somehow *won*. Sennacherib was abandoning his gains along the trade-rich coastline of Khor. Permanently. It was an inexplicable decision.

"Why?"

Taharqa's expression curdled briefly before adopting its expansive smile once more. "Captain Pisaqar. Is this turn of events displeasing to you?"

"No. This is most welcome news. I congratulate you warmly." Pisaqar knew he had badly mis-stepped. He'd nearly trodden again on his former student's titanic pride. "The failing is mine. I lack the wisdom to see why a warmongering king would end a successful campaign season by vowing not to repeat it. Bloody conquest, tyranny, enslavement, sacrilege—these are the things that Assyria has taught the world to expect of her. But never peace."

"Your concerns are heard and well understood, my old friend. Indeed, it is just as you say: Sennacherib has waged a successful campaign. When he returns to his court, he can boast of sacking forty-six cities. He can rightly claim that he made King Hezekiah a cage of his own capital. He has extracted annual tribute from the Kingdom of Judah. And our dear ally Hezekiah will of course forswear any further ... disorderly stirrings. So as not to provoke further Assyrian intervention. Does this satisfy you, Pisaqar?"

It was a sensible enough explanation. Pisaqar could think of no reason to question it—but his gorge rose at the thought that he had spent Pakheme's life to secure what his own general described as an Assyrian victory. He could have wept at the thought.

"This satisfies me, General," he said, nonetheless.

Taharqa stopped again and laid his enormous hands on his shoulders. "You have earned Egypt's thanks for your most worthy service. That service is at an end."

Pisaqar's mouth hung open at such a casual dismissal. Taharqa smiled coolly and tossed his chin. "Senanmuht, see to it that my old friend is accommodated."

A hand took his elbow. The time had come to leave. Touching his heart in salute, bowing, Pisaqar followed his new minder through the crowd, which quickly closed behind him again. Taharqa turned his back, the matter forgotten.

Senanmuht. Of all the servants at his disposal, Taharqa had chosen a Saite to eject Pisaqar from his presence. Pisaqar knew the man: a lesser son of a noble family hailing from the Western Delta. The Saites had a storied history of blue-blooded intrigue. Supposedly that had ended a decade ago when Kushite arms had tipped their patriarch, one of a batch of pretender pharaohs, from his flimsy throne. Pisaqar had played something of a role in that. In fact, he suspected one of his arrows had given Senanmuht his limp, a deduction the Saite nobleman had never confirmed aloud.

But that would go a long way toward explaining the outright contempt that dripped from Senanmuht's every syllable. "You've drawn Taharqa's ire, sellsword," he said as he led him through the dwindling edge of the crowd.

"Say what you mean, Senanmuht. I am in no mood for your petty maneuverings."

The Saite clicked his tongue as if scolding a child. "My, my, such a rebuke! I've barely said anything to you at all! Pisaqar," he said as the other man made to brush past him, "stop. I'm to deliver the general's decision. It's one you'll wish to hear."

Pisaqar faced him. Whatever Senanmuht was about to tell him, he meant to do it with soldiers in view.

"Speak, then."

Senanmuht's smile hadn't dropped. "It's really quite simple. Taharqa has already deemed it to be in Egypt's interest that your commission be withheld. When his decision is brought before Shabaku, the pharaoh will naturally agree. You are released from his service. With Egypt's boundless gratitude, I'm sure." He paused, searching for a reaction. Offered none, he shrugged. "Perhaps I should be clearer. There will be no payment for your little mercenary band."

Pisaqar's ears rung. His mind, struggling to absorb the totality of the betrayal, sought to understand a piece of it. "This is why Taharqa marched from Jerusalem without us?"

The Saite pretended to cover a laugh, the courtly equivalent of mocking applause. "Pisaqar, you speak as if this exclusion surprises you. Our great general wants nothing to do with your sordid ways of war. You, who slinks through the night like a fangless snake and slits men's throats as they sleep. The methods of a coward."

"This was our plan! Taharqa endorsed it! Your lies besmirch what little credit you still possess, Senanmuht. Tell me the truth. Did Taharqa convince himself that he would shatter the Assyrian lines? That was never the intent of his attack."

Senanmuht considered his answer. "He lost many warriors. Had he not broken off the attack when he did, it might have become a second Eltekeh."

Only with no Crown Prince Shebitku to blame.

"He casts the blame at my feet?"

"Naturally. You swore you would cut the Assyrians' bowstrings."

"There were thousands in that camp. Knowing this, I promised I would do my best to thin their arrows before the morning assault. Wreak havoc, then escape. That was the task. You were *there*."

"Yet the enemy resisted strongly. All you achieved, through your vermiform nocturnal maneuverings, was to coax Taharqa's spears into a strong Assyrian line."

"Whoever is to blame for that episode, the end result is unchanged. My Desert Mice broke the siege. They opened the way for the peace Taharqa just concluded. Now he proposes not to pay us?"

Senanmuht shrugged, apparently seeing no point in arguing over details. "That is, indeed, the general's decision. Not a proposal. A finality."

"This is a mistake. Releasing me from his service is Taharqa's right. But to renege on his word … this cannot be." He took a step forward, half-pleading despite himself. "Senanmuht, tell me you will ask him to reconsider. My people—"

"This has all been discussed and decided upon. Egypt has promised Assyria annual tribute. A *generous* one. That tribute comes straight from the royal treasury. I fear there will be little payment left afterward for the likes of sellswords."

"My Mice number eight. We were nine before, except that one of mine perished bringing Taharqa his victory. If you must forgo his payment, so be it. The dead have no need of wealth. But surely the pharaoh can spare some pittance for the ones who remain!"

Senanmuht stroked his chin as if he was actually mulling this over. "As I've said, the agreed tribute was … quite generous." He closed with an indulgent smile. Deeming his work done, he turned to leave.

"What of Pakheme?"

The Saite half-turned. "What did you say? Is that a name?"

"Pakheme is the one who fell at Jerusalem. Did Sennacherib say anything of his body? The Assyrians snatched it up when they abandoned the siege. I sent ahead a missive in hopes that Taharqa would ask for its return."

For the first time, something approaching pity flashed across Senanmuht's features. "I know of the missive. I'm afraid the general never intended to ask."

The Desert Mice had made their camp on the beach, far from the reek and racket of the army. Pisaqar had walked the whole way back, but he still didn't know how to deliver the news.

Embittered as he felt, his heart lightened with a sense of homecoming. The sea breeze bore the scent of roasting fish and a peal of Tariq's infectious laughter. As he drew near, he could see Nawidemaq silhouetted against the orange glow of the fire, scrutinizing the flaming tongues for the face of one god or another. Ermun was dictating his daily journal to Kalab, who was practiced enough after twelve years of tutelage that he could trade barbed jests with Tariq even as his stylus wagged. On the beach, Amani stood ankle deep in the surf and watched the Philistine sunset in a rare moment of tranquility. Yesbokhe searched the dunes for seabird feathers to use as fletchings. Among the donkeys the Judeans had gifted them as a mark of gratitude, Qorobar lay in the sand, an Assyrian helmet covering his face.

In his more tender moments—and admittedly, those were coming more frequently as he edged into his waning years—he could imagine them his children. Whoops rose as they spotted him, calling his name in the same way children greeted their father. It joyed and saddened him. Their love made his failure all the more unforgivable.

"Pisaqar, look! We caught a shark for dinner!" yelled Tariq.

Amani tapped the top of his head. "*I* caught a shark."

"You lured him into the shallows. Yesbokhe shot him. Ermun roasted him. I say we call that a group effort."

"Which you had no part in whatsoever!"

Pisaqar interrupted them. "Children, children." That drew some queer looks—not the form of address so much as the way he spoke. "Let us eat. After that, we must discuss matters."

The shark meat was tough but delicious. Tariq boasted of strangling some Assyrian officer and lifting a few choice items from his strongbox, including a jar of saffron. Ermun's culinary touch had done the rest. The conversation was loud and bawdy as it ever was with veterans, but the pauses were a touch too long. They were waiting to hear their captain's news.

When he delivered it, the reaction was the best Pisaqar could have hoped for.

Qorobar leapt to his feet and hurled his bowl into the fire. "That *fucker*!"

The others shouted their recriminations or else stared sullenly at the flames, imagining in them a thousand ugly deaths for their treacherous general. Thankfully no one voiced a wish for violence.

"Let's kill him," growled Amani.

"We'll rip our gold straight out of his earlobes," Tariq said in heartfelt agreement, which was a first for the two of them and a sign that the others were thinking the same.

Pisaqar tamped down on the talk straight away. "In what way does murdering the pharaoh's best general further the interests of ma'at? We fight for order. Justice. Good faith. To seek out vengeance is the opposite of ma'at—it is *isfet*. I will not brook any more mention of it."

The pair of them lowered their heads in penance, but their wrathful expressions remained fixed.

Ermun asked, "What next for us, old friend?"

"I have pondered on it. I fear there are no pleasing answers."

"Tyre isn't far," said the redhead.

"They pay tribute to Assyria. Tribute bleeds a city white."

Egypt, too, if Senanmuht is to be believed. "There will be no gold for us in Tyre or any other place in Khor."

The acolyte scratched his whiskers as he mulled this over. "To the north, then?"

"There will be work for us there, as there ever is. Reaching the northern kingdoms is the difficulty. Either we travel overland—"

"Through Assyrian territory," muttered Qorobar.

"—or by sea."

"Which we can't afford," finished Tariq. "Thanks be to Taharqa."

There was a weighty silence as the mercenaries dwelled on the only remaining option. Ermun gave voice to it. "We go home, then. We return to Kush." Heads nodded around the fire.

"Back to guarding merchants," sighed Amani.

"And boats," said Tariq.

Kalab spat an impressive gobbet of beer spittle into the flames. "Least those pissers pay up when it's time."

"*Fucking* Taharqa," muttered Yesbokhe. That this came from their taciturn archer lent considerable weight to the sentiment.

Pisaqar massaged his hands. "The fault is mine," he said with finality. "I put my trust in my former student's word when I ought to have known better. You have all been on campaign for the better part of a year with nothing to show. You all lost a dear friend at Jerusalem." His voice caught. A circle of eyes bored into him. Qorobar's hollow gaze was particularly difficult to meet. "I have proven myself an unworthy captain. I will not ask any of you to follow me again. If you choose to leave my service, then you will be given a mount," he nodded to the dozing asses, "and we will part as friends. For my own part, I will cross the Sinai and return to Egypt."

He stood on protesting knees. Ermun, ever loyal to a fault, made to stand as well, but he waved the old priest back down. "I will leave you to look to your own hearts. Good night."

Then he retreated to seek out his bedroll. There was no more conversation around the fire, only the dreary silence that falls over a group as they ruminate over a pitiful turn of events. One by one, the Desert Mice downed the dregs of their beer and abandoned their places. Soon, the only one who remained was Nawidemaq, his chalk-smeared face hovering over the flames, trying to discern within them the will of the gods. Pisaqar could have told him not to bother. He had always tried to serve the greatness of Egypt, secure in the belief that a righteous god would adopt and bless him in turn.

Now his error was clear. Any gods that deigned to notice him did so only for their own entertainment.

THE BLACK PILLAR

ASHURIZKADAIN FLEXED HIS knuckles and savored the ache in his tendons, the hallmark of a good night's work. His was a not an easily mastered profession. The nights were always long, the work itself quite strenuous, and recognition often lacking. The latter point, though, was no longer salient. He was in the king's service now. Perhaps not under the circumstances he would have chosen, but still.

The creases of his fingers, he noticed, glistened with blood that had not yet dried. He scrubbed at the joints with a cloth, annoyed at his own sloppiness. It would have been unprofessional to appear before the king disheveled.

The tent flap opened. He went still at the interruption. The servant's eyes lingered on his bloody hands. "The king summons you."

Sennacherib lounged on his portable throne, studying the wooden box laid at its foot with peculiar ferocity—an expression Ashurizkadain already knew quite well. His former master had worn it often. A family trait, then. Or a mark of the divinely touched.

He came to a stop before the throne and prostrated himself.

"Your Majesty." The floor, a multicolored tessellation of tiles, muffled his voice. To someone who did not understand their provenance, the decoration might have appeared unseemingly plain for a king's own tent. But the floor itself was both a trophy and a monument. Each individual tile had been pried from the ruins of a razed city. They easily numbered in scores.

The king spoke. "Up, Ashurizkadain. I am told you come bearing tidings."

He regained his feet. Sennacherib's intense gaze rested on him. "I would speak plainly if you should allow it, Your Majesty."

"How I shall miss plain soldierly speech. Soon, I shall have more than my fill of dissembling from the wretches who fill my palaces." The king smirked as he said this, although there was no humor behind the words. "And my cousin was fond of you. Speak without reservation."

Ashurizkadain hid hands moist with Egyptian blood behind his back. "The deserter talked without much prodding. The ones outside Jerusalem were mercenaries from Kush. They call themselves the Desert Mice. Their leader is a man called Pisaqar. He once served as advisor to Pharaoh Shabaku himself during the uprisings. It seems that he taught the chariot to the boys at court, young Taharqa among them."

"Master of Horse, then," Sennacherib mused. He ran a gold-sandalled foot along the hinge of the wooden box. "Why would a man forsake such an esteemed position, I wonder?"

"The deserter's talk became looser the more I worked on him. I expect he was speaking falsely," warned Ashurizkadain.

"And?"

"There was a misunderstanding, it is said. Perhaps with Taharqa, perhaps some other nobleman. He was ejected from court some years ago. It appears a similar event has just taken place."

This piqued Sennacherib's interest. "He has been banished once again?"

"If the deserter is to be believed, yes."

The king ran his fingers through his beard. He was barely twenty, and his facial hair required a good deal of cultivation, but it would have been unwise to judge Sennacherib on age alone. The scars on his face spoke of many battles fought, and his dark eyes gleamed with intelligence.

"Thus, this Pisaqar, this leader of rats, is without the pharaoh's protection. How fortunate. How *just*." He began to pace along the trophy floor. "This man has wronged me greatly, Ashurizkadain. It is thanks to him that Jerusalem yet stands. Thanks to him that the sons of my most trusted courtiers lie dead outside its gate. Thanks to him that my royal court is thrown into flux. The perfidy of *one man* forces me to quit my campaign in my moment of triumph. I am compelled to return to Nineveh. To what end? That I must spend the next year putting to rest the squabblings of the great houses?"

Sennacherib's shook his head with such profound contempt that he seemed on the verge of crippling laughter. His abrupt change in fortune beggared belief. "And on top of this, Taharqa will return to Egypt claiming victory over me! Despite never defeating me in battle! Taharqa won nothing!" His voice exploded. "*His verminous sellswords stole my victory in the night!*" The bellowed words seemed to inflate the sides of the tent. The camp beyond fell silent at the king's wrath.

Ashurizkadain stood unmoving, considering the manifest possibility that Sennacherib would strike him dead.

The king steadied his breathing with visible effort. The rage was still there, but he had yoked it to his will once more. "These decrepits, these rats, must be punished. All of them. This lone prize shall not suffice." He gave the box a rough kick. Its cedar lid thumped heavily.

Ashurizkadain bowed, mostly out of true deference but partly to hide his excitement. He sensed the hand of Ashur steering him toward his destiny. Opportunity was beckoning. "I await your command, Your Majesty."

Sennacherib didn't seem to hear him. He remained infatuated with the wooden box—the start of his new collection. "When I return to Nineveh," he whispered, "I shall erect a pillar. I shall carve it from polished granite, the same that the Egyptians use to build their obelisks. Its inscriptions shall be inlaid with the finest onyx, and the names of my victories shall be of poured gold. I shall set into its pedestal these tiles beneath my feet. To my pillar I shall nail the skins of my enemies. I shall stretch them and stitch them together so that the pillar is wholly covered. Let my courtly rivals look upon my pillar and tremble. Let the Kushites wander the afterlife skinless, weeping. Let them explain to their old, soft gods, 'My flesh commemorates Sennacherib's triumph.'"

The king at last deigned to notice his servant. "Ashurizkadain, I commission you as the instrument of my justice. Avenge this dishonor. Deliver Ashur's justice to the wicked. Bring tranquility to Nineveh. I charge you with this task: hunt Pisaqar of Kush to the ends of the earth. You shall capture him. You shall skin him and his men alive. You shall bring these tokens to me as proof of your deeds. Your reward shall be a place beside my throne." He stooped, and with slow relish, opened the box. Inside lay a neat roll, black and glistening by the torchlight: the first of his collection. The Kushites had left one of their own behind, and the king had made a trophy of his skin.

Ashurizkadain, the Flayer of Caleh, looked on his handiwork with no small measure of pride. "Your will be done, Your Majesty. I shall not fail you."

Sennacherib's smile was etched with malice. "Good. For in the event that you do, I shall be leaving space for one more skin at the top of my pillar."

YAHWEH'S GIFT

NAWIDEMAQ ROTATED HIS reedy arms and felt the chalk creak between his shoulder blades. He would let the sun fall half a palm further, and then he would ask one of his fellows to smear a fresh layer onto his back. Perhaps whoever did him this kindness would listen to him at last and allow their flesh to be coated in turn, and thus ward off the scalding gaze of the Utu, who watched by day and night alike. But probably not.

"Shit," groaned Tariq. "My head is pounding." He swatted at the air about his face as if to bat away flies, although there were none. The creatures of the desert were wise enough to take shelter. Only men, foolish men such as they, would choose to brave the noonday heat.

Nawidemaq knew what to do for pains in the head. He leaned around Tariq and held out the remedy.

The redheaded man regarded the proffered egg with bewilderment. "Uh. Thank you, but I'm not feeling hungry."

"Smash it to your head," said Nawidemaq. He mimed slapping a palm onto his brow. "It makes the ache less."

Tariq returned his eyes on the shimmering path ahead. "Maybe later, Nawidemaq."

He put the egg away with a quiet sigh. The others were not friends of the desert as he was. Of course, to Tariq, the desert was a place of hateful fear. He was not Nawidemaq, who had dwelled in the dry places for many years, who counted the scorpions and jackals and carrion birds as dear friends. To his companions, the Sinai Desert was a godless land, bereft of their sight and blessings.

But he knew better. Gods inhabited the world in the same way that men dwelled in cities. For certainly, some god was responsible for sculpting the rocks of those towering peaks, just as a mason would. Another god stirred the wind and coaxed the dust spirals into being. Yet another danced between the flapping wings of the ravens overhead, guiding them toward water like a kindly elder brother. And surely there another god presided, a shopkeeper doling out portions.

Nawidemaq pointed to the birds. "They go to water. We ride maybe one, two hours. Then you drink. Head stops aching."

Tariq squinted back at him. "How do you figure about the birds? Oh. Wait. The gods."

"The land sings to you, also, if you learn to listen."

"Maybe you'll teach me. Long as the lesson doesn't involve wasting eggs."

Nawidemaq beamed. Tariq made a joke of too many things, but his heart was good. "Nothing is forbidden. Make payment to gods, gods gift you knowledge."

"What sort of payment do they need to get rid of chapped lips?"

Before Nawidemaq could dispense more wisdom, Pisaqar rode up from behind. Their captain was the only one who still rode alone. The Mice, with no other goods to barter, had been obliged to trade away their donkeys at each stop in return for water and bread. "The next station is not far. We will stop for the night."

The captain rode off, and Nawidemaq patted Tariq's thigh. "You see?"

The supply station was nestled in the shadow of a split cliff face, little more than a grain silo and a pair of huts. The only evidence of water was a few squat trees protruding from a shallow depression. Desolate as the place seemed, some ancient pharaoh had seen the potential of the wadi and deemed the oft-dry stream bed worthy of a permanent outpost. The keeper came out to meet the approaching horsemen, exchanged some words with Pisaqar, and had his wife prepare lodgings while his children fetched jugs of water.

The mercenaries drew up. Riders and asses both hung their heads with fatigue, their bodies crusted with sand. They groaned as they slid from their mounts. A boy hurried up and offered Nawidemaq a jug, which he accepted gratefully. "Gods bless you, child." Even though the words squeaked out dry, he made a point of tipping some water onto the sand. Only with the spirit of the wadi appeased did he dare to rinse the grit from his teeth.

Tariq nudged him. "Can you ask the gods which donkey the captain will give up next?"

Nawidemaq lifted his hands. He took the bridle and led their thirsty animal toward the trees, where a trough awaited. He patted its neck, murmuring his appreciation for its labors. The boy who'd brought him water approached shyly.

"You wish to make friends?" Nawidemaq asked.

The boy's eyes darted to avoid the sight of his nub-toothed grin. He nodded. Nawidemaq knew what he looked like and took no offense. He made for a wild figure, with his bald head, his kilt of braided grass, and his skin dusted with chalk. He kept his smile up and beckoned the boy forward.

"You stroke his cheek. Here, this way. But not so close to the eye!"

The donkey tensed at the first touch, but relaxed once he realized the stranger posed no threat. The boy smiled at last. "I like him," he said, which was when Nawidemaq realized why he had come. Pisaqar had made his opening offer. The animal was being inquired after.

He stifled his sadness, for although life in the Sinai would be difficult for this most pleasant animal, his years would be shorter still in the employ of soldiers. He asked the boy, "Does your family raise animals?"

"Only that," said the boy. Without taking his infatuated eyes off the donkey, he pointed. Nawidemaq followed his finger along the dry stream bed and saw a great beast half-hidden among the brambles, nibbling at the thorny branches.

He passed the lead line to the boy and crept toward the beast, his bare feet cracking the parched earth. "Only that" was a bull whose best days were evidently behind him. His sagging hide was an echo of vanished youthful breadth. His horns were easily ten cubits from point to point—an impressive span, yellowed and pitted with age though they were. His hooves were worn down, his nostrils swarming with flies, his hide caked with unwashed dust thick enough that its color was undiscernible but for his ridged spine, which still bore vestiges of white. *An albino*, Nawidemaq thought. A most blessed pigment.

The bull raised his enormous head to regard his visitor, chewing thoughtfully on a mouthful of thorny branches.

Nawidemaq felt a wave of compassion for the neglected bull. He blinked away tears.

The bull shook away the biting flies and clomped toward him, his head swiveling with curiosity.

Nawidemaq cradled his snout and ran his thumbs gently along the dried ruts. He rummaged through his satchel until he found a jar of fat. "I am called Nawidemaq," he told the bull as he massaged the lard into its wounds. It rumbled its appreciation and nuzzled him like an outsized dog, eyes closed and ears flapping. Even there, the medicine man could see the swarms of lice wriggling in the crevices. There were marks on its flanks from years of merciless whipping. He could have wept to see the abuse this kind soul had endured.

"Worry not. The gods have remedies for all of it," he promised the bull. "Now come along! You and Nawidemaq will be the best of friends."

"You will not sell?" Nawidemaq's voice grew shrill with disbelief.

The station's keeper crossed his arms and shook his head. "Not if it means you taking the animal, no. I will accept your coin if you agree that I slaughter it tonight. Your friends will have its meat. I will keep the remains. Its bones will make for good broth."

"I offer good pay!" Nawidemaq once again held out his handful of Lydian coins.

"And I will accept," said the keeper, "in exchange for the bull's bones."

"Bah!" The medicine man stomped out of the cave dwelling. Outside, the others had gathered in the shadow of the grain silo, backs pressed to the bricks which, while hot to the touch, were still cooler than the air itself. They looked dispirited, even more than when Pisaqar had delivered his news a week before. Perhaps Amani had a few scraps of shiny metal hidden in the pockets of her mouse-skin vest, or Qorobar had stuffed an onion or two into his sack of Assyrian helmets—commodities Nawidemaq could add to his offer. But a week in the desert had taken so much from them all that he couldn't bear to ask for more. Not even to buy his new friend's life.

Sadly, he trudged back to the grove where the bull still nibbled contently on his barbed supper. He stroked its neck and sank to the desiccated earth. He dug a clean cloth from his satchel and unrolled it on the ground. Then he set down his leather bag, unbound its cord, and piece by piece laid its contents across the cloth.

"The bag of gods," his companions called it, and there was some truth in what they said. Nawidemaq's journeys had taken him all across the world, and in every little corner of it, he had found new peoples—tribes and villages and cities, each with its own language and customs, each convinced of its own paramount importance. Because each had the protection of its own god. Who was Nawidemaq to question the truth of such things? Everywhere he visited, he prayed to the god that held sway. Sometimes on a hilltop beneath a certain cluster of stars, other times among chanting priests at some great city's temple, and still other times in little mudbrick shrines in anonymous hamlets. From each place of worship, Nawidemaq had taken a small token. Tiny shards of clay and sandstone and marble and obsidian—the fragments of local gods the world over.

Which god would he call on today? His white-streaked fingers traced over the divine collection. "Ah, you," he whispered, though he dared not speak this god's name. He gently picked up a lump of white stone taken from the tallest hill of Jerusalem, where the Judeans had built their temple. "Perhaps you help, mighty one. For it was my companions who saved your people. I offer what I possess. In return, I ask one small favor of you."

He pulled out half a loaf of stale bread: the last of his food. He buried it in a shallow hole, mouthing—but not speaking—the god's name. Then he looked to the east, where the god had made his true home, and waited for his answer.

The Sinai stretched out before him, with its rock-strewn sand and its steep ochre mountains. A stir of wind had kicked up a pall of dust, which the afternoon sun caught at an angle and stained the sky. If not for the rocky peaks, the heavens would have been indistinguishable from the desert. This leg of the journey had carried them inland, but Nawidemaq could still smell the salt of the distant sea. He shut his eyes and inhaled the scent, basking in the varied glories of creation.

The Judean god's answer came as the first tinges of violet appeared in the eastern sky. Out in that rock-strewn expanse, a dark speck shimmered in and out of view, as if the god remained hesitant to give up his secret. Nawidemaq stood as he recognized the movement of a horse.

The lone rider was at the end of his strength. He slouched, holding the reins loosely, his head lolling with each clomp of his panting horse's hooves. By the time he drew close enough for Nawidemaq to observe his poor state, the other mercenaries had noticed his approach as well. Yesbokhe clambered atop the silo and strung his bow while the others formed a line, their bows held in ready hands. Their thirst would have to wait.

Amani glanced Nawidemaq's way as he took his place. "Where've you been hiding?"

"I pray at the wadi. I make new friend."

"You mean that bull sniffing at your ass?"

"Yes, him."

"Isn't that lovely." The girl jerked her chin at the approaching rider and said to no one in particular, "Must be a messenger."

As if in answer, Yesbokhe called down in his terse way, "Blue cloth."

At that, they drew their weapons. Nawidemaq wondered why the god of the Judeans would send an Assyrian as his emissary.

But whatever the interloper had in mind, it wasn't combat. He swayed in the saddle as he drew near, clearly very weak but with enough presence of mind to keep his hands in sight. He didn't call out to the warriors arrayed against him. He halted a stone's throw away. His mouth moved soundlessly as he tried and failed to speak, his haggard eyes pleading.

Pisaqar, ever a man of quality, stepped forward. "If your heart is peaceful, come down from your horse, and this is yours." He held out a waterskin.

With clenched teeth, the man slid off the horse's back. His legs failed him. He crumpled on the ground. At Pisaqar's gesture, Tariq and Qorobar moved forward and grabbed his arms.

"Amun! It's the twice-traitor!"

"Eleazar?" Pisaqar became equal parts worry and suspicion. "We agreed our business concluded in Jerusalem. Let us bring him inside and give him the chance to explain himself."

Inside the cave quarters, Eleazar gulped down two full waterskins without heeding the priest's warnings. He immediately vomited it all up, provoking outraged cries from the Desert Mice as they scrambled away. They were now condemned to sleeping amid the stench of fresh bile. The Israelite—or Assyrian, they'd never quite agreed—pressed his hands together in penance.

Pisaqar squatted in front of him and offered a cup of beer, which Eleazar eagerly accepted. "Now that your throat is wetted, you can tell us what important errand brings you alone across the Sinai."

The man drank deep and wiped the foam off his beard. "A mad venture, I agree," he said, "but one you will all find of interest. I offer you the chance to save Egypt and win riches beyond your wildest dreams."

Amani clapped her hands. "A strong opening offer," she jeered. More than anything, Amani prized loyalty among friends. To keep company with a man who'd betrayed not one, but two peoples revolted her, an opinion she didn't bother to hide. She wasn't alone in her scorn.

Qorobar spat. "Let me put my axe into him, Pisaqar," he said, clearly relishing the thought.

Even Ermun, the hale priest, voiced agreement. "This one is a betrayer, and a leopard cannot change his spots."

Pisaqar kept his eyes on Eleazar. "I hope you will understand our suspicion. The last time we worked with you, we lost a dear friend. Now we make the journey home empty-handed, only for you to mysteriously cross our path once again. Through mere happenstance, I am certain."

"I followed," said the traitor. "For people who make a profession of killing in the night, you are not difficult to find."

"And why have you followed us? Did you not win enough plaudits to live out your days among your people?"

"I have no people. I know it is the reason you all scorn me. I am at peace with it. Let us all benefit from my duplicity.

When I first left Assyria's service, I took *this* with me." He reached into his tunic, then froze as the mercenaries around him coiled up. "I mean no harm, you fools! Look!" He withdrew a papyrus scroll and held it out to Pisaqar.

The captain took it with a frown. Without unrolling it, he passed it to Ermun. He and the traitor watched each other's eyes as the priest carefully unrolled the papyrus and studied the script.

"By Osiris! This is a royal mortuary scroll!"

Tariq spoke the question almost everyone else was thinking. "A what?"

Ermun stared at the apparent treasure in bewilderment. "This is a set of instructions for the caretaker of a tomb. So that the caretaker and his descendants can make the correct offerings to the *ka*." Nawidemaq recognized the Egyptian word for a shade, a spirit. "This ensures the ka's well-being in the afterlife. Possessing this scroll is a capital offense."

"Kill someone for owning a few lines of script?" said Tariq in confusion.

"Yes," the priest said patiently, "because in order to make an offering at a resting place, one must know where the resting place is. And this is the resting place of a pharaoh." Nawidemaq's spine tingled as the other Kushites murmured among themselves. He'd had his doubts that of all people, the Judean god would send a betrayer to carry out his will. But this was beginning to smack of divine providence.

Pisaqar leaned toward the traitor. "Where did you get this papyrus?"

"I stole it from King Sennacherib himself," Eleazar said proudly.

"Why would the king of Assyria take interest in a dead pharaoh's tomb?"

"Is it not obvious? He aimed to plunder it! Assyria does not conquer lands by the sword alone. It infests the lands it covets with treachery first. What better way to do this than with gold? If Sennacherib can corrupt a nation's elites without ever touching his own treasury, well then so much the better. And you Egyptians, with your extravagant burials, provide just such an opportunity. Sennacherib meant to poison Egypt's halls of power with the wealth of one of your own dead god-kings. He delights in such cruel absurdities."

Pisaqar said, "And now you have robbed Sennacherib instead. What is your intention? Will you give this scroll over to Pharaoh Shabaku for a reward?"

"Shabaku would hurl me onto a wooden stake for merely possessing this, just as your priest says," scoffed Eleazar. "No, I sought *you*. The Desert Mice. I chose to reveal this knowledge to the men who plucked Sennacherib's victory from his hands. You are mercenaries. You understand opportunity. This papyrus offers a chance every hired blade only dreams of: to retire rich. You will no longer be forced to sell your bows and risk your lives for masters who care not whether you live or die."

Ermun methodically rolled up the scroll. "We are soldiers, not thieves. What you propose is without honor. It's beneath us. We should turn this man and this papyrus over to the pharaoh. Let him decide the wisest course."

Tariq jumped up, his red braids bouncing. "Now wait a moment. There's a reason we're skulking in this desert cave, covered in sunburn and infested with sand mites and with four donkeys between the eight of us. We could have been up in the ass crack of Memphis, drowning in girls—"

Amani rolled her eyes. "That's lovely."

"—but no! The pharaoh *fucked* us."

There were hisses around the fire, Nawidemaq's included, for it was never wise to profane a living god.

Tariq spat with contempt. "Saying it nicely won't change the facts."

"If blasphemy is the way you choose to comport yourself," said Ermun calmly, "that's your business, Tariq. My issue is your reasoning. We cannot withhold news of this plot from the pharaoh out of pure spite. There is nothing noble in it."

"Maybe giving Shabaku the papyrus is the right thing to do. But didn't you just finish saying that merely having the thing is enough to get you executed?"

"Pharaoh Shabaku is a wise ruler. He wouldn't kill a man who shows him loyalty." Ermun said this slowly, doubting his own words.

"Shabaku doesn't rule, Ermun. He's just an old man. An old man who puts people like Taharqa in charge of things. And if there's one thing we know for sure about Taharqa, it's that he doesn't value loyalty for shit. We tell anyone else about this, we die with stakes up our asses."

"Then what do you propose?" demanded the priest.

Eleazar set down his beer with a *thunk*, reclaiming the group's attention. "This is where I must remind you that robbing this tomb was King Sennacherib's plan. If you Kushites do not see it through, he will."

The deep silence that followed seemed meant for Nawidemaq to break. He stood, massaging the white stone from Jerusalem between his hands.

"Before sun fell, I make offering to the god of Israel. I ask for his favor. After, this man comes from the desert, near dead from thirst." He peered at Eleazar, whose black eyes were filled with surprise. "If this does not tell you our fortunes change, remember what already happen to us. We deliver the last city of the Hebrews from its doom. Our general refuses to pay us. Now a man of Hebrew birth comes to us and offers greater reward still. If we take it, we defeat our enemy Assyria once again. We take revenge for Pakheme. We save Egypt." He looked to the priest. "Sometimes to serve a greater good, we must do a small evil. This is one such time. God of the Hebrews, gods of Egypt—they speak now. We must be wise. We must listen."

Everyone simply stared at him until Kalab clapped his hands on his knees. The acolyte pointed at Nawidemaq, declaring, "Fuck me if that isn't the most sensical damn thing the man's ever said. I'm sorry, Teacher," he added to Ermun, "but our medicine man is in the right."

Pisaqar stood as well. "Our course has not changed," he announced. "We still make for Memphis. Any who wish to leave my service are still free to do so then. Whoever stays with me," he looked to Nawidemaq with a smile in his eyes, "we will go forward with the gods' blessing. Eleazar, come outside. We have more to discuss."

Eleazar came up to Nawidemaq in the wadi as he scooped the last damp soil out of a hole. The filthy bull loitered at the medicine man's hip, snuffling curiously at the water jug he'd brought.

"Thank you for speaking for me," the Israelite—Assyrian?—said.

Nawidemaq touched his heart cordially and emptied the jug of water into the hole. He patted the bull between the horns as it happily guzzled away.

Eleazar tossed his chin. "You have made a pleasant new friend."

"Animals know honest hearts," Nawidemaq said.

"That is not my experience of them. Though I suspect you are not speaking of the bull."

"I am not."

Eleazar shifted his weight, his expression hidden in the darkness. "Do you doubt my honesty?"

Nawidemaq burped out a chuckle. "Mistrusting a breaker of oaths is only wise. I believe, also, you know even more than you say. But I trust in the gods. I trust in my captain."

Eleazar opted not to address the accusation further, but asked instead, "Will the other Desert Mice follow their captain's lead?"

Nawidemaq ran a thumb along a growing crack in the bull's horn. He would need a farrier to fasten a metal band around it to stop the crack from growing, or else remove the horn. Then he remembered with a pang that the bull would not be coming with him. He told Eleazar, "I do not know my companions' minds. Men are not honest, least of all with themselves. But Pisaqar? Good man. He tries to do right. Rare to find a man such as he. One to follow. I know it. My companions know it. If they have wisdom, they will come."

"And hopefully the unwise are greedy. That redheaded fellow, for instance."

"We are all mercenaries," agreed Nawidemaq, being purposely opaque. He left it unsaid that Tariq was much cleverer than the traitor seemed to think. Any experienced warrior knew it was better to be underestimated by one's enemy—and Eleazar could yet prove to be one.

He clapped the soil off his hands and stood. With an affectionate pat on the bull's shoulder, he headed for the cave, where the notes of a bawdy group song could be heard drifting through the seam.

Eleazar remained at his shoulder. He asked in bafflement, "You would leave your bull outside? Without a tether?"

"He does not belong to me. This is where I found him."

The traitor turned the words over. Then, at the entrance to the cave, he caught Nawidemaq's arm. In his free hand, he held a small purse. "If you wish to leave here with the bull, take this."

Nawidemaq opened the purse and found a handful of polished carnelian stones inside. For the first time that evening, he was completely surprised. "Why?"

Eleazar's teeth showed through his beard, but the smile didn't quite reach his eyes. "Because treasure is heavy, and bulls are strong. Consider it a wise investment." He winked and ducked inside, where the singing dampened.

Nawidemaq weighed the purse, wondering if accepting it would leave him indebted to a man who'd proven himself untrustworthy twice over.

Somewhere in the night, a jackal yowled. Accepting this as a sign, Nawidemaq closed his fist and strutted over to the cave where the keeper lived.

CRIMSON SANDS

THE MARCHING COLUMN spotted them at last just as the sun passed its zenith. Up until then, Ashurizkadain and his men had kept their distance, lurking behind the waves of shimmering heat, their horses tightly clustered so that even if the mirages failed to flatten their images completely, it would be impossible to gauge their numbers. The horse tribes made an art of hiding in the open, and years of quelling them had taught Ashurizkadain many of their tricks. The most important, by far, was knowing when to drop the charade and strike.

When the Egyptians kept up the march and missed their customary noon halt, he knew the time had come.

"Nimrud!"

His second rode up, his armor and skin dusted ochre by the Sinai sand. "I serve, my lord!" He panted the words like some sort of beast.

Ashurizkadain made no secret of his revulsion. Nimrud immediately remembered himself and clicked his jaw shut. Behind his sweat-moist beard, his throat worked instinctively, trying to summon up some saliva to swallow. "Apologies, my lord."

"Ready the men. We attack."

Nimrud squinted at the distant prey, their forms reduced to wavering smudges as they labored east through the arid valley. "Perhaps it would be wiser to wait some hours, my lord," he suggested. "This way we would strike with the sun behind us."

"And allow them time to pick ground to defend? No. They are in the open, laggard from thirst. Perhaps instead of wagging your overeager tongue, you shall hold it still and allow your captain to lead. Do as I have commanded."

If Nimrud reddened, the dust caking his skin made it impossible to tell. He nodded and rode away, barking orders to the others. They numbered forty, veterans all, but months of unopposed pillage in Judah had made them soft. A few days in the Sinai were ample proof of that. It took an embarrassing amount of time for them to gather and swap onto fresh mounts. The archers strung their bows with hands that fumbled from dearth of water. Managing the task, they slid behind their riders, who groaned as they hefted their shields. Then the archer-rider pairs all sat on their mounts and awaited the word, watching Ashurizkadain from beneath their helmets with fevered eyes. No bloodlust, no hint of motivation, just weariness. Assyria expected much of its servants, and these men had thus far shown themselves lacking.

Whatever their mediocrity, the Egyptians soldiers' quality somehow managed to be poorer still. They barely reacted as the intruders cantered through the heat-distorted air and resolved into the shapes of twenty horses. The Egyptian detachment numbered fifty or so, and reacted as a herd would: by going still. The heat-stricken men were agog as the mysterious horsemen closed the distance, perhaps convincing themselves that these were friendly outriders, or more likely, failing to think much at all. Only as the approaching horses broke into a gallop did they awaken to the threat. Then they managed to shamble into a semblance of a line, spears lurching to the ready. Slingers stumbled to the wagons to find their stones, but needn't have taken the trouble.

All around Ashurizkadain came the clatter of recurve bows, the twang of heavy strings. The shafts rushed into the sky, wriggling at first, then straightening once their fletchings tasted the air. The blinding sun caught them and rendered their arcs invisible, but the first impacts were unmistakable. For all their faults, the archers had judged the range well. Arrows slammed into wagons amid explosions of wicker. Oxen flinched and sank, baying, onto their forelimbs. A servant boy tumbled in the dust and lay still.

Ashurizkadain, seeing his men had their range, looked to Nimrud and made a circle above his head. Nimrud blew a horn, and the riders hauled on the reins, guiding their horses into a broad circle. The archers seated behind them twisted on the horses' backs, loosing their arrows at will into the coalescing enemy ranks. The Egyptians had succeeded in planting some of their round-topped shields in the sand, but not enough to matter. They fell, screaming, with shafts plunged all the way to the ends in their bare chests. Sling stones hurtled back in reply, but the Assyrians were well outside their range, and they plopped down between the two sides with harmless puffs of sand. That left the Assyrians to spend arrows at will, taking careful aim, felling more Egyptians with every volley. Sometimes one would drop in a heap, dead before he hit the ground. But more often they sank and wailed, painting their comrades with sprays of blood as they flailed in their death agonies. Those who tried to pull the arrows out only deepened their misery. The barbed arrowheads resisted their efforts, and when they did come loose, it was amid loops of sinew.

Ashurizkadain felt himself grinning wide. His parched mouth split at the corners and began to bleed, but he didn't mind the pain. The Egyptians' woe and despair more than made up for the inconvenience. What a shame that none of these sorry men would live to tell of their annihilation by a small, exhausted band of Assyrian cavalry. The king, though, would be pleased when Ashurizkadain told him of it.

His men felt it too—the intoxication of victory. They sent their arrows with whoops and taunts. These Egyptians' bodies would lie in the desert until the sun shriveled their flesh and laid their bones bare. Their souls would wander here, far from home, until the ruin of their bodies consigned them to oblivion. And one day soon, Assyria would visit that fate on all of Egypt. That was a lesson worth knowing, and Ashurizkadain's men made sure that as the Egyptians began to die in earnest, they learned it well.

The desperate survivors broke, abandoning their shield wall. Some kept enough presence of mind to cluster around the wagons for cover. The rest fled into the open desert. The heat would certainly claim them there, but Ashurizkadain took no chances. He went after the runners personally, leaving his men to annihilate the last stand at the wagons. Methodically, joyously, he trampled them one at a time, splitting their bodies beneath his horse's hooves, not bothering to sully his spear with their blood. His own now ran freely from his split, grinning lips. This was the triumph Assyria had been denied. Now he had the honor of reclaiming it for his king, one sundered corpse at a time.

His triumphant men stood astride their massacred foes and cheered their captain's approach. Even dour Nimrud managed a gracious bow. "Your course was wise, my lord. I was wrong to offer counsel where it was unneeded."

Ashurizkadain's magnanimous smile tasted like metal. "I serve the king. And you serve me. Remember it, Nimrud. Have you remembered to take prisoners?"

Fortunately for Nimrud, he had. Three cowering Egyptian soldiers, wearing linen kilts and headbands with white feathers, were huddled beside the wagon. The prisoners hid their faces behind their locks, shivering. One was babbling an entreaty to Egypt's weak gods.

"Good." Ashurizkadain swung off his horse and retrieved his leather pouch from his belt. His tools clattered inside. "I will begin questioning these ones while you bring the spare mounts. Have the men gather up the arrows, every last one. Leave no evidence of our involvement in this. When that is finished, you are to strip the bodies. We will require unsullied clothes for the next phase of our journey."

Nimrud made a quick survey of the bloody, arrow-riddled bodies around them. "That shall not be a simple task, my lord. Nevertheless, I shall ensure that it is done."

As the men dispersed to see to their duties, Ashurizkadain squatted in front of his captives. He licked the blood from his lips. "Do any of you raise animals?" They looked at him, questioning and fearful. He cocked his head. "You understand me, yes? It has been some time since I spoke your language." Receiving reluctant nods, he continued, "I am told the process is somewhat similar. The process of skinning, that is. Of course, I have never skinned an animal myself. As such, I would not know from experience. Husbandry is not my profession. My skills are in a different vein. Only slightly, however, if what I am told is true. That skinning a man and skinning a goat or a cow are somewhat similar."

Judging that he'd enthralled his audience, he told them, "One begins by hanging the man upside down. There are several advantages to this. It minimizes the amount of blood. It also keeps the man awake longer, I find. Finally, less work. It is easier to tug." He mimed the motion, at which his prisoners flinched.

"One begins by slicing the wrist all the way around. Not deep enough that you cut the veins, but enough to expose the muscle. Then one draws the knife up the bottom of the wrist and slices all the way to the armpit. One now faces a choice: does he skin the man whole, or a little bit at a time? I would say the latter, in your case. Your skins are not very aluable."

They were all breathing hard now, their eyes fairly bulging from their heads. The praying one had ceased his mumbling.

"Again, one cuts all around the upper arm, close to the armpit. Then he arrives at the reward. He takes the wrist, just at the base of the long cut, and he begins to peel. The skin is delicate here. He must be gentle. Sometimes he must cut beneath the skin as he peels, so that it separates cleanly from the muscle. Then he pulls more, a little bit at a time, a little harder as he works his way up the arm. By the time he has reached the elbow, the skin becomes more difficult to separate. This is where we begin to tug. You will be surprised how little strength is needed. Only persistence. There is very little blood, either, provided one has not cut too deep. The process is much the same for the legs, although, I confess, this is the part you will enjoy the least. The genitals tend to become a distraction, so before one begins, he must…" He made a slice-and-toss motion.

"What do you want from us?" the faithful one cried, finding his voice again at last.

"Answers. I am certain you shall give me all I need. As a reward, whoever tells me the most shall go to the underworld whole. The others, I shall flay alive. The last sight you see shall be your moist hides smoldering on a fire. And so. Which of you shall tell me of Pisaqar, captain of the Desert Mice?"

They shouted over one another in their desperation to dribble out every scrap of rumor that had made its way around the army camp. He listened intently until their shrieks devolved into gibbering pleas. By that time, his men had finished their duties and gathered around to grin at the spectacle, carrying armfuls of pinkish rags. When the prisoners' voices broke and they could scream no longer, he left them sagging against the wagon wheel.

He murmured into Nimrud's ear, "Force them to strip before you kill them. Make it clean."

"As you wish, my lord."

Ashurizkadain heard the unasked question. "Flayed men are too obvious a calling card, Nimrud, and I would rather not delay in this cursed desert any longer. They gave me all the information I require. It seems the Kushites are indeed without

Taharqa's favor. They have separated from the army and made for the Nile." He looked west, where his quarry lay, perhaps a day's ride ahead of him. The king's favor was within his grasp.

"Pisaqar is alone."

THE PITS BY THE RIVER

YESBOKHE HAD ALWAYS hated Sena. You smelled it before you saw it, and once you'd seen it, you couldn't wait to leave. He couldn't think of any other places like that—so he supposed that Sena, with its overpowering reek of stagnant piss, was a singular marvel.

The Senaites knew their reputation and had done their best to allay it by placing the dyeing pits on the outskirts of the coastal town, but the constant push and pull of the Great Green Sea's breeze made their efforts tragically useless. Since there was no point in trying to avoid the pervading stench, Yesbokhe had gone straight for the source.

Up close, the pits were quite beautiful—pools of fierce blue liquid that sat tranquilly in their shallow brick enclosures. The rest of the operation didn't have the same appeal. Just beside the dyeing pits were neat rows of amphorae buried to their necks, uncapped, with the cloudy yellow urine inside bared for all to smell. Into these amphorae, industrious workers dipped their ladles and splashed generous helpings of putrid piss all over the freshly dyed sheets, which they left sopping on the clotheslines. Stripped to the waist, the workers' bare backs glistened from the heat of the ever-burning kilns.

Not that Yesbokhe pitied them. While he'd been off fighting the pharaoh's war, the dyers had spent the entire campaign season dyeing their precious *irtyu* cloth. Now, with the war won and commerce set to pick up again, they'd soon bundle their wares onto ships and caravans setting out east. These stinking men were all going to be rich.

The Desert Mice, on the other hand, had a long way to go before their payoff.

Which made this haggling even more of a challenge. And a debasing one at that.

The merchant remained politely indifferent to the lead pieces in Yesbokhe's outstretched palm. Reluctantly, he added a knob of carnelian. The merchant smiled and bowed and—infuriatingly—made no move to take the offer.

"I am sorry, my Kushite friend, but as I have already said, these," he indicated the bolts of bright blue cloth on his table, "are promised to Adon of Tyre. I am to finalize the sale tomorrow."

Yesbokhe jangled his handful of trinkets. *I'm offering you payment* now*!*

He realized he was coming across as petulant. Exchanges like these were the reason he didn't say much. He really was no good at this sort of thing, or at talking in general. Better to speak seldom and be thought a taciturn professional than open his mouth and reveal his impotence to the world.

Doing his best to hide the way he fumed, he added his last bit of carnelian to the handful.

The merchant remained steadfast. "Adon is an irascible fellow, I'm afraid. Your offer must be quite generous to be worth his ire."

Yesbokhe had to physically restrain himself from hurling the whole handful in the merchant's smiling face. When the tinsel had cleared from the edges of his vision, he dropped the money back into his purse and unslung his quiver. He drew one of his handmade arrows and displayed it to the merchant. He tapped on the shining arrowhead. *Iron*. He pricked his finger, drawing a bead of blood. *Sharp*. He traced the reed shaft, then bent it between his hands. *Straight. Flexible. Strong.* He stroked the eagle feather fletching. *Neat.*

The merchant clearly had no grasp of archery, because his skepticism was clear. He had no idea that Yesbokhe's arrows were without equal.

The scout winked at him. Without warning, and in one motion, he drew his bow and nocked the arrow. The merchant shrank with warbling cry, but Yesbokhe had no intention of harming him. He sent his arrow whistling straight into the sky.

With deliberate movements, he pulled five more arrows from the quiver and laid them neatly on the table. He slammed his purse down beside them, then coolly stepped back just in time for the hissing arrow to come back down. It sank into the center plank with a hard *thunk*.

The merchant shrieked and scampered backward once more, his saucer-like eyes fixed on the vibrating arrow.

Yesbokhe slung his longbow. With a satisfied nod, he slid past the stunned merchant and pulled a bolt of blue cloth off the cart. He walked away with a bolt over his shoulder, humming contently, while the merchant tried to work out what had just happened.

The land beyond the cluster of kilns was marshy and devoid of vegetation, save an intrepid bush or two. Yesbokhe traversed the network of duckboards with enormous care, because his nose told him the swamp wasn't made of mere river water. The spidery blue filaments spreading across the mud confirmed the awful suspicion. This was no place to lose one's balance.

But he almost did exactly that when he chanced a glance up. Ahead, standing on the thin causeway that rose above the floodplain, a man was waiting on him. He was shaven-headed, wearing a white kilt. A sword dangled at his hip. He held the reins of a vast horse that could only be of Nubian stock.

Yesbokhe stopped dead, clutching his bolt of cloth. He knew the sight of an Egyptian cavalryman, but something about the man was wrong. This one meant him harm.

The scout took a slow step back. The man tensed in response, the fingers on his sword hand twitching.

Without a second thought, Yesbokhe hurled the bolt aside and sprinted back the way he'd come. His hard-won prize was left to unravel in the pissy swamp. The duckboards thumped under his hard footfalls as he veered from one to the next. He threw a hunted glance over his shoulder. To his horror, the man had not only followed him, but was whirling a loaded sling about his head.

He bent low, but knew it wouldn't do him any good against any halfway proficient slinger. There was one last pair of duckboards between him and the relative shelter of the kilns, joined into a bent elbow. With no other choice, he leaped the gap between them. He misjudged and only just managed to land heavily on one knee. He found both hands plunged wrist deep into the yellowish muck. In the same instant, the sling stone hurtled over his bowed head and into the marsh with an odd sucking sound, spattering him with brown and blue flecks.

Gagging, he scrambled to his feet and dashed into the baking heat of the kilns.

"Kushite thug!" The merchant shook a fistful of arrows at him. "Come to rob me again, have you?"

Yesbokhe cast about desperately for a place to hide. To his dismay, nothing presented itself—nothing, that was, except the blue dyeing pits. For an instant, he considered simply putting an arrow into his pursuer. But no. He couldn't stoop to killing a fellow Egyptian soldier, not if he had a choice.

He hurried up to the merchant, who shrank again in fear as he removed his bow and quiver. "Sorry," he mumbled, pressing both into the man's reluctant hands. He yanked one arrow from the quiver, snapped off the arrowhead, and put the reed shaft into his mouth. Then, with the astonished merchant looking on, he lowered himself into the nearest pit and lay down. He squeezed his mouth and eyelids shut as the revoltingly warm liquid closed over his face.

As his perception of the world shrank into darkness and a soup of muffled voices—and an earthy, metallic taste he tried his best not to think about—he couldn't help wondering if the gods had chosen this as his squalid end. He supposed Osiris would laugh to see a man with pigmented skin like his own, only blue instead of green. That might work in his favor, when the time came to blunder through the Deathless God's trials, vying for an afterlife he wasn't sure he deserved.

The voices above went silent. Yesbokhe breathed lightly through the reed tube and hoped desperately it wasn't making a whistle.

Then the side of his head exploded in a blaze of agony. Yesbokhe gasped through his straw, inhaling a mouthful of dye. He catapulted himself out of the dyeing pit, blind and coughing. His first sight was the soldier, his kilt splashed with blue, struggling to pry his sword free of the vat's soft clay bottom. A stroke of good fortune that Yesbokhe wasn't going to pass up. He tackled the soldier with a grunt. There were shrieks all around as the grappling men rolled on the stinking ground. They punched wildly at each other, but with one simple difference: Yesbokhe was punching with a dagger in his hand. He stabbed in a frenzy, making a pink mess of the other man's midriff. He only stopped when his dagger drove into a rib and snapped at the hilt.

Panting, the top half of his ear dangling by a flap of skin, he got up shakily. He let the useless dagger handle drop. The man was wearing a pair of Assyrian boots, he noticed. Odd choice of souvenirs. Yesbokhe's trophy dagger had been the wiser choice, though he supposed more decorative than practical. As he retrieved his bow and quiver—the merchant had evidently dropped them when he scampered—he noticed that the dangling paw of his cloak had been stained a vivid blue. He groaned to himself. His leopard skin was ruined. The others would never let him hear the end of it.

Cursing silently, pressing at his nearly severed ear, he made to turn away. Before he did, he snatched another bolt of cloth from the merchant's stock. Adon of Tyre wouldn't miss it, filthy rich bastard that he was.

He crossed the piss marsh again, head turning in search of more crazed soldiers, and though the horse had disappeared, no more threats presented themselves. Warily, he moved onto the causeway and started upriver.

The Nile was near flood, and the people of Sena were busy with preparations. Ditch diggers toiled on the roadside, readying the irrigation canals that would carry the lifegiving waters to every corner of this branch of the Delta. Farmers with their wives and children fanned out across the fields, raking out the dead roots from their previous crops. Wagons trundled past, piled high with bricks and reeds that would shore up the town's buildings. Sena was built on an island, and if the gods were good, their flood would be generous enough to warrant some precautions.

Yesbokhe didn't pay any of this undue attention. He was busy thinking about how much his ear—or lack thereof—bloody hurt. He tried to distract himself with thoughts of the oasis at Siwa, and this lovely blue cloth he'd be bringing as a homecoming gift. Kasaqa had always been one to appreciate the finer things. His wife, with her nimble fingers, would work this unadorned cloth into something breathtaking. Maybe a new cloak.

His ever-roving scout's eyes fixed momentarily on a cloud of dust to his left, beyond a line of palm trees. In that instant, he found himself back at Eltekeh, amid the smashed chariots and the shrieks of dying horses, blood squishing in his sandals. He shook his head to clear the sudden memory. That dust was probably just a team of oxen trying to free a stuck wagon. But he kept looking, just to be sure. He'd decided he was in no mood to face Osiris colored blue.

He followed the road south along the river. Though the dock hadn't come into view, he knew it would soon. He imagined the others had boarded the boat already and were cursing as they waited on him. That wouldn't be too bad; mostly he just hoped he'd missed loading the asses, which never failed to be a chore, especially if the one doing it was bleeding from a halved ear. The fact was he'd never gotten along well with asses, or people for that matter—Kasaqa being the notable exception. And those Judean donkeys? They were biters. The thought of their chomping teeth made his neck prickle with anxiety.

Wait—that wasn't why.

He stopped in his tracks.

When he snapped his eyes back to the palms, there was a line of horsemen shaded between the trunks, ten in all, two riders sat atop each steed. They were far, at least thrice an arrow shot, but his sharp sight picked out the sparkle of bronze gorgets in the dappled sunlight.

He gasped through his teeth. Tits of Mut! More cavalrymen!

Before he could complete the thought, the mounted men sprang into the open. Whether they'd noticed his bow or his blueness, they had picked him out as their target. The entire squadron was charging straight at him.

Why the pharaoh's men were this intent on murdering him, Yesbokhe couldn't even begin to fathom. But he didn't think twice. He cast his second bolt of cloth onto the dusty road and broke into a sprint. His sandals pounded dirt as he unslung his longbow. He scrabbled through his jostling quiver for an arrow and pulled one free. The enemy was closing with ferocious speed, and the boat still wasn't in sight. He had to delay.

He nocked an arrow and skidded to a halt, legs splayed and bow bent, his clawed right hand holding the taut string to his right ear—the intact one, gods be thanked. The wind was against that same ear, he noted, so he adjusted his aim in that direction and angled upward for maximum range, eyes flicking constantly between his arrow's shaft and his target.

He released the string and his breath simultaneously. He was already back to running full tilt while the arrow whistled high into the air, its feathers guiding the shaft straight and true. He glanced back in time to see a rider expertly catch the projectile on his small shield. The rider lowered his buckler before stooping over his horse's neck to allow the bowman perched behind him to take a return shot.

Yesbokhe swerved off the road and crossed the line of palm trees just as the enemy arrows began to fall. They hammered into the trunks with explosions of stringy bark. Others pulped themselves on the hard-packed road. The shots were *close*, far too close for Yesbokhe's peace of mind. He was up against professionals. And they'd be on him in twenty heartbeats.

Unless he could dissuade them. Huffing, he dashed back up the embankment and perched on the roadside, half-shielded behind a tree. More arrows sliced through the palm fronds but he paid them no mind. He loosed three, four, five arrows at the rapidly approaching horsemen. The first shot was long, the second flew wide, and the rider managed to take the third and fourth on his shield—but the impacts weakened the buckler enough that the fifth punched through the planks and stapled his arm to his breast. He tumbled off the horse's back with a squawk, the reins still clutched in one hand. The horse swerved in obedience, and the archer soon followed his rider ignominiously to the ground. They both rolled in a tangle of limbs amid an upswell of Egyptian dust.

The other cavalry witnessed this and adjusted tactics. The riders began to circle, their archers loosing arrows as quickly as they could nock them. They meant to throw off Yesbokhe's aim, which would have worked admirably—except he was no longer there.

He hurtled back through the trees and into the field beyond, making for the thick reeds. He crashed through them with the desperate strength of a hunted man. Using his bow as a club, he whacked the stalks aside, breathing hard through bared teeth. Hooves sank into the damp soil behind him. He heard jumbled shouts. But no arrows followed. The reeds were tall and thick enough to obscure him.

He waded into the warm green water until he was sunk to the navel, deep enough that he could dive if he was spotted. Glancing constantly shoreward, he battled his way through the shallows. He didn't dare make a sound. If the gods favored him, his friends would hear the yells and make themselves ready.

When the boat appeared through a gap in the reeds, he could have laughed with relief. It wasn't much to look at—just a mass of reed bundles lashed together into the rough approximation of a hull and covered over with planks, encircled with wooden railings, with a little lean-to hut sat precariously in the middle. Yesbokhe's heart sank to see that there was only one person aboard: the boatmaster, a fat Egyptian called Pepy-Nakht. Standing amid a cluster of nervous-looking asses, the rotund man hauled on a line, which led to another ass that had anchored itself obstinately in the muddy shallows. The Desert Mice were pushing the stubborn animal's flanks, to little avail.

The scout whistled frantically at them as he thrashed out of the shallows. "Horsemen!"

The mercenaries immediately understood his tone. They drew their weapons as one. Over the chorus of oaths, Pisaqar yelled, "We cannot withstand cavalry! Board the boat!"

"What about the donkey?"

The captain's face hardened with indecision. Then he drew his sword, and for an awful instant, Yesbokhe was sure he would slay the animal to deny it to the enemy. Instead, with one swipe, he cut the reins. Then, with a backhand motion, he smacked the flat of the blade across the donkey's rear end. In a flurry of hooves, it vanished through the reeds. The small herd of goats nibbling at the undergrowth bleated in alarm and scampered out of its way.

With visible relief, the mercenaries clambered onto the rickety dock. They hurried for the boat. The albino bull clomped along after them. Weapons and bags were tossed unceremoniously onto the deck as everyone made to board. Kalab added his khopesh to the growing pile and offered Yesbokhe a hand up.

"What happened to *you*?"

Yesbokhe gestured hopelessly back the way he'd come. He handed the acolyte his bow—which he'd kept meticulously dry—and let himself be pulled from the water. The others, lined up on the dock, did double-takes at his blue skin.

Qorobar made to hop aboard the boat first, but Nawidemaq's screech brought him to a halt.

"No boat! No! We appease the river first!"

This despite the clearly audible hoofbeats. The enemies must have spotted the fleeing ass. For now, the tall reeds hid Pepy's boat from view, but they'd soon find the branch in the road and charge through. The peril of the moment was clear—but Nawidemaq, for all his eccentricities, was rarely wrong when it came to the gods.

Amani gesticulated wildly between the medicine man and the road. "Don't just talk about it, holy man! Do it!"

Nawidemaq dug through his bag of holy trinkets, clicking to himself in the bastard tongue of the deep southern plains. He pulled out a polished red stone carved into the shape of some sort of shellfish and cupped it to one ear, his eyes squeezed and tongue between his teeth. The dock planks creaked as the mercenaries hopped impatiently. Beyond the tall reeds, hooves beat up and down the road, seeking a way in.

Then the medicine man's eyes snapped open. "An offering of warm blood!"

"The beast!" cried Tariq. But Nawidemaq's white bull was already sitting on the boat, watching the scene unfold with bovine serenity.

The others cast about with despairing eyes for some sort of mammalian sacrifice. Qorobar growled, leaped off the dock, and promptly vanished into the reeds. He soon emerged holding a struggling goat by the neck. Eyes afire, he stomped up to the water's edge, then wound back, and with an almighty effort, hurled the goat into the air. The animal flew in a high arc, bleating and flailing, before splashing down in the Nile.

"Well?" bellowed Qorobar.

The medicine man nodded sheepishly. "That will work."

Quickly as they could, the group scrambled aboard the boat. Pepy-Nakht, clearly aghast at his poor choice of passengers, handed out a few oars, which they used to shove off from the dock. Slowly, laboriously, the loaded boat brushed out toward the wide expanse of the Nile.

Then came the hiss of arrows slicing into the water. Those who held poles pinched their shoulders and hunched, while everyone else hugged the cabin. The enemy horse pairs milled in the shallows, loosing arrows at their escaping quarry.

Pisaqar grabbed Eleazar by the neck and roared in his face, "Why are they here? What have you done?"

"I know nothing!" insisted the Israelite.

Meanwhile, Yesbokhe stood aft and loosed arrows back. His quiver was running low and the rocking waves made his platform unsteady, and the riders kept wheeling their horses about to throw off his aim further. Those arrows that reached their targets landed on well-placed bucklers.

Rather abruptly, the incoming volleys thinned out and ceased altogether. The enemy had run out of arrows. All that came the Kushites' way now were clucking noises and obscene gestures.

The Desert Mice made a show of their escape. They danced around the deck, whistling and lifting their kilts, mocking their foiled pursuers.

Alone among the groups, two men remained silent. Pisaqar stared over the Nile at the man who could only be his opposing counterpart: a thin-chinned man wearing a crimson cloak. Even a furlong away, with facial features reduced to smudges of color, there was little mistaking the malevolence that burned in this man's gaze. Yesbokhe might have shuddered, but Pisaqar studied his new enemy with sublime composure. For the first time since Jerusalem, the captain resembled himself.

The breeze caught the sail. The Nile drew the Desert Mice to her breast and bore them on toward their destiny.

Pepy-Nakht heaved an explosive grunt as he took his place at the campfire. His knees throbbed, and his fingers too, his body spent after a long day and half a night of overuse. There was still much hard labor to come, he was certain. He studied his Kushite passengers sidelong while they settled onto their logs. The mercenaries kept their weapons near to hand, caring little for his many reassurances that they were safe in this isolated niche of the Delta. These were troublesome passengers he'd taken on. And—for the moment—poor ones, too. Between the nine of them, they had only a single loaf of bread. The priest, Ermun, tore off hunks, which his acolyte Kalab distributed, each topped with a slice of onion.

"Where did you come across that?" Qorobar asked appreciably as he was handed his meager dinner.

"The blue fellow found some growing wild," replied Kalab, jutting his chin at their scout.

With his mouth full, the big man asked Yesbokhe, "Where exactly? Might try to dig up some more."

The scout pointed to a grassy mound, one of the many scattered across the tree-covered little island.

Qorobar rumbled his thanks and went back to his meal, such that it was.

"Here." Pepy-Nakht found the acolyte holding out a fist-sized chunk of bread and thick slice of onion.

The boatmaster took the generous portion with amazement. "It's more than any of you have gotten," he observed, puzzled.

Kalab shrugged. "To each according to his need," he recited without much care.

Pisaqar saw the exchange and said across the fire, “We are soldiers, accustomed to short rations.”

Pepy guffawed. “Good, because I was getting the impression you were feeding me more because I’m fat. I understand. I’m only soft.”

Tariq grinned slyly. “Good to keep you fat ones around. Spares us the trouble of drawing lots when the starving times come.”

The mercenaries gaped at the redhead in horror, but Pepy’s roar of laughter broke the silence.

“Aye, and on the day, I’ll hop cheerfully into the pot!” The flickering ring was filled with chuckles. The Israelite failed to join in, but looked out warily into the night.

“Should we not make some passing attempt, at least, to be quiet?”

“Eleazar,” said Pisaqar patiently, “our boatmaster assures us of our safety. Let his word suffice.”

Pepy rolled his eyes at the anxious foreigner. “We’re deep into the Delta, and a seldom-visited corner of it, at that. Those horsemen can’t have followed us, even if the gods told them where to look. Out there are only fish, fowl, and crocodiles.”

Amani clutched her heart in mock terror. “Not crocodiles!”

“Aye, they come dragging themselves onto these islands at the scent of foreign blood. You’re safe, dear girl. But you, my Israelite friend? You’ll be torn limb from limb and shat out by morning.”

“An improved form! Gods be praised!” Kalab shouted, adding to the mirth as Eleazar glowered.

“Quit tormenting the man,” Pisaqar ordered. The laughter stilled.

In the bout of silence that followed, the old priest addressed Pepy with a curious question.

“What is this island called?”

Pepy chewed his bread. “I don’t know. No one’s ever cared to ask. It’s just a hiding spot far from prying eyes. I doubt it ever had a name.”

"Oh, it surely did in the past. Those humble mounds were walls, once." He indicated the place his acolyte had, where Yesbokhe had found the onions.

The others peered at the place Ermun pointed to. "How do you come to that?" asked Tariq.

"The coast is dotted with ruins such as these. Great cities ruined in some forgotten cataclysm, fallen into decay. Why, Pisaqar and I have made our camps in many hollow walls over our decades." Pisaqar nodded with a distant expression. "I am certain you've encountered such places in your travels without knowing, Pepy-Nakht."

"Ah, but you see, priest, sailors of Egypt who venture out into the Great Green do not live to grow old and fat like me," teased Pepy. "I suppose that's the reason those cities are ruins. Their people trusted the sea, and the sea naturally betrayed them."

"Still," Ermun said amiably, "I wonder what this island meant to whom, and how long ago."

"I say it's the spot where Osiris's tree grew," Qorobar said with a spray of half-chewed onion.

Kalab grinned. "No, no, this is the site of the Lord of Life's long-lost prick!"

"His *what*?" the Israelite said, appalled.

"He doesn't know the tale," said Pepy in awe. "Let's regale the man! The night is young."

The mercenaries adjusted their positions with eager looks, glad of the excuse to retell the story beloved of all Egyptians. They looked to their leader, who leaned forward and clapped his hands on his knees, grinning at the dismayed foreigner.

"We begin with Osiris," he thundered, "the best and goodliest of all gods. He and his perfect wife, Isis, ruled together over Egypt, having saved the people from war and cannibalism by teaching them to farm, and bake, and brew, and play music, and write poetry. With each gift they gave, their people's love for them grew. Osiris served Egypt well. The land prospered."

Ermun took up the tale. “But watching this was Set, the younger god, wicked and jealous. He wished fervently to surpass his brother’s accomplishments. When Osiris departed on a long trip to spread the knowledge of civilization to other lands, Set saw his chance to supplant him. After much time, Osiris returned, and Set was the very first to welcome the god-king home. He did so—”

“—by throwing a party!” cried Tariq. “It was a spectacular thing. All the best food you could think of and more, the palace decked in splendorous things from across the world—”

“Which had only just been civilized,” muttered Amani.

“—filled with music and dancing and beautiful half-naked girls—”

She smacked the back of his head and stole the tale as he rubbed the sore spot. “But apart from that nonsense, in the middle of the party there was a chest, really beautiful. It was made of expensive woods like ebony and cedar, little bits of ivory. This was a priceless treasure. Everyone couldn’t help staring at it while they mingled, even the guests of honor, Osiris and Isis.”

Kalab swept in, still chuckling at the redhead’s setback. “Once the god and goddess had grown sedate, and not a little drunk, Set called everyone’s attention. He announced that he would hold a game, and the gorgeous wooden chest would belong to whoever won. He lifted the lid and proclaimed that this luxurious gift would belong to the one who fit inside it perfectly. One by one, the guests tried to cram themselves inside, but nobody quite fit.”

“Some were too big,” said Qorobar.

“Others too thin,” added Amani.

“And still more,” boomed Pepy-Nakht, “too fat!”

The priest continued. “Finally, Osiris, overcome with curiosity, inquired if he might try the game. The god-king wriggled down into the chest, and his brother rubbed his hands in anticipation. For in truth, this was what Set had planned.

He knew his brother well, and so had built the chest to his precise dimensions, from head to foot and from shoulder to shoulder. Osiris fit into the box exactly. Believing he had won the game, the god-king cried out—"

"*The chest is mine!*" yelled Pisaqar.

"*Indeed, my brother*," Qorobar said forebodingly, "*and forever shall it be yours.*"

The Kushites clapped for the miniature performances. Then Ermun went on. "At that, Set slammed the lid down, and as poor Isis looked on in horror, he nailed the lid shut. This was no chest, but a coffin! Then Set hurled the sealed chest into the Nile. The coffin floated downstream for a time before beaching itself on the shores of a foreign land."

Eleazar crossed his arms. "Which this island is not."

Amani shushed him sharply.

Ermun inclined his head. "The chest stopped at the base of a tree. Quickly, the tree grew and flourished from Osiris's divine power, hiding the coffin within its trunk. The king of the land soon noticed that a particular tree had grown more beautiful than any other. On his command, it was chopped down and brought to his palace. No one realized that the trunk still contained the coffin of Osiris."

"Isis," intoned Tariq, vying to redeem his earlier misstep, "was heartbroken at the loss of her husband, but she was determined to find him. The goddess turned into an eagle—"

"Falcon," said Amani.

"—no, an *eagle*! She flew north along the river, searching far and wide until her path led her to the stump of the tree. Then she disguised herself as an old woman and went to meet the king."

"Why would she know to do this?" asked Eleazar, struggling to keep up with the story.

"Because she's a goddess! She understands these things! Everyone stop interrupting me!" Tariq cleared his throat. "So, the king met this old woman and was so impressed that he took her on as a nursemaid for the newborn prince. Isis grew fond of the child. She decided to make him immortal by bathing him in flame."

The Israelite rubbed his brows.

"But when the queen saw the old nursemaid feeding the child into the fire, she attacked her, not realizing that Isis was actually bestowing a great gift. With the ritual interrupted, the child lost his chance at immortality."

The priest revoked Tariq's storytelling privileges by abruptly taking up the thread. "In that moment, Isis threw off her disguise and revealed her true nature. The king and queen prostrated themselves in terror, asking what they could do for the goddess to win her forgiveness. Isis asked only for the tree. When she retrieved her husband's body from the trunk, she found him dead inside. Weeping, she returned to Egypt with the body, and placed it in the silt of the river while she worked to find a means of restoring it from decay. Before she could devise a solution, Set discovered what she was doing. Enraged, he set upon Osiris's body and hacked it into forty-two pieces, which he then scattered all across the land of Egypt.

"Isis had lost her husband for a second time, and although she wept once more, she did not give in to despair. Again, she searched, this time traveling up and down the Nile in a boat. Piece by piece, she recovered the parts of her husband's body. After she had gathered as many as she could find—"

"Not his prick, though," mentioned Kalab, but a hiss from Yesbokhe silenced him. The scout motioned to Qorobar, who had grown suddenly solemn. Pepy-Nakht gazed on with interest, wondering if the big man had suffered some fresh loss of his own.

Gently, Ermun continued the telling. "Isis performed a ritual, which made her husband's body whole once again. Osiris sprang to life. However, their joy was brief, for Osiris had passed into death, and therefore could not remain in the land of the living for long. In little time, he would be forced to depart for Duat, the realm of the dead, there to rule instead of Egypt. Before he left, however, he conceived a son with Isis, whom they named Horus the Younger. Horus would bear Osiris's legacy and one day avenge him." He smiled at his companions. "A story for another time. Well, Eleazar, now you know it. The myth of Osiris."

Eleazar seemed to be chewing his tongue. "Quite entertaining."

Kalab snorted. "He thinks it's stupid drivel."

"How did the god and goddess conceive a son without his..." Eleazar motioned between his legs.

"Prick," Amani said, very loudly. "We aren't gentle souls. You're allowed to swear."

Tariq added, "It's a myth, Eleazar. It doesn't have to make sense."

Qorobar had apparently recovered enough to rejoin the conversation. "Don't listen to him. His people think the first man came from mud, and the first woman was one of his ribs."

The girl grimaced. "They would, wouldn't they?"

"Well then, what do Egyptians believe?" demanded Eleazar.

Pepy-Nakht settled back and chewed his calluses while the bickering went back and forth. Troublesome customers, this mismatched little band. But he'd spent a lifetime hauling brick and straw. He was ready for an adventure. Especially one that made him rich enough to retire, give his aching bones some rest at last.

All the same, the boatmaster couldn't help but wonder whether these ones had fought themselves free of Set's treasure chest already, or were presently blundering into it.

OSIRIS'S DUE

ERMUN RAN THE whetstone along the arc of his khopesh. There was an art to honing the curve of a blade, a commitment that required patience and precision. The priest had been bringing the gods glory for nearly forty years by now, and knew the task well. Well enough that between passes, he could stoop over for a squint at the papyrus laid on the planks.

All through the five days they'd sailed the Nile, Ermun had plied the text, and yet the papyrus stubbornly kept its secrets. A good deal of the scroll had rotted and crumbled away over the centuries. What sections remained were largely blank, the ink smudged from countless fingertips tracing crucial lines of text. Only a few parts could be made out, and among them, one name in particular.

"Sethherkepeshef Meryamun," muttered the priest. It had been his constant refrain ever since Eleazar had passed the scroll into his care, and the only fruit the decayed text had borne.

By midday, they would reach Memphis. The other mercenaries were cheery at the prospect of civilization after a long campaign season. Reed boats passed with growing frequency, all rowing downriver for fresh loads of festivalgoers. Kalab shouted greetings, eagerly asking after the availability of girls and beer in the city. "Plenty of both!" the boatmasters called back, tossing over some of the flower garlands that festooned their hulls. Although the morning was young, the mercenaries' necks were heavy with strings of blue lilies. Yesbokhe, still looking a bit blue himself, had busied himself fashioning flower crowns for everybody, but Nawidemaq had claimed them all for himself. A good dozen of them teetered on his head as he wound garlands around his bull's horns. The animal eyed the flowers hungrily but contented himself with nibbling at the loose petals coating the deck. Further aft, Amani whirled her sling and cast a whistling stone across the water. Her deftly aimed shot caught a heron mid-flight. The other mercenaries whooped as the bird flopped into the Nile. Tariq dove in to fetch it. He swam the full distance submerged and at last surfaced directly beneath the fallen bird, an astounding feat which the rest applauded. The girl thief watched him sidelong while he swam back, a fact that the rest of them pretended not to notice. Except Qorobar. "Young love," he said softly. He added a wriggling perch to his basket and cast another line.

Then there was Pisaqar. The captain had been leaning on the railing ever since the gleaming white pyramids had appeared through the haze of dust. Even the younger mercenaries had seen the great edifices enough times by now that they no longer noticed them, but Pisaqar gazed on them with such unblinking raptness that his eyes must have been aching. Ermun spoke again, more out of concern for him than a desire to make conversation.

"Have they changed since the last time you saw them?"

Pisaqar smiled over at him. "They have been there for almost two millennia, my friend. They will always be there. I still enjoy gazing on their majesty. And what of your work on the papyrus? Any revelations?"

"None whatsoever. I know the same things I did the first time I laid eyes on this cursed thing. The man buried was King Ramesses, Eighth of His Name. He was fond of onion bread.

And astronomy, also. No mention of tomb or temple. We know the offerings he demanded for his *ka*, but not the offering place. Maddening." He set his khopesh down so he could stand. When he stretched his arms, his aging bones creaked. "Truth be told, I'm not altogether disappointed in this scroll's lack of answers."

"There are other ways to glean the information," said Pisaqar.

"Yes, there are indeed. But that isn't what I was speaking of."

Pisaqar made a face. "I know that. I was giving you an out."

"Were you, now?"

"To spare us both an awkward talk."

"Yet it's one we must have. Matters have changed, Pisaqar. To be released from the pharaoh's service, that was not unexpected, not after Taharqa moved on from Jerusalem without us."

"It came as a surprise to *me*," Pisaqar muttered bitterly and—Ermun thought—sadly, too.

"But now we find that we are being pursued, it seems by Taharqa's own cavalry. Should that not give us pause?"

"I did take pause, my old friend. Two days we spent winding through the Delta, and there has not been a sign of those horsemen in the three days since. We have shaken them off. You know that. Just as I know that you have harbored doubts about this venture from the beginning. Thirty years together, Ermun. Your heart is not a secret to me."

Ermun looked out over the shimmering green waters. Beyond, on the highest swell of the western bank, loomed the necropolis and its jewels: the pyramids. The great monuments jostled for space on the plateau, each more enormous than the last. The rising sun cast their smooth white limestone sides into relief, and shone brightly on the golden capstones surmounting each. The mind struggled to reconcile their mountainous scale with their human artifice. And their age was a fact that defied easy comprehension, even for a learned man such as he. The pharaoh whose resting place they sought had walked the land some four centuries past, a long enough span. Yet the pyramids had been built by the greatest of pharaohs some fifteen hundred years prior to Ramesses the Eighth's birth—and so predated humble Ermun by nearly two thousand years. That impossible span was more staggering still when one saw how little affected the huge pyramids were. Their limestone casings looked to be every bit as smooth as the day they'd been anchored in place. That men—ancient men—could build such things was a fact that had never failed to stagger Ermun.

Yet his acolyte didn't seem to notice them at all. Kalab was busy trading wicked jests with Tariq in a vain effort to win back Amani, a struggle he wouldn't admit he'd lost. Girls, beer, and swordplay. He thought of little else.

"I worry for the boy," he told Pisaqar. "That's the root of it."

Pisaqar followed his gaze, puzzled. "Kalab, you mean."

"Yes."

"He can scarcely be called a boy," his friend chuckled. "Twenty-five Inundations, he's seen! Nearly half of them with you."

"Oh, he is grown, true enough. He has a strong arm, that boy. And he's a better fighter than you were at his age."

"Let us not say things we will regret," smiled Pisaqar.

"But his mind! So very uninquisitive. He might know the prayers, but he has never cared about the reasons we say them."

"I daresay you have just described most priests in Egypt, or anywhere else for that matter."

"And that is likely true," admitted Ermun. "Maybe my age has made me prone to bouts of lament. Even so, that boy is an acolyte, meant to honor the gods and their laws. Yet he was the first to jump at the chance to rob a god-king's resting place. Have men always been this easily corruptible?"

Pisaqar mulled this over. "I feel you judge your acolyte too harshly, Ermun. After all, you agreed to this venture too."

The priest wagged his finger. "Ah, but I made you work hard to convince me!" His smile faded. "Pisaqar, I must be serious. I am deeply troubled. Nawidemaq has persuaded you all that we still serve a higher cause, but he is mistaken. This thing we do, it's simple greed. We rob the pharaoh for our own benefit."

"Which makes us no different from anyone else," Pisaqar told him steadily.

"Such cynicism fills me with dread. A nation of selfish people is rotten, Pisaqar. Brittle." He looked at the other mercenaries, still occupied with their play. "I fear for them all."

Footsteps announced Eleazar's approach. "How long before we reach Memphis?"

"Another hour," said Pisaqar.

"Excellent. Priest, have you made progress with the papyrus?"

Ermun exchanged an entertained look with Pisaqar. The twice-traitor seemed to fancy himself some sort of authority figure. Doubtless, that would make for an amusing spectacle when he tried to inflict himself on someone who wasn't in the mood for him.

"The papyrus hasn't yielded any useful information," Ermun told him. "I daresay King Sennacherib's plans would have been foiled from the start, thanks entirely to his lousy recordkeeping."

Eleazar had a quick laugh. Probably it was one reason he'd won himself into the Assyrian king's trust. "I assure you, priest: keep the faith, and your reward will be great. Whatever information that papyrus lacks, my contact in Memphis will deliver."

Ermun stooped on creaking joints and carefully rolled up the papyrus. "Your man will be no help whatsoever."

The Israelite raised his thick brows. "Is that so?"

"If he is a tomb builder, as you say—and it seems you are ever brimming with half-truths, so that's a matter of debate—then he will know how to break into one. That doesn't mean he'll know where to find it in the first place."

"Come now. He and his forefathers built in the Valley of the Kings," the Israelite noted sourly. "Of course he will know where the tombs were built. It is his profession."

"You fail to understand: this pharaoh died over *four centuries ago*. Tombs in the valley are well hidden. Those who build them are sworn to secrecy. No one living can give us the information we seek. I assure you, your man is quite useless in this matter. No, if we're to know where to look, there's only one place to go." To find their answer, they would need to venture into the house of the gods. "The temple of P'tah."

Memphis. The White Walls. City of a Hundred Doors.

The Heb Sed festivities were in full swing by the time Pepy-Nakht jostled his boat into a vacant dock, a feat that required the full breadth of the plump sailor's vocabulary and not a few unsubtle threats besides. It really was remarkable how persuasive a few part-drawn blades could be—Kalab's khopesh prominent among them.

The moment the dockhands lashed the boat, the other mercenaries sheathed their weapons again and hopped ashore, elated to be on solid ground once more. Pepy laid a ramp and descended into the open hold, where he began to tie the restless donkeys together.

"What will you do with them?" Kalab asked.

"Sell the stinking things," Pepy replied, though there was no real bite behind the words. "These beasts will chew through the hull if I leave them to it!" He stroked a mane. "I'll find a dealer of repute, young priest, don't you fret. They'll be treated well."

"Long as they don't end up in a stew. They bore us across the Sinai without complaint." Kalab thought. "Well. Some complaint."

"But remember. These beasts of burden will only fetch so high a price. We'll have enough bread and beer to get to Thebes, no further. I won't be able to linger there long without provisions." The boatmaster's obsequious grin belied the canny words. "Remind your captain of that, won't you?"

Kalab clapped Pepy on the arm. “Pisaqar doesn’t need to be told anything twice,” he assured with a grin that was every bit as false. “Farewell.”

He joined Ermun at the far end of the dock, where the old priest was conferring with Pisaqar. The captain handed Ermun a wad of cloth. “This ought to serve as an acceptable offering to Osiris.”

Ermun half-unwrapped it. Inside was a miniature hoard of precious stones—several rubies and an emerald the size of a fingernail. Pisaqar chuckled at the way their jaws dropped.

“Jerusalem may have emptied its treasury to pay Assyria its tribute. But King Hezekiah at least saw fit to scrape together this reward for us.”

Kalab told him, “This could buy us passage all the way to the Second Cataract.”

“Pepy-Nakht’s payment will not be an issue as long as you succeed in your task.” Pisaqar bunched Ermun’s fist around the gemstones and clasped it tight. “Give this up to the Eternal Lord. Do not return with it. Understand?”

The captain spoke with such firmness that Kalab glanced between the two men, wondering what sort of interesting conversation he’d just missed.

Ermun nodded assent. Pisaqar touched his forehead to theirs, then went to gather the others. They would have their own mission to perform that day.

Ermun pulled up his scales to allow Kalab to stuff the treasure into his tunic. Then they set off into the city, toward the looming walls of the great temple.

Pharaoh Shabaku’s jubilee, the Heb Sed, was well under way, and the full population of many tens of thousands thronged the streets. There were minstrels on every corner, their competing tunes echoing down the avenues where listeners flailed and swayed to whichever song caught their fancy. Naked children splashed in the reed-filled canals under the doting eyes of their parents. Packs of adolescent boys swaggered along, each youth trying to outshine the next in a largely fruitless effort to capture a girl's interest. Men and women alike crowded around the many beer stalls. The drinks were courtesy of the pharaoh himself. Everyone was raring to get their god-king's money's worth.

Kalab and Ermun drew more than a few eyes as they pressed through gaps in the crowd. It was little surprise; the pair made for a wildly incongruous sight. Their black-as-night skin marked them out as Kushites. Their shaven heads and leopard-skin cloaks made them priests—but also warriors, because each wore the white feather of a soldier in his headband. And then there were the Assyrian scales they'd donned, which no one had a clue how to interpret. If anyone thought of troubling them, though, they refrained. Would-be heroes held their tongues, prostitutes kept to their doorsteps, and the masses evidently decided it best not to ask khopesh-wielding priests for a word of blessing. For the second time today, Kalab counted himself amused at the power of a sheathed blade.

The crowds gradually parted. Up ahead, the Temple of P'tah beckoned them closer. Its monolithic walls were at least the height of ten men, easily dwarfing any other structure in the city. Painted hieroglyphs proclaiming the deeds of gods and kings graced the upper reaches of each facade, while above them, countless pennants of every hue slithered on their poles. Kalab had been to this temple countless times but couldn't help being overawed at the sheer audacity of the structure, built on such scale upon the soft silt of the Nile's banks. Carved steps lifted him from the casual squalor of the city, eyed the whole way by rows of vigilant sphinxes. To either side of the main entrance, itself wide enough for two wagons to pass through side by side, were a pair of obelisks hewn from polished basalt, adorned with tall columns of hieroglyphs limned in gold. Beyond these stone sentinels, common folk were not permitted to pass, so the platforms were piled with offerings of food, garments, and candles—the modest sorts of things low-born Egyptians could afford. And of course, beside each gift was a tablet or scroll that asked the gods for a boon in return. Religion could be quite transactional, Kalab found. Not that his purpose was any different.

The Temple of P'tah was not a single structure, but a grand complex that housed both the gods themselves and the bureaucracy that sustained them. The main entrance brought Kalab and Ermun into an office space rather than some holy sanctum. Scribe-priests were ensconced behind vast desks heaped with offerings, which they meticulously logged on papyrus scrolls before passing them to servants to be organized and warehoused. The whispers echoing through the chamber were not chanted prayers, but arithmetic. Festivals were busy times for these administrators, surpassed only by the harvest.

They passed through the busy offices and onto a colonnade, whose thick pillars buttressed a ceiling crowded with painted scenes from myth, the background colored in dazzling blue to mimic the sky. The courtyard outside, like the foyer, was a practical space. Vacant silos awaited the coming grain tax, Egypt's true source of wealth. Since the harvest wouldn't come for many months, the priesthood had converted the space into a paddock, where goats and cattle nosed around every cranny for stray kernels left over from the past season. Acolytes tended to the herds, carrying staves and shovels and looking hideously bored. They scrutinized Kalab's armor and sword with undisguised envy.

As they drew nearer to the heart of the temple, statues began to appear between the columns—humanoid shapes with the heads of falcons, rams, lions, bulls, jackals, crocodiles. All were studiously clean from the morning rituals, with bread bowls and beer mugs laid at their feet. There were amulets about their necks, and cloaks of animal skins draped across their shoulders. Ermun and Kalab played their small part in the observances by bowing before each statue.

After much meandering, they arrived at the House of

Sekhmet. The lion goddess's place was a surprisingly modest building on the far side of a square courtyard. Her house was rather nondescript, but the half dozen alabaster sphinxes guarding the courtyard made it unmistakable. Each statue was nearly thrice Ermun's height, with such astonishingly lifelike features that they seemed likely to pounce given half a reason. As a precaution, the two of them bowed carefully to each sphinx they passed. It didn't pay to take the risk of offending such deadly creatures. The pair made a final obeisance in front of the dwelling place of the warrior goddess herself, leaving a jar of beer and a bronze dagger on her doorstep to appease her bellicose spirit.

Beloved as Sekhmet was of the Kushites, they hadn't come with her in mind. It was her son, Osiris, that they sought. The entrance to his vaults was sequestered in the corner of the courtyard, where steps descended steeply into the temple's foundations. It was possible to make out maybe the first ten steps before darkness swallowed up the rest. The sconces hadn't been lit; evidently visitors were not welcomed.

Ermun took the plunge with hardly a pause. Kalab savored one last look at the open sky before following his teacher into the bowels of the temple. Within moments, he found himself enveloped in growing blackness, which squeezed him tighter with every step as he drew further from the sunlight. At the same time as sight abandoned him, his hearing conspired against him, amplifying his and Ermun's footfalls into a muffled cacophony. Wind drew at the tunnel entrance, sounding for all the world like some vast creature's breathing. Ahead and below, in the invisible depths of Osiris's domain, he could hear whispering—whether real or imagined, he couldn't quite guess. The musk of dry decay and salt singed his nostrils.

Kalab gripped his khopesh tightly and trusted his feet, which twelve years of swordplay had made sure and precise. Soon enough, his heel came down hard on level ground. Ermun hissed as the acolyte bumped into his back.

"Wait." After a pause, the priest struck a flint. A shower of sparks illuminated the tunnel for just an instant, enough to leave the afterimage of a narrow, straight tunnel etched into Kalab's eyes. He placed a hand on Ermun's shoulder and stepped past him into the lead, gripping his weapon handle. He slowly paced down the passage with his fingertips grazing the smooth walls. Here, deep in the house of the Undying Lord, even the sound of the sucking breeze had vanished. Kalab's rasping breaths were loud in his ears. He timed them to match his careful footsteps. The rhythm lent him some welcome calm.

When he saw light ahead, he almost mistook it for a trick of his mind. "Is that torchlight?" he whispered.

"The sanctum."

The sanctum was a round chamber with a domed roof and seven doorways, all open except the largest: a double door, barred and chained. Its brass panels were reliefs depicting Osiris's death, dismemberment, and resurrection. The air was hot and thick from burning sconces, the first sign that any other souls were present in this place. But if the mortuary priests were here, they didn't show themselves.

They bowed to Osiris's door and then circled the chamber to inspect the open doorways. Most of the rooms were rather banal—sleeping quarters, a few storerooms. The chamber they sought stood apart: the vault. It was filled with not riches, but knowledge—logged on papyri and crammed into hundreds, even thousands of round niches chiseled into the sandstone walls. Claustrophobic passageways with low ceilings branched off, their depths lost in a maze of right angles despite the ample torchlight.

"Beer?" Ermun inquired. He held out a skin.

"What? We have work to do."

"Aye, and it'll take a good while. No, then?"

"I'd rather keep my wits," Kalab said. "The sooner we're out of this place, the better."

The priest chuckled. "Ah, the callowness of youth. Suit yourself." He took a deep draught and stepped into the vault, already peering into niches as he corked the beer.

However dim their expectations, the task proved more daunting still. Without a catalogue to guide their search, Kalab and Ermun were obliged to pull the papyri from their niches by the armful, unroll each one, and read the hieratic script by flickering firelight. The exhaustive work devoured the hours, though the only way to guess at the passage of time was by how often they had to pause to feed the flames. The papyri were remarkably uniform in terms of content: they were mortuary scrolls, listing the names and last wills of the dead, logged with all the meticulousness and formality of a bureaucratic apparatus. The scribes had paid special attention to the funerary rites, logging the gifts of grain, beer, and treasure the departed took with them to the afterlife—for the temple was owed a portion of each. Death was no escape from taxes.

As they combed through the archives, they slowly deciphered the way the priests had organized the records. The most recent scrolls were those nearest the door, so the pair slunk into the further reaches of the labyrinth, where the papyri were old enough to flake apart as they were unrolled. Commoners' scrolls were relegated to niches near the sandy floor, while the ones closer to the ceiling, where the air was driest, were reserved for the high-born dead. Kalab was constantly teetering on a stool, armpit deep in recesses. His shaking fingers brushed aside cobwebs and scorpions to dig out papyri half-buried in centuries of dust. His armor and sword he removed and left piled together at a junction beside Ermun's. His white tunic became streaked with dust, which turned to dark grime as his sweat soaked through the linen. His coughing kicked up dust, which he inhaled, provoking more of the same—a fine addition to this ouroboros of misery.

And then, finally—*finally*—they found the mortuary scroll they sought. It was a plain thing, outwardly indistinguishable from the thousands that packed this cursed library. Whichever priest had stored it hadn't even bothered to put it in the correct niche, but rather a middle one among papyri perhaps three hundred floods old.

"Sethherkepeshef Meryamun!" exclaimed Ermun, jabbing a knobby finger at the pharaoh's cartouche, his stylized name. "Well done, boy! This is the one!"

Kalab clapped his hands, not out of joy—he was far past any semblance of positivity at the moment—but to rid his protesting joints of some caked-on dust. "Let's take the thing and be gone."

"No, boy. This belongs to the temple. We needn't be quick to deepen our indebtedness to the gods. We copy this down, word for word. After that, we may leave."

They placed the papyrus on one of the desks built into the wall and unrolled it with infinite care. The scroll was warped from centuries of dry rot. It bulged out, so that they had to lay twenty stones along its edges to persuade it to lie flat. They winced every time it cracked. The archaic, faded script defied easy reading. The two resorted to reading troublesome sections aloud in order to agree on the wording.

"What's this say about grain?"

"I'm still stuck on this passage here, teacher. Something to do with taking away ... difficult vapors?"

"Removing troublesome vapors, I would hazard. I come away with the suspicion that our Ramesses was especially fond of drink."

"I refuse to think it. I won't believe we've spent all this time chasing down some dead guy's favorite beer recipe."

"There's a little more. See here—*ta dehent*, it says. The Peak."

"Awfully vague. Which peak? Egypt has a few of them."

"The one that watches over the Valley of the Kings. And look, see this passage? There's mention of a slope."

"And a cleft. Suppose we'll be looking for a hill shaped like an ass."

"Well, there's no need to be vulgar, boy."

"You're not the one covered in dust and scorpion bites!"

"Ah, see, now this part could prove be useful. A star chart. Here the author references the Pole Star. During Inundation ... place above the left shoulder..."

Kalab sniffed. "Do you smell burning?"

They exchanged a troubled look and swiveled their heads back the way they'd come.

A humanoid figure was standing in the passage, jackal-headed, smoke curling from its shoulders, its fingers ending in long black talons. An Anubis. Watching them.

A lance of atavistic terror stabbed through Kalab's heart, driving all thought from his head save the urge to flee. That same terror rooted him to the spot, helpless as a lamb on an altar. The gods had seen his sin-laden heart and come to claim him.

Ermun's voice drew him back from the verge of animal panic. "Why do you trouble us?" he asked the Anubis. Somehow, his voice didn't waver.

The figure spoke in a low, echoing voice. "That is for the Lord of Life to ask of you."

A priest of Osiris. Kalab could have perished of relief.

Ermun gathered his thoughts for a moment. "We've come to inquire after a *ka*, in order to pay tribute. We've brought an offering of our own."

The jackal priest said nothing, but lifted one palm in a half-circle, indicating they should finish their task. Relieved, the two turned back to their work. They conferred in rapid whispers.

"How long has he been standing there?" hissed Kalab.

"I have no idea. We must assume he was watching us for a good while."

"He might have heard it all. What do we do?"

Ermun sighed glumly. "What option is there? We must wait and see what happens."

When they were confident they'd finished transcribing the full text, they rolled the mortuary scroll up again and placed it back in its niche. Then they went to join the visitor, who hadn't moved a muscle the whole time. He led them back through the passages, pausing midway to allow them to gather the items they'd discarded. If he noted their foreign armor, he didn't see fit to question it.

Back at the sanctum, the double doors were opened, and the statue of green-skinned Osiris was bared. There were glistening entrails laid in bowls at his feet, and he wore necklaces of precious stones. Kalab and Ermun approached him, stopping and bowing every three paces. They prostrated themselves before the god, the earthy scent of intestines heavy in their nostrils. The jackal priest's heavy presence lingered behind them while they paid their respects. Beneath the gaze of a god and his sinister representative, Kalab felt his neck hairs standing on end. The place reeked of magic.

"You have come in pursuit of a *ka*," boomed the jackal priest. "Speak its true name, then, and Osiris will summon it before you."

Kalab was glad to have his face pressed up against the floor; it hid his wince. "You wily bastard," he mouthed.

Ermun faced the priest and said deferentially, "I'm pleased to say that we've learned much from the scrolls we found. We need not trouble the Lord of Rebirth."

"Speak the name!" barked the jackal.

Ermun's expression was full of despair, though only one who knew the man well could have seen it. There was no question of lying in the physical presence of Osiris, who alone possessed the power to raise souls in the afterlife. And the reverse was equally true. Faced with the obliteration of his immortal *ka*, Ermun had no choice.

He raised his chin. "Sethherkepeshef Meryamun."

The jackal priest, though motionless, seemed to coil up on hearing the royal name. For long moments, he stood rigid. Without a word, he started toward Ermun. Kalab scuffled to his feet and went for his khopesh—but the priest skirted around and retrieved a box from Osiris's pedestal, whispering unintelligibly in the confines of his mask. He opened the box to reveal a fine powder, the same pallorous green as the god's skin. He moved with slow purpose, sprinkling it in a circle around Ermun's feet. He replaced the box, faced him once more, and spread his arms wide.

His shriek tore through the dense air and shattered the quiet. "Osiris! Lord of Rebirth! I summon the *ka* of Sethherkepeshef Meryamun! Bring him forth from the twilight! Make him a home of my flesh! This we ask of you!"

He threw his head back. All at once, he began to shudder. His torso writhed, his limbs flailed, his fingers bent into claws. His deafening scream reverberated around the sanctum. The air rippled, and the flames guttered in their sconces. The priest's scream assailed their ears for an unnaturally long time. Even when his lungs were empty of air, his throat still fought to produce sound.

Then he slumped onto his knees, motionless. His ribcage flexed. He drew a harsh, rattling breath, as if it was his first. Then, still bunched into a ball, he whispered, "Who disturbs me?" His voice was different—high pitched and reedy. "Who has brought me forth?"

Fresh rivulets of sweat ran down Kalab's spine. He could have no doubt that they were facing a pharaoh's *ka*, hauled back from the afterlife to confront the men who were about to deprive him of it forever.

Ermun visibly swallowed, undoubtedly wrestling with the same knowledge. "We are supplicants," he replied. "We have come bearing tribute." The words were vague enough that they managed not to qualify as lies.

The *ka* swayed on its knees and spoke haltingly. "Long have I lingered without tasting tribute. My form is without vitality. I am withered." It raised one arm and turned the hand, studying it with jealous curiosity. "Why have you come after so much time, when I am reduced to a husk?"

Kalab saw the opening and rushed to answer. "You're diminished because your resting place has been forgotten. No one knows where to make sacrifices for you."

The *ka* didn't react in any way. It continued to rock on its knees and stare up at Ermun in wary expectation. Kalab remembered the green circle. "Tell it what I just said!"

Ermun repeated the words. This time the *ka* seemed to hear.

"You seek my tomb?" it rasped. Ermun and Kalab looked at each other, uncertain how to reply. "You seek my tomb!" The voice gained strength and volume as the *ka* grew wise to their game. It pointed an accusing finger at Ermun. "Liar! Thief! You wish to desecrate me!"

Ermun could only stand aghast, unable to contest the accusation—because it was true. And Osiris was watching.

The *ka*'s anger deepened into apoplexy. "Your wickedness shall carry its own reward, heretic! In the name of Osiris—"

"Shit," Kalab and Ermun muttered.

"—I curse the fruits of your foul endeavor! He who profits by me shall reap his own end! May his triumphs crumble to ash. May his wives be made barren. May his children perish. May his allies betray him. May his lands be ripped from him and given to his enemies. May he die without comfort or honor. May his *ka* be severed from his form. May he wander sightless for all eternity. Let utter ruin be the price of treachery! The Lord, Anubis, shall make it so!"

The two of them stood transfixed in horror, which only became more abject with every word. With a long hiss, the *ka* departed. The jackal priest visibly regained his form, his shoulders losing their slump and his back straightening. He shook his head to clear the fog and pushed himself standing, regarding them with benign interest through his mask. He appeared unaware of what had just happened.

"Now. Is there anything else I can help you with?"

Ermun shambled up to him and opened Pisaqar's purse with trembling fingers. "For Osiris," he mumbled, emptying the plundered jewels into the priest's outstretched palm. The priest bowed gratefully.

"A generous contribution. Osiris is well pleased."

Then they fled without a backward glance, Kalab clutching his copied scroll tight against his pounding heart.

The jackal priest watched the visitors go. "Knumhotep, come over here." His voice was an undignified squeak, broken thrice over. It had been a difficult session. He reflected, not for the first time, that he was far too old to be doing this much yelling.

He drew off his mask and headdress as his acolyte hurried out of the office.

"Teacher," the boy piped. "Forgive me for failing to chain the door. It won't—"

"Quit scraping, child. Help me close up the shrine. Then I need you to bring a message to Senanmuht."

"Taharqa's man?" his acolyte asked in complete befuddlement. "Forgive me, master, but why not the pharaoh's sandal bearer? Or the high priest?"

He sighed. The boy was dutiful, yes, but oh so dull. "A wise man keeps his finger to the winds. No, Taharqa must learn of this. It seems some of his fellow Kushites have come calling."

THE MOB FEASTS

"BLESSINGS UPON YOUR hearts, noble warrior!" The old man thrust a beer under Tariq's nose, shouting to be heard over the baying crowds.

Tariq took it with a grin and a bow. "My thanks for your thanks, good sir!" He took a hearty quaff before turning away. Then he dumped the rest. It was a shame, really, pouring out good beer. But he had a job to do. Maybe if they did it well enough, Pisaqar would let them enjoy the Heb Sed later on.

And what a festival it was. Memphis swelled with jubilation. The raucous masses packed every street, dancing to the riotous music of pipes and drums. It was the loudest din Tariq had ever heard—and he'd fought in *wars*. The people's glee was positively orgasmic. How could it be anything else? Mighty Assyria was defeated. Egypt stood at the cusp of a long and prosperous peace.

The presence of the pharaoh's warriors was not lost on the people of Memphis. They gathered around Pisaqar's mercenaries, reaching out to brush the white feathers tucked into their headbands. Together with the veneration came foamy beers. And *girls*. Memphis's girls were a fine sight, decked in all the splendor their middle-class fathers could afford. Whenever a gaggle of them sauntered past, Tariq plucked one over for a dance. They weren't shy with their kisses, either.

"By Horus," he yelled to Qorobar, "this city knows how to live!"

Qorobar walked with a doughty woman under each arm. To his credit, he looked like he was doing his best to act cheerful. "Think Pisaqar will turn us loose when we finish the work?"

"No chance of that!"

"Oy, what's happening with Nawidemaq's bull?"

Further back, the little procession was swamped. The crowd was thickest around the white bull, all of them raising the same chant as they laid their reverent hands on its white hide. "Apis! Apis!" They heaped its neck with flowers and tossed palm fronds beneath its hooves. The bull accepted this praise with calm puzzlement, which turned to joy whenever a garland swung close to its maw.

Tariq leaned close to Qorobar and bellowed, "They must think we're a temple procession!"

Amani suddenly appeared beside him. "Hold onto this." She palmed him a bag that clicked and rattled with what sounded suspiciously like jewelry. Then, with a wink, she slipped back into the crowd, headed for their counterfeit Apis bull, her obsidian knife hidden against her wrist, her braided head swiveling in search of more bracelets to cut.

Qorobar frowned after her. "That one's going to get her hand chopped off for thieving."

"Amani? Naw, she'll give them the eyes. If by chance that doesn't work, she'll just pin the blame on us."

He heard a shrill whistle. Pisaqar was beckoning from the front of the cavalcade, indicating a side street. Eleazar was already waiting there with their informant, a conniving little shit whose false leads had coaxed them into some of the nastiest brothels and taverns in Memphis. But Tariq *still* trusted him more than their Israelite—and the locals seemed to agree. His long-sleeved blue tunic earned him a wide berth.

"You're drawing some unfriendly looks there," Tariq told him as he sidled up.

Eleazar donned his customary smile. "If I give offense, it is beyond my power to remedy."

"That's plainly untrue. You could round out the beard, at the very least. People are taking you for an Assyrian. Which, I ought to add, isn't necessarily wrong of them."

Qorobar lumbered up, having finally shooed off his disappointed lady friends. "You'd best have found the right place this time, Assyrian."

Tariq raised his brows. "See what I mean?"

"It's the right place," Eleazar promised the big man, ignoring the point.

Qorobar patted their foreign guide's ringlets. Affably, he said, "I rather hope so."

The rest of the Mice freed themselves from the crowd and joined them on the corner. The only ones missing were Kalab and Ermun, who were still attending to their business at the temple. Pisaqar conferred with the Israelite and the shifty local, then said to the rest of them, "There is a tavern along this street where our man ought to be. Same roles as the last ... however many times. But keep your blades near to hand. This place is quite ill-reputed."

Indeed, the guide grabbed his pay and darted off with palpable relief. The Desert Mice didn't have to go far down the street before they saw why. The day had brought them to some foul spots already, but this one was particularly heinous. It wasn't a street so much as a sewer. The column of mercenaries snaked along haphazardly placed duckboards, which shifted underfoot and threatened to send them sprawling in the vomit-colored mud. Tariq batted at bloated flies, trying not to dry heave at the putrid stench. Somehow, people *lived* here. Prostitutes leered at him from their doorsteps. Drunken men pissed out of windows, aiming for the shallow ditches and missing wantonly.

The tavern was only recognizable by the amphorae lying tipped by the door. A bouncer stood ankle deep in the frothy muck. "Going in?"

Pisaqar told him, "We're looking for a man called Nibamon."

"The Nose? He's in there." He pointed at the captain's sword. "You'll need to leave that outside."

Qorobar spoke loudly. "Or what?"

The bouncer gave him an indolent stare. "Or there'll be a fight."

Pisaqar waylaid any further outbursts with a cutting glance. "There will be no need of that. Yesbokhe, you keep watch. Everyone else, leave your weapons." Reluctantly, the Mice deposited their blades in the basket beside the door. Tariq cast a longing glance at the main avenue, where the celebrations had reached a new pitch and any number of girls waited to reject his advances.

Heaving a mighty sigh, he followed Nawidemaq through the door. At the sound of hooves clomping after him, he turned incredulously. His reward was a face full of hairy snout. "Argh! Shit! Stop that!" He put a firm hand on the bull's nose. It mooed querulously and stomped in the mud, straining to cram its horns through the sagging door frame.

"Nawidemaq! Your stupid animal keeps trying to nose its way in here!" Tariq dug in his heels and pushed hard with both hands. One of his thumbs slipped into a slimy nostril. "Fuck!" The bull wagged its head. It pressed forward, neither noticing nor caring how its horns gouged deep furrows out of the mud-brick door frame. The patrons in the dim barroom watched the unfolding drama with interest that failed to rise to the level of actual concern. As if a full-grown bull plowing through a doorway and undermining the roof over their heads was nothing to worry over.

Outside, the other mercenaries were jabbering in alarm. They hauled on the bull's harness and tried to get a grip on its horns, but the beast paid them no attention. It only had eyes for its friend. Fortunately, Nawidemaq jangled out of the barroom with his arms aflutter. He shunted Tariq aside with remarkable ease and put soothing palms over the beast's eyes. He made hushing noises until its hooves quit scraping. The bull allowed itself to be pushed back. Nawidemaq then pressed on its hindquarters, putting his full body into the effort until, to everyone's amazement, it sat down heavily in the mud. Its enormity was enough to lever sogging duckboards into the air.

Nawidemaq pulled some garlands from its neck and laid them between its forelimbs. "You wait here," he instructed at full volume and with broad motions, which he apparently thought the bull could understand, "and eat flowers." He patted its head reassuringly before filing after the others into the tavern. By what could only be divine will, the bull stayed loyally put.

The side street had been fetid. The tavern was far worse. Scant light filtered in through the tiny windows. Men slouched at the center bar, clearly capitalizing on the glut of cheap beer from the Heb Sed. They retained enough wit to keep away from the crumbling, stained walls where overflowing piss pots were lined up. The tavernkeeper didn't seem inclined to take advantage of his sobriety and empty the makeshift latrines. Instead, he kept his gaze on the newcomers and thumbed the knife openly slung on his belt.

Pisaqar nudged Eleazar. "Let us not remain here an instant longer than the task demands. Find your man."

The Israelite swallowed his nausea and jutted his chin at a pitiful figure huddled alone at a table, snoring gently. He, Pisaqar, and Tariq slid onto the benches beside him. When he failed to stir, the redhead snapped his fingers next to the man's head. He jolted awake and looked up.

They all nearly recoiled at the sight of his face. There was no nose—just a moist, bifurcated hole. His small eyes flitted between the three men and correctly gauged them to be a threat. He raised his pudgy hands.

"Please. I don't have anything to give you." The nasal slur seemed to buzz out of the gaping wound in his face. It was a singularly awful sound. "Tell Sabef I need more time. Please."

Pisaqar listened dispassionately. Eleazar opened his mouth to speak, but Pisaqar put a hand over his and looked to Tariq.

Tariq put on all his bluster. "Why should you have more time? You've been given enough, haven't you?" He fought to look the man—Nibamon—in the eyes, not at his mutilation.

Nibamon fell for the ploy easily. "I can pay it back! I haven't heard back from my sister yet, but she has the silver! I swear! I'm worth nothing to you dead. Just let me be!"

"If your sister hasn't answered you by now, she has no plans to, Nibamon. You'd best find another way. What about your Assyrian friends?"

Nibamon's jaw fell slack. "*Who?*"

Tariq and Pisaqar looked at the Israelite, who immediately sensed his credibility was now at stake.

Eleazar leaned in. "You were previously approached regarding a heist. You were to assist in robbing an old tomb."

"Yes. Yes, I was asked," sputtered Nibamon, "but not by blasted Assyrians!"

"Who, then?"

"I don't know! Some nobleman. He didn't give his name. Why..." His beady eyes narrowed. "What is this? You don't work for Sabef, do you? Who are you?"

Tariq sighed to himself. Mentioning the Assyrian involvement had been a sloppy move. Then again, Nibamon hadn't known that his prospective employer was a foreign invader, and that was an interesting tidbit in itself. It meant the Assyrians hadn't approached him directly.

There were traitors at work in Memphis.

Pisaqar chose to tip his hand. "We are not your creditors, and we have not come for money. We are here for you." Qorobar ambled over and *thunk*ed a fresh mug of beer in front of the noseless drunk, before flicking away the dusty froth and moving back to the shadows.

Nibamon grimaced at the beer, silently agonizing over whether he wanted to indebt himself to yet more dangerous strangers. His indecision resolved itself quickly. He groped for the cup, raised it in a trembling hand, and quaffed it down. Half missed his mouth.

He burped, nauseatingly, through his nose hole. "You need me for the tomb robbery, then?"

"I have yet to decide. Prove your worth and perhaps I will give you a part in it."

"I'm not interested," Nibamon said peevishly. "Your redheaded man here intimidates me with all sorts of lies, scares me half to death—"

Tariq shrugged. "I didn't need to say much at all to get you squealing."

"—and now you propose to involve me in a crime whose punishment is slow impalement. I'd rather not. Just leave me alone." His sudden bravado wilted quickly under Pisaqar's level gaze. "Please."

The captain gestured for another round. "It is plain that you have made some questionable choices in your life. Sending us away would be the poorest one by far. This man Sabef will come for you before long; you are already looking over your shoulder, after all. Allow me to solve that problem for you. I offer you my protection. As you can tell," he gestured to his mercenaries, "my promise carries some weight. Far more than a few local thugs."

Despite Nibamon's mutilation, his skepticism was clear. "I only see a mismatched collection of ruffians. And a girl."

Amani's bared teeth flashed across the room. Pisaqar spoke for her. "That *girl* has personally killed more men than you see gathered in this room. My name is Pisaqar, captain of the Desert Mice. I assume you have heard of my deeds in Jerusalem?"

"What I'd heard was that a horde of mice swept over the Assyrian camp. Ate all their bowstrings and shield straps. That sort of thing."

Tariq sat back, affronted. "That's the stupidest thing I've ever heard. Who told you that?"

"It's only rumor. Admittedly, that never made much sense to me. Mercenaries, though…" Nibamon pondered for a moment. "Very well. I believe we might be able to work together. But first I'll need—"

"No, please, allow me," Pisaqar interrupted. His calm assertiveness silenced the man at once. "I would like to hear more about this pharaoh's tomb."

Qorobar delivered four more beers. Tariq sniffed his before taking a cautious sip. Pisaqar's went untouched, as did Eleazar's, though out of preference rather than sobriety. The Israelite had Assyrian tastes; he only drank wine. One more reason to mistrust him, as far as Tariq was concerned.

Nibamon finished his in a couple of gulps. Wiping his chin, he considered his reply. "Well, I should begin with the obvious. The tomb belongs to Ramesses the Eighth. He was buried in the Valley of the Kings. It's something of a legend among tomb builders—"

"Of which you're one?"

"Yes, I'm a foreman," he said, growing a bit annoyed at the interruptions. "I was… I made some mistakes." He pointed to his conspicuous lack of a nose.

"Angered the wrong people?" suggested Pisaqar.

"I was commissioned to build a new gateway in the precinct of Mut, at Karnak. The foundation wasn't set properly. The pillars buckled. The roof came down. Many workers died. An accident—very unfortunate. The priests felt I was at fault."

"But you were not, I am sure."

"No! I've been disgraced, disfigured! All over some idiot mason's laziness!"

Pisaqar nodded with studied indifference. "So. The tomb of Ramesses. What makes it a legend?"

"Well, it hasn't been found, for one."

"I should hope not."

"Because, the story goes, the builders were made to disappear. It's said that Ramesses was a man consumed by greed. The Robber Pharaoh, some call him. He spent the entirety of his short rule robbing the graves of his forebears. Raided neighboring lands for wealth. Taxed the priesthood into poverty. He used all this misbegotten wealth to fund a lavish project in the Valley of the Kings, a tomb unsurpassed in its ambition. He conscripted half the builders in Upper Egypt for it. They say he worked them day and night. Many of them perished. Ordinarily, a pharaoh's tomb takes years to excavate, but cruel Ramesses saw his finished in just two. But that was still not enough for the Robber Pharaoh. When he himself went west to Duat, he took the builders of his tomb with him, thus ensuring that the secrets of its construction would remain hidden forever."

"Rather curious that this story is so well known, then," observed Pisaqar.

"In Set-Ma'at, we still spit at the mention of that pharaoh's name."

Eleazar asked, "Set-Ma'at?"

"The Place of Truth," Tariq translated. "It's the village of the tomb builders, just outside the Valley of the Kings."

Pisaqar said to Nibamon, "It seems to me that your people have a score with Ramesses the Eighth. Help us, and you will be the man to settle it."

"It's an appealing notion, don't mistake me. But it's also impossible. As I told you, this tomb is a secret. No one knows where to find it. It's been sought many times, by far cleverer men, without success."

"What if I were to tell you that we have found the pharaoh's mortuary papyrus?"

Nibamon rocked back on his stool, mouth agape. "You lie again."

"I do not," the captain said, which Tariq supposed qualified as a half-truth. He wondered how Ermun and Kalab were faring in the vault of Osiris.

The noseless foreman collected his wits. "If that's true, and you've located the tomb, why do you need my help?"

The Israelite chimed in. "Because the only task more difficult than building a tomb is robbing one. We are a band of soldiers, not engineers. We know nothing of this place, this Valley of the Kings. We must be taught how to dig properly, how to navigate the tunnels, how to avoid traps."

Pisaqar said, "There are many unknowns that we cannot possibly fathom. For all this, we need an expert. The Assyrians seemed to believe that expert was you. Were they wrong?"

"No," Nibamon uttered, licking his lips. "I'm the one you want. But there's a slight problem." His eyes flicked from side to side. Slowly, he rose off his stool, hands spread.

A group of men were filing out of the back room. Tariq immediately knew from the way they moved that these were fighters. With deadly coordination, they split and swung out to the sides of the room, their drawn swords leading the way. The mercenaries found themselves pressed against the bar, unarmed and surrounded.

Pisaqar pushed cowering Nibamon behind him. "Speak your business," he demanded of the plainly dressed intruders. Their only reply was to tighten the knot, blades pointed inward.

Tariq cast about for a weapon. There were only clay cups. He smashed one and snatched up the biggest shard he could find. Pisaqar grabbed the remaining bits and flung them in the face of the nearest assailant. The man stumbled back. Amani and Yesbokhe picked up on the tactic and began emptying the shelves, hurling cup after cup at their attackers, who faltered under the unexpected onslaught.

With an unearthly shriek ululating from his throat and his eyes fairly popping out of his head, Qorobar launched into a charge, his enormous fists flying. Tables and stools skittered out of his path along with startled enemies, their discipline crumbling beneath the berserker's onslaught. One unfortunate failed to move aside fast enough and was lifted aloft, feet kicking, before being slammed into the ground with an audible crunch.

Tariq tossed his pottery shard aside and took up a broken stool, which he swung just in time to knock aside a chopping blow meant for his collar. Wood thudded hollowly against iron. The enemy stumbled and brought his sword back around to catch Tariq's reverse. The stool knocked the blade from his grip. They met each other's eyes, each calculating whether he could reach the fallen sword between them first.

Before they could come to a decision, Amani slid in and scooped it up. In the same motion, she tossed it backward. Pisaqar snatched it out of the air. Twirling it, he rushed to aid Qorobar, who was fighting off three assailants through sheer bluffery.

Nawidemaq was similarly pressed. He swung about with his gnarled staff, forcing back his attackers with difficulty. He fought alongside Eleazar, whose table leg was faring poorly against the swordsman he faced.

The mercenaries' ferocity could do little against sharp iron. Their attackers recovered, and before long had forced them back to the center of the tavern.

"What now?" called Tariq, trying to find a gap in the tightening ring of bruised, angry faces.

Pisaqar made no reply. He bounced his stolen sword in his grip, which was answer enough.

From outside, there came a loud crash. Dust sprinkled from the rafters. The second crash was accompanied by the rumble of falling masonry. The flap at the door billowed. All eyes fixed on the spot.

The white bull erupted into the tavern amid a cascade of pulverized brick, baying its outrage. With a terrifyingly light toss of its horns, the attacker nearest the entrance was flung against the wall. Bones crunched. The man beside him did his best to stumble out of the way, but the incensed bull reared up, and with a twist of its huge head ripped his legs from under him. He landed on his side, stunned. The bull immediately gored him, ramming a gigantic horn into his ribcage and dragging him savagely from side to side. His limbs went slack, but the bull continued to grate the lifeless body into the floor, leaving a smear of arterial blood clearly visible even in the wan light.

The other assailants scrabbled as far from the frenzied animal as they could get. The cordon gave way in the midst of the blind panic, leaving the front entrance wide open—in a very literal sense.

Pisaqar shoved Nibamon toward the yawning breach where the door had been. "Run! Everyone go!" They needed no further urging. With a last salvo of cups and stool legs, they all stampeded into the daylight, hauling their new companion behind them. The bull's continuing rampage gave the mercenaries ample time to escape through the alley and vanish into the festive crowds.

"It could only have been Sabef," Nibamon insisted. The group was gathered again on Pepy's boat, which rocked soothingly in the lapping river. Evening had fallen, and the city's convulsions were beginning to quiet down at last, but no matter how much Tariq yearned to stretch out on the deck and sleep, it was clear that the night was going to be an eventful one.

Ermun patted the air placatingly. "You wouldn't rest on that conclusion if you knew what we do already. Taharqa wishes to make us vanish."

"I cannot understand him anymore," Pisaqar said. The captain scarcely seemed to believe his own words. "Taharqa's vanity has consumed him. If he wanted to kill us, best to have done so quietly in the Sinai. Instead, he chooses to ambush us in Sena, on Egyptian land! And worse, far worse—to pursue us into the capital itself! His audacity verges on lunacy. He must have the pharaoh in thrall. I can think of no other way.

Shabaku is too old to enforce his rule, Heb Sed be damned. Crown Prince Shebitku forsakes his duty as co-regent and hides behind the curtain. Taharqa is given free rein to trample the rule of law."

Ermun muttered, glowering, "It seems no one holds ma'at sacred anymore."

The noseless foreman said, "But why would he want you dead? You helped him, didn't you? Weren't you the ones who freed Jerusalem?"

"You have answered yourself," Pisaqar told him gravely. "Taharqa wants sole credit for the victory. He will share it with no one. It has become clear to me what he seeks to do: he positions himself to take the throne once Shabaku goes west. In his mind, we Desert Mice stand between him and the double crown."

Ermun leaned on his knees, his expression grave. "Forgive my presumption, Captain, but it seems that we've timed our venture in the middle of a royal power struggle. Perhaps it's best to lie quietly until Taharqa's anger has cooled."

That piqued Tariq's interest. Both the priest and the acolyte had been uncharacteristically gloomy since they got back from their temple sojourn. Libraries were boring places, certainly, but they'd come out with exactly the information they'd sought. They'd found the means of locating Ramesses the Eighth's tomb.

Which made it doubly odd that Ermun was openly naysaying every point of discussion.

Pepy-Nakht cleared his throat. "If that's become your plan, where will you wait? For how long?"

Tariq winced. The boatmaster's questions sounded benign enough, but what he was really saying was, *Pay me or get off my boat.*

The implication wasn't lost on Pisaqar. "There can be no delay. Inundation is barely three weeks hence. We must make Thebes before the river swells, or else be stranded in Lower Egypt. Where Taharqa is already looking for us."

"We can't be certain of Taharqa's intent," argued the priest.

"My friend, everything you've just said is speculation. I can't believe your own former student would wish you dead."

Tariq snapped, "You weren't at the tavern with us. Those men were closing in for the kill. If not for Nawidemaq's bull, they'd have had us."

"How is our Apis faring?" Pisaqar asked the medicine man.

"There are some cuts. That is all. He sleeps peacefully."

Nibamon clapped his hands on his knees and stood up. "Good for you and your pet bull, but this all sounds rather more perilous than I'd been led to believe. So, if you don't mind—"

Qorobar shoved the foreman back onto the bench. "We mind."

"You don't understand," pleaded Nibamon. "I'm in a great deal of debt. If I were to suddenly vanish, Sabef would quickly start asking questions, and as you all might remember, everyone in that tavern saw you take me. Maybe Sabef decides to tip off the authorities. Next we know, there will be chariots chasing us through the Valley of the Kings." He exaggerated a hopeless shrug. Nibamon had an odd habit of signing much of what he said. Apparently, he'd gathered that his mutilation made his expressions difficult to read. "I'm a liability to you. It's unfortunate, I know. But really, it's not that bad. Before I go, I'll tell you anything you want to know about your tomb. Your priests here can write it down. Then Sabef is spared the trouble of looking for me, and you all escape south. Everyone wins."

Pisaqar nodded as if he were at all convinced. "It's commendable, your concern for us. You make a reasonable argument, Nibamon."

"Oh." Nibamon's shoulders slackened with relief. "Wonderful. I'll just go ahead and—"

Qorobar pushed him down again. "Nope."

Pisaqar couldn't hide a grin. "Of course, though we would solve many problems by letting you go, Pepy-Nakht must still be paid for our passage to Thebes. I fear we will need your help with that. The good news is, if you play your role well, your debt will be cleared, Taharqa will be off our trail, Pepy will be amply rewarded, and in the end, all of us will be rich beyond imagining. Everyone wins, just as you said."

"Oh, I like the sound of that," Pepy beamed.

The mercenaries exchanged growing smiles. "Captain's scheming again," Amani laughed. "I missed that."

Pisaqar said to Nibamon, "Tell us where to find Sabef."

Which was how Tariq found himself up to his chin in the Nile, stark naked. The water was cool, still, and black except for the occasional white tendril. Somehow, Nawidemaq was *still* shedding chalk.

"I hope my friend does not worry much," the medicine man whispered earnestly for what must have been the twentieth time.

Tariq swished at the water to dispel a chalky curl, glad that the night concealed his scowl. He'd have been hard-pressed to come up with a worse skinny-dipping partner. Pisaqar could have paired him up with Yesbokhe, who could be counted on to shut up, or Amani, who was not unpleasant to look at. But no—he'd gotten Nawidemaq, who was exactly the opposite of Yesbokhe and Amani in both respects. He was half certain that the splotch of white on the man's forehead was going to get them spotted, which meant he'd finish out this terrible day with a spear up his ass.

In truth, Nawidemaq was a well-meaning fellow, and he was only worrying for his friend, so for possibly the twentieth time, Tariq answered politely, "I'm sure your bull is fine."

The two watched the torchlit docks in renewed silence. Nibamon's creditor, Sabef, ran his operation from a barge near the granaries, an important spot that hinted they were about to tussle with someone who had political clout. He kept an appreciable number of armed thugs in his employ—six roaming the docks, another on the barge, and probably an equal sum guarding the boss inside.

The Mice were about to tear down Sabef's whole racket.

Tariq supposed they'd had worse odds before. Then again, they'd never done it naked.

If only the bull wasn't literally licking its wounds on the boat.

"I do wish he was here, though," Tariq whispered.

Nawidemaq wiped fiercely at his eyes.

Pisaqar appeared at last. He and noseless Nibamon slowly threaded their way along the docks toward the barge, flanked by a pair of burly men. "Looks like the captain got his meeting."

Nawidemaq bobbed his head. "They take his sword away."

"We expected that, don't worry. Time to go."

He bit down on a dagger and pushed out of the reeds. Nawidemaq followed him, with a little clay jar balanced on his head. Tariq had noticed it but knew better than to ask questions when he'd only get gibberish in reply.

At first, the water was shallow enough for him to walk along the riverbed with the mud squishing between his toes. As the bottom gradually dropped away, he transitioned to hopping along, then to swimming. He hoped dearly that he wouldn't bump into a crocodile. Nawidemaq had made the appropriate offerings to ensure otherwise, but still, Tariq retained a healthy fear of being pulverized and dismembered simultaneously. He didn't think that unreasonable.

Fortunately, they didn't need to go too far before they reached the first support struts. Tariq was glad to have the planks overhead to shield him from the torchlight. The pole was sheathed in a layer of slime. There was no question of stopping to catch his breath. Instead, he pushed from one to the next. His hard exhales whistled around the dagger, loud enough that he was certain a thug would hear. When he heard footsteps approaching, he submerged down to his ears and treaded water, his lungs aching, until the gangster was gone.

The barge had been impressive enough from a distance, but up close, its enormity became apparent. The reed hull had the footprint of a temple, and the cabin was, in essence, a two-story house. The massive vessel was so heavily loaded that its bottom had settled into the riverbed. Silt had collected around it, high enough to walk on. Fish that made their homes in the pitted hull flocked to their new visitors. At first they nibbled curiously, but soon enough they were biting. Hard. He'd have loved nothing more than to push off and circle the barge at a distance, but the railings were lined with a frankly ludicrous number of torches. The only way to remain undetected was to hug the waterline, brave the hungry schools of fish, and hope dearly that they didn't latch onto something important. He and Nawidemaq paddled along the hull, stifling groans of pain.

They breathed a little easier once they'd made the far side, the one turned out to the open Nile, where no patrolling guards on shore could spot them by chance. Voices drifted over the water. Tariq could make out the captain's deep, calming tone speaking in the interrogative. A door slammed, and the voices grew muffled.

"He's in the cabin with them," whispered Tariq. He peered along the curve of the hull. There was no sign of anything but glimmering water. He waved speculatively into the darkness, where he caught the flash of teeth. "There's Amani and Qorobar." Further along, there was a staccato yellow blink as a blade caught the torchlight. "Ermun and Kalab. That's everyone." He held up his dagger and turned it to reflect the torchlight. Glistening human shapes hauled themselves from the water and began their climb.

The bundled reeds made good handholds. Tariq's fingers were soon touching the deck planks. Slowly, he raised his eyes over the edge.

A thug sat on an upturned pot, facing him. His heart throbbed in panic, but the man was occupied swatting at flies and didn't notice him. He ducked back down. He gnawed on his dagger as he mulled over his next move. Nawidemaq elbowed him and tossed his chin at the others. Tariq followed his gaze and saw, to his horror, that Amani was already swinging a leg onto the deck. Before he could think of a way to stop her without giving them all away, she'd clambered aboard. Then she dropped her dagger point-first onto the planks and sidled into the open.

Her low whistle instantly drew the guard's attention. He shot to his feet, axe in hand—and went still, baffled at the spectacle of a naked young woman leaning against the cabin.

"Evening," she drawled. "I'm afraid I'm somewhat lost."

The thug mouthed at her. Then Tariq was on him. One arm wrapped around his neck while the other plunged a dagger up through his ribs, wriggling around in search of the heart. The victim writhed, trying to bring his axe to bear, but Nawidemaq swept in and hauled it out of his grip. Once he'd gone limp, the two of them dragged him to the side and lowered him into the water by his feet. The lifeless body flopped into the water with a quiet splash.

Amani peeked over to watch it sink. "Not bad, Tariq," she complimented, punching his arm.

"Nice distraction. Try that trick more often."

"Oh, ha-ha. You'd love that, wouldn't you?"

As endearing as her nudity was, the appearance of the other mercenaries—also naked—comprehensively killed the effect. They quickly set to work extinguishing torches, which plunged the area into merciful darkness. Even so, Tariq kept his eyes trained above shoulder level as they all gathered around the door, knives drawn.

Inside the cabin, Pisaqar was in the midst of negotiations with Sabef. They didn't seem to be going well.

"I must be sparing with details," the captain was saying. "It is for the safety of everyone involved. I hope you understand."

The other voice, which could only be Sabef's, replied in a tone laden with skepticism. "That's the problem. Without details, there's nothing to understand at all. There's only this vague promise of a big payoff, coming from a man I don't know.

And because I don't know you, your word is worth shit to me."

"That is an unfortunate position, Sabef."

"For you, it is. Because the fact is, while you're a stranger, this ugly fuck-stain sitting beside you is one I'm very well acquainted with. And I'll tell you, this one isn't worth the scum under your sandal strap. Nibamon's the worst kind of customer. Not only does he fail to honor his commitments, he does it so spectacularly that he actively harms the reputation of anyone he's in business with. People are less inclined to borrow from me because they know I treat with shits like Nibamon the Nose. What a bad joke. What a pity. The Nose blunders into my place of business, not to finally pay up, but to ask—through you—for my permission to disappear."

"Let him."

"What's that?"

"If Nibamon is such a burden on you, let him go. Tell everyone he is dead. Let him disappear and serve as a warning. I will take him off your hands."

There was a pause, which Tariq imagined hid a sigh. "In my line of work, appearances matter. People don't get the idea unless you put on a show. In this case, I'm going to need to make an example. I suppose I should cut off the man's lying tongue, make him wear it around town for a couple of days. That will get people thinking."

Another pause, this time on Pisaqar's end. The mercenaries readied their knives. Nawidemaq uncorked his little jar.

"I will not allow that to happen, Sabef. Nibamon is under my protection. Let him go, as I said, and I promise, you will soon be repaid in full."

"I'm sorry we failed to reach an understanding."

The line was drawn. With a shout, Qorobar reared up and kicked in the door. To everyone's surprise, Nawidemaq was the first to charge through the cascade of splinters, still fist-deep in his mysterious jar. The mercenaries rushed in right behind him, howling and brandishing their knives.

Pisaqar and Nibamon were sitting at a table across from Sabef and his lieutenants, who'd risen from their seats with their knives drawn. They gaped, flabbergasted to find themselves squaring up to half a dozen Kushites, dripping wet and naked.

The captain dragged the foreman off his chair. At the same time, the medicine man yanked out a fistful of reddish powder, leaped onto the table, and—with a mighty lungful of air—blew the powder all over the gangsters' stunned faces. They staggered back, frantic hands waving to dispel the orange cloud hanging about their heads. Then their eyes rolled into the backs of their heads. They toppled over, unconscious.

It took an embarrassingly long time for everyone to realize there wasn't going to be a fight. They lowered their daggers and hid their teeth.

"What the fuck?" Qorobar said.

Nawidemaq looked a little sheepish. "Magic Ionian dust."

"Some warning would have been nice." Pisaqar actually sounded entertained. "Did you kill them?"

"No. They wake in a short time."

"Well then, let us not take chances. Bind them." They quickly hog-tied the gangsters with scavenged rope and let them lie. Outside, they found several more thugs lying on the deck with arrows sticking out of their necks, either gone west or in the process of leaving. Yesbokhe had done good work.

Once the dead were dumped and the living safely locked inside, they waved torches to signal Pepy, then set about searching the barge. The cavernous hold was mostly filled with sacks of barley and wheat, onions and beans, as well as beer amphorae straight from the pharaoh's breweries. All these commodities were mightily welcome, either as rations or barter. But there was more. In Sabef's lush quarters, they found a strongbox that brimmed with glass beads, turquoise, rubies, and even a few silver bars.

Pepy had soon drawn up on his boat. They crammed the cargo hold with as much loot as they could fit, then piled more sacks on the deck. By the time they'd finished, the boat had a visible list. Even Pepy insisted they stop at that point.

Still, even after taking more than their fill, the barge held an ample amount of cargo. For Pisaqar, there wasn't much question of what to do with it.

"Leave the grain sacks in a pile at the end of the dock," he ordered, pointing to the small but growing crowd of curious onlookers gathering there. "Let the people take their fill."

Ermun was perturbed at this. "Pisaqar, is that wise? Serpent though he may be, Sabef holds much sway in the city. To defang him completely, toss his wealth to the winds—it will throw the city into flux. *Isfet* will reign."

Pisaqar considered this counsel. "I spent all my life upholding ma'at. I always did what I thought best for Egypt. I obeyed my masters. Only now do I realize the stains my service left on my soul. There is much I must answer for when I go before Osiris with my heavy heart in my hands. And look. See how little good it did anyone." He looked to the crowd of commoners, their sunken cheeks, their threadbare clothes. "Those people are hungry, my friend. It is in my power to help them now. Therefore I must."

They spent the remainder of the night throwing the grain sacks onto a great pile. Ermun insisted on one last trip to the temple, where he and the acolyte left several more sacks as an offering to Osiris. The sun was rising before the barge was finally emptied out, and by then, the gaggle of onlookers had swollen to a crowd, all come to ogle at the new pyramid by the river.

With crew and cargo loaded up, Pepy's boat dropped sail and labored onto the open river. Pisaqar cupped his hands toward the crowd. "A gift of grain from Sabef the Generous!" The people burst forward in a joyous onrush. The sack pyramid promptly vanished beneath the crawling swarm. It had been demolished completely before the docks even faded from view.

BABYLON'S GARDENS

THE REEDS WHISPERED against the hull as the boat neared the shore. "Stroke! Stroke!" Pepy-Nakht cried from the prow. The Kushites strained at the gunwales. Their oars clattered together, ever out of sync. Effective warriors they were, and strong swimmers—but terrible sailors. As if to demonstrate that a week on the Nile had taught him nothing, Qorobar vaulted over the side the moment he deemed the shore close enough. He judged poorly. He vanished with a splash and came back up sputtering. Cursing breathlessly, he paddled after the boat.

The bow rose as it cleaved the riverbed. "*Now* you can jump," Pepy said with clear exasperation. The mercenaries pulled in the oars and splashed down in the shallows. Eleazar took his place beside them and grabbed a fistful of the bundled reeds that formed the hull. Qorobar waded past them to lift the prow on his shoulder—a feat that ought to have taken three strong men, but one he managed alone. Together, as the plump Egyptian gave the count, they heaved the laden vessel halfway onto the steep bank, far as it would go. They propped up the stern with rocks and logs to prevent it from drifting away in the night.

Then they set about making camp. Pisaqar chose a thicket of thorny trees as the campsite. The word didn't mean much; as far as Eleazar could gather, Kushites didn't think much of tents, preferring either solid roof or open sky. They hacked away a clearing, then built a fire and arranged their woven bedrolls around it.

"Wouldn't it be a fine thing," redheaded Tariq mused aloud, "if we could all spend the night in a cozy tavern?"

"With soft beds," said Amani, a suggestion that caused both Tariq and Kalab to study her closely. Eleazar gathered they were competing to woo her, though she seemed less than receptive to the acolyte's advances.

"And as much beer as you could drink," added Nibamon.

Qorobar shook his head. "You ought to open one if you want it so badly, Tariq."

"Don't tempt me with dreams, big man!"

When the camp was made, Yesbokhe slipped off to scout the immediate area. He returned bearing a clutch of quails, much to Eleazar's relief. He was sick to death of picking miniscule fish bones out of his teeth. And chewing Egyptian bread was almost worse. Though it tasted fine, it always had a sandy grit that Eleazar couldn't bring himself to trust.

With another long day of sailing behind them, the Kushites settled down around their fire. Jugs of beer were passed around as the priest began to roast the birds. He tossed some onions onto the coals as well, but Qorobar didn't bother waiting for his to blacken. To Eleazar's horror, the towering axe man snatched one up and chomped into it, crinkling skin and all. He caught Eleazar staring at him in disgust.

"Is this a problem for you, little traitor?" he said, chewing with his mouth open.

Eleazar sipped his wine while the others chuckled. He'd grown weary of tolerating their unsubtle jabs. From the big one, especially. "Eat your onion and be still. Your armpits squelch whenever you move."

There was a moment of awed silence, then uproarious laughter.

"The Israelite has some balls, after all!" Tariq cried, slapping his knee.

Qorobar scowled as the mirth rippled around the fire, his eyes narrowed to slits. "Funny little man."

"It is not I who flopped into the Nile like a sack of clay. A good show."

"Aye, I fell into the water. I also lifted the prow of that great boat as if it were nothing. You ought to save your jests for someone your own size."

"It was a titillating feat of strength, to be certain," Eleazar mocked.

Pisaqar spoke up. "Be calm, the both of you. This is not productive."

The circle went obligingly quiet. But the acolyte couldn't resist getting another rude word in. "You ought to watch yourself around our foreign friend, Qorobar. This one's a slayer. He breaks whole cities."

Amani scrutinized Eleazar. "What's that mean?"

"I did some asking in Jerusalem," said Kalab, clearly thrilled to have her attention. "That's what they called him. They say he was with the Assyrians at—"

"Babylon," Eleazar finished for him. He regretted saying anything in the first place. When he failed to break the expectant silence, Amani did instead.

"Are you going to tell us about it or not?"

"She's never been to Babylon," said Tariq. "Call it curiosity."

Nawidemaq massaged a knob of bronze in one hand. "City of Marduk. It was beautiful."

The thief girl told him, "That's very nice, Nawidemaq, but I want to hear it from *him*."

Eleazar looked to Pisaqar for intervention. The captain regarded him levelly. "Tell them, Eleazar. Make them see why I have chosen to trust you."

The Israelite understood that he was being ordered to bare his soul. He hesitated, weighing his words. When he replied, he spoke to the fire. "We of Sennacherib's army marched on the city to quell the usual troubles. The Babylonians are proud people, not overfond of paying tribute for long. To lay eyes on their city, one understands why. Imagine for yourselves building a city in the midst of the scorching desert, between two rivers, and then rutting the space between with a network of canals to rival Egypt's great delta. Into these canals flows trade from across every land, such that the city spreads and spreads until there is nowhere to go but up. The buildings themselves stretch into the sky. Even the merest hovel in Babylon is three, four, five floors tall. Atop every one, the people built—of all things—sun terraces. So great is Babylon's prosperity that when its people tire of their cool paradise, they venture onto their roofs to entertain themselves with the heat of the desert. As a novelty.

"We, Assyria's soldiers, did not think much of this. When we took the city, we drove the Babylonians into the streets so that we could pillage their homes without their wails filling our ears. We took all we could carry. After this, we went among the people to find the strongest men who would make for good laborers. We sent them into the desert in chains, toward Ashur. Once the men were gone, we picked out the most beautiful women to become our wives. The heavens shook with their lament.

"We used great lengths of rope to pull down their prized terraces. We dragged them off the roofs. We spilled their fragments into the street, onto the heads of the ones we had driven there. We took care with our task. A great many were crushed. Those who tried to flee, we chased back with whips and clubs. My comrades laughed to watch them scurry to and fro. It gave us pleasure to watch the upstart Babylonians punished by their own wealth. Once Sennacherib deemed the city appropriately humbled, we took our plunder and slaves and wives, and we left Babylon cowed beneath a pall of dust."

He looked up to find the Kushites staring at him in open amazement. Their discomfort made him smile. "These are the masters I chose to abandon. For this, you call me traitor. I wear the title gladly."

Qorobar dusted the rinds off his hands. "And you gave me shit for eating an onion."

Ermun kept his expression neutral, but contempt smoldered in his eyes. "What a deed. How did it feel then, to participate in such a heartless culling?"

"One does not feel much at all," shrugged Eleazar. "It was work. A farmer does not consider the wheat stalks he scythes down. Only much later did I dwell on what we had done. I remembered that before the Assyrians took me from Israel, they merely killed my father with an axe. A mercy, compared to the way we killed the Babylonians." Eleazar was somewhat surprised to note that his vision swam with tears. "I could not bring that fate on Judah. Not on my own people."

Pisaqar gripped his shoulder. Loud enough that his Kushites could hear, he said, "I could claim that I am proud of all the deeds I have done for Egypt. But I would be a liar, then." He looked around at the rest of them. "It is no cowardly thing to cast off an unworthy master. It is a lesson I have now learned for myself. If Eleazar is a traitor, then we are as well."

Amani, though, wasn't satisfied. "What about your wife?"

Eleazar's heart throbbed at the memory of poor Nidi. Her lilting laugh, her agonized moans. Her gentle caresses, her desperate grasp. Her amber eyes—so full of joy, so horribly vacant. "She died in Assyria. She died giving birth."

"You raped and murdered her."

"No!" The horror of the accusation stole his breath. He couldn't find the words to contest the lie.

"Exactly the same way you did her home."

"I loved… She… I had no…"

"No choice?" Amani's eyes reflected the flames. "There's always a choice, Israelite. You might have made the right one in the end. That doesn't excuse the things you did before."

"It was expected of us," protested Eleazar. "I did not wish to take a wife. Had I refused my reward, another would have claimed her in my place, someone cruel. There were many who enjoyed what we did to Babylon."

"His reward, he says," sneered Amani.

How could he possibly begin to explain what they'd shared? They'd been children stolen from massacred nations, forced to build new lives in a wicked land. She should have despised him as a coward, Nidi, but she had chosen to love him instead. Her strength had been so great that it had outlived her body, swept him away from Assyria even as he grieved her, borne him back to the land of his people. If he managed to do any good with his pitiful life, she was why.

But when he saw the look Amani reserved for him, those words died in his throat. Nidi had looked at him the same way when he'd carried her from smoking Babylon.

Qorobar spat a gobbet of phlegm between his feet. "What a shitty stand-in for Pakheme."

Tariq hid his face behind his braids.

Pisaqar jumped to his feet. "Your willingness to judge Eleazar does you no credit. You are not the first man to have lost everything, Qorobar. And you, Amani! A person is more than the worst thing he—or she—has ever done. I know it well. But you, of all people, should have learned that best."

Qorobar snatched up his axe. Eleazar stilled, certain he was about to be hacked into screaming chunks. Instead, the big man stomped off into the night. The *thunk*ing of an axe head on wood rose, punctuated by wheezing grunts. A splintering crash announced the felling of a tree. Then the *thunk*s started up again.

Amani, for her part, accepted her captain's rebuff with unnerving calm, belied only by the tears shining at the corners of her eyes. Tariq reached out to her, but she slapped his hand away, in no mood to be touched. She stared into the flames, sniffing. Eleazar could only guess what she saw.

"Here." Kalab was holding out a spitted fish to him. Eleazar took it in a shaking hand, scarcely caring that the quail had already been shared out. He saw Pisaqar looking his way, but couldn't find it in himself to meet the man's gaze. Not for the first time in his life, he was trapped in a land among foreigners who'd happily see him dead. He had a dreadful feeling that he would finish his long journey as a bloated corpse in the Nile, sour nourishment for Egypt's crops.

Tariq had been acquainted with Amani long enough to know she took solace in water, just the same way he did. It was little surprise to find her ankle deep in the river. She was watching the ripples as they gleamed in the moonlight, her arms crossed and expression hard.

"Are you alright?" he asked.

She accepted the beer he offered, signaling her willingness for company. "I've never taken fatherly scoldings that well," she admitted.

"Fathers usually mean well by it."

"My first one didn't." She swilled her cup. "Sometimes I wonder if I should've just listened to the old shit, stayed married. Farmed cats."

Tariq was taken aback, and not a little amused. "You. Married. Raising cats."

"That's the way I felt about it. The instant I spoke the vows, the whole thing just seemed so damn bland."

"You're telling me that you divorced your husband in the same breath that you married him."

She gave him a defensive look. "Is there a rule saying when I get to divorce?"

"Well no. There isn't. But I think a scolding might have been a little warranted."

"A little," she laughed. "Would you like to guess how much my father would've gotten as a bride price if I'd kept my end?"

"Two cows," Tariq said promptly.

"That was… Who told you?"

"People talk, you know." He raised his hands as she narrowed her eyes. "Pakheme, I think."

"It sounds like you were asking Pakheme about me. Interesting."

"I like to be in the know. When I look at a girl, I ask myself, 'How much would this one's father want for her hand?' You, I took one glance, and I decided straight away you were out of my price range." Her smile became a simper, which was the signal for the backhand of the compliment. "But then I got the truth from Pakheme."

"Little shit!" She went to punch him, but he darted out of reach.

Eventually, when their laughter died down, she turned back to the water. "I wouldn't fetch two cows nowadays," she sighed.

A fresh joke died on Tariq's lips as he saw how the humor had gone out of her. Trepidly, he asked, "Is this to do with what Pisaqar said?"

"Suppose so."

He waited on her.

At last, she said, almost offhandedly, "Only embalmers use knives like this, you know." She held out her blackstone dagger. "They're heirlooms. I got this one from my uncle."

"I didn't know women embalmed."

"That's because they don't."

"Oh."

"So when my father couldn't get the bride price back, he was obviously angry with me. He sent me to Memphis to live with his brother. Turns out my uncle was none too pleased to be caring for some wayward niece." She paused a moment, trapped in a recollection. "Let's say I spent some time locked in tight places."

"He didn't," Tariq said, dismayed.

"I think you have the right idea," she said grimly. "The thing I did—the thing Pisaqar was talking about—was stab my uncle while he snored, with his own fancy knife. It was onto the streets after that. If you want to eat, you need something to trade. Most girls in that situation only have the one thing. But luckily for me, I was somewhat prepared. I had this sling. I'd spent a lot of my childhood picking off jackals when they came sniffing after the cats. I got very, very good at shooting rats. If I got tired of greasy meat, felt like a change in fare? All I had to do was find a sack of grain to cut. Of course, you can only steal so many times before you get caught. That's how Pisaqar came across me: with my wrist on the axe man's block."

She lifted her shoulders, a movement that was flippant and false. "All told, farming cats would have been easier."

Tariq glanced at the obsidian knife tucked into Amani's belt. He'd always wondered how she'd acquired it. Now, he wasn't sure he was better off for knowing. "That's what Pisaqar was talking about? The worst thing you've ever done?"

"It's in the running." She forced a smile. "Alright. Your turn."

Ropey pink intestines that dangle about Pakheme's knees, quivering as he screams, swords hacking him down in crimson sprays…

He swallowed hard. The moment drew itself out while he fumbled for words, sifting through one awful memory after the next and realizing, in the process, how much willpower it must have taken for Amani to tell him what she just had. It was a feat he couldn't hope to match.

To his amazement, she took his hand. "It's fine. Don't worry."

The answer came to him. "It's not the worst thing," he confessed, "but I think it qualifies as bad."

"Tell it."

"This one time, there was this girl I was sweet on. But she never looked my way, and besides that, she'd just stopped seeing some prick and I didn't want to bother her. It was tough on me, you know. People saw it. Someone came up to me and he said, 'Tariq, I have just the solution. You need to brew up a love potion.'"

Her mouth opened. "Come on, now."

"Well, I didn't think it would actually work. So, I went to the only priest I knew. He told me that, fine, he'd put together the love potion, but he needed a certain ingredient. Something from the girl."

"Tariq, I'm warning you, if this goes the way I think it is, I'm going to stab you."

"Spit."

"*What*?"

"He said he needed some of your spit. It wasn't all that tough to get, honestly. You drool in your sleep."

"Tariq, did you fucking feed me my own saliva?"

"No—by Amun, put the knife back! This was supposed to be funny!"

"I was supposed to be hearing the worst thing you've ever done, not this horrifying shit!"

"That's what I'm telling you! *You* didn't drink the potion, *I* did."

She paused with her knife half drawn. She snorted an accidental laugh. "You drank my spit."

"Right. And the other vile shit Ermun threw in. Eye of crocodile. Shank of cat fur. Flat beer."

She turned his way with a swish of water. "And the potion worked?"

"If you've ever found yourself wondering why you've fallen suddenly and madly in love with me, there's your answer."

"That's just stupid. You're the one who drank it, not me."

"And here's you, acting as if magic potions behave in some sensible way."

She dumped out the rest of her beer and waded past him onto the shore, her head wagging in disbelief. But she was smiling. "I'm going to sleep now."

"Wait! This conversation was supposed to end with you on top of me!"

"Pleasant dreams, Tariq."

"Good night, Amani," he grinned. He looked out over the lapping shore. On the far bank, a pair of palm trees swayed, dancing together in the light breeze. "You, raising cats. Can't believe it."

"Explain what you mean by *rampage*."

Senanmuht flexed his aching leg, glad for his full-length robe. Behind his kneecap, the arrowhead was biting again, just as it always did this time of year. A wholly objectionable means of sensing that Inundation was upon the land. The old wound was courtesy of a certain Kushite savage some ten years past.

The infuriating irony devoured him as he watched Taharqa lift his next potential bride's chin. The girl—a cousin of Senanmuht's—wrung her hands as the Kushite afflicted her with his scrutiny. Surely in that moment she wished for her true husband, but he was beyond her reach—slain along with many more noble sons outside Jerusalem. All thanks to Taharqa's folly. The desire to smite the man was overpowering. For a moment, Senanmuht forgot he'd been asked a question. Until Taharqa let the poor girl's chin fall and glared at him with the malevolence so typical of his kind.

"I merely suggest," Senanmuht said, bowing and hating the act, "that Pisaqar's commitment to the Divine Order is not as strong as he has led us all to believe."

"And you base this suggestion on the word of some grasping priest from the bowels of Memphis. What is your name, girl?"

"Iput," the young woman said, her voice quavering with what Senanmuht imagined was indignant fury.

Taharqa chuckled kindly. "Come forward, Iput."

The general moved on to the next prospect as she stepped out of line, visibly trembling now. Her beauty had damned her. Perhaps Taharqa would invite her to sup with him and her father. Or perhaps he'd wish to gaze on her nude form before he made his final decision. Senanmuht wasn't certain which was more humiliating for a daughter of Sais. As if being gifted to a Kushite invader wasn't degrading enough.

Senanmuht stifled his roiling anger. There was still a game to play. "I agree that the priest's news alone is not cause for alarm. However, we must keep in mind broader events. In the Sinai, a column of your men has been massacred. In Sena, shortly after, a cloth merchant reported being robbed blind by a Kushite bowman. In Memphis, *isfet* is unleashed. A false Apis is paraded through the city. A tavern is demolished. Food riots at the docks."

Taharqa ambled past the next prospects—proud widows of Eltekeh and Jerusalem—with disinterest. "Old. Plump. Plain." He clicked his tongue. "Sais runneth dry." He turned to face his advisor. "Of your family's meager offerings, your counsel manages to be the most distasteful by far, Senanmuht. All you've done is scrape together a handful of random troubles and presented them to me as evidence of ... what, exactly?"

"Of a mercenary who seeks to sow discord in the nation you've brought peace," asserted Senanmuht.

"What madness, Senanmuht. Pisaqar has always served ma'at. His self-proclaimed virtue would never allow him to stoop even to simple theft, much less murder."

"With utmost respect, General, Pisaqar is no longer your teacher. He is a sellsword. One whom you have deprived of payment."

"An act I regret deeply, necessary though it was. Pisaqar knows this."

Senanmuht dared to play his best piece. "You could not trouble yourself to reclaim his man's body."

Taharqa became very still. The women lining the walls shrank back as they sensed the great man's rage nearing a boil.

Fully aware of the danger he was in, Senanmuht quickly added, "That is how Pisaqar views the matter, dear General. He told me himself." A lie, but not an unreasonable assumption. "The forfeited payment was an offense, true. But allowing the Assyrians to keep his man's corpse for whatever unholy purpose ... that was an affront, whether you intended it or not. Pisaqar will never forgive you for it."

Taharqa paced the room, contemplating. At last, he pointed at Senanmuht. "I want Pisaqar found. You will neither approach nor attempt to apprehend him. Discover his intent. Only once I know the truth of the matter will I move against him."

Senanmuht carefully kept the anger from his face. "General, as your trusted advisor, I must recommend strong action. You have made an enemy of this man. If he is allowed free rein, there is no telling what havoc he might wreak."

"No, Senanmuht. Pisaqar was as a father to me, once. I owe him restraint."

"General—"

"I have given my command. See it written. Let it be done."

"But of course." Senanmuht bowed deep. The ache in his knee had become a steady throb, as if Pisaqar's arrowhead was stirring at the mention of its master.

"And Senanmuht?"

"I serve, General."

"Send for Iput's father." Taharqa gestured to poor Iput, who turned ashen as her worst nightmare was brought into being. "Tell him his lovely daughter has managed to charm me. I shall dine with them both this evening to discuss the bride price."

THE PLACE OF TRUTH

NIBAMON'S FACE WAS torture to gaze upon. Ever since the day of his punishment, he'd carefully averted his gaze from pools of water, polished metal, anything that cast a reflection. It was a rule of life, a thing he'd gotten used to. He'd learned to live with the pain, too. Having one's nose sliced off was an agony he'd have wished on no one. Himself least of all. He still remembered the sound of crinkling cartilage as the knife sawed in, how the blood had gushed down his throat, obliging him to swallow it down in order to breathe, how he'd been slowly deafened by his own screams. A hard day. And though the wound had healed and the pain had dulled, it had never quite faded.

The desert made it worse. The murderous heat clawed at the hole in his face. Sand got past his mask and stuck to his exposed sinuses, where it dried into a pale crust. His breathing produced a moist whistle that made the battle-hardened mercenaries cringe around him. He would have pitied the Kushites if he hadn't been fully preoccupied with his own misery. It felt as if an embalmer was wriggling a rod into his skull in a fruitless search for his brain.

"Must be nice to see home again, eh?"

Nibamon glanced at Qorobar, adjusting his mask reflexively. The hulking axe man was caked in dust from their column's uphill march. He knew from his reluctant years of living in this desolate place that the bottom layers of dust had mixed with the man's sweat and turned to paste. Without a bath, it would be impossible to wipe away completely. And there were no baths to be had here. Not in Set-Ma'at.

Qorobar frowned down at him. "What's this place called again?"

"The Place of Truth. Set-Ma'at."

"Shit, that sounds pretentious. That can't be what you chiselers actually call it."

"No. To us, it was always the Village."

Qorobar grunted and turned his eyes forward again, back to the wretched place whose many names could never capture the reality of living there. Nibamon was home, and it was of no consolation at all.

Set-Ma'at was situated in an arid bowl high above the Nile, which a poorly placed hill neatly blocked from view. The hill also stymied the cool northerly wind that might have been a balm for the inhabitants' suffering. And—to add to the insult—the hill wasn't even high enough to offer shade from the searing sun. The only shelter was in the village itself: a cluster of a few dozen homes, each touching the next, arranged in neat rows along the contours of the tiny valley. A rectangular wall surrounded the community. Heaped against it were shards of broken pottery, the debris of centuries of daily journeys to the river and back in a constant struggle for water. There were no wells, no smattering of rain, only the distant Nile.

Nibamon blew out a long sigh through his nose, provoking a flinch from Qorobar. "I'm sorry." The big man only grunted. "To answer your initial question: no. I'd hoped never to see this place again. No one who lived here was fond of it."

"I thought you told me your sister still dwells here."

"I said she might. And if she does, it's because she was the only one stubborn enough to stay. Everyone else scampered once the renovations were complete." Receiving a questioning look, he explained, "Some pretender to the throne wanted to lighten his heart for his journey to the underworld. He figured the best way was to restore some old tombs. He commissioned workers from Thebes for the job. My father was one of them. I spent most of my youth in this place. Soon as I was old enough to take commissions of my own, I left."

"Ah." Qorobar nodded. His black, emotionless eyes flickered down to Nibamon's mask, as if to say, *That went well for you.*

Nibamon stopped to cast a final longing look back at the Nile before trudging into the desiccated valley, toward his detested childhood home. The Desert Mice marched ahead in column, setting an unwavering pace that he found hard to match. He could only gaze after the bull-drawn cart, hating himself for not taking Pisaqar up on his offer to let him ride. Now he lagged behind with Qorobar acting as his increasingly sullen bodyguard, both of them breathing more dust than air and suffering tremendously for it.

"You wait—" Nibamon began to say before thinking better of it and stopping.

"Wait for what?" demanded Qorobar.

"Nothing." He'd been about to tell him that their sorry state was nothing compared to the months of digging ahead, but he supposed it was even odds that Qorobar would slay him on the spot. He was a man who veered between sullenness and murderous violence, with only his captain's will holding his proclivities in check. At the moment, Pisaqar was a tad too distant for Nibamon's liking. Best be quiet.

When they caught up to the rest of the column, it had drawn up to the base of the guardhouse. The blocky structure was the largest in the community and looked much the same as Nibamon remembered it. The roof was caved in and the interior gutted. His father had always maintained that his great-great-great-great-great-great-grandfather had torn it down during the famous strike, while his mother had shrugged that it had probably burnt down in a Bedouin raid. Either way, the guardhouse remained a deserted ruin, because there was little left to guard. It'd been that way since the line of Ramesses had ended three centuries before.

Pisaqar led them through the open north gate. At the head of the main street, he motioned toward Nibamon. The foreman hastened forward at a shuffle, his legs protesting after the long climb under the stern sun. The captain, by contrast, didn't even sound winded as he asked, "Which of these houses is Senet's?"

Nibamon studied the long rows of houses rising up on either side of the street. Their facades had once been plastered smooth with mud, painted white. But the years had flaked the surface off to reveal the bare mud brick beneath. The doors had been plundered for their valuable wood. Beyond the yawning frames, every house was empty. The awning that had once covered the street was gone as well—stolen or blown away. As much as Nibamon had hated living here, it wounded him to see his home abandoned to the indifference of the ages.

"That one used to be ours." He pointed to the fifth house on the left. It was afternoon, and he knew the inside would be cooking as the sun blazed through the high windows. There was no sign of life. "If she's still here, she moved houses. I would guess she went to the foreman's house." He could picture his elder sister sitting against the wall in the morning shade, wiggling her toes as the line of sunlight crept nearer, then retracting her legs just in time. He smiled despite his melancholy. "Senet always chased after the shade."

The foreman's house would be one of the larger buildings deep within the village. Soon as they'd turned the first corner, Nibamon saw the linen sheets flapping overhead, casting the street into orange shade. Potted fig trees lined the walls. There beside them squatted a middle-aged woman in a dress streaked with dirt, her thick hair gathered in a top knot. She was humming to herself while she sprinkled water around the tree stems. Nibamon watched her a moment, remembering his mother's lullabies.

"Hello, Senet."

She looked around with a quizzical expression, recognizing his voice without quite placing it. Then she saw him—and shrieked. Her body recoiled an in instinctive effort to bolt, but there was no room. She rolled across her pots, snapping the modest stems, and went tumbling in the street amid a cloud of dust.

Nibamon hurried over, stooped. "It's me, Senet. Your brother."

She looked up at him with frightened eyes. "Nibamon?" They filled with tears as he helped her up. "What did they do to you?"

Only then did he realize his mask wasn't on. He'd pulled it down at some point. "I was punished. I'll explain later. There will be time. We plan to stay for a while."

Her handsome face grew pinched. "You've brought soldiers." The mercenaries were clustered on the nearby corner to watch, like a gaggle of children. "Kushites." She spat the word.

Pisaqar came forward with his hands spread at the waist. "Kushites, yes. But also friends. As friends, we ask your hospitality." He correctly read her growing furor and added, "Or at least your indifference while we take up residence in some of these abandoned houses."

After a steadying breath, she told him, "I'm going to stay angry and suspicious for a little while."

The captain grinned. "I take no offense." He instructed his mercenaries, "Yesbokhe, Kalab, search the rest of the village, make sure there are no surprises in store. The rest of you, go back to unload the cart. Move all the grain and provisions into one house. Choose places for your lodgings."

The mercenaries scampered off with much whooping and yelling. Again, like children.

Senet whispered to Nibamon, "They brought food for themselves?"

"Plenty of it. And beer. Another long story for later."

"I was sure they were going to rob us. That's what soldiers always mean when they talk of hospitality. Why have you brought them here?" Her eyes widened with understanding. "The tombs."

"The tombs," confirmed Nibamon. "That of the Robber Pharaoh, specifically."

She snorted a laugh. In that instant, she became her teenage self again. "A stupid legend. They'll die of thirst before they find it. Better men have tried." She practically yelled the last sentence. Pisaqar, conferring with his priest friend, stifled a smile but otherwise ignored her.

"They're decent enough people, Senet. And we know where to look."

"Oh yes, yes, I've heard it all before. But not from you. Not from my little brother. The Nibamon I know builds great things. He doesn't pick over ruins for flakes of tarnished silver. Did they take your honor from you along with your nose?"

He wanted to snap at his sister, remind her that honor had never meant much to her. She was the one who'd raked Father with scorn for dutifully laboring on when the pretender king stopped sending bread, even after the other workers had left. She was the one who'd broken off her first engagement in favor of a younger, comelier suitor.

But bickering would only aggravate her more. "How is Rukhmire? And the children?"

Realizing that no one was going to rise to her taunts, she threw up her hands. "It's hot out. Come inside. I'll pour us water." She blew her cheeks and added, "Bring your brute friend."

Pisaqar followed them around the next corner. He pointed to the broken fig trees as he went by. "I am sorry about your plants."

"I'll grow more," she said curtly.

"It cannot be easy to grow things in this heat."

"I'll try harder." She stopped beside her door and ushered them into the parlor, quickly hauling the door shut so the cool air inside wouldn't escape. One look around the interior told Nibamon that, dismal setting considered, Senet had done quite well for herself. The floor was made of mud tiles, not the hard-packed earth they'd grown up with. There was a straight staircase that provided easy access to the roof terrace, as well as a ceiling vent for the hot air. The plaster walls were painted white on the top half and decorated with murals left over from the previous owners, although Senet had taken the trouble to repaint the faces to resemble her own family: her rakish husband Rukhmire, her son Meri, and her daughter Yem. The wall tables below the murals were crammed with pots and baskets—filched, he was sure, from the many abandoned homes. The shelves and benches held a rather astonishing variety of herbs and houseplants.

Senet pointed her guests to a couple of often-repaired chairs and disappeared up into the back rooms. She returned with a jug of water on a tray, which she propped between their armrests.

"You keep a beautiful house," Pisaqar complimented as he accepted a mug.

"You'll want to blow on that," she said brusquely. "I just finished boiling it." She cleared some pots from a bench and spread a mat to cover the mud bricks. Before she could sit down, a pair of children darted out of the back room and bounced onto it, giggling and screeching, their gleaming eyes alternating between Nibamon and Pisaqar, but mostly fixing on the latter.

Pisaqar waved at them, his teeth shining bright in the dim room. They returned the greeting with bubbling enthusiasm as their exasperated mother scooted them aside and sat in the narrow space between their wriggling forms.

"Who's that?" screamed the girl, Yem.

Nibamon said, "This is Pisaqar. He's one of the pharaoh's soldiers."

"You're too old to be a soldier," cried Meri, the boy.

Pisaqar clutched his heart. "This poor old man! What can I say to such mean children? Should I..." he suddenly reached out, making claws of his fingers, "crush their little heads?!"

The children reared back, screaming with laughter. "Nooooo!" they shouted in unison.

Senet's expression softened somewhat. She gathered her children and pointed to Nibamon. "And that is your uncle, Nibamon. Remember him?"

The girl nodded while the boy asked, "Why's he wearing a thing on his face?"

Nibamon opened his mouth but found he had none of Pisaqar's easy charm, and no way to deflect from the mutilation the priests had inflicted on him. Lost for words, it was left to his sister to cover for him.

"Don't be rude, Meri. Now go back outside and play. We adults need to talk."

The children jumped up and scurried toward the back room. "Can he come?" Yem pointed to Pisaqar.

"No! Shoo! And drink some water," she yelled as her children vanished. She turned back to her guests, shaking her head. "They're yours, if you want them."

Pisaqar cackled. "Do not tempt me."

"You have children?"

His smile took on a brittle quality. "Once."

"I'm sorry." It sounded like she meant it. She had warmed to him. Not for the first time, Nibamon understood how Pisaqar won loyalty from his people. Even him, he realized. He'd sprung to the man's defense when his sister questioned his character.

Pisaqar cleared his throat. "So. You had questions for me."

"Just one, really, and not exactly a question. My brother tells me you've come for the lost tomb." Receiving a nod, she continued. "Before you start, you'll need to have a conversation with my husband, Rukhmire. You see, Rukhmire is the last guardian of the valley. The others left over the years, but my husband chose to stay."

Nibamon observed, "Just as Father did."

"Duty makes men feel important. Makes them do stupid things. In truth, I would love nothing more than to get out of this gods-forsaken place. Move to Thebes. Memphis. Anywhere. But my husband won't hear of it. He just disappears for days at a time and squats in his little hut with his little sword. As if he'd stand a chance against any robber who's halfway serious."

Pisaqar said, "We are fully serious. Ramesses' tomb is in that valley, and we intend to pick it clean. It might be best for everyone if we simply scared your husband off."

She smiled despairingly. "He won't run away. He'll die before he lets you get past him. No, best to wait until he comes back for water. Then you'll have your chance to speak sense to him. You might succeed where I've failed."

"And if I cannot?"

"I don't know. Tie him up?" There was no humor in her laugh. "It'll break him, but at this point it's probably for the best. The pharaoh used to send a sack of grain every week. Now it comes once a fortnight, if that. Sooner or later, it will stop coming at all. Rukhmire needs to hear the hard truth from someone who hasn't already told him a thousand times. Preferably someone with a sword."

In the end, although Senet assured them her husband would return in a day or three, Pisaqar decided it was better not to wait. He was a man of action. The idea of sitting inert, beholden to the loose schedule of a total stranger, galled him. Once again, Nibamon was condemned to a long uphill march. Thankfully, dusk had fallen, and the cooling air made the effort bearable. The ochre sand darkened to umber as the sun neared the end of its circuit, the cloudless sky all crimsons and violets. The shrunken column lit torches as night approached. Pisaqar had specific errands in mind and had opted to bring a smaller crew: the two priests, the Israelite, and Nibamon.

They scrabbled uphill in the gathering dark, their torches guttering as they made their way over the rocky ground. Ahead of them lay a cliff face, tall and sheer. The setting sun cast its jagged lines into harsh relief. Any one of those innumerable shadows could have easily been mistaken for a canyon mouth. In reality, there was but one way into the valley—and Rukhmire guarded it.

His hut first announced itself with a red flicker. Fire must have been one of his scant joys, because his dwelling place was a depressing sight. It was little more than a semicircle of rocks piled man-high and topped with thatch. A pair of eyes peered out at the approaching visitors through a window maybe the size of a fist. The eyes disappeared, and out stumbled Rukhmire, bent copper sword in hand.

The robust young man Nibamon remembered had fallen prey to the ungentle years. His head of curls was reduced to a mop of limp strands. His smooth bronze skin had turned swarthy from far too many lonesome patrols in the sun. His fine teeth had been stained brown and worn flat by sandy bread.

"Halt!" he cried hoarsely, brandishing his sad family sword. "Halt in the name of Shabaku!"

Pisaqar said out of the corner of his mouth, "Nibamon, calm your brother-in-law."

He remembered himself and hastened to the head of the column on creaking legs. "Brother! Put down your sword. It's me, Nibamon."

Rukhmire lowered his guard with clear relief. "Nibamon!" He grinned, and in that moment, the raffish boy who had wooed Senet out of her first engagement was visible once more. He shook his head and laughed at the sight of Nibamon's unlikely company. "Amun's sake, man, what've you gotten yourself into this time?"

He couldn't help but chuckle in return. "New job, new friends," he replied.

"Come sit, all of you. It's a little cramped inside but you ought to fit. I daresay I can scrounge up enough bread for us to nibble on... Gives me an excuse to head home early, I admit..." Still jabbering, he stooped and disappeared through the door. Nibamon was no longer sure whether he was talking to his guests or himself.

Somehow, Rukhmire had managed to exaggerate the size of his living quarters. The round hut was only a few paces across. A stone bed encompassed half the hut, and the remaining space was cluttered with baskets and pottery, all empty. Their host pulled a threadbare blanket from a cubbyhole and spread it on the bed, which he offered as a seat. Nibamon exchanged a wincing look with the others, but Rukhmire was so excited to have company that no one raised a complaint. They squeezed awkwardly onto the bed while he dug through his baskets for presentable food, muttering and grinning all the while.

Eventually, he pressed a few hardened heels into their hesitant palms, then sat on an upturned basket with a happy sigh. He smiled between them. "How's the bread?"

The stiff crusts crackled as the men, remembering themselves, gnawed into them. "It's much appreciated," Ermun told him after a moment, kindly.

"Good, good. Well, brother, catch me up on your news. I'm very keen to hear how you've come to surround yourself with such formidably armed company. Does it have anything to do with the…?" He tapped his nose speculatively.

Nibamon opened his mouth and found he hadn't considered such an obvious question. "The priests at Karnak did this to me. Some men were killed on the job. I ended up taking the blame."

"Were you in charge?"

"I was, yes."

"Well then." Rukhmire shrugged apologetically. "Shame they decided on the nose, though. It was always your best feature. Same nose as my Senet."

Nibamon's gaze fell. He'd forgotten that he'd once been handsome, and with prospects. Then again, his sister still had her beauty, and she hadn't exactly prospered either. For all their aspirations, they'd ultimately wound up back in the parched heights where only dead kings still dwelled.

Rukhmire pointed at Ermun and Kalab. "Wasn't you who did it to him, was it?"

The acolyte swallowed his bread with a grimace. "We aren't those kinds of priests."

"You sure? Those sickle swords look awfully mean. I didn't think anyone even used those anymore."

"We raise them in defense of ma'at," said Ermun.

"Oh. I see. That explains the feathers on all your heads." Rukhmire frowned as he noticed Eleazar's conspicuous lack thereof. "Except you! No offense, friend, but with that beard, you have a bit of a foreign look."

Eleazar spread his hands and bowed but wisely chose not to speak. But Rukhmire didn't need to hear his accent to draw conclusions.

"You aren't the pharaoh's men, are you?"

Pisaqar said, "Not anymore."

Nibamon's brother-in-law seemed to deflate as the good cheer left him. "I'd worried about that." He looked at his sword leaning against the doorway. The men's muscles tightened, but Rukhmire didn't make a move. Neither did they.

The guard blew out his cheeks. "This is a shit day."

"I must be honest with you, Rukhmire. We have come to recoup a debt by way of a dead pharaoh. We require entrance to the valley. I am aware that this puts you in a difficult position, for which I apologize. I hope we can come to an understanding." Pisaqar touched his heart to convey his good intent.

"And me, I hope you can see what you're asking me to do. It's one thing to bribe a man. But my many forefathers have guarded the valley for two hundred years. With *this sword*. You're asking me to set it down and look the other way and let you rob the place my ancestors protected. You'd make me put a price on their honor, and mine. I'd rather you killed me."

Nibamon pleaded, "What about Senet? Your son and daughter?"

"You'd take care of them, brother." Rukhmire spoke as if that were a matter of fact, which it was.

Pisaqar broke in. "Your family is exactly that: yours. Do not pass them into another man's keeping so willingly. It is not fair to them, it is not fair to Nibamon, and you will go to the next life for no good reason."

"At least I could tell my grandfathers I kept my oath," said Rukhmire.

"Your forefathers were amply rewarded for their service. You cannot possibly say the same. We passed through that forsaken village down there. I spoke to your wife. She is thin as a reed, and hoarse from thirst. She receives a sack of flour every fortnight, this when the pharaoh's bureaucrats trouble themselves to send it. She fears for the future. She is right to do so. Pharaoh Shabaku is an old man, likely to perish sooner than later. I know the man who will take the throne in his place. I helped raise him. His name is Taharqa, and I tell you now, while Shabaku may fall short on his pledge, Taharqa will not trouble himself for you at all. These dead kings you guard, them and their ransacked tombs, they mean nothing to him. I am giving you the choice to recognize your abandonment now rather than later. Let me help your family prosper."

Rukhmire slouched on his basket, nodding along dejectedly. "I suppose this is the part where you offer to pay me off."

"Indeed, let us speak of payment. Our work will take us some months. Throughout that time, you and your family will be supplied with all the provisions you need. Water, bread, beer, we will bring it up from the river daily. These are the things the pharaoh has never been able to provide for you. It will be as easy a life as your family has ever lived here."

"Fair enough. But when you leave, I'm trapped in the same predicament. What am I supposed to do after your work is done?"

Pisaqar smiled. "You are no fool, Rukhmire, are you?"

Rukhmire smirked back. "Lately, I've been looking more and more to the future. That tends to happen, when you've children to think of. Tell me. What can you do for us after you leave?"

"There is one unspoiled tomb left. In that tomb are enough riches that we could divide it into a dozen parts and still be unable to spend it all. I can offer you wealth to pass to your children, and they to theirs. The chance to begin anew."

Rukhmire massaged his hands, apparently mulling it over. Finally, he asked, "Which tomb are you after?"

Pisaqar shook his head. "I am afraid I cannot say. It is for your protection as well as ours."

"I understand," the man said. "I'd like to guard the canyon while you work. At least then I can rest knowing I've earned my share." He stood up. His beaming face left Nibamon with no remaining doubt. Rukhmire hadn't truly meant to sacrifice his life for a bunch of empty tombs. The man had been playing Pisaqar all along, extracting as much as he could. Rukhmire had always been a clever one.

"Finish your food, boys," he told them. "Then I'll show you into the Valley of the Kings."

The full moon shone down on the still-warm rocks, bathing the valley in blue light. As many times as Nibamon had visited the royal necropolis, clinging back then to his stern father, it baffled him how small the valley was. In most places, the valley was narrower than a city street, only widening slightly in the center. Even then, a stone tossed underhanded would have cleared the gap easily. Steep limestone hills crowded in on both sides, some deceptively smooth—his child self had scaled them frequently enough to know better—most jagged and forbidding, and nearly all topped by cliffs many times the height of a man. Branching paths cut into the hills with regularity, ascending toward the distant mountains without ever coming close to them. There were only a handful of well-hidden entrances to the valley, which made it an easy place to guard. The pharaohs had chosen this as their resting place because of the defensible layout, the murderous heat, and the isolated locale, counting on these combined factors to protect their graves for eternity.

Almost comprehensively, they'd failed. Walled entryways were nestled into the valley walls, open invitations to the tombs they framed, invitations that opportunistic men over the centuries hadn't failed to pass up. The thick stone portals had been battered open, the rubble-filled passageways beyond cleared, the inner sanctums gutted not just of their boundless treasure, but of any object that might carry an iota of value—up to and including the pharaohs' corpses. The guarantee of theft was the reason pharaohs of more recent dynasties no longer chose to be buried here, but in humbler tombs across Egypt.

Nibamon's father had devoted his life to sealing the tombs once more, but in the mere decade since he'd died, more robbers had returned to undo his work.

Kalab pursed his lips in distaste as he ran his fingers along the chisel marks that disfigured one portal slab. "All this effort to scrape at empty tombs. One imagines how they must have reacted once they got in."

"Not well," Rukhmire said grimly. "They spent their wrath on the inscriptions."

The old priest hissed in dismay. "As if it weren't enough to obliterate a man's body. But his epitaph, too? What evil spite."

"Aye. Better that the tombs had never been restored in the first place. At least then, they wouldn't have attracted attention."

Eleazar spat on the ground. "This crooning is without point."

Ermun retorted, "A man lives on as long as his name is still spoken. Your previous master understands that very well. How curious that you do not."

The Assyrian traitor looked supremely untroubled by the erasure of foreign kings. "Let us do what we came here to accomplish. Afterward, we can return to Set-Ma'at and resume our bickering."

Kalab let out a burst of mocking laughter. "Listen to the tyrant's cup bearer. He pretends as if finding a lost tomb is the work of minutes."

"I appreciate the difficulties we face," Eleazar said—slowly, as if speaking to a small child. "What I fail to understand is why you priests whittle away our time mewling over hollow ruins."

Sandals scuffed against hard sand as Kalab whirled, fists bunched and nostrils flared. Eleazar reflexively grabbed for his knife, but there was no need. Ermun placed a hand on his acolyte's shoulder and brought him back to himself.

"His words may sting, but he isn't incorrect. Now give me light."

Kalab rolled his shoulders, and with a final glare at the Israelite, held a torch aloft for the elder priest. Ermun leaned through the open door and into the dim tomb, frowning at the worn hieroglyphs within. His feet remained just beyond the doorstep, and Kalab kept a firm grip on his belt to ensure he kept his balance. Neither man was willing to risk bringing down the wrath of a departed pharaoh by entering his tomb.

Eleazar's lip curled. "And they return to their idle studies."

It was Nibamon's turn to lose his temper. "Oh, will you shut your mouth? How is it not obvious they're doing this for a reason?"

"I see that they read over inscriptions, which your brother *just said* were erased, in a tomb that *plainly* is not the one we seek. I fail to see what this accomplishes."

Ermun cried out with excitement. "Here! This cartouche! Usermaatre Setepenre Meryamun!"

Eleazar lifted his hands, aghast. "Just as I said. Wrong tomb."

"No, this is the marker we sought," the priest told him. "This is the tomb of Ramesses, Seventh of His Name. The predecessor of the king we seek. From here, we look to the stars. They will point the way." Kneeling, he pulled a bolt of cloth from his satchel and unwrapped it to reveal a papyrus: the copy of the mortuary scroll from the Vault of Osiris. He spread it on the ground with eager hands.

Kalab looked up at the cliffs that rimmed the valley. "Someone should call Nawidemaq off." He pointed to the reedy-limbed figure dancing madly on a rocky outcrop, his limbs flailing and twisting as he bellowed a lyrical entreaty to some unknown god. The white bull was there too, plopped on his rump and watching his friend with patient curiosity.

Kalab cupped his hands. "Nawidemaq! Stop! We don't need the rain anymore!"

The medicine man's gyrations came to a teetering halt. His arms dropped disappointedly. The syllables drifted back down. "I go back now! Sleep!"

The Israelite watched him vanish. "Why was he asking his gods for rain?"

"Well, they aren't his. He only borrows them," Ermun explained.

Nibamon said, "Rain is how robbers normally find tombs. In the wet seasons, they'll sit and watch the water flow. If they see some disappearing, it means there's a hidden void. A good indication there is a tomb beneath."

"Does it ever rain in this place?"

Kalab seemed to take enormous satisfaction in chastising, "Of course not. That's why Nawidemaq was asking."

Nibamon concealed his smirk by squatting down beside Ermun to study the scroll. By the torchlight, he could make out Kalab's script, so exactingly neat that he could have sworn a royal scribe had written it all. Amid the archaic, formalized words, the acolyte had sketched out a table that could only be a star chart. Ermun traced one column until he found the appropriate row.

"There. It's as I remembered. During the first week of Inundation... Israelite, make yourself useful. Stand here on the threshold. Very good. Now face north."

Eleazar frowned up at the Pole Star and followed it downward. "If this is a joke, it is a terrible one." He was facing a wall of smooth limestone.

"This is where I want you." Ermun placed himself in front of the reluctant Israelite and squinted over the man's shoulder, searching the hills.

"What exactly are you doing?" demanded Eleazar. He was immediately shushed.

Kalab looked in the same direction with an increasingly perplexed face. "The papyrus tells us to look for a cleft hill. Except..."

It dawned on Nibamon what had gone awry. The terrain they were scrutinizing was a jumble of slopes that crowded each other out as they competed for height, merging and splitting, their slopes dotted with jagged rocks. He couldn't pick out a feature that he might describe as a cleft or a seam—a shallow draw here, a divot there, but nothing remarkable enough to warrant scrutiny. If the priests had translated correctly, and it was a cleft hill they sought, any of those gradual inclines could have been made to fit the description.

Rukhmire, true to form, broke the dejected silence with a joke. "A good time for rain, no?"

WATERFALLS

"FOLLOW THE TRICKLE all the way down!" Nibamon's shouted instructions carried down the slope. "All the way! Don't let your eyes wander!"

Amani yelled back up at him. "We know damn well what to do by now! Stop yapping and tip it out already!"

The top of the hill was already lined with empty amphorae. Qorobar hauled a fresh one into view and balanced it on its tapered end. At the foreman's nod, he pulled out the clay stopper and tipped the jug over. Water gushed out and began to work its way down the slope. Amani had thought this a stupid plan when they'd first begun a few days ago, believing the water would just soak into the sand. But the earth had been completely parched for so long that it rejected moisture. The trickle of water flowed speedily down the contours of the hill, rushing between the divots and ruts that the sun's brightness had obscured.

New possibilities—new areas to search.

Up the slope, Tariq scurried to the right as the water abruptly shifted course. He plopped down a blue-painted stone to mark a point of interest. Amani mimicked his course, as did the Mice further down the slope. The water found another dip and cut back the other way. Tariq threw down another marker. Then the water reached Amani. She scuttled down the hill to keep pace, hugging her small armful of stones. Her eyes were reserved for the water alone, and her feet suffered for her diligence. Sharp rocks bit into her raw soles. She ignored the pain. The better she did her work, the sooner it would be over. She was somewhat incensed when the water carried straight past her and into Yesbokhe's lane without doing anything remarkable at all.

She dropped her armload with a grumble and sat to inspect her feet. Days of water chasing had rubbed her calluses away and left the exposed skin a tender crimson. She counted the three toenails she had left. The rest had fallen off. Tomb robbing was already proving a tough line of work, and they'd barely gotten started.

"Any more broken toes?" Tariq said. The noonday sun haloed his head and left only his white grin visible.

Amani squinted up at him. "Are you going to offer me a hand up, or just stand there gawping like a prick?"

"The second thing." With his free hand, he gestured to the empty amphora balanced on his shoulder.

She made a show of grimacing while she pushed herself up onto the swollen balls of her feet. Pitying her, Tariq gave up on the bad joke and reached for her, but she dashed his hand away. Then she grabbed the amphora off his shoulder, stuck her tongue out at him, and carried it downhill, where Yesbokhe waited his turn.

They ferried the empty vessels down to the valley and loaded them onto the bull cart, trading them for the various picks and mattocks piled on the bed. Nawidemaq used the last full jar to replenish their waterskins before driving the cart away on another trip to the faraway Nile, his stolid bull's nose scraping the soil in a useless search for a tuft of grass.

The remaining Desert Mice gathered in the shade of a rocky outcrop. "You all look a sight," Amani told the tired men. None bothered answering, too exhausted to come up with a jest. Everyone was layered in brownish dust, from their cracked palms to the cloths wrapped around their heads and spilling down their shoulders. Their dress was a trick they'd learned from the Bedouins during the Libyan campaigns. Qorobar and Nibamon, who spent the most time on the scorched hillcrests, had swathed themselves completely in threadbare curtains pulled from the shells of houses in Set-Ma'at. Almost everyone had smeared chalk across their exposed skin at Nawidemaq's suggestion. None of these measures seemed to help matters much. The only reliable way of dealing with the sun was water, and they were pouring most of that out in an increasingly frustrated search for Ramesses' tomb.

Five days and nights they'd been at it. Five days since the dead pharaoh's scroll had pointed them to these rocky hills. Assuming the whole papyrus wasn't just a litany of lies, and there was in fact a tomb here, the builders had hidden it well. For the first couple of days, the Mice had scaled and descended the slopes line abreast, poking with long sticks in search of loose dirt, prying up rocks, searching for anything that didn't belong—any sign of the supposed cleft hill. When their efforts failed, they'd turned to more traditional methods of tomb robbing. Or what noseless Nibamon assured them were traditional methods, anyway.

Amani was a city thief. She'd spent her latter youth on the streets of Napata, surviving off of fat pilgrims. She could slice open a purse and slink back into a crowd unseen without breaking step. She could wriggle soundlessly through a window smaller than a dinner plate and burgle a landlord into shit-eating poverty. But rummaging around arid landscapes in search of centuries-lost tombs? That was outside her skillset.

What she did know for sure was that there were riches beneath her feet. Gold, cedar, turquoise—she could smell the stuff. In her spare moments, she imagined she could taste precious metal.

That might have been blood, though. She got nosebleeds when she was angry. Which was a lot of the time, these past days.

Still, Nibamon's assurances helped convince her that she wasn't going mad. Building a tomb into an existing terrain feature was exactly the sort of thing his ancestors would have done, the foreman claimed. Especially when they were pressed for time. And if Ermun's memory of history served, they'd been on a short schedule when it came to Ramesses the Eighth's resting place. The pharaoh hadn't ruled long—a few years at the most. It was entirely possible that one of these hills had originally been split by a deep crevasse, and the time-strapped builders had constructed the tomb at its base before filling the whole thing in.

Evidence of such a project was exactly what the Desert Mice were seeking. Water was their best chance, but with Nawidemaq's gods steadfastly ignoring his pleas for rain, the mercenaries had been forced to bring their own. The process of hauling water uphill and chasing it back down all day would have been arduous already. In the swimming heat, though, Amani wasn't sure how much longer she could bear up. The men sprawled in the dust around her looked like she felt. They nursed limbs that were rigid from heat cramps. They poured as much water as they could spare over their cracked feet and quaffed down the remainder as fast as they could without puking. Their forms had literally shrunk, they were so parched. Their collective misery was almost a physical thing. Even the Sinai hadn't been this bad.

Pisaqar knew it. He knelt in the spot where the shade was smallest, leaning his head against his staff in meditation or prayer. She watched as, minute by minute, the sun edged over the wall and obliterated the captain's shade. Once it was gone, he hoisted himself up, tottered, and trudged back into the open. She got up to follow him.

"Rest a while longer," he told her in a voice tightened by thirst.

She pushed aside the pounding in her own temples. "I've been rested. I was waiting on you, old man."

There was true gratitude in his smile, however unneeded. She owed him. Pisaqar was the one who'd rescued her hand from the axe, who'd given her a place in his band—a chance to prove her worth. He hadn't even expected her to fuck him in exchange. As far as Pisaqar was concerned, there was no debt between them whatsoever. She was one of his people, and that was the end of it. Loyalty was the only way she could begin to repay him, and he hadn't even asked it of her.

The watery trails had already been scorched away. All that was left of their work was the painted rocks planted haphazardly along the slope. Amani and Pisaqar scaled the hill, leaning on their staffs. With every labored step, the sun beat down on their headscarves. They knelt beside the first marker, eyes casting about for the reason Eleazar had dropped it. She saw nothing that could have caught the Israelite's interest, just pebbly ochre dirt. She scraped at the top layer regardless, using one of the bronze mattocks Pepy-Nakht had bought in Thebes. The tight-packed earth budged reluctantly, as always. Pisaqar stabbed the butt of his staff against the larger rocks she uncovered. A loose rock, Nibamon had claimed, might be a sign of a buried rubble pile—which, if the gods were good, might prove to be the backfilled tomb entrance.

As Amani and Pisaqar began their excavation, the others roused themselves from the shade and climbed up with their tools. They gathered around and lent a hand, raking the soil and prying rocks free. Debris skittered downhill. The foreman made his rounds between them, inspecting the ground with prodding fingers. For the first few days, they'd pestered him with hopeful questions. "See anything? What about this spot here?" But now the only sounds were the metallic scrapes and their labored breathing. Soon enough, as they reached the dry ground the water hadn't touched, they began kicking up dust in quantity—enough to irritate Nibamon's nose hole. His awful retching and wheezing joined the discordant noise. Amani gritted her teeth every time the man drew breath.

"Tariq!" she hissed.

The redhead looked at her wearily. He rasped, "Can we just not?"

She kept her voice low. "I can't fucking stand that sound!"

"Stuff some rocks in your ears. I don't know. I can barely talk, Amani. I don't have it in me today."

"Like fuck you don't." She sighed. "You want me to ask nicely? I'll even beg."

"No... That'd be too odd." Tariq licked his desiccated lips and raised his voice for the group. "Alright, boys. Any requests?"

Amani said, "Nothing about girls."

At the same time, Kalab called, "Something about girls! And water! Mostly water."

The redhead snapped his fingers. "'Thief on the Nile,' then! I know for a fact that Amani hates that one." Amid the chuckles, he began with the chorus, with the others quickly lending their voices.

"Hold thine oar, o' courtly lady
Row, row, a charm of jade be
My heart aches as
the river takes thee
Pharaoh steals her down the Nile.

I saw her sat on tranquil waters
Row, row, my courtly lady
A fish net dress and a golden collar
Pharaoh steals her down the Nile.

She leans o'erboard to spy a glimmer
Row, row, her charm of jade falls
Slips between her grasping fingers
Treasure sinks beneath the Nile.

She wails, she weeps, she cries in sorrow
Row, row, the pharaoh pities
She'll have a new charm on the morrow
Leave her woes upon the Nile."

Amani knew the words, somewhat, but didn't bother joining in. It was an old tale, one of the oldest—of Sneferu, greatest of the pharaohs, who took pity on a handmaiden who'd lost her necklace in the river and ordered one of his magi to part the waters to get it back. She'd never been much for singing, least of all when the lyrics were lovesick lamentations about half-clothed girls. This particular song was one of the least egregious in Tariq's repertoire. The rest always seemed to rely on the manly idea of romance: that love was best depicted in the form of an over-muscled, bearded murder machine bent on sucking the face off some delicate waif.

Those songs annoyed her shitless, which was precisely why the men sang them. But at least it was better than listening to Nibamon's breathing. Without that aggravation to worry about, she could concentrate on finding the treasure.

Which was right beneath their feet. The deeper she dug, the more certain she became: this hill *reeked* of gold, one handful of which would eclipse the sum total of her ill-begotten earnings in Napata. Or, for that matter, the earnings from their grand misadventure outside Jerusalem. But she tried not to remind herself of that too often. Whenever she thought about Pisaqar's former student betraying his trust, her stomach flopped over in outrage.

Pisaqar tapped her leg with his staff. "Your nose is bleeding."

She held her nostrils. "Damn it."

"Go rest a while. No, I insist."

Back at the outcropping, the shade had shrunk to a mere sliver. She flopped down there anyway. She was too irked to bother venturing further. But the mere act of sitting was enough to prick her bladder. "Now?!" She hadn't had to piss all day! The tingling fed on itself and grew into a painful throb. Her bladder seemed to think itself more important than her resounding headache and her bloody nose. She heaved herself upright, gritting her teeth against the urge to bawl out of sheer aggravation.

There was no question of relieving herself this close to the shelter. She hobbled out into the sunlight again and snuck as best she could along the foot of the hill, her clawed fingers digging into her belly. Gods be thanked, she didn't have to go too far. She rounded a bend, which shielded her from the men's view. Just for added privacy, she folded herself into the shadow of a teetering boulder. Its flat side gave her something to lean against. She dug out a handful of sand and squatted over the hole, spacing her feet so the puddle wouldn't wet her heels. She groaned aloud as she let go. Pissing in a state of intense thirst was anything but pleasant. It stung like a young scorpion. She huffed through the spasms and squeezed her eyelids.

As her bladder haltingly emptied itself, she noticed something odd: the boulder had lines. Though its flat side was badly weathered, she could just about form the impression of two straight lines forming a narrow triangle. Even to her unpracticed eye, the old chisel marks were unmistakable. They distracted her enough to see her through the rest of her minor ordeal.

When she was done, she hauled her kilt back into place and knelt beside the carving. Untold years of sandy ballast had coagulated at the base of the flat-sided boulder. Switching between her mattock and her fingertips, she scraped at the top layers. The rubble was packed down tight. Progress was halting. Nevertheless, she didn't have to dig far to figure out what she'd found: the crude likeness of a staff-wielding Anubis. It wasn't an official inscription so much as a worker's graffiti—a stick figure, nowhere near the artisanship she'd have expected of a pharaoh's tomb. Even so, the fact remained that the pharaoh's builders had been in this secluded part of the valley. They'd lingered long enough to make their mark on the stone.

Maybe this wasn't a mere boulder, but the fallen capstone of a wall, inverted to reveal a workman's idle carving.

She quickly got back up, dusting her hands. She had to tell the captain.

Then it occurred to her that her pissing spot was about to be crowded with men who'd happily leap at the smallest opportunity to make fun of her. She wasn't about to let those cocky shits ruin her moment. She kicked at the dirt to cover up the evidence of the deed, only to realize there was almost nothing to conceal. There was only the palm-sized hole she'd dug, still damp. Her water had disappeared into the earth, just as the noseless foreman had said.

She tore back into the open at a dead run. Who cared if they joked about the piss hole? She'd found the entrance to the tomb; she'd never been more certain of anything in her life. She hurtled around the bend and grinned at the sight of the men, still scrabbling in the dirt, still singing their idiotic song. "Oy, assholes!" They paused and squinted at her through the drifting dust. "I've got you beat! I just took a piss on Ramesses' head!"

BEST LAID PLANS

THE DESERT MICE met in the ruined guardhouse. The Lion had risen in the sky, giving proof to the lateness of the hour. Not long ago, the constellation had roused itself to witness their near destruction outside the gates of Jerusalem. Its presence tonight was lost on no one, though what it might mean was up for interpretation.

They crowded around a table, their faces suffused with candlelight, as if they had come to participate in some ancient rite. Perhaps they had. The Kushites were a disparate enough group on their own, with little in common but their allegiance. But standing alongside the black-skinned mercenaries were a disgraced foreman, a boatmaster, an impoverished guard, and a two-time traitor. They'd all been drawn together—whether through the will of the gods, the intervention of fate, or a happenstance alignment of ambitions. They'd all gathered to hear what destiny had in store.

The table had been laid with a curious amalgam of items. The mortuary scroll was spread out, its script indecipherable to all but a handful. Drawn onto the table with charcoal sticks was a rough map of the area—the broad crescent of the Nile with stylized likenesses of Thebes, Set-Ma'at, and the Valley of the Kings. In the middle of it all sat a curious framework of twigs and twine, with crisscrossing pegs of clay carefully arranged within. Beside it was a painted statuette with folded arms and a blue headdress.

Pisaqar spoke. "Welcome, my friends. Before we begin, I must make one last offer. You are all aware of the task we have set ourselves. There are deadly perils involved, not least of which is getting caught. If anyone here has remaining qualms, speak now and take your leave of us."

He surveyed the group's stillness with approval. "So be it." He indicated the charcoal map. "The Valley of the Kings. This is the place Egypt's greatest pharaohs chose to rest for all time. Three and sixty tombs in all, carved deep into the earth, all the way beneath the bedrock. Sealed with thick portals, laid with traps, covered over. All to protect riches vast beyond the comprehension of the common man.

"Almost without exception, these efforts failed. The tombs have been cracked open and made hollow. Such is the fate of men who grasp for more than they need. But there is one pharaoh whose tomb has escaped the attention of his subjects. Until now."

He pointed at the figurine. "This is the one who is to repay Egypt's debt to us: Sethherkepeshef Meryamun. For all his obscurity, and despite the briefness of his reign, the Robber Pharaoh will have taken to the afterlife such enormous wealth that but a small fraction of it will give your families generations of prosperity. He will have cedar chests crammed with gold, silver, and gemstones. Chariots. Artisan-crafted daggers and bows. Armor. Provisions for the next world, stored in jars that will themselves be invaluable treasures. His royal corpse will be encased in three, four, five sarcophagi, plated in gold and electrum.

"We are going to take it all. In order to do this, we will smash the tomb open and haul out the loot. A simple enough plan. But the execution—this will take some finer expertise. Nibamon?"

The foreman cleared his throat with a sickening wheeze. “Somewhat unfortunately, Ramesses the Eighth was one of the last pharaohs to be buried in the valley. The men who built the tomb were the heirs to a trade perfected over the span of five hundred years, here where we stand in Set-Ma’at. They knew the Valley of the Kings intimately. This means that we’re about to contend with the most elaborate tomb complex ever constructed.”

He pointed to the uppermost section of the miniature scaffold, where a clay block was balanced. “First, we come to the door. Solid limestone, at least a cubit thick. Once we chisel through that, we run into what should be the entrance stairs, but in actuality is a wall of rubble. This is the backfilled entrance. All gravel left over from the dig. The last thing the builders do before they seal the tomb is pack the rubble into the corridor, tight and as far back as they can. Once we clear away this backfill, we hack through another portal, thicker than the first. We breach the first room: the entry hall. This is where we might come to the first traps.”

“What sort of traps?” asked Tariq.

“Sand chambers in the ceiling are common. You don’t want to find yourself beneath one of those when it empties out. I expect we’ll find more elaborate things. Like false floors. Stake pits. Weakened pillars. That sort of thing.

“Judging by the location of the tomb, they’ll have needed to dig down a good ways before they got below the bedrock. Past the entry hall will be several more switchback tunnels, most of which will be linked together by decoy chambers. Every room we come to, they’ll want us to believe it’s the true burial chamber.”

“That seems an obvious ploy,” Eleazar noted.

Nibamon nodded. “They’ll have done their best to convince us otherwise. The decoy chambers will have a bit of treasure in them, and I’d wager at least one fake sarcophagus. And in the likely event we don’t fall for it, we still have to waste time searching the walls for the next hidden portal. Could be we’ll be delayed long enough that we get caught. Could be we chip through the wrong portal and find there's a trap behind it."

"Wait, wait, wait." Qorobar leaned over the table and jabbed a finger at the model tomb. "What are all these *probably*'s and *could be*'s? Do you mean to tell us that everything you just said was your nearest guess?"

"Well. Yes." Nibamon raised his voice to be heard over the general muttering. "Eventually, if we're persistent, we'll win our way through. Then we'll reach the antechamber. There will be several more portals to crack open before we reach the burial chamber."

Pisaqar took up the thread again. "From that point, our job becomes simple. We take everything in the burial chamber and haul it out. By hand. We load it onto Pepy-Nakht's boat, and then we escape south to Kush."

Kalab spoke up. "Say we accomplish all of this. We manage to steal past all the traps without getting killed and then haul all this heavy loot up these twisting tunnels. What happens after that? Do we simply walk out of the tomb with the sum total of a pharaoh's worth on our backs?"

"My acolyte raises a fair point," said Ermun. "The amount of treasure involved poses a difficulty in itself. Removing it all could take weeks. We can't expect Pepy-Nakht's boat to sit on the riverbank all that time, laden down with an ever-growing pile of stolen gold. We'll be noticed, for a certainty."

"Agreed," said Pisaqar. "That is why we must simplify the process. Bringing everything to the surface is the most time-consuming task, as it must be done by hand. We will surmount it by bringing all the treasure up to the entry tunnel. Only then do we involve Nawidemaq's bull. We will empty out the tunnel in a single night. Once daylight comes, we seal the entrance. Whatever is left inside, we can return for at a later time."

"What if we get spotted in the middle of the lift?" asked Amani.

"Then we will face a choice between abandoning the loot or fighting it out. I know which choice I will make."

Silence descended on the group as they considered the arduous, prolonged work ahead of them. Tariq slunk off and returned with a jug of beer. With a stoic face, he poured them each a measure. He raised his cup.

"To the Robber Pharaoh," he intoned, fighting a losing battle against his grin. "And the flummoxed look on his face when we swagger into the afterlife decked in his finery. To Pisaqar's Mice!"

Idleness was vice. Ashurizkadain had always felt this way, for every brush with luxury had served to confirm the notion. He was reminded of its basic truth now, surrounded as he was with the trappings of stagnant wealth. The cool night air wafting across the veranda played with his curly locks. Vile Memphis was attempting to seduce him just as surely as the fishnet-clad servant girl who flitted between the couches to refill his golden goblet, though he had not called for more wine. Her kohl-rimmed eyes looked him up and down as she bent with her jug. She curved her lips into a tempting smirk. Pointedly, he averted his gaze. She sauntered away, giggling behind her hand.

He raged silently at the depravity of Egypt, where even the servants did not understand their place.

His foul mood was not lost on Khaemon, his corpulent host. The opposite couch squeaked as Khaemon shifted his bulk. "If the vintage is not to your—"

"Your wine is acceptable," Ashurizkadain interrupted tightly, not wishing to hear another guttural word. The titanic nobleman shut his mouth with an audible clack, deadened as it was by the rolls of fat encasing his jaw.

To think that this contemptible specimen would one day rule Egypt in Assyria's name revolted him beyond expression. Better to burn it all down. Submerge the fragments of their once-mighty civilization in their treasured river. Cart the population off to the north to be hardened by the lash, redeemed into something worthy.

A task for another day. He would remain beholden to this Saite traitor for as long as it took to pick up his quarry's scent. Khaemon's people had been making inquiries in the city for weeks now, seeking the Kushites' whereabouts. Following the debacle in the tavern, the mercenaries had melted into the city—and, likely as not, were doing just as Ashurizkadain was: hiding. Or they had gone. But where? Back to their nation's capital, Napata? Meroë? North, into the Delta? A frustrating array of possibilities, and Khaemon seemed little better equipped to explore them than his Assyrian guests.

All they had found was rumor. Of a bleeding white bull staggering through the streets on a painted man's lead rope. Of a pair of scale-armored priests making sacrifices at the temple. Of corpses floating down the river.

The last tidbit was the most interesting, and he had spent a good deal of silver pursuing it.

"How long until your men return?" he inquired of Khaemon.

"Soon enough. Patience, my friend."

"I have been patient for three weeks. A score of days waving aside your Lydian-piss wine and your grubby whores. I weep to watch my men brought low by these decadences, while your menials scatter my king's silver across Memphis's stinking alleys. How much more time and money must I squander before you can persuade this creditor to meet me?"

Khaemon frowned as he considered whether or not to answer. He chose unwisely. "You seem unaccustomed to the nature of bribery. It is a long game you have chosen to play, Ashurizkadain. In order to advance, there is a transaction. Sometimes—"

"Do you truly believe I care to listen to these sordid details? I have no interest in these. They matter not. I want only your results. If the process does not yield results, then it is without worth."

Khaemon could not help but protest. "Your words wound me, Ashurizkadain. Am I not your ally, after all?"

"You are not," barked Ashurizkadain, his forbearance breaking at last. "You are your own ally. A cynical fool forever spinning schemes in service of your own ends. Woe upon Egypt, for you are but one among countless many. You are a nation of skulkers who know no master greater than themselves. There is no unity in this place, no greater vision. Only men jostling for space upon a single ladder, fumbling for the next rung. Fat. Slovenly. Greedy. Indolent. This is the reason Assyria will win in the end. What?" He rounded on Nimrud as he emerged from the lower floor.

His lieutenant bowed. He glanced curiously at Khaemon as he straightened, likely wondering if he was about to be ordered to execute the man—a command he would, of course, obey without question, qualms or no. He was a good soldier. "We have word, my lord. There is a man downstairs who claims to have seen the Kushites leave. He says they were passing out grain to the rabble. He is willing to share more. For a price."

Ashurizkadain launched to his feet. "Bring him before me. You!" The scantily clad servant girl turned quite pale as he pointed her way. "Fetch my knives from my chamber." She scurried down the stairs after Nimrud. He paced, massaging his tingling hands.

"You mean to torture a man on my property?" demanded Khaemon, horrified and indignant. "On my balcony, no less!"

"That is my precise intention, and if you do not cease your mewling, you will lose your promised place in the new Egypt. Instead, you will dwell in Assyria for the short time it will take to spit you upon an iron spike. I will skin a hundred of your countrymen this very night if I must. One way or another, I will ride on the morrow. Pisaqar has eluded my king's justice long enough."

PAKHEME

"Ow! Fuck!" Qorobar hobbled to a stop.

"Are you alright?" Kalab asked from behind him.

"Fine. Just got another bloody shitting rock in my sandal." Qorobar alternated between flexing and shaking his foot until the irritation came loose. All the while, he kept the water jar balanced on his skull, a feat he was certain would have made his mother proud. *Big Legs*, the other villagers had called her. She'd made a profession out of trekking to the riverbank to fetch water for the community, with one jar atop her head and two more dangling from a pole laid across her shoulders. A great woman, she'd been—in a literal sense. Like mother, like son.

Kalab clapped his shoulder. "It's good to see you smile again."

The shoulder pole lifted with his shrug. "Heat's getting to me, I suppose."

They continued their winding way through the valley, past the alcoves of empty tombs. Dawn had just broken, and the dim indigo light deepened the shadows at the entrances. Though the mummified corpses had been smashed and stolen long before, Qorobar could almost imagine the pharaohs' accusing eyes boring into the valley's newest set of plunderers.

At least you tasted the afterlife, he thought. Pakheme's face came to him for just a flash of an instant, and—in that same instant—he saw it cleaved open and blood-doused. He blinked, stifling a moan. He tried to remind himself that he needed to treasure these fleeting glimpses. They were a sign—had to be a sign—that some fragment of Pakheme's *ka* still existed, despite the loss of his body. That they would find each other again in the next life.

When they arrived at the hill, the five who'd drawn night shift were already clustered at the entrance. He called out, "Tough night?" Still reeling from the vision of Pakheme, his voice broke on the second word. They burst into laughter.

"Better count your balls, big man!" said Amani.

Only Pisaqar didn't join in. He searched Qorobar's eyes as he helped unlimber the pole. If he saw what was amiss, he did him a courtesy and left him be. Instead, he beckoned to the others who had just come up the hill. Kalab, Nibamon, and Yesbokhe gathered around the two of them to hear the news.

"We made little progress in the night. We sought to clear out the rubble in the entrance tunnel. However, the stones refused to budge. We spent our efforts on widening the tunnel. It is nearly broad enough for two men to fit, now. Well, as long as one of those men is not you, Qorobar." The chuckles were kinder this time. "You ought to be able to make more progress than we did. I wish we could have done more. Ah, yes. And the torches keep going out." The captain looked exhausted. He gestured to the others. "The tools."

Tariq gave Qorobar his bronze mattock. As he grabbed it, a seam running down the handle pinched his hand. "This bloody thing is broken, you toss rag."

"You don't say." Wearily, the redhead held up his palms. They were covered in blood-filled welts.

"You could have wrapped it up in your kilt or some such."

"What, and let Amani poke fun at naked me all night? I'll take the welts." Raising his wounded hand in farewell,

Tariq joined his group and began trudging off, headed for Set-Ma'at and a much-needed bedroll.

Nibamon clucked his tongue disapprovingly as he made his rounds and inspected their digging implements. Ramesses' tomb hadn't been any kinder to their tools than it had to their bodies. The chisels were dulled, the mattocks were warped and cracked and nearly unusable, and the rock basket was full of new holes.

"We'll need to visit a blacksmith in Thebes, soon."

The scout cleared his throat and mimed a drinking motion.

The acolyte nodded. "I'm sick of flat beer myself, Yesbokhe. That's not to say I won't drink it gladly when we get back to Set-Ma'at."

The tomb entrance didn't look like much. The leaning slab Amani had found had turned out to be the capstone of the tomb alcove. Plunging into the earth beneath it was a round bolt hole they'd dug, surrounded by fresh piles of gravel. A passerby would have found Ramesses' tomb almost indistinguishable from the bare slopes around.

They slunk through the hole one at a time. In Qorobar's case, it was a tight squeeze, but he managed. He dropped into the small cavity they'd excavated around the door of the tomb. Kalab passed out torch sticks, which they wrapped with greased linen and struck alight. The flames guttered as the yawning mouth of the tomb sucked the air, as if it were trying to draw them in even as the hieroglyphs carved into the frame warned them away. Centered above the door frame was the circled name of Ramesses the Eighth, an elaborate arrangement of symbols: a moon, a jackal staff, an ankh, a seated god, an obelisk, a boat, waves, and an altar.

Nibamon whispered the name like a prayer as he ducked within. "Powerful is the Ma'at of Ra, Helpful to Amun."

Qorobar eyed the cartouche. He nudged Kalab. "You remember that boy in Libya? The one who got in with the quartermaster's daughter?"

"Oh, I remember that one." The acolyte grinned. "He stole her scarab amulet. She thought he'd secreted it about himself someplace. So, she—"

"—thought he'd hidden it in his kilt," finished Qorobar. They bent over with laughter. "Amun, that boy's face!"

"The way she kept fumbling around! She really wanted that scarab back," squeaked Kalab. He wiped tears from his eyes.

"What was his name, anyway?"

The acolyte pinched his brows. "I honestly can't remember."

"Me neither."

Kalab followed his gaze to the cartouche. "It isn't fair, is it?"

"Never was. If we ever remember, maybe you'll do that boy a favor, carve his name in stone."

"I'll do that," promised Kalab.

"Ought to leave the scarab out of the inscription, though."

"I wouldn't dream different," he said with a renewed grin. "Let's get to work."

They slipped through the cracked portal and into the tomb.

Ramesses had been a minor pharaoh, a far cry from the legendary king for whom he'd been named—but clearly he'd meant his tomb to give the opposite impression. The entry tunnel was two arm-spans across, wide enough that the builders had needed to install center columns to shore it up against the weight of the hill above. The line of columns descended steeply into the earth until the darkness swallowed them up. But Ramesses' ambitions had gone beyond merely filling in a split hill and digging an overlarge tunnel into its bowels. He'd advertised his greatness on every clean surface. The walls were etched with careful rows of hieroglyphs, the columns too, all exquisitely painted—golden chariots and red concubines and white-robed courtiers. The decoration even spilled over onto the deep blue ceiling, where the builders had painted an orderly firmament of stars meant to guide the pharaoh out of his resting place and into the heavens.

And—this was what baffled Qorobar—no one had been supposed to see any of it.

Ramesses hadn't wanted visitors, but he'd expected them. His front door had been nearly three cubits thick, an obscenity that even the pyramids couldn't boast of. Chiseling through stone that thick, even soft limestone, had been a horrid bitch of a job. Then, Ramesses had filled in his foyer with gravel, an obstacle his guests were still contending with nearly two weeks after arriving on his doorstep. The rubble itself was all pulverized limestone leftover from the tomb construction, loose stuff that was easy to scoop up and pile in baskets. The trouble was getting it out. Because Ramesses had ripped up the stairs.

Even getting down the tunnel was a pain in the ass. Qorobar picked his way along the guide ropes they'd strung between the columns, using the demolished remnants of the stairs as footholds. The angle of descent was just steep enough that it couldn't be traversed unaided, which he felt certain was by design. He plunged into the earth on unsteady feet, trying to ignore the empty gazes of the carved gods.

The nature of the task became apparent toward the end of the tunnel, where the pall of dust hung thick. His torch flame flickered and shrank, obliging him to stop until the fire caught its breath again. There was more gravel underfoot by now. Then the rope ran out, and his feet scrabbled on loose rock.

"Reached the bottom," he told Kalab over his shoulder. He offered a hand and helped the acolyte onto the heap of stone and sand. They waved their torches around so they could inspect the previous shift's handiwork. The others had managed to fully excavate another column, only to run into a veritable wall. The least of the stones was the size of a man's head, while the largest could have passed for a millstone.

Qorobar scratched his brow. "This is going to be a shit day."

Nibamon and Yesbokhe scuttled off the rope next. The foreman surveyed the scene by tapping on the stones with a hammer. "This appears to be a cave-in," he pronounced.

"Appears?" said Kalab. "*Is*."

"Not exactly. Look at the arrangement of the stones. It's too orderly. There are no gaps between the stones. And the way the crevices are all packed with sand and pebbles. No, this was built." He patted the wall and stood back, adjusting his mask. "As to why, I only have guesses."

"Then guess," Qorobar told him.

"I suspect we've found a backstop. A barrier meant to hold the backfill in place, prevent it from collapsing inward."

"Inward into what?"

Nibamon shrugged. "More tunnel. The entry hall. Who knows? It could be either or neither."

The archer asked the question none of them dared voice. "The pharaoh?"

The foreman had to raise his voice to be heard over their excited jabbering. "It's not possible. We haven't gone deep enough."

"*Pfff*." Kalab waved his hand in mock dismissiveness, though they all knew he was right. "There's no joy in this fellow. Don't listen to him."

The work was tough and unrewarding. The tomb builders had known their craft well. To begin with, they'd packed the stones tightly into the passage. The many tons of rubble they'd piled against their wall had compressed it into a solid mass. No matter how the robbers tried, there wasn't the slightest chance of wriggling a mattock into a crevice to lever a stone loose. They had to rely on brute force and persistence. Painstakingly, they drove dull chisels into the stones using hammers that bit hard with every blow. Welts stung Qorobar's hand. He removed his mask and wrapped up the bloody palm, which helped a bit. Only now, he had to keep stopping to cough and retch and spit. Nibamon, scurrying about the three Kushites' feet to scrape up the rock fragments, constantly reminded them not to touch their eyes. Qorobar knew that if he gave in to that ever-present urge, he'd only succeed in rubbing the tiny rock shards into his eyeballs, blinding himself.

He gripped his hammer and kept on striking. Gradually, the reverberating blows became one with the ringing in his ears. This was ruinous work. He didn't like it, he didn't understand how any man could inflict it on himself as a *profession*. Soldiering was the safer job, as far as he was concerned. At least wars ended.

Still, being the strongest man in the group had some perks. When the big stones at last started coming loose, he was the only one who could heft them. He would pile them on a sledge and haul them up the tunnel. At the top, he transferred the rocks to baskets and lifted them out of the bolt hole, then dumped them on the already huge rubble pile outside. He finished each journey doused in sweat, but accepted it as the price for a few precious gulps of fresh air. Then he'd start the painstaking descent, lowering the sledge in front of him by fits and starts.

Nibamon helped—distractedly. The foreman made the climbs bearing a basket, complaining of the dust every time Qorobar passed him. To be fair, Nibamon's basket was always overflowing with gravel, and Qorobar didn't envy him his lack of nostrils. But then the man would *linger*. Several times, Qorobar found him paused along some stretch of wall with his fingers tracing the hieroglyphs. The foreman would tell the passing mercenary in a tone that was both apologetic and surprised, "I was wrong about him!" He would summarize the inscriptions. "There was famine, but he gathered grain for the people." "There were invaders on the borders, but he rode out and destroyed them." "There was plague, but he performed rites for the dead."

After the umpteenth revelation, Qorobar's patience ran out. "Why give a shit?"

"All knowledge is valuable," Nibamon recited.

"This isn't knowledge. It's lies."

"You can't simply assume that anything written down isn't true."

"Why wouldn't I? I've seen how great men work. They let the common struggle along, then whenever something big happens, they act as if they were behind the whole thing."

"What's written on these walls is an exaggerated telling, I agree. All that means is we need to be skeptical of what we read. Not that it isn't worth knowing."

Qorobar made a dismissive grunt. "What I know for sure is that we've got work to do. We don't need you standing around, and what's more, we don't need you feeling sorry for the asshole we're about to rob."

They gradually blunted their chisels into uselessness breaking down the wall. But one chunk, one basket at a time, they succeeded. They knew they'd done it when a piece crumbled into an unseen cavity. Their whoops of elation echoed through the tunnel. They'd chipped through the wall.

Nibamon, summoned forward, stuck a torch into the hole and cast about. "It's open space on the other side," he confirmed.

Kalab offered another torch to Qorobar. "You ought to be the first in, after all the work you've done today."

Qorobar reached out to take it, but Yesbokhe grasped his wrist. The scout shook his head, his eyes full of concern.

"We should attempt to widen the breach first," agreed Nibamon.

"How? All the chisels have gone to shit. Only way forward is to start prying rocks free, and in case you weren't paying attention," he slammed the ball of his fist on unbudging stone, "these aren't going anywhere. Might be they're looser on the other side. Any disagreements? Don't bother."

Before they could raise an argument, he tossed his torch into the hole and went in after it, headfirst. A brief struggle later, he spilled out at the other end and rolled down the rocky incline before coming to rest on a reassuringly level floor. Breathing hard, he gathered up the torch and stood.

The acolyte called through the hole. "Qorobar? What's happening?"

"I got through!" He lifted the torch for a better look at the wall. "The stones aren't packed as tight on this side. I think I can yank them loose by hand."

"What about the space beyond? Can you describe it?" asked Nibamon.

Qorobar turned, torch aloft, and allowed himself the briefest glance at the swallowing darkness before turning his back on it once more. "Tunnel. Lots of tunnel."

He heard Kalab mutter to the others, a smile in his voice. "Big man's regretting his choice."

"The fuck I am! Alright, I'm making a start at it."

He scaled the sloping wall and got hold of the highest stone he could reach. He hauled on it, and then immediately dodged as it rolled past his head. The surrounding stones fell away as if they were eager for freedom. After weeks of scraping at gravelly soil, the relief of making visible progress was as invigorating as the rush of battle. A steady avalanche of rocks went rolling down the tunnel, smashing the deceptive hieroglyphs and bouncing off the support columns. He winced at that. He slowed, fearing that if he did his job too well, he'd send a mite-too-large boulder smashing into a column and cave the whole tunnel in.

Evidently, he wasn't the only one with concerns. He saw Yesbokhe peering through the small gap developing near the ceiling, but the scout wasn't looking back at him. Rather, his eyes were turned upward. "Stop."

"Why?" Qorobar asked, but complied.

"I hear something."

"Can't hear shit but the ringing in my ears."

Yesbokhe's voice became suddenly taut. "Get out." The gravity of those words, coming from a man who rarely troubled himself to speak at all, clutched at Qorobar immediately.

He dove for the gap. The rocks elbowed at his ribs and knocked the air from his lungs, paralyzing him for a few precious heartbeats. In that silence, he finally heard what the alert scout had: a ceaseless hiss, growing louder with each passing instant. The image came to him of cobras writhing into the crevice after him, latching onto his ankles and calves. And he felt it, too. A cool trickling sensation on his back as their venom clawed through his veins and toward his heart.

Then he remembered the sound. He'd heard it years before, on some damn fool march across the western desert, stomping across the hot dunes.

Not cobras. Sand.

Yesbokhe and Kalab were jostling each other in their urgent efforts to reach for his hands. Their mouths formed yells, but Qorobar could hear nothing. The hiss became a muffled roar, and the trickle of sand on his spine erupted into a flood. He tried his damnedest to crawl free, but found that his legs were utterly immobile, already encased in sand. His almighty effort to pry his lower body free only succeeded in slamming his skull into the roof. Dazed, he fought on, but the sand swelled through the cavity before he could make it another palm's distance. The last thing he saw before it closed around his head was his brothers' horrified faces.

And then, darkness. His eyes were still open. He knew this because he could feel the sand scoring his exposed eyeballs. He tried to close them against the sickening agony but couldn't. The immense pressure made the tiniest movement impossible, even the flutter of his eyelids. He couldn't move. Couldn't breathe. Sand filled his nostrils, his mouth.

His mind descended into panic. In its midst, he struggled like the trapped beast he was—tried to struggle, and failed. His mighty strength was nothing against the tons of sand encasing his body. Couldn't move. Couldn't see. Couldn't breathe. His own muffled screams were the lone sound that reached his sand-filled ears, and these only deepened his primal desperation. The more he screamed, the more he struggled. The more he struggled, the greater the need for air. And when he found there was none, he screamed even more.

Something scraped his hand. The pressure around it had abated. Fingernails scored his skin as they frantically dug around his arm. Someone hauled on his wrist. They were yelling his name. Again, they pulled—hard. His shoulder popped from its socket. He barely felt it. The ache in his lungs, too, was less insistent than before. The darkness had become multicolored. It coalesced around a body he no longer inhabited. He watched, almost curious.

Pakheme smiled at him.

"Qorobar!" Someone slapped him across the face. Only then did it occur to him to suck in a lungful of dusty breath. The pain returned. It stabbed into his lungs, filled them, and spread through his body in a molten wave.

"Get up! We have to move!"

He heard hissing. That awful sound, more than his brothers' cries, got his legs back under him. He hacked and retched as they half dragged, half pushed him up the tunnel. Trails of mucus-crusted sand rolled down his chin. He couldn't see a thing. His eyes were twin blazes of distilled suffering. Several times he collapsed, but his three companions wouldn't let him lie. They bellowed at him as they pulled him up by the armpits, cursing his sluggish legs.

The heat built as they climbed. Then he felt the blessed sun hot on his flesh. And water, life-giving water was being sloshed over his face. He gagged but didn't give a damn. He blew out his nostrils and rubbed it fiercely into his eyes. They kept on pouring until he was able to blink.

The moment he locked eyes with Yesbokhe, the scout embraced him. Kalab knelt and rested his forehead against his. They were laughing and weeping.

"I saw Pakheme," Qorobar told them. The water made his voice blubbery.

Yesbokhe nodded. "He guided us," he swore.

Qorobar caught his breath and looked to Nibamon. "What the fuck was that?"

The foreman shrank with guilt. "It was a sand trap. That's why they put the wall there. To hold the reservoir in. The moment you undermined the support wall… I'm sorry, Qorobar. I should have seen it right away."

Qorobar pushed himself up on Kalab's and Yesbokhe's shoulders. Then he grasped Nibamon's. "You have nothing to be sorry for. You warned me not to go in. It's my own stubborn fault." He patted the foreman's cheek. "Tough part's over, eh?"

The acolyte looked at him, bemused. "Praise be to Amun. You really did see Pakheme."

"Aye, and I don't want to see him again for a good long time. Dying is shit."

THE PIT

ERMUN STIPPLED THE wall with his horsehair brush, attempting to poke the muddy clod loose. The obscured symbol remained reluctant to unveil itself, as if the tomb itself balked at divulging its secrets. He could have dispensed with the brush and scratched at the hieroglyph with his thumbnail, but truth be told, he'd never been fond of grit beneath his fingernails. It was one of the reasons he'd become a priest in the first place. Better the life of an erudite scholar than a potter, however esteemed his family business had been.

Of course, if he'd known scholarship was out of the question, he might have consented to a life of humble clay sculpting. For in Kush, if a man was not born upon a staircase, he must ascend it from the bottom step. Not for a grasping commoner the privileged role of a healer or a dream interpreter or temple steward. No, in these difficult and uncertain times, the priesthood needed one thing above all else: accountability. Men who would fight in the pharaoh's battles and report his doings to the starch-robed masters in Napata.

He'd done this for a long time. Long enough that he'd outlived his teacher, only to be assigned a young acolyte of his own. It was then that he'd finally realized he would never be permitted to ascend past that bottom step. A life of bloody campaigning stretched out behind him, and all he had to show for it were the scraps of knowledge he'd gathered up of his own accord. How to seal a gushing wound. How to break a spear with a khopesh. How to read, and more importantly, analyze. These were the things he had sought to teach Kalab, his acolyte of now twelve years, and his dearest companion. And the most important lesson of all: that the high priests did not serve ma'at at all, but themselves.

At last, the crust of dirt fell away and revealed the word scratched into the wall.

Robber.

An accusation. Was it meant for him? He shook the frivolous thought away. The placement was interesting, however. The lone word, written in the low hieratic script, had been deliberately set amid the opening lines of the Trials of Osiris—as if to remind the passing pharaoh's *ka* of some awful sin as he went to stand before the Lord of Rebirth, to offer up his heart to be weighed on Osiris's scales.

The graffiti was a desecration, to be sure. But it gave Ermun some hope that perhaps the Ramesses, Eighth of His Name, hadn't been in much position to lay curses.

"Ermun!" The summons carried up the passage.

"I answer," he called back. He put his brush away and started walking, nibbling at the crescent of dirt under one thumbnail.

The source of Ramesses' wealth may have been a matter of contention, but he had spared none of it on his resting place. The backfilled tunnel they had spent almost three weeks clearing was just the start. It led into the entry hall, a small chamber crowded with ornately decorated columns. Its four walls each held a doorway, blocked in turn by portals that had once borne ferocious curses. The Desert Mice had bludgeoned them all into oblivion. The pieces piled around the door frames were still spattered with the blood of sacrificial goats, bought in Thebes for the purpose of appeasing the hungering gods.

Of course, then came the obvious question: which was the correct door? After much debate, they'd chosen the right-hand one. Ermun ducked through the shattered portal with a brief prayer, his torch leading the way, and arrived at the tunnel Nibamon had dubbed the 'Serpent'—a series of plunging, square-cut passages joined together by hard corners. Ermun descended the narrow steps sideways, bracing himself against the walls and lamenting the dusty cobwebs that soon gloved his hands. He fed the balled-up webs to his torch, which flared up and illuminated the watchful Anubis statues standing guard in their niches. The presence of these divine sentries was the only evidence there was something worth protecting at the end of this labyrinth. Otherwise, the rough-hewn look of the tunnel was hardly befitting a god-king.

Amani was waiting impatiently for him at the final corner. "About time, you old knob. Come on. We're about to break through." The thief glanced back at him. "How are your knees?"

"Quite useless, same as always."

"That's what you can spend your share on, then. A stuffed couch and a house full of servants. You'll never need to walk again."

"Don't torment an old man with such dreams. But tell me, would you be a part of this excellent arrangement?"

"I thought you said not to torment you."

She brought him along the next stretch of tunnel, which was level and much longer than the previous descending passages. At the end, they found Tariq, Nawidemaq, and Eleazar gathered around yet another portal. Ermun was beginning to feel that Ramesses was overfond of these obstacles, considering how little they'd done to dissuade his robbers.

Kneeling in front of the portal was Pisaqar, who was in the final act of breaking it apart with the one good chisel they had left. Eleazar bobbed as he grabbed chunks of broken limestone off the floor and tossed them into Tariq's and Nawidemaq's outstretched baskets. Several filled ones already lined the tunnel. Curiously, many of the fragments were blackened on one side. The priest scooped one up to study it.

"Soot," he said bemusedly. "They must have burned a great fire here to have made this much of it."

With a sharp *crack*, the portal split open. Pisaqar leaped back. The top half of the portal crashed to the floor and broke apart. An impenetrable cloud of dust swelled to fill the tunnel. Everyone held rags to their faces and covered their eyes, well accustomed to this sort of task by now.

They sprinkled water on the walls and waved damp rags to encourage the dust to settle, casting eager looks into the opening they'd uncovered. Though the dust began to clear, the room beyond stayed impenetrably, disconcertingly dark. The acidic stench of burning was close to overpowering.

Comprehension dawned on Ermun. "It's all covered in soot," he said with awe. "They set the entire chamber alight before they sealed it up." He began to make out details: a rectangular room with a tapered ceiling that evidently made columns superfluous. On the other side lay—surprise of surprises—another tightly sealed portal. None of this was noteworthy or unique. But on the floor was the strangest obstacle Ermun had yet seen.

The floor sloped into a deep trench, perhaps the height of three men, which spanned the center of the chamber, wall to wall. The oddity was that it didn't appear to be an obstacle at all, more of a mild inconvenience. One could simply walk into the pit, cross the room, and climb back out. Ermun doubted it would pose any trouble even for him, despite his knees.

"What's the point of that?" Tariq said, voicing the question they all had.

Pisaqar climbed through the broken portal and knelt at the lip of the trench, squinting and holding out his torch. The bottom of the trench was covered in light gray ash. "I do not like it," the captain muttered. "If it were filled with sharpened stakes, it would make some sense. This is only a fire pit. At the bottom of a tomb." He shook his head and looked at Amani. "Go back to Set-Ma'at and wake Nibamon. We must hear what our tomb builder has to say. The rest of you, let us clear away the passage."

As Amani flitted up the tunnel, Ermun touched the captain's elbow. "Pisaqar, look." He nodded to the opposite side of the blackened chamber. "I see a mark above the door."

"Tariq, a torch." Accepting one, Pisaqar wound back and flung it underhand across the trench. It bounced off the door with a burst of sparks, then rolled back down into the pit. The flames immediately snuffed out and plunged the chamber back into utter darkness.

Pisaqar sighed and beckoned for a second torch.

"No," Ermun said, "I saw what I needed to see." He smiled at his old friend. "That mark is the circled name of Ramesses the Eighth." He watched Pisaqar's face go from consternation to happy disbelief.

"We've found the burial chamber!" He pulled Ermun into an embrace and kissed his cheeks as the tunnel was filled with joyous cheers.

Ermun thumped Pisaqar's back, glad for his friend after having watched their many travails quenching his noble soul. "That's what this place must be. It's the antechamber. The builders must have burnt offerings here once they'd sealed the burial chamber. May I go take a look?"

"The honor is yours, Ermun. We never could have done this without you." Pisaqar turned away to grasp his men's wrists, beaming like he hadn't in a long time.

Ermun hobbled into the room. He only had eyes for the cartouche above the door. It represented the end of his life's servitude, a chance to return something of value to the land he loved rather than prolong its irrelevance. He could build a temple to Thoth in the far south, bring the written word and its accompanying enlightenment to the illiterate tribes there, ones who would benefit from it most. Perhaps he could give his own patronage to men like Pisaqar, the sort of men that could remake Egypt into the beacon it had once been. The priesthood, after all, put enormous stock in its ability to make or break powerful men, to steer Egypt in a way that benefited them. Now, he could do the same.

All finally within his reach.

With careful steps, he shuffled down the gentle incline and into the pit. Flakes of ash crumbled into his sandals and turned his toes gray. He couldn't help smiling at that. Amani was right. One servant wouldn't be too much luxury for an old man. It would be a pleasant change to have someone wash his feet every evening, certainly.

His heart skipped a beat as he slid on the loose ash. Catching himself, he lowered his torch slightly to get a better gauge of his footing. The flames abruptly went out. They didn't even gutter. Odd.

He turned around and took a breath to ask Pisaqar to throw him another torch. There came an instant of all-encompassing dizziness and nausea that ripped the feeling from his legs and folded them under him. The last sensation he ever knew was of that sickening plummet from which he would never rise.

Then his *ka* was rinsed from his body and borne west.

APIS

NAWIDEMAQ SAW THE gods take his friend. He watched how they emptied his limbs of strength so that he dropped like a stone. The old priest toppled soundlessly with his eyes rolled upward, for it was the nature of certain deities to draw the life essence from a man's pupils and up into their dwelling places in the stars.

"Ermun!" Pisaqar hurtled for the broken portal, his beer cup spilling forgotten from his fingers to shatter on the floor.

Nawidemaq hugged his captain tightly. "Do not go near! You will die!" The captain, in the first throes of grief, tried to break his grip.

"I must help him!"

"He is gone," Nawidemaq told him sadly. Pisaqar's struggles ceased. Only then did the medicine man release him. He warned, "The pit is death. Do not go in."

Pisaqar knelt at the edge of the blackened trench, crestfallen. Thick ash dissolved in his bunched fists. Tariq took his side, tears flowing down his cheeks. How many times had Ermun mended their wounds? Calmed their hearts in times of trouble? A good man, one who always sought to give more than he received. Now he lay folded in the ash, and they couldn't help him. They could not even close his eyes.

"How will I tell Kalab?" Pisaqar whispered.

Eleazar came up, his expression deeply disturbed. "What happened to him, Nawidemaq?"

"I hear tales of this," the medicine man whispered to him. "In the deepest south are lakes that turn to poison in the night. I know a story of a man and his son who go to fish. At the lake shore, the son falls dead. The father bends to help him. He dies also. I hear of villages punished by the lake gods for laziness. Those who oversleep die in their beds. Those who awake with the sunrise live, but are not permitted to sit, or they too die."

Eleazar nodded slowly with dawning comprehension. "This is no divine punishment. It is a trap." He fixed his eyes on Ermun's corpse. "A pit filled with invisible poison."

Pisaqar got up, wiping his eyes. He reached out to the Israelite. "Torch," he said tightly. Eleazar handed one over. Pisaqar sidestepped close to the pit and lowered the torch in headfirst. Soon after it passed the lip, the flame went out. "Oh, my poor friend," Pisaqar told Ermun. "You could not have known."

Tariq sniffed and let out a thick wheeze. "It was quick. He didn't feel a thing." He looked up at his captain. "We have to get him out somehow."

"We use a rope," suggested Nawidemaq, miming a pulling motion.

Pisaqar growled, "I will not have my friend dragged on a noose like hunted game."

Eleazar rubbed his beard. "Perhaps we fashion hooks out of some spears. Little more dignified than a noose, I admit. But Pisaqar, I must say that no matter how we extract your friend, we are still left with the problem—"

"—of how to get across ourselves, I know."

The redhead paced along the lip of the trench. "Gods know we have plenty of rubble. Why not fill it in?"

Nawidemaq shook his head in earnest. "It is the same as dropping a rock into a full cup of water. The water flows out."

Pisaqar and Eleazar seemed to come to an identical realization, because they exchanged a look.

"The poison behaves the same way as water," the Israelite said.

"We can scoop it out, as if drawing from a well," finished the captain. "Tariq, go after Amani. Gather the Mice. Have them load the cart with every amphora, every vessel you can find."

"Qorobar still has that stupid sack of helmets," said Tariq.

"That as well. The rest of you, go with him. I will stay here."

Tariq was clearly perturbed. "I don't like the idea of leaving you alone in this place."

"Then you will understand how I feel about leaving my oldest friend here. I will not do it. And there is little purpose in any of you loitering when there is nothing to accomplish. Leave me." He returned his gaze to Ermun, lying contorted in his open grave. "The worst that can happen already has."

Tariq burst into Set-Ma'at. His sandals flapped about his ankles, ruined after a dead sprint down the rocky trail. It wasn't yet dawn, and Amani was the only one he found. She was sitting on Nibamon's doorstep while she waited for him to get dressed. Between gulps of air, he gave her the news.

Amani blanched. She rushed from door to door to wake the others. They were sleepily emerging just as Nawidemaq and Eleazar got there.

They took it well. Qorobar dashed his water jug against a wall, raging at the departed pharaoh's greed. Yesbokhe wept in silence. Amani held Kalab's hands while he numbly absorbed what he could only see as his own failure. His teacher was dead, and he hadn't been there to protect him. His twelve years as an acolyte were at an end.

But there was still work to do. Nawidemaq woke his bull and hitched the cart, where they loaded every conceivable water vessel they could get their hands on. Tariq found himself repeatedly trying to explain the nature of the task before them, but only received uncomprehending looks. He wasn't certain he understood, himself. Ramesses had played a trick on them all.

And the pharaoh wasn't done. As they started loading the cart, the wind began to stir. It came from the north, feeding on itself, gathering force as it spilled through the gaps between the hills.

Senet rushed out of her house. "It's a sandstorm coming! You must get inside!" she cried.

Tariq was vehement. "We can't leave the captain alone in that tomb!"

But then the wall of sand erupted over the mountains and hurtled into the valley. Its blast knocked Tariq off his feet. Flying granules stung his face and forced themselves between his pressed eyelids, into his ears, up his nostrils. The others were similarly afflicted. Even Qorobar had to fight to remain standing. Their albino bull, stalwart as he was, brayed loudly and sought escape.

In the end, the question wasn't of willpower. It was a matter of physical endurance, and theirs was no match for the raw strength of the elements. Left no choice, they retreated into Senet's house, the only intact building in the village. She graciously allowed the bull into her parlor.

"This storm can't last," Tariq said. "Pisaqar won't know what happened to us."

Amani handed him a beer. "He'll know we have a good reason for not coming."

"That won't be much comfort to him. The poor man's stuck in a dark tomb with *at least* two corpses."

"Tariq," she hissed angrily, "fucking stop it."

Only then did he remember Kalab. The acolyte—no, priest—set down his fresh cup and disappeared into a back room, his expression murderous like Tariq had never seen, not even in the heat of battle.

"I'm sorry," he told the group at large. "But really, how long can this storm go on?"

Senet shrugged hopelessly. "A few hours. Days, if the gods aren't good."

Eleazar said, "There is plentiful food and water in the entry hall. He will survive."

A terrible thought struck Tariq. "There aren't enough torches to last another day." The image of their captain groping blindly through the silent, pitch-dark tunnels was too awful to dwell on.

Nawidemaq glowered at the pile of trinkets he'd emptied in front of his stool. "The gods of the sea send a mighty wind. It will be a terrible storm."

The awful wind howled through the village. The gusts were not merely air, but sand, even rocks—and that transformed the storm into a physical obstacle. It blasted the ruined walls and ripped away chunks of mud brick, adding these to its strength. As Kalab struggled down the street, rocks the size of marbles pummeled his shins, and the gritty wind stabbed at his exposed hands like innumerable needles. But if he let go of the grain sack that covered his head, it would be torn away in an instant, and the sand would soon blind him.

Through the rough fabric, he could see little. There was only shrieking brown nothingness. The best he could do was keep sidestepping along the street and have faith that Qorobar was still ahead of him. Behind, Nawidemaq would be in the same predicament. Kalab was left to wonder how they would all fare once they left the dubious shelter of Set-Ma'at's walls.

And that was if the storm would allow them that far. For a moment, the shrieking dulled, and he caught a glimpse of the axe man's bulk. Gladdened, he quickened his pace to close the distance. But the storm had deceived him. An almighty gust caught him mid-step and smashed him into the wall. Dazed, breath knocked from his lungs, he crumpled. The wind tried to whip off his hood and almost succeeded, but he pulled it back below his chin and hunched there, rasping, until rough hands hauled him standing again.

"We must go back!" Even though Nawidemaq bellowed the words into his ear, his voice was barely audible.

Kalab gestured hopelessly in front, where Qorobar had just been. Turn away or forge ahead, they had to stay together. They couldn't risk losing anyone else.

"Find Tariq," he yelled. He had to repeat himself twice more before the medicine man understood him. Nawidemaq pulled on the bull's lead line and drew the animal alongside them, shielding them from the worst of the wind. Kalab huddled against its white hide, and they resumed their way, heads bent against the raging sandstorm.

Even with the bull's bulk to protect him, the storm found ways to multiply his woes. Sand forced its way beneath the scales of his Assyrian armor, where it crawled incessantly like the lice he'd once burned from the seams. Particles got into his sandals and rubbed his feet raw. Every crevice of his body was invaded. Sand stung beneath his nails, lined his gums, slithered into the crack of his ass. Every step forward was a battle against the wind, and the price of success was pain.

Neither Ermun nor Pisaqar would have asked this of them, Kalab was certain. But they needed them. Until the task proved impossible, the Mice needed to make the attempt.

As Kalab passed the hollowed-out gatehouse, he realized once and for all that they were doomed to fail. Unhindered by walls, the sandstorm redoubled in strength, its winds so pernicious that even the doughty bull now strove to keep its footing. The swirling sand was a near solid mass that no longer dulled the sunlight, but blocked it altogether, swathing the land in darkness. Kalab felt, rather than saw, that his exposed hands and feet were crisscrossed with tiny cuts.

Out of the roaring darkness staggered Qorobar, with Tariq clutching his belt, his hood torn away, eyes and mouth all stuffed with sand. The big man was waving for them to go back. The acolyte turned around, filled with guilty relief. His only comfort was knowing that his teacher would have wanted no one else to die for his sake.

The wind let up again. Kalab, knowing this meant it was about to shift once more, set his stance and doubled over—only for the new wind to sweep up from directly behind him. The strength was terrifying. There was no chance even to stumble before he was blasted prone. His teeth clacked together as his jaw was driven into the rocky soil. He spat out rocks and perhaps teeth, and haltingly pushed himself back up.

He could see again. Then he realized, dreadfully, that he shouldn't have been able to. His grain sack hood was gone.

No, not gone. Flapping at his shoulder, its drawstring tugging at his neck.

He snatched at it. Too late. The wind got hold of it first.

With a jerk, the string whipped tight around his neck, and his world became a blur of multicolor and screaming darkness. Between bursts of awareness, in which he clawed frantically at the tugging string, he keenly felt the sharp rocks raking his body as he was dragged, gyrating, across the ground. Knobs of stone punched into his armored torso, bruising his ribs. He dug in his heels but only managed to tear off his sandals. Even as the earth sought to bludgeon him to death, his loose makeshift hood did its utmost to strangle him. He managed to roll to his knees, only for the storm to blow him back down. But in the process, he got his fingers around the string, and after much desperate tugging, the bag came away with a ripping of fabric. It flapped off into the storm and left Kalab to pant in great sobs.

He was alone. There was no way of knowing how far he'd been dragged, or in which direction. "Help! Anyone!" he screamed into the surrounding darkness, which was broken only by the glitter of swirling sand. Already, the stuff was forcing itself into his eyelids, cramming his sinuses. It hurt. He knew without doubt that he was meant to feel this pain. The gods had brought him here to sentence him.

On his knees at the mercy of their hateful storm, he found he could recall none of the prayers Ermun had taught him. Instead, he thought of the words on Ramesses' walls, the Book of the Dead—the Forty-Two Judges he would face as the god Osiris weighed his heart, the Negative Confession he was expected to give them.

I have not stolen, he would falsely claim. *I have not lied. I have not slain. I have not raped. I have not slain. I have not stirred up strife.*

Morosely, he came to the recognition that he would not pass the Judges' scrutiny. Despite a dozen years at good Ermun's side, he hadn't troubled himself to learn anything valuable. He would go to the Lord of Life with a heavy heart, and his *ka* would be annihilated.

"Spare me," he pleaded to the storm. Sand coated his tongue, his teeth. He didn't care. "Let me be who my teacher wished me to be. Show mercy. I beg you."

The wind blew his tears dry as he shed them, turning the sand in his eyes to crust. And then, as blindness began to overtake him, Ermun walked from the swirling sands. He wore all white, and his arms were spread wide in greeting.

"Teacher!" Kalab cried. He labored to his feet. The wind tore at his clothes, forgotten in his exultancy. As he rushed to embrace his true father, Ermun's pale shape resolved itself into that of a white bull with its broad horns. He stopped in amazement. The bull plodded up to him and nudged his heart with its enormous snout, snuffling in greeting. The lead line was strung on the ground behind it. Nawidemaq was nowhere in sight, but the bull didn't seem troubled. With a snort, it turned its head as if to offer the acolyte one of its vast horns.

"You truly are a divine beast," he said wonderingly as the gentle bull led him away, though the storm deafened his words.

The journey back was agony, but the bull stayed with him every step, guarding his battered form against the brutal wind. They battled together through the murky, stinging brown until at last, through a gap in the billowing sands, Set-Ma'at came into view. Of the other mercenaries, Kalab saw no sign. Not until they rounded the second corner of the main street, where Senet's house was. Two human forms rushed from the doorstep where they'd been huddled. With hurried hands, they took hold of Kalab and the bull, hauled them to the door, and shoved them through.

He staggered into the parlor. As his legs gave way and he sank to the floor shaking, the combined efforts of half a dozen straining people succeeded in pressing the door shut. The storm lashed apoplectically at the planks, infuriated by their escape. Gusts vied to suck the rattling shutters off their hinges. Senet ran from one window to the next with an armful of damp rags, which she stuffed into the cracks in an attempt to keep out the sand. It was a valiant struggle, largely in vain. She stabbed the mercenaries with brittle-eyed glances as they clustered at her front door, having ruined her home and exhausted themselves into uselessness.

Tariq crawled up to Kalab. "We thought you were gone," he panted.

The acolyte would have agreed, but a violent fit of coughing interrupted his reply. Someone handed him a waterskin, which he alternated between gulping and pouring over his face.

"The bull, too," continued the redhead. "The damn thing broke loose. It just ran off. How'd you get hold of him?"

Kalab pointed a trembling finger at the albino animal, where it sat peaceably in the foyer while Nawidemaq rinsed its eyes. "That's no bull." The others gathered as he recounted how it had rescued him from certain death. "It's not an ordinary beast of burden. It's Apis himself."

A small voice asked, "Is that a god?" The little boy—Yem, Tariq thought he was called—had emerged with his sister from the back of the house. Hugging their dolls, the children gazed wonderingly at the blessed bull.

"Yes," said Kalab. "Or if not Apis, a herald, at the very least."

With a clatter of hooves, the white bull lurched standing—and, swishing its tail, shat on the floor.

Qorobar laughed with all the rest. "The gods work in mysterious ways."

Senet wasn't entertained in the least. The woman squealed in outrage and whacked the bull with a broomstick, god-sent or no. Intrigued, it chomped speculatively at the bristles, at which point she gave up and swept the mound of bullshit away.

A fresh outburst from the sandstorm rattled the door, stilling the group's chuckles. The children cried out, and Nibamon drew them to him.

"Will you try again?" The foreman hadn't gone with them into the storm, which was just as well. Tariq and the other Kushites had plenty of sand crammed up their nostrils, but noseless Nibamon likely would have been smothered to death.

"Yes," said Tariq.

There was an immediate uproar. "Tariq, no," Amani asserted over the various shouts. "We aren't chancing it again."

Qorobar agreed. "It took Apis himself to get us out of that shit. We have it from a priest."

"What about the captain?" demanded Tariq. He looked at Kalab. "What about your teacher?"

"They're in the gods' hands."

Tariq barked a laugh. "Why does that answer fail to surprise me? Leave it to Kalab to wash his hands of doing the right thing."

The acolyte launched at him, only for Qorobar to shove him back on his ass. Then the big man spun around and shoved Tariq against the wall. "Take that back," he snarled.

"I won't," gasped Tariq.

"The two of you, always with the bickering. Like Osiris and Set. Except with them, it was clear which was the bad one.

Then there's you, both of you, taking turns being wrong. Just stupid boys. Amani would be better off without either of you. Say you're sorry."

Tariq sucked in some breath. "Sorry," he said to Kalab without quite looking at him.

"Now you!" Qorobar snapped at Kalab.

"What for?"

"Gods' sake! Apis gave you a second go, and you're just going to keep acting like an ass?"

Kalab breathed deeply to calm himself. "Fine. Tariq, I'm sorry."

Qorobar lumbered off. The redhead hunched, holding his ribs. Amani stomped over, gave him the briefest of inspections, and went to sit on the other side of the room, plainly furious at the situation they'd collectively foisted on her.

"Now," said Qorobar, "let's all sit in peace while we wait for this shit to blow over. No one's going anywhere."

Ashurizkadain had ordered the camp made behind a hillcrest, amid a circle of wind-hewn stones from a savage age long forgotten. The locals seemed to think the ruins cursed and so avoided them, which gave the Assyrians solitude. The Flayer was glad of it. No longer could his men find whores or wine to tempt them. Enfolded within ancient stones, the only means of whiling away the long hours was vigilant duty.

Through the valley below swirled the waters of the Nile's First Cataract. Clusters of rounded boulders jutted from the river, channeling its flow into fierce rapids, whose black depths and frothing white caps hid submerged rocks that would easily gut any boat foolish enough to blunder in. This Cataract was the first of five infamous obstacles that had stymied glory-seeking pharaohs ever since the birth of Egypt. They were nearly unnavigable, even when the Nile was not at flood. And until just a few days ago, the Inundation season had been at its height. Only now was boat traffic beginning to resume once more.

From his perch in the stone circle, Ashurizkadain watched a team of workers coaxing a vessel through a calm channel using ropes and poles and their own straining bodies. The boat carried mud brick, to his disappointment, but he'd sent men down to inquire regardless, just as he did every time a new arrival was sighted. The Kushites' boat would be carrying sacks of grain. He knew as much from the wretch he'd left skinless in fat Khaemon's house. And from his own encounter with the Desert Mice on the Delta, he knew that their boat was far larger than the one he looked on now.

Seven weeks. Ashurizkadain clenched his fists. That made it nearly two months since Pisaqar had slipped from his grasp in that Memphis tavern. How much longer must Ashur's justice be delayed?

Just as he had done seemingly a hundred times every day, he reviewed what he knew. From Memphis, the mercenaries had fled south by boat. This could only mean their destination was their homeland of Kush. In order to get there, they must pass through the First Cataract. Thus far, they had not. He had pressed enough silver into enough Egyptian palms to be certain of this. A boat as large as theirs would not go unnoticed, and besides that, the inundated river had choked off traffic until recent days.

Pisaqar would come. All Ashurizkadain had to do was sit patiently.

He gnawed his lip until he tasted blood.

Spitting on the foreign earth, he looked to the north, searching the river for approaching boats. To his fury and dismay, the waters were nearly devoid of traffic, except for the occasional fisherman. The horizon yielded nothing but the dirty smudge that had lingered there since the previous sunset—a brown haze whose faded heights were infrequently lit by flashes of lightning. He knew the sight well from Assyria. A sandstorm.

"My lord!" Nimrud was striding up the hill, holding the damp hem of his Egyptian kilt.

Ashurizkadain folded his hands behind his back and stood impatiently while second-in-command struggled up the slope.

"My lord," Nimrud said with blowing cheeks, "there is a great storm in the north."

The Flayer indicated that direction with brittle patience. "I can easily see the storm from this vantage. It is one of the tame southern variety. It shall pass soon."

"Forgive me, my lord, but the men on the boat have told me different. It is a wind of peculiar strength. It has blown stiffly for some days. All Egypt is held in thrall, from Thebes to the Delta. This is to be the last boat for a long while."

His first urge was to erupt, but he held his tongue and forced himself to think. "The land is brought to a standstill," he mused.

"That is so, my lord."

"And thus our quarry is held fast, as well." Ashurizkadain rang his tongue over his desert-chapped lips. "We may hunt once more."

Nimrud furrowed his brow in consternation, a state into which the man descended with dismaying regularity. "If I may suggest, my lord... This plan you have already devised is a sound one. The Kushites must pass through this narrow point to journey home. Our men hold the advantageous ground. The enemy shall be penned in the Cataract. They shall make for easy prey. I must recommend that—"

"Nimrud. I am confounded as to the reason you display this incessant need to offer your counsel. I have never asked for it."

"Of course. I beg your forgiveness, my lord."

Ashurizkadain inclined his head. "It is yours. Do not place yourself in a position to ask it of me again."

"Shall I make the men ready?"

"See it done. We ride for Thebes." As Nimrud retreated with much scraping, the Flayer returned his attention to the north, where the sandstorm was trapping his quarry. No more idle sitting for the warriors of Assyria. They were the hunters, and theirs was to seek.

The sandstorm howled for a full week.

It was a once-in-a-generation gale. Neither Senet nor Nibamon had seen its like in the Valley of the Kings. Sandstorms were a regular affliction in Kush, and the mercenaries were much better acquainted with them than their Upper Egyptian hosts. But this storm had still made a mockery of their proficiency. They didn't dare test it again.

For seven days, they stunk up Senet's house. There wasn't much option of returning to their own lodgings; the storm had ripped open the makeshift doors and filled the rooms with sand. They passed the time any way they could think of. They sang songs, told stories, played with Senet's small children. Kalab, when grief loosened its hold on his voice, recited the myth of Osiris—murdered by his own brother, divided into pieces, scattered, reknit, and resurrected. The tale of death and rebirth was a poignant one in the aftermath of their loss, and a reminder of the observances the storm was preventing them from keeping. Even now, Ermun's *ka* lay trapped in limbo. It would not find its way to the next world until his body was properly interred.

They, like their departed friend, were captives of events beyond their control. There were nine of them confined to a few rooms, and two children, and a bull. Space was tight. Tempers were short. Scuffles broke out over the shrinking water rations. The few sips they were allowed were barely enough to wash down their bread, and then, they gagged. The overpowering reek of literal bullshit made a chore out of eating.

A bad week. The experience was every bit as awful as roasting in the Sinai, or chasing the Bedouins across Libya, or breaking against the Assyrian lines at Jerusalem. Those shared tribulations had bound them into a tribe. It was the only reason they got through without turning Senet's house into an abattoir.

When they awoke to silence, they burst outside like men and women reborn. The village was covered in a cubit of sand. They waded into their houses and shook off their scant possessions. Nawidemaq drove the cart down to the Nile as quickly as the bull could trot, and returned just as Amani and Tariq reappeared from a secluded house, having leaped at the long-awaited chance for privacy.

With the group fed and watered, they thanked an exhausted Senet and started their ascent to the Valley of the Kings, where their captain awaited rescue.

SHATTERED DOORS

"PISAQAR!" THE CALLS echoed through the vacant halls of the tomb. "Pisaqar!"

Tariq skidded down the first tunnel. He didn't bother with the ropes dangling between the center columns; they'd only slow him down. And after seeing the stoppered water jugs and sand-covered bread baskets at the entrance, there was no thought whatsoever of caution. That Pisaqar had left his meager provisions untouched could only be a bad sign. Tariq kept scanning the floor for footprints, but the thin layer of sand had not been disturbed. Dread parched his tongue. Any number of nightmare scenarios flitted tauntingly through his mind.

"No, no, no," he muttered. "Pisaqar!" He slid to a halt where the floor leveled out, relieved to find their wooden braces still in place below the sand trap. He had imagined Pisaqar groping through the dark and knocking into a beam and being buried alive—only unlike Qorobar, without friends nearby to pull him free.

One nightmare less—a dozen to go.

He dove through the portal into the columned entry hall.

"Pisaqar! We're here!" But his captain wasn't. The hall lay empty. There was one difference, though.

Someone had broken the two remaining doors open.

Tariq stared at the smashed portals with chilled blood. "Oh *no*."

Kalab rushed in and bumped him, provoking a startled yelp.

"Sorry." The acolyte gaped at the sight. "*Shit*. How did that happen?"

Qorobar lumbered in next, followed shortly by the rest of the Mice. The sight of the broken portals provoked a wave of hysterics, to which Nawidemaq contributed a babbling torrent of prayer.

Yesbokhe proved himself the most courageous of them all by daring to approach the breached doors first. He knelt by one and traced the floor. He mimed a walking person with two fingers. *Tracks*. He checked the other door and made the same sign. *More tracks*.

"Pisaqar's?" asked Qorobar.

The scout lifted his hands, at a loss. He jabbed his finger at various spots. *Very many tracks*.

Tariq swallowed down a lump of atavistic terror. "Alright. We won't find him by just standing around like assholes. Yesbokhe and Nibamon, you come with me. We'll look in the Serpent Tunnel. Like as not, that's where he'll be. Nawidemaq—Nawidemaq?"

The medicine man snapped out of his prayer trance with a click of vertebrae. "Yes."

"You and Kalab take this left tunnel. Qorobar and Amani, you take the center."

Amani said, "I want to be in your group."

"Wha—is this really the time? Fine. Qorobar and Yesbokhe take the center. Amani, Nibamon, and I take the Serpent. If anyone finds him, make noise. When your first torch burns low, turn back. We'll all meet here. Questions?"

To his surprise, no one balked at his leadership, not even

stubborn Qorobar. They split off into their groups and stepped tentatively through the portals with their torches up and hands on their weapons.

He snaked down the hard-cornered tunnel with his sword leading. What he expected to encounter, he had no idea. But he had to put his tongue between his teeth to muffle their chattering. At least having a firm grip on two cubits of iron eased his state of mind somewhat. He hated today. It'd been a bad week. Shit, the whole year had been a string of catastrophes. Losing Pisaqar on top of it all—he could barely countenance the thought.

"Should have taken a contract in Lydia..."

"What'd you say?" Amani hissed behind him.

"Just that I'm flattered you wanted to join me, not Qorobar."

He didn't see her eyeroll, but felt it. "I didn't ask because of *you*. You said Pisaqar would be down here. I agree. So, here I am."

"Alright, then."

Nibamon, bringing up the rear, remained politely quiet.

But Pisaqar wasn't in the poisoned chamber. That wasn't to say it was empty. Ermun still lay where he'd died, looking much the same—not bloated or purple or decayed at all, just pallid. Beside the door was a bunched blanket, an empty waterskin, and their captain's sword. There was no sign of Pisaqar himself.

Nibamon peered down into the black pit. "I've never seen its like," he murmured. "A pit of ash that kills. Incredible." He gestured at its opposite end. "How did you make it across?"

"We didn't. We—" Tariq's jaw dropped. The portal on the other side of the room—the one that had lured Ermun to his death—was wide open. His heart threatened to erupt through his ribcage. "It wasn't like that when we left. I don't understand. What's happening? What the shit is happening?!"

Amani clutched his hand tight. "Stop that," she said with pointed calm. "Now look. There's broken rock around door. That means he chiseled through. This isn't the gods at work."

Tariq nodded fiercely and willed his heart to be still. "I'm glad you came."

"Didn't come for you," she reminded him, but smiled. "Let's find out how he got across."

Nibamon walked the edge of the pit until he came to the left-hand wall. "Here. He carved handholds for himself." The wall was pockmarked with holes, gouged in a rough line. Tariq couldn't imagine how anyone could have had the endurance to hang on one-handed while he hammered out the next hole. One would have needed to stand on something. Then he saw the planks lying in the pit amid tangles of rope.

"He must have made a bridge out of those planks. Lashed them together." Tariq looked at Amani. "Those came all the way from the entry hall. Why wouldn't he just keep going to the surface? What could have driven him back down here? To risk *this*?"

Amani was probably the bravest person he'd ever met, but she couldn't help a perturbed glance back the way they'd come. "I don't know. But he barely made it. That last stretch of wall gave way. While he was hanging off it, looks like."

"He must have made a jump for it. That's why the bridge fell apart." Sure enough, on the far side of the trench, the soot had been scratched away down to the bare limestone. Pisaqar's lower half must have been hanging off the ledge, his legs immersed in poison. He'd fought an almighty struggle to claw his way onto the ledge. He'd made it, only to confront the fact that he had no way back over.

And they had no way to reach him.

Tariq cupped his hands toward the cavernous dark of the yawning portal. "Pisaqar!" The syllables echoed into the void. There was no answer but ringing silence.

Nibamon said, "My torch is going out."

Tariq jammed his own torch into one of the handholds. "I'll leave this burning for him, in case he comes out. Maybe he heard us and can't answer." To Pisaqar, he yelled, "We'll come back for you!"

Then they backtracked up the Serpent Tunnel until they again reached the entry hall. The others were already waiting for them.

He explained what they'd found in the poison room. The others visibly relaxed at the news that their leader might still be alive.

Tariq asked, "What'd you find, Qorobar?"

The axe man gestured to the middle door, the one he'd investigated. "Nothing in there but a dead end. Some sort of pyramid room. Rough stone. Looked unfinished."

Nibamon scratched under his mask. "That sounds like a relieving chamber. A sign of a large void beneath. Odd to find that in an underground tomb."

Tariq waved his hand. "That's not important now. Kalab, what about you and Nawidemaq?"

The medicine man made a sign and spat over his right shoulder.

Kalab pursed his lips. "An unholy place. I think you ought to see it."

The door on the left brought them through a short tunnel, devoid of decoration, that ended in another rough-hewn square chamber. Its walls were carved with horizontal niches. Inside each rested a cloth-wrapped human figure. Clearly whoever made the niches had paid more attention to their number than their dimensions, because the bodies hadn't fit. Most had their shins or heads smashed in so that they could be crammed into place. The bandages were blackened and grimy. They hung loosely from the bodies, exposing cracked skin and white bones. The air held a sour tang that invaded the nostrils and rested on the tongue.

"Decay," said Nibamon. He, like the rest of them, covered his nose—or lack thereof, in his case. "These mummies weren't properly prepared. The embalmers skipped steps." He stepped between the niches. "They're all done the same way. Interred at the same time. They have no headdresses. I see no amulets. A royal corpse wouldn't be treated this poorly. Rushed. All of it rushed. Why?"

Kalab pointed above the door. "'Blessed be the laborers, who shall serve me in Duat.'"

The hole in Nibamon's face emitted a long crooning noise. "The builders! The stories were true! That shit pharaoh dragged them all to his grave beside him!" He kicked the wall. "Bastard!"

Qorobar edged for the door. "This tomb is cursed."

"Yes. It is." All eyes turned to Kalab, whose own gaze remained rooted to the floor. "Ermun and I knew of it since Memphis. Ramesses himself appeared before us in the vaults of Osiris. He pronounced the curse on us for seeking to disturb his rest."

A collective moan of horror filled the crypt. To be cursed by an embittered enemy, that was one matter. But by the apparition of a god-king, one who had sown misfortune in life—this was grim news. Suddenly, their string of misfortunes made sense. The sand trap, Ermun's death, the epic storm, the loss of Pisaqar—all these events were at the behest of a vengeful pharaoh.

Qorobar jabbed his finger at the shrinking acolyte. He bellowed, "Why would you keep that from us?"

"Because Ermun believed in Pisaqar. He knew whatever mission the captain set for himself was a righteous one. He didn't want to deter the captain."

"And now," growled Qorobar, "Ermun is *dead*. The captain is gone! What'll happen to us now, eh? Who dies next? Suppose it doesn't matter to you! Because you decided it wasn't worth mentioning in the first place!"

Tariq stepped between them and shoved Qorobar back. "Oy! Enough of that! This doesn't help anyone!" He looked around the circle of wan faces. "Why is Kalab the one getting the blame?"

Kalab looked at him in astonishment.

"Amun knows how many portals we smashed open to get into this place, and let me remind you, *every single one of them* warned us—in no uncertain terms—that we'd be cursed if we carried on. Well, we did, and now here we are. We're in it up to our necks. We can't outrun the curse. We can't bargain our way out. Our only choice is to push through and finish it. Anybody else have a mind to complain? Let's hear it now. After you're done, we've got a job to do. Anybody?"

He met their eyes, one by one. When no one spoke up, he nodded in satisfaction. "Pisaqar needs our help. Let's work."

THE RIVER OF DUAT

OVER THE NEXT day and night, Tariq oversaw a singularly bizarre operation. Nibamon and Nawidemaq, who each fancied himself an expert on the subject, agreed that the poison filling the trench acted the same way water did. The only way to drain the pit of this not-water was to bail it out.

Qorobar brought down the sack of Assyrian helmets he'd carried with him since Jerusalem. Using them as buckets, they would kneel beside the pit and scoop out a helmet-full of poison, then tip it into a waiting amphora. Some careful measurements on Nibamon's part determined that an amphora could hold eighteen helmets' worth of water. After some discussion, Tariq judged that twelve was a reasonably safe number. Whenever the amphora was 'full,' it was carried all the way to the surface and dumped a safe distance from the tomb entrance.

Simple enough, Tariq surmised. The trouble was that the stuff was literally invisible. The sight of hardened soldiers dipping upturned helmets into an empty trench, rising with infinite care, and pouring the contents into a jar, all with sweating brows and tongues stuck between their teeth—it put him in mind of children playing pretend. Any of the mercenaries might have laughed at themselves if not for Ermun's body lying cold just out of reach.

Gauging progress was an interesting quandary. They solved it by accident when Eleazar lost his footing at the edge and very nearly fell to his death. Catching him by the sleeve, Tariq hauled him back to safety. The Israelite's fallen torch rolled a little way, then abruptly went out. After that, Tariq would periodically dip a lit torch in and mark its terminus with a line of chalk. Progress was slow, at first. Infuriatingly so.

"It's like playing bloody make-believe," whined Qorobar after what must have been his fiftieth trip to the surface with a double load slung on his shoulders. Similar grumblings were constant. The seemingly foolish nature of the task grated on the mercenaries. Tariq was put in mind of the occasion when the nomarch of Hesbu had insisted on their company—then whole—marching through the streets of Poubasti in endless circles all day long to impress his people with a show of strength. Except Kushites were a rarity in that corner of the Delta, and the locals became wise to the game almost immediately.

But at least the nomarch had paid them in the end. Maybe the same would be true when they finished with Ramesses.

They made faster headway the deeper they went, thanks to the way the trench tapered toward the bottom. The space between Tariq's grade marks grew. Once the poison level dropped out of arm's reach, the mercenaries had to scoot down the sides on their asses with ropes tied at their belts, the lengths carefully measured to be sure they couldn't descend too far. The self-imposed restriction hampered progress somewhat, but Tariq had no intention of losing anyone else. He knew Pisaqar would have agreed.

They shouted his name at intervals, pausing their work so they wouldn't miss a reply. They never heard anything back.

At long last, the trench was emptied to knee level, low enough to safely cross. But the first thing they did was retrieve Ermun. They hoisted his rigid corpse in careful hands and brought him out on their shoulders, Kalab leading the way. They set him down in the entry hall. At that point, they looked very much like he did: gray with ash, hunched, drawn. To their shame, they couldn't fix their friend into a posture that befitted his dignity. The best they could do was wipe the ash from his face and cover him with a blanket. And though Kalab wanted to remain in the entry hall with his teacher, they were all cognizant of the fact that Pisaqar had done the same, only to be forced into the depths of the tomb for unknown reasons. There was no circumstance under which Tariq would permit anyone else to be alone. Kalab didn't question the decision. Planting kisses on Ermun's covered brow, they made the descent as one—down the Serpent Tunnel, across the poison pit, and through the portal into the dark labyrinth beyond.

The elaborate warren of passageways put the ones that had come before to shame. One passage split in two. Each snaked off in opposite directions, branching in turn into yet more tunnels that thankfully ended in single rooms. As for the purpose of these rooms, Nibamon could only offer guesses. Decoy burial chambers, perhaps. Or, more likely, they'd been meant as supplemental burial chambers for Ramesses' family. If that was true, the absence of royal sarcophagi was a heavy indication that the pharaoh's plans had gone badly awry. His wife, concubines, and children had not followed him west. They'd gone to oblivion instead.

The twin passages joined and split, joined and split, yielding chamber after barren chamber. Their yells and whistles echoed between boastful rows of hieroglyphs. Pisaqar did not answer them. But neither was there any sign of his body. The only indications of his passing were dragging footprints in the otherwise undisturbed dust, and once, a discarded torch. Yesbokhe sniffed it and judged it to have been out for many days.

The effort took on new urgency after that discovery. On through the subterranean maze they went, breaking up walls and building cairns to ensure they could find their way back, even if all their torches went out. The troubling lack of such precautions on their captain's part didn't go unnoticed. Had he been arrogant enough to think he could retrace his steps blind?

Or had something prevented him from stopping?

The tunnels joined together and leaned into a gradual descent—straight as a sunbeam, far as an arrowshot, before unexpectedly terminating.

Then the mercenaries encountered a wholly unexpected obstacle: water.

At the end of the long tunnel, the floor dropped away into a pool of lusterless water, the same yellow as the sandstone. It was utterly still, such that Tariq at first mistook it for a stone landing and almost stepped onto it.

Kneeling, he shone his torchlight on the murky yellow depths. "Pisaqar, please tell me you didn't swim into *that*."

Eleazar leaned past him with an incredulous look. "Have we gone all the way to the Nile?"

"Impossible," Nibamon's nasal voice said from behind him. "We'd have needed to travel leagues."

"Well then, where did this water come from?"

Nibamon replied, "I don't know. There's no water in these hills. It doesn't matter how far one digs."

"Rain?" suggested Kalab.

"You have rain in Kush, yes, but Egypt? The Valley of the Kings, no less! Never. This must have been brought up from the Nile. By hand. The audacity confounds." The foreman's tone was wonderstruck. Even envious.

"It doesn't matter how this water got here," said Tariq. He pointed at the opaque brown. "We have to go in. It's the only place Pisaqar could have gone."

"All of us?" asked Nibamon. He had never shared the Kushites' comfort with water.

"No. There's no telling how far it goes. Or—" Tariq swallowed, "or what we'll find in there. One of us has to go alone first. It should be me. I'll go."

Amani looked astonished. "Why you?"

"Because this is my fault. I let Pisaqar stay."

Qorobar put a hand on his shoulder. "Let me. Amun knows I've wronged the man enough times over the years. Let me make it right."

Tariq dashed his hand away. He forced a grin. "You can fuck off and make amends some other way. I'm the best swimmer. Besides, your fat, wrinkled head will only get you stuck. No, I'm the one. The rest of you are staying. That's all there is to discuss."

Yesbokhe came up with a rope. He tied a secure knot around Tariq's ankle. He pointed to Tariq and yanked twice. *Meet trouble, haul on the rope.*

Tariq faced the water. He took a steadying breath, but before he could finish mustering his courage, quick footsteps came up from behind him. Amani grabbed his cheeks and kissed him fiercely. The other Kushites hid smiles and turned away.

"They're finally out with it," Qorobar said with what sounded suspiciously like pride. "Young love."

Amani pulled away. "More when you get back," she promised. "Go get him."

He nodded. He waded into the water. Its coolness prickled at his skin. With a few deep breaths, he shut his eyes and made the plunge.

Opening them, he saw only solid brown. The light dimmed with his first cutting strokes, and then, almost instantaneously, fled altogether. He swam in total darkness, keenly aware of the walls hemming him in, because he scraped his head or his hands against them every time he moved. Without sight, it was impossible to swim in a straight line. There was only the cold water that pressed against his skin, whose rush filled his ears. Whenever he bumped his forehead on the ceiling, he recognized—or imagined—that he was still swimming ever deeper. His lungs raised the first hint of protest. He ignored the discomfort. He continued to fight the water, kicking and scooping.

The press against his ears grew. He wiggled his jaw, alleviating the discomfort. But still, he had to contend with the growing ache in his lungs. His body was warning him to turn back. He couldn't—not yet. He'd barely gotten started.

He ran face first into a wall, mashing his nose with a crinkle of soft bone. His chin stung insistently enough that he was sure he'd cut himself. Still, he was relieved. He'd blundered into an upward bend. He fumbled around the walls until he was sure of the angle. Then he propped his feet and launched himself diagonally upward. He couldn't be far now. Up meant air.

Until the rope around his ankle went taut. He kicked to loosen it and tried to lunge, but it caught again. He grasped the problem: the rope was getting snagged on the rough-edged corner of the ceiling. The choice was clear: forward or back.

It was an easy decision. He drew his knife and sliced through the strands with a few practiced cuts. Snagged in place, the others wouldn't have felt his signals for help even if needed it. He left the useless rope floating in his wake.

His lungs were burning by now. He clenched his teeth with the effort of holding his breath. He scuffed the chiseled sides of the tunnel with his toes and raked it with his fingers, tearing the softened nails, but the effort seemed to win him additional progress. Up and up he battled, until the weight on his ears began to relent. He could feel the surface coming close.

He exploded out of the water with a deep intake of breath. He padded in place, hearing his harsh, grateful breathing reverberate on stone.

"Who's there?"

He almost wept to hear Pisaqar's voice. "It's me, Tariq."

Pisaqar spoke with an identical flood of relief. "Praise Amun!" The chamber they were in was devoid of light, but Tariq heard his captain scrabbling over. Hands felt at him, found his armpit, and pulled. Though there was little strength behind the effort, it lent Tariq a welcome sense of direction. He flopped onto level ground with his limbs flailing.

Blindly, he and Pisaqar shared an embrace. Pisaqar shook in his grip. The man's skin was clammy, taut against straining bones. But he was alive. That was enough.

Tariq asked, "What happened to you?"

Pisaqar's heavy silence spoke loudly while revealing nothing. After a few moments, he said with a false laugh, "I could ask the same of you."

Tariq pitied him—understood, even. Nine days in the dark. He wouldn't have wished it on anyone.

He told Pisaqar what had happened in his absence. The sandstorm, the clearing of the poison tunnel, the blind swim. He came to the end of the tale and fell silent. Pisaqar never gave an indication of hearing, but sat silent in the dark the entire time. Tariq didn't even hear him move. He wished he could see the captain's face, if nothing else. An imaginary terror came to him—that he wasn't talking to Pisaqar at all, but some evil spirit that spoke with his voice.

"Pisaqar, how did you end up here? Why?"

"They were long days, Tariq. When I realized you wouldn't return, I began to work. If only to ease my mind. And then … I…" He trailed off into a haunted silence. "I found a way across the pit. And I had to… I ran. I hurt my leg." Another pause, in which Tariq imagined a hopeless gesture. "I ran until my feet hit water. I swam until I found air. And then … I waited. I knew you would come." He sobbed. "I knew you would. I am sorry I could not wait."

Tariq's heart broke to hear such hollowness in his captain's voice. He was glad, suddenly, that he couldn't see his expression. But he had to ask the question. "Why didn't you wait?"

"Nine days. You would not believe me if I told you, Tariq. The things… You would not believe. Take me away from here. Take me back." Pisaqar made a sound that could have been the merest approximation of a laugh. "I need a beer. By the gods."

"Yes. We'll go back." Tariq looked around. It was an instinctive motion. He still couldn't see at all. There was only pure darkness, the musty scent of moist stone, the light lapping of water. "Where are we?"

The question stirred Pisaqar's mind again. "This was the burial chamber. This was where the Ramesses the Eighth rested."

Tariq's leaping pulse slackened again at the dejection in the other man's voice. "Was?"

"It is empty, Tariq. Someone else broke into the tomb long before us. Everything was all for nothing."

THE HUNT

"NONSENSE," ELEAZAR HEARD the noseless foreman mutter to himself, the word just audible above the rumbling creak of the cartwheels. "Utter nonsense."

Eleazar glanced at Kalab, but the man paid him no mind except to bow his head lower and whisper his prayers more fervently. The shrouded corpse beside him in the cargo bed wasn't much in the mood to talk, either. Eleazar let off pushing the tailgate and leaned around for a look at Nawidemaq, who guided the bull by the bridle along the river path. The medicine man walked with even more hop in his step than usual, glad to be under open sky and the comforting gaze of his thousand gods.

"I won't believe it!"

Eleazar sighed. "Nibamon, if you wish to unburden yourself, come help me push, and I will listen to you."

Nibamon fairly jogged over. "Thank you, Eleazar. These blasted Kushites won't listen to me. As if I, a builder by trade, wouldn't know better than them."

"You have tried speaking to Pisaqar, I assume?"

"Pisaqar is huddled in Senet's house. The man barely speaks at all!"

Kalab's prayers stopped. "Neither would you, if you'd been through what he has. Have some respect, man."

Nibamon raised his hands. "He needs more time, I know. But while he recovers, the four of us travel to Thebes, where we will barter off more valuable grain to have our chisels sharpened, and to have your dear friend embalmed. Our supply is growing scarce. We can't keep this up longer than two, three weeks."

"Tariq is confident we can drain the water in that time," said Eleazar. "We did it in the poison pit. We can do it again."

Frustration suffused Nibamon's voice. "He's been at it for a day, and he's managed to drop the water level by what? Two fingers? Think about how far we have to carry the water just to get it out of the tomb! It'll take a year at this rate. Half of us will die of exhaustion trying. Now, suppose we succeed. Suppose we can finally get dry torches into that chamber. Suppose there *is* a false wall, as you've all convinced yourselves. Who's to say what it leads to? There might be more tunnels! More traps! More water!"

Kalab threw up his hands. "Then leave. We're almost in Thebes. We'll give you a sack of grain, and then you can make a new start."

"That's ... not what I'm saying. I'm trying to tell you that this maze of a tomb is nonsense. Tombs are supposed to be easily navigated. This way the *ka* can find its way out to the surface, on to the afterlife and the Trials of Osiris. Ramesses' tomb is so needlessly complex, it makes a mockery of that aim. His *ka* could never escape."

Eleazar mused, "Perhaps the Robber Pharaoh feared the Trials. Perhaps he knew his heavy heart would unbalance Osiris's scales. His *ka* would be annihilated. Undeath may have seemed preferable to nonexistence."

The medicine man hissed at the thought. "To seek such a fate is unforgiveable to any god."

Kalab gave up entirely on praying. "For men who seem to know all this of Egypt's religion, you understand little. For us, there is no such thing as undeath. A trapped *ka* is doomed to waste away. Ramesses would have been the worst fool imaginable to try to elude Osiris's judgment. His priests would have deterred him from the attempt."

The foreman nodded rapidly. "We know that Ramesses sought the afterlife. The Book of the Dead is carved on the tomb walls. There is also a list of his earthly deeds, which he is to recite before Osiris. He appointed a caretaker to make offerings to his *ka*. The tomb inscriptions show that he made sacrifices of his own in his final days. Most importantly, he built a robber-proof tomb. In fact, he made it *so* robber-proof that he rendered all his precautions useless."

Eleazar finally understood what the foreman was trying to say. "You are telling us we have been following a false trail."

"Yes!" cried Nibamon. "Finally, someone understands!"

Eleazar couldn't help a gratified smile. "Tariq is a decent man. But rather unimaginative, and not especially clever, I fear. Tell me, then. Where is Ramesses truly buried?"

"In the tomb, certainly. We've simply been following the path that he left for us. Instead, we must seek the one he meant for himself. Think of the entry tunnel with its roof full of stars. Think of the mortuary scroll, the way it led us to the tomb using the Pole Star. Ramesses was an astronomer. He would have wanted to keep his eye on the heavens."

Thebes bustled in the midst of Inundation. Nibamon pushed his way through the crowds with a grain sack bunched on his head. Jealous glares followed him. All around him were farmers who'd abandoned their flooded fields for the city in search of seasonal work. There was never enough of it. And hungry mouths made greedy hands.

Fortunately, Nawidemaq's exotic looks were just frightening enough to give them second thoughts about acting on their lack of scruples. The medicine man strutted along behind Nibamon in his heron gait, a satchel of dull chisels jangling on his shoulder.

They'd visited the smith half a dozen times by now, and the man knew them by name. Spotting their approach, he left his furnace and ambled over. Into his waiting arms, Nibamon dropped the sack of grain, and atop that, Nawidemaq plopped his satchel.

"Come back this afternoon?" Nibamon inquired.

The smith nodded and turned away. That left a few hours to whittle. Besides, that ought to be enough time for the priest and the Israelite to hand Ermun's body off to the embalmers.

Nibamon raised his brows at Nawidemaq, who grinned with his mouthful of nubby teeth and gestured expansively down the street, where their favorite beer stand awaited. The brewer, unlike the smith, had not learned who they were and didn't seem inclined to ask. His was a simpler craft, however, and he deposited two mugs of his sole product on the counter as they sat. A pair of onions sufficed as payment.

Between the mugs, Nawidemaq set down their usual drinking companion: Wabatabahu, the pot-bellied god of plenty, who hailed from a place in the deepest south whose name would forever remain beyond Nibamon's ability to pronounce. They raised their mugs to him and to one another, then drank deep, for Wabatabahu took much offense to moderation. That sat fine with Nibamon. Three beers were the minimum he required to dull the ache. Three, coincidentally, was Wabatabahu's favored number. Nawidemaq preferred to take his time on his third beer, but Nibamon plowed on.

Around the time he started on his sixth, Nawidemaq looked partway over his shoulder. By his eighth, the medicine man pivoted on his tool and began actively scrutinizing the passing crowds.

He was just reaching for his ninth when Nawidemaq abruptly said, "We must go."

"I need to finish this one," Nibamon protested, slurring a bit.

"We are being watched."

"What?" He twisted around, but Nawidemaq slapped his thigh—hard.

"Be calm! Leave the cup. Come." Nawidemaq dragged him off the stool by the elbow. Mewling, Nibamon made a grab for his beer, but it was out of reach. Before the crowd closed, he saw some bastard sliding onto his seat and swallowing it down for him.

The medicine man bobbed from side to side, fairly swatting people out of his path. Over their heads, Nibamon saw the smith's chimney jutting in the air. "The chisels won't be done yet. It's too soon."

"Better to have them than not," said Nawidemaq. He kept glancing backward. Nibamon followed his gaze but couldn't see anything of note.

His slowed mind grasped what the chalk-dusted man had just said. "Wait. You mean we can't come back?"

"I do not think so."

Nawidemaq strutted right up to the smith at his sharpening wheel. "The tools," he chittered. "Need now."

"Job's half done," the smith said. He saw Nawidemaq's expression, shrugged, and rolled up the half-sharpened chisel with the rest. He held it out, then twisted it away as Nawidemaq reached for it. "Can't give back your payment."

"Fine." Nawidemaq snatched it and hauled Nibamon back onto the street.

"We're going the wrong way! The ferryman is—"

"We must lose him first."

"Who?"

"Him!" Then Nibamon saw their pursuer: a bald man dressed in a blue tunic. He was lean and sinewy, his right arm noticeably more muscled than the left. Nibamon had spent enough time with the black mercenaries to know a soldier's build. The man's painted eyes were fixed on the two of them as he shoved through the crowd.

Nibamon staggered after the Kushite, doing his best to keep up without treading on his heels. "Who is that? One of Taharqa's men?"

Nawidemaq shook his head, which could have meant that their pursuer didn't serve Taharqa, or that he simply didn't know. Nibamon was about to ask him to clarify, but his companion dragged him onto a side street. They hurried down its length, dancing over the outstretched shins of workers resting in the shade. Nibamon was too drunk to manage it gracefully, and pained, angry squawks marked their progress. The bald man appeared at the mouth of the street. Spotting them, he broke into a run. That was all Nibamon saw before Nawidemaq tugged him into an alleyway.

No men asleep here, just mounds of shit and puddles of piss-soaked mud. They were splattered to the knee with both by the time they'd burst, revolted, into the open. They plowed through a queue of women at a well, found themselves hemmed in by houses, swept through a draped doorway, crashed into someone's parlor.

"Is he behind us?" asked Nawidemaq, shouting to be heard above the housewife's shrieks.

"He's near! Just outside!" At that, he was stopped and shoved unceremoniously onto a stair landing.

"Go up!"

Nibamon obeyed. Drunk, heaving for breath, he struggled up the steps. Nibamon drew a reed tube from his belt quiver and slid a long, feathered dart into the end. At the sound of commotion at the doorstep, he raised it to his lips. He sucked in a hard lungful of breath, and then, almost at the same time the door flap was thrown aside, he forced the entire lungful into the tube. Evidently, he hit his target, because a man's cry joined the housewife's screams. Without waiting to see what his feather dart had accomplished, Nawidemaq bounded up the stairs.

"Go!"

Nibamon stepped onto a rooftop terrace, its shelves and railings covered with potted plants.

"Lovely garden," he remarked. Nawidemaq grabbed a fistful of Nibamon's necklace and hauled him bodily toward the divider. They hopped from one house to the next, swatted at every step by palm fronds and fig branches, raising a cacophony of breaking pots and barking dogs. Nawidemaq periodically stopped and blew another dart back the way they'd come, but the bald man—now hobbling on a paralyzed leg—had learned the trick and ducked into cover every time.

Atop the eighth house, they smashed through a woven sunblind and made to vault over to the next house, only to find themselves facing a two-story drop.

Nawidemaq spoke with his hands as well as his voice. "Hang over," he motioned. "After that, you fall."

Nibamon moaned. "I'm a builder, not a damned acrobat!"

"Tell *him* that!"

The bald man was still slinking over the balconies, only now they were close enough to see his snarl. And his sword was out.

"Fall or die!"

Simple choice, then. Nibamon slid one leg over the mud-brick wall, then the other. As he lowered himself beneath the ledge, he saw the medicine man blow his last dart, then hurl the empty tube at their assailant. Then Nibamon was dangling at the end of his reach, legs kicking ineffectually for purchase on the smooth wall. With a shuddering breath, he let go.

A sickening lurch of the stomach, a fall. His feet hit the ground, his knees buckled, and he was left sprawling in the dust. Nawidemaq hurtled over his head. As he landed, he tucked his head into his sternum and rolled. Coming smoothly to his feet, he hurried over to Nibamon and helped him up. The two of them limped down the street and cut around a corner.

Just before they did, Nibamon looked back. The man was watching them from the railing. He was wincing as he held his shoulder, a feathered dart protruding from between his fingers, his other arm hanging limp by his side.

"He's gone," he told Nawidemaq.

"Wabatabahu is a generous god," the medicine man said matter-of-factly. He patted Nibamon's back. Together, they made tracks for the docks, where the ferry waited to take them back west across the Nile, toward the safety of Set-Ma'at.

The coiled lash sat heavily in Ashurizkadain's grip. He circled the one who had failed him, who at this moment stood lashed by his wrists and ankles against a tree, his bare back turned outward.

"Tell me what you have told Nimrud," he ordered, his voice weighted with quiet menace.

The failure's voice was muffled against the ribbed bark of the palm tree. "There were two of them, my lord. One brown, one black. One Egyptian, one Kushite. The Egyptian was small and fat. He wore a mask. He did not have a nose. The Kushite had painted himself white, but his hair was in a coif, as the Kushites wear it. I saw them drinking on the street. They saw me watching them. They fetched their wares from a smith's shop. After that they fled into the city. They hit me with darts as I chased them. I lost the use of my arm and my leg. I could chase them no further. When I last saw them, they were running toward the river."

The man's silence was broken by the crack of a barbed whip against his naked back. He flinched and tensed, but he was an Assyrian soldier. He did not permit himself to cry out.

Ashurizkadain stroked his beard. Though he had commanded his men to shave theirs in order to pass as locals, he had kept his. He felt it important to differentiate himself, even as they dressed in Egyptian rags and hid their curled locks behind wraps of cloth. Without strict hierarchy, there could be only vile chaos.

"They sought to return to their boat," he mused aloud. "They are not staying in the city."

Nimrud cleared his throat. "We are fortunate they were here at all, my lord. Had they come tomorrow instead, we would have been on the road south, and missed them."

Ashurizkadain didn't reply. He merely tore another gash into the failure's back. The soldier rocked against the tree, but said nothing. He stood rigid as the rivulets of blood ran thick along his spine.

"You mentioned a smith. Tell me, did it cross your mind to visit him afterward?"

"I did, my lord!" The failure spoke between clenched teeth. "They gave him chisels. He was to sharpen chisels."

"Oh?" Ashurizkadain cocked his head and lowered the lash. "It seems Pisaqar is cutting stone. How many chisels?"

"Two hands," replied the failure. He was rewarded with a third lash.

Ashurizkadain rolled up the whip and slapped the coil into Nimrud's chest. "I am finished. Untie him. Bind his wounds. Bread and water for a fortnight."

"My lord."

He cast his sight west, up and down the hills and mountains that lined the bank. "He is cutting large quantities of stone, to put such strain on so many tools. Hmm." There, in the distance, his eyes came to rest on the jagged promontories that crenellated the fabled resting place of the Egyptian kings. The Royal Necropolis. The Valley of the Kings.

"A mercenary bites the hand that feeds. How very trite." He smiled to himself. "Nimrud! Prepare the horses! It appears our Kushite friends have gone rummaging around in old graves. Let us see if they require our assistance."

SLITHER

IT WAS JUST as the noseless one had said: Ramesses had wished to look upon the stars. The mouth of the shaft had been easy for Eleazar to find, as simple a matter as it had been to steal out of Set-Ma'at while the exhausted Kushites slept. At the base of Ramesses' hill, the moon had illuminated the broad trail of stones that ran up the slope—not unlike any number of dry riverbeds Eleazar had marched along as Assyria sought the hidden villages of the mountain tribes. But this was no riverbed, he knew. This was the remnant of the ravine the pharaoh's builders had filled in. And the only reason he'd found it at all was because the gods had scoured the hill clean, their sandstorm laying bare the work the Robber Pharaoh had tried his utmost to conceal forever.

He'd followed the rocky trail up the slope until it tapered to a point. There, he'd found the cairn. Its stones had been stacked into the approximation of a pyramid, for the Egyptians were ever enthralled by their own faded grandeur. Nibamon had even confided that the greatest pyramids were said to have star shafts of their own, a feature Ramesses the Eighth would have sought to emulate.

Eleazar had made short work of demolishing the sad facsimile. Beneath it, he had found a square hole three fists wide. It descended almost straight down into the earth. How deep, he couldn't be certain. But he dropped in some pebbles and heard them bouncing for a long time. He wanted dearly to slide a torch down, except for the small fear that it would fall into the burial chamber and catch light. What an end to King Hezekiah's ambitions that would be.

What next, then?

He sat beside the hole and allowed the question to consume him. It would have been an easy matter to sneak back to bed, pretend he had found nothing, and allow the Kushites to spend their efforts on the waterlogged tunnel until they at last gave up. He could return later with a small group of Judeans whose loyalty was assured, who shared with him and Hezekiah the dream of Israel—united and powerful, able to repel the groping of Assyria and Egypt alike.

Your will be done, Lord, he prayed. But whose? Was he following the will of Yahweh? Ashur? Or even Amun? One or all of those gods was at work here, of that he was in no doubt. In strange moments such as these, he imagined that all three gods were one and the same. He felt the weight of a divine gaze pressing on his bowed head—righteous, stern, reproachful. He had been granted an extraordinary blessing. The more he dwelled on it, the more clearly he realized that none of these mighty gods would countenance using their gift treacherously, not even in the pursuit of a noble cause.

He would not be here without the Kushites, nor they without him. They were bound together. Twice, he had betrayed. The gods would surely punish him for the third. But moreover, he wished to share this bounty with the Desert Mice because the choice was just.

Satisfied, he made to stand, reaching for his sword.

It was gone.

His confusion spoiled at once into foreboding. "Ah," he said.

"That was no god's gaze I felt on me, but an earthly one." He turned to find the girl, Amani, poised a few leaps away. There was a loaded sling in one hand, a black gleaming dagger in the other, and in her eyes, murder. Unmoving, she watched him.

He took a deep breath as the sling began its slow twirl. A good shot, that girl. He'd seen her kill birds midflight. He had no doubt she'd end him before he took two steps. But she didn't release her stone. Not yet.

"How long have you been standing there, Amani?"

She didn't answer, except to shift onto her back foot and twirl her sling faster.

"I suppose this was a long time in coming. It is true, I have committed many sins in my life. I am certain I am owed death. I do not begrudge you this thing you are about to do. You will not hear me beg. But please, allow me to only ask you a favor. When you see Pisaqar, ask that my share of the treasure be set aside and delivered to Jerusalem."

"You won't have a share," she said. "What use does a dead man have for gold." The words were phrased as a question, but she spoke them as a declaration, and dared him to rebuff her.

His heart sank. He watched her leaden sling, awaiting death, but she didn't release her stone. She was still willing to hear him.

"I never meant to keep my share for myself. It is all for Jerusalem. Judah must gird itself for the day Assyria breaks the peace. I want my people to endure and prosper. Surely even a street urchin can understand such a thing. Do you not wish the same for Egypt?"

"Not particularly."

"Then Kush. The land that bore you. Your friends. Pisaqar. Think what he would say, if he saw the cold-blooded murder you are about to commit against me."

She grimaced. "You promised you wouldn't beg."

He almost smiled, except for the dreadful thought of that heavy stone hurtling into his brow, and that girl closing the distance with her knife, plunging it into his guts again and again until his blood flowed free down the shaft that had borne Ramesses' soul to the stars. But still, for an instant, he found the humor in the moment. "Forgive me, I did."

She considered him, her sling atwirl. She lowered her chin, tensing.

He closed his eyes.

With a terrific crack, the sling stone smashed into the rock where he'd been sitting. It ricocheted off into the night. As the whine faded, he opened his eyes and found Amani face to face with him, her knife pressed against his throat.

She smiled. "I like the new you. Keep him around. Next time?" With a click of her tongue, she gave the blade a twitch and let it nick him. Cool wetness trickled down his neck. "The stone doesn't miss, and the knife cuts to the bone." Lowering the weapon, she stepped back. "Let's go see Pisaqar. Tell him about your find."

"Ah! Not so tight!" winced Amani as Yesbokhe cinched the knot against her ankle. Yesbokhe squinted up at her, jutted his chin toward the hole bored deep into the mountain, shrugged. Amani made a trembling sigh. "Tight is good."

She looked out over the crest where the men were strung out, performing their final inspection of the rope as Qorobar gathered up the coils on his broad shoulders. Tariq stopped him and bound up a frayed section with thread. The depth of his concentration was honestly touching. At the mouth of the star shaft, Nibamon wriggled a notched stone into the sand until he'd seated it firmly, then dipped his hand into a jar of lard and rubbed a fresh glob onto the sanded groove. And, just to be sure, Nawidemaq stood over him and raised a hymn to Wisbin, whose caring hands wove the threads of life and whose gnashing teeth severed them. Amani thought it was an appropriate choice of deities. The rocks beneath the medicine man's feet were coated with the blood and feathers of the chicken he'd sacrificed to ensure her success.

And still, Pisaqar kept trying to talk her out of it. "I do not ask this of you, Amani."

"I know," she said. "I'm going to do it anyway." He hadn't liked the idea when she'd put it forward, and he liked it still less after laying eyes on the exceedingly narrow star shaft, not even a cubit across. Amani wasn't overly enthusiastic either, truth be told. But she was the slimmest of the lot. It only made sense that this task should fall to her.

"We can widen the shaft," he suggested, just as he had before.

"That'd take weeks. We don't have time. Not with Taharqa on our trail again. And our food is already running low. And regardless, there's no guarantee widening it would work. We'd risk collapsing our only sure way inside. Or at best, we'd fill the bottom with rubble without any easy means of excavating it. I have to go in now. It's the best way. The only way."

"I know," Pisaqar said quietly. His heavy gaze rested on her. In his eyes, she saw the sorrow that had been there ever since Jerusalem—and added to that, fear. Whatever he'd seen in the darkness of Ramesses' tomb, it had cut him to the core.

But he'd survived. She would, too.

Qorobar lumbered close, burdened with heavy loops of rope. "The line is good," he informed them.

Yesbokhe gave the knot one last tug and stood with a nod.

Pisaqar pulled her into a hard embrace. Into her ear, he murmured, "It is not the shades in that tomb you must fear, but the ones you bring inside with you. Leave them here, in the sunlight."

Her brothers all hugged her in turn, even Eleazar, perfunctory as his embrace was. Tariq held her the longest, until embarrassment overcame her fright and she pushed him away with a forced laugh.

"When I come back up, we'll all be rich," she promised.

He contorted his face into a passable grin. "Well then, hurry up and get in there, you lazy shit."

She punched his sternum and faced the dark, square notch carved deep into the earth. The others surrounded her, somber faced, as if it was her own tomb she was about to enter. She wasn't one to give much thought to curses and the like, but the Robber Pharaoh had already taken Ermun from them, and he had almost gotten Qorobar and Pisaqar too. She was putting herself squarely in his gaze.

They'd come so far together. She wouldn't let them fail, not on her account.

Squatting before the borehole, she steadied her breath. Then she got onto her belly and wriggled in headfirst. She only got a glimpse of the four-sided shaft plunging nearly straight down. Then her body blocked off the light and left her in the blackness. Someone had a firm hold on her ankles.

"Are you ready?" Pisaqar's muffled voice asked.

"Yes. Let go." Her words rang down the shaft. The grip released. Her slow, halting slide began.

The warmth of the sun on her feet vanished. The tight space reverberated with her methodical breathing, the clanking of the hammer and chisel strung on her wrists, stretched out in front of her. The blood gathered in her hands. She flexed her fingers, which helped slightly, but her head was growing heavier as well, and she couldn't do anything about that except try to hurry. The shaft's narrow walls clung to her shoulders. She wriggled constantly to free herself, which drew a sweat and slowed her down as the dry stone sucked at her moist skin. Also slowing her progress was the rope on her ankle, which slackened only reluctantly whenever she yanked on it. Her brothers were anxious for her.

"Faster!" Her own yell exploded in her ears. She stopped, her mouth opened in a silent howl of pain until the ringing lessened. The rope stayed taut. Either they hadn't heard, or they wouldn't listen. Angrily, she hauled on it hard enough that she grazed her knee on the limestone, skinning it. "Fuck," she panted. She stared ahead, sightless, as the pain slowly dulled.

This might have been a bad decision.

The rope let off, allowing her to writhe further down. How far, she didn't have the faintest clue. She could have gone just a few cubits, for all she knew. There was no way of marking progress in this lightless place. She could only wriggle in deeper and try not to think too hard about what she'd gotten herself into.

Her sweat began combining with the dust and gradually formed a paste that clung to the walls. She found herself stuck fast. The walls tightened around her ribs. She screwed her eyes shut to stop the darkness boring into her pupils. She bit hard on her lower lip, preventing herself from crying out. She twisted and thrashed, raking her fingers on the stone, pummeling her body into numbness in the effort to free herself.

At last, her body came unstuck. She wept with relief and fatigue and terror. A small voice tried to remind her that her brothers wouldn't let her die wedged in this tiny borehole. If she got stuck, they'd pull her out. Simple.

But what if the knot comes loose? She retched at the horrible thought.

No. She couldn't allow herself to think of that.

It came anyway. She imagined herself pinched in place, upside down, unable to move forward or back, with the blood pumping into her head until it was practically bursting, trapped here for days until she finally died of thirst ... all in complete darkness.

Unable to bear it, she stopped crawling and took some time to sob.

"Stop it," she ordered herself. She shook the tears away. "Stop it." She drew in a ragged gulp of stale air. Then she tugged on the rope for slack and kept moving.

Down and down and down she went. She whistled to try to get some sense of how far the shaft went, but the darkness yielded nothing. The space was nauseatingly narrow. Even freeing herself enough to fall took abominable effort. The dust tore her throat; she tasted blood. She hummed one of Tariq's bawdy tunes to keep her mind somewhat distracted. Whenever the rope dragged her to a stop, she tried to remember that it was because someone she knew was hanging onto the other end. She wasn't alone.

At some point, the sounds in the tunnel changed. Quizzically, she stopped and blew a speculative whistle. Sure enough, her note came back to her in a faint, distorted echo. She was nearing the end. Invigorated, she pushed onward. Then her hammer clattered on stone. She spread her hands on the flat surface and tugged twice on the rope. It went taut immediately. She signaled again, and the others pulled her back a few palms' distance. At her third signal, they held her fast. Now she had room to work.

Regaining her breath, she felt at the stone, just as Nibamon had instructed. Too smooth for limestone. There were etchings in it, probably another shitty curse written in hieroglyphs she wouldn't have been able to read even if she could see.

Still—not limestone. Basalt, maybe. She wouldn't be able to break through that, not without blunting her bronze chisel. Keeping her wits about her, she felt around the stone for edges she could exploit. She found none. But the walls were porous, which meant they were made of limestone. That, she could breach.

She unlimbered her hammer and chisel and got to work. With space at a premium, progress was agonizing. Her arms were pinned straight in front of her and unable to move, restricting her movements to tiny wrist swings. Every iota of progress added to the pile of rock fragments on the slab, hindering her progress. There was no getting rid of the pile except to brush it to one side. Rock chips flew into her face. She kept missing the butt of the chisel and smashing her fingers. The tediousness infuriated her. Whenever her rage boiled over, she'd stop to gather herself, then resume. Bit by bit, she whittled into the wall.

Then, abruptly, her chisel drove into open space. She caught the handle with a hiss, which—she realized—might not have been her, but the suction from the hole she'd just made. Along with the tangy smell of broken rock, she detected a different odor—something musty and dry.

She bound her tools to her wrists again, so that she couldn't drop them, and resumed work. One hammer blow at time, she elongated the breach. Her fingers swelled around her chisel—from smashing them or from blood flow, she wasn't sure, but she wasn't about to give up. It must have taken hours. The others kept tugging on the rope to check on her, and she'd return the signal, wishing she had some way of telling them what she was doing.

I made a hole.

It's the length of a forearm now.

Working on the second corner.

I smell treasure.

The stone is coming loose.

All at once, the basalt slab dropped away beneath her. Almost immediately, she heard the crash and splinter of wood, the skittering of gravel on a smooth floor. Then silence, except for her hard breathing.

She hauled on the rope again. As it let up, she slid out of the shaft and swung into the open, dangling by her ankle. Her outstretched fingertips found stone, and the rest of her body crumpled onto the blessed floor after them. She almost cried with relief as the blood flowed back into her curled legs. Once she was certain she could move without passing out, she pushed herself to a kneeling position.

"I made it," she murmured. She raised her head and shouted toward the surface, "I made it!" She wasn't certain anyone had heard her until she caught the sound of wood bouncing and clattering down the shaft. She scuttled backward just in time for a torch to land where she'd been kneeling. A flintstone skipped off the floor just afterward. She groped around, cursing, until she found the thing.

At the first strike, the chamber briefly lit up bright as day. The darkness returned, blacker than before, but her second strike banished it.

Her breath caught. She began to stand, only to find herself unable to.

Riches. Riches beyond counting, comprehension, or imagination.

She sank down on her haunches again, dazed and trembling.

From far, far above, Pisaqar's voice drifted down the shaft, the syllables drawn out to help her understand through the echo. "Amani! What do you see?"

She couldn't find the strength to call back. To herself, she whispered, "Wonderful things."

A COPIOUS BOUNTY

"WHAT DID SHE say?" Tariq asked.

Yesbokhe lifted his ear from the hole with a broad smile. He clasped his hands together in triumph.

The group burst into cheers and dancing. Tariq narrowly dodged a rib-cracking hug from Qorobar.

Pisaqar asked, "Did she say anything else?"

The scout shook his head.

Tariq said in earnest, "Is she alright? Did she sound hurt?"

He shook his head.

Tariq turned to the captain. "When we get back to Napata, I want to swap him for somebody who talks."

Pisaqar smiled at him. For the first time since Jerusalem, there was surety in his eyes—the sense that there truly was some justice in the world, and they were its beneficiaries. Pisaqar grasped his wrist. Just as he released him, he turned Tariq's palm over. The skin was red-raw, testament to the death grip he had kept on the rope the entire day.

"She'd be glad to hear how concerned you were," Pisaqar told him.

Tariq laughed. "But she'll also make fun of me till the day

I die, and in the next world too."

"The rope! Many tugs!" Nawidemaq's announcement drew a hush over them all. Amani wanted them to pull her out.

They hurried back to their positions and began to haul in unison, only to stumble back on the first pull. The acolyte swore. "There's no weight to it! The knot must have come off her."

"Keep pulling," Pisaqar ordered. He'd recognized something they hadn't. As the coils of rope grew into a heap, it became evident: there was a metallic thudding coming from the hole. It took a stunningly brief amount of time to get to the end of two hundred cubits of rope, making the day's effort seem an insult. But the thing tied to the end gave meaning to Amani's struggle.

It was a tall scepter plated in gold from its jeweled pommel to its spade-like head. Its ribbed handle was etched with miniscule hieroglyphs whose meaning escaped Tariq completely, while the head depicted a mythical scene featuring Osiris and a cadre of Anubis warriors. Though he was no craftsman, Tariq could appreciate artisanship when he saw it, and this was quality beyond anything he'd encountered throughout his travels. The artifact gleamed blindingly in sunlight that hadn't touched it in four hundred years.

Kalab's trembling hands hovered over the staff. "A *sekhem*! Borne by a pharaoh and imbued with the power of Osiris! She chose this out of all the treasure surrounding her. It can only be a sign of favor."

Pisaqar held it out to him. "Then it should be yours, Kalab. Such a blessed thing belongs in the hands of a priest." Kalab took the sekhem with reverence he'd never have displayed just weeks before.

They tied a basket to the rope and fed it back into the hole, weighed down with a rock to ease its transit. When Amani sent it back up, she'd packed it with statuettes—female figures each about a cubit tall, carefully painted in lifelike colors with their headdresses inlaid with silver.

"Lebanese cedar," said Tariq, rapping a knuckle against one. "You won't find this stuff anywhere these days. Priceless."

Nibamon hissed, "Don't abuse them like that! These are *ushabti*! They're meant to serve you in the afterlife."

"Eh? How?" Qorobar turned his own ushabti in his hands.

"They're servants. They'll cook for you. Sweep your house. Tend your fields."

The big man's confusion became a slow smile. "I get fields?"

"That's right. Everyone does. And an ushabti will take care of them for you. Happy to do it. Look at the way she smiles!"

Qorobar patted his ushabti's head. "Nice to meet you, too."

The bonanza had barely started. Amani sent up treasure after treasure, each more stunning than the last. Ramesses must have expected to encounter some old foes in the next life, because he'd taken an arsenal to his rest—swords, khopeshes, and axes. They were all forged of the finest copper, gone green with age. Their handles were made from alternating bands of ebony and ivory, and their pommels were nuggets of solid gold. Even more exciting for the Kushite men were the bows, dozens of the things—composite bows made of layers of laminated wood, with golden handles and horns. Anyone in Kush would pay a lifetime's wages for one of these. A prospective buyer might even get a few ivory-headed arrows as part of the bargain; there were plenty to spare.

There were jars of perfumes and spices whose scents baffled the mercenaries and the Israelite both, despite all their travels. There were polished chests limned in electrum, themselves works of art. Some contained intricately worked sets of jewelry—rings, necklaces, armbands, bracelets, crowns. It seemed Ramesses' lust for fine things outstripped his artisans' ability to produce them, because many other chests were merely stuffed with tiny bars of gold and silver, or precious stones that hadn't found a setting. Clearly, the pharaoh had expected courtly female company in the next life, because he'd packed dresses of fine white linen and golden fishnet, a frankly ludicrous number of wigs, and enough kohl to blacken Sneferu's pyramids.

As the sun set and the night deepened, Eleazar gave a cry. Alarmed, Tariq and the rest rushed to the cart where he'd been sitting. The Israelite was clutching an amulet the size of two spread palms. Its stippled golden surface glittered white in the moonlight. The man was babbling, seamlessly transitioning between Akkadian and Hebrew.

Pisaqar shook him. "What is the matter? You are frightening the men."

Eleazar remembered himself and spoke Egyptian. "It is just as Isaiah told me. This treasure—it was taken from Israel! Look at this script." He held up the amulet. "All in Hebrew!"

Tariq rolled his eyes. "It's a good ploy, Eleazar, but everyone knows where the pharaohs get their gold from: Kush. You don't see any of *us* scheming for a bigger share."

Eleazar's excitement soured. "I am not *scheming*. I am telling you that this pharaoh took from my people. Who is to say how many of these baubles were forged from Israelite gold?"

"What would it matter?" Qorobar said. "That's what money does. It changes hands. We're taking from Ramesses. Ramesses took from the Israelites. The Israelites took from whoever. Back it goes, all the way to the beginning of everything. There's no such thing as thieving. Everyone's just trying to get their shit back."

Kalab leaned into the cart and pulled out a clay jar. "Not everyone, Qorobar. Look at the name on this vessel."

"You know damn bloody well I can't read."

"It says, 'Usermaatre Setepenre.' Do you know that name?"

Pisaqar took the jar from him with careful hands. "*The* Ramesses. Second of His Name. Ramesses the Great." Disbelief clouded his words. "The Robber Pharaoh stole from his own forefather, the very best among them. What foul audacity!"

Kalab nodded. "None of this treasure belongs to the Robber Pharaoh. The walls in that tomb chronicle times of pestilence, famine, and war. Maybe the inscriptions are accurate, and Ramesses truly worked to rid Egypt of its troubles. But the workmen entombed in that secondary chamber? Stolen trinkets like these?" He indicated a jar, inscribed with the name of a different king. "These things tell another story. They tell us that this pharaoh spent his reign exploiting Egypt's troubles to rob the land. I would bet my share that this Israelite amulet came from some other pharaoh's pillage. The same goes for every scrap of treasure, right down to his royal headdress. He snatched it all from other tombs. He only bothered to scratch out the former owners' names and replace them with his own."

"Robber Pharaoh, indeed," said Pisaqar. "Then let us balance the scales. Eleazar, any item that bears the mark of your people will be yours to keep. What else would you bid of us?"

Eleazar bowed gratefully, still clutching his amulet. "I would like to make a gift of a lamb."

The basket swung out of the shaft and thumped Amani on the head, jolting her at the precise moment that her nodding had transitioned to a doze.

"Damn it!" She rubbed her head as she checked the basket. Along with the usual bread and beer was a bundle of red-soaked cloth. She unwrapped it quizzically to find a lamb shank, still seeping blood. She yelled at the ceiling, "You could have cooked it first, you bastards!"

A voice drifted down in reply, distorted by echoes. She had to demand it repeat itself several times before she could make it out. "The jug!"

"Huh." The nearest jug to hand was the one they'd sent down. She turned it over and found a symbol etched roughly on its side. A tree? Upside-down spider? It didn't mean anything to her. Shrugging, she unstoppered the jug to take a swig, but spat as the liquid inside touched her lips. More blood! In a fit of disgusted rage, she very nearly flung the thing away. Then another shout came.

"Paint the mark!"

"Oh, shit on that," she grumbled. "Is this honestly the time?" She looked around in hopeless aggravation.

She stood at the bottom point of an inverted pyramid, its four walls sloping away from her and carved into broad steps, all of which were cluttered with artifacts she'd barely begun to sample. For Amun's sake, there was an actual *chariot* stuffed into a corner. She hadn't started to figure out how to get that out of here. Because first, there were all the treasure chests, pipes, staffs, baskets, bowls, shields, sandals, chairs... All that and more, and she hadn't even cracked open Ramesses' sarcophagus yet. The gargantuan thing was set into a recessed alcove opposite a plain door, which presumably led back to some part of the tomb complex. But that was an assumption she wasn't in the mood to test. Ramesses had played enough tricks on them already.

That left the star shaft as the only way out. Even working at a toad's pace, she would soon run out of items that would fit through. She'd have to start smashing things before long. A shame—but gold was gold.

Might as well get started.

She waded toward the enormous sarcophagus to the racket of smashing porcelain and splitting cedarwood. Her foot nudged metal, which she discovered to be some sort of many-pronged lantern. Recognizing its shape, she whisked it up. She held it beside the painted jug the others had sent down. Identical. Not a tree, then.

"Pretty. I'll keep you."

Reaching the sarcophagus, she pressed the strange lantern up against the carved hieroglyphs, and with a deep breath, sucked a mouthful of blood from the jug. She blew a spray of lamb's blood all over the lantern, then a second mouthful, just to be sure. She moved the lantern aside and found a perfect outline.

"Not bad, Amani," she grinned through crimson teeth. Sucking at them, she went back and plopped the blood-spattered lantern into the basket, plus a few other random items near to hand. She gave the rope a couple of tugs. As the basket disappeared into the starry ceiling, she set her eyes on Ramesses' chariot with its sidings of woven gold thread. Delicate things, chariots.

She hefted a gilded mace.

BETRAYAL

ASHURIZKADAIN SAT ON his horse and listened as the struggle in the distant hut reached its crescendo. His guest was proving most reluctant to meet his acquaintance. The crash of pottery and furious bellowing gave credence to the fight the Egyptian was putting up.

A body blocked off the light of the tiny window and hung there, flinching, until it crumpled away. Then three figures emerged into the gathering dawn, one supported between the other two. Ashurizkadain frowned, wondering if the Egyptian guard had somehow managed to repel the Assyrian veterans. Then the fire in the hut died and the fourth man came out to join them.

"He fought, my lord," Nimrud informed him, though his limp told the story well enough.

He nodded. "Bring him. Leave one man hidden to watch the canyon. And cover our tracks as we leave. These Kushites have keen eyes."

They rode back to the house on the riverbank and tied their horses among the copse of date palms, their hooves stamping deep into the fresh graves there. The bloodied prisoner was dragged inside and flung on the dirt floor. They bound his wrists to his ankles. He made a last attempt to struggle, but a few swift kicks to the belly persuaded him to lie still while they tightened the bindings.

Nimrud set down a stool before him, where Ashurizkadain promptly sat. "I am the Flayer of Caleh," he said.

The Egyptian grinned at him through swelling eyes. "Good one. Wait. You're serious! Nice to meet you, Cally. I'm Rukhmire the Goat Tickler. Since we're giving ourselves shitty nicknames for some reason." His bravado won him the flat of a sword to the kneecap.

"You misjudge your situation, Rukhmire. I introduce myself as the Flayer because I am the one who skins my king's enemies. It is my profession. One could say it is my foremost talent."

"That's well and good, Cally, I just don't know what any of that has to do with me, a humble goat tickler."

Another sword slap, this time to the elbow. The Egyptian made his cry of pain into a high cackle.

Ashurizkadain made a conscious effort to relax his fists. "If you continue your mocking, I will be forced to gag you."

"That just means you've lost the argument," chuckled Rukhmire.

"Ah. I see. You believe I have brought you to this place for a conversation. I have not. We are about to have dealings, you and I. You will provide me with answers. The better they are, the less pain I inflict upon you. Perhaps I will even let you live, should you behave."

Rukhmire wriggled into a more comfortable position on his side. "Shitty way to do business," he panted. "Doubt I'll be a repeat customer."

Ashurizkadain stood and swaggered away. He thrust his hands into his thick felt gloves. He tapped on the tools spread in front of the fireplace, perusing his options. He returned to Rukhmire with a cluster of oval shells clacking on his open palm. Rukhmire gazed at them levelly, albeit with shallower breaths.

"Oyster shells," Ashurizkadain said. "Abominably crude, I must own. However, I have no qualms about damaging a hide so worthless as yours."

"That's a mean thing to say," Rukhmire said tightly.

"Indeed. As I am an honest man, I shall admit that you have angered me somewhat. Consider this your penance." At his nod, his men came forward and clasped the Egyptian in iron grips. Ashurizkadain knelt and guided the edge of the oyster shell against Rukhmire's shinbone, where the flesh was thin and the cut easiest.

"Wait!" The Egyptian shrunk beneath the shell's kiss. "You haven't even asked me a question yet!"

Ashurizkadain inclined his head. "Quite so." Then the cutting began.

Coarse tools produce inelegant results. Given the sad hut in which Rukhmire had lived much of his life, Ashurizkadain expected he had learned that lesson already. But he carved that same message into the man's legs with serrated shells—sawing, scraping, scooping. After an hour, Rukhmire's feet were hidden beneath bloody tatters of skin peeled from his lower legs.

Ashurizkadain removed his gloves and rinsed his hands in a bowl that Nimrud offered. He tossed his chin at his captive. Nimrud stooped and allowed him a gulp of the scarlet water. The Egyptian promptly spat it in his face.

Rukhmire turned his burning eyes on his tormentor. In a voice that warbled with dulling agony, he yelled, "You told me you were good at that, you lying heap of shit! Look at this mess!" He sank his head and wept soundlessly, his bound hands thumping the earthen floor.

"Now is the time for questions. Where in the valley is Pisaqar? What work has he undertaken there? How many men accompany him? Where is the boat they sailed down the river?"

"Cram your cock in an anthill," growled Rukhmire.

"I shall ask once more. After that, I shall finish with

your legs. Do not tempt me, Egyptian, or you may lose your manhood as well."

That, at least, persuaded Rukhmire not to blurt out whichever retort he thought wittiest.

Ashurizkadain repeated himself. "Where in the valley is—"

Hoofbeats sounded outside, cutting off his questions. The Assyrians drew their swords. There came a knock on the door. "My lord! Gallu returns from the canyon!"

The soldier came in, saluted, his eyes avoiding the quarter-flayed specimen curled on the floor. "I searched the hut more thoroughly, my lord. I felt this would be useful to you." He held out a straw doll and a tiny roll of cloth.

Rukhmire's breath caught as Ashurizkadain took it. "A girl's toy," mused Ashurizkadain. "How touching, Rukhmire. Were you fashioning a gift for your daughter?"

His eyes darted all over the room, anywhere but at the doll. "No. For my niece. She lives in Thebes. With my brother, Nodj."

"I admire your quick wit. Would that you were born Assyrian. A worthy servant you would have made. Alas. Nimrud?"

"I am yours to command, my lord."

"Take half the men and go to the village beneath the pass, the one we thought deserted. See if you might find a little girl there. Bring her."

"And if we encounter the Kushites?"

"See to it that you do not."

"Your will, my lord."

Ashurizkadain turned back to his captive as his second-in-command left with his party. The Egyptian was breathing hard, trembling but trying not to show it. Though his captors had been conversing in Akkadian, the context had been clear enough.

"I regret that a child must see her father in such a sorry state." Ashurizkadain paused. "Perhaps it would ease her woes to share in his suffering."

What little color remained in Rukhmire's face fled. "Please don't. Please leave her alone. Skin me the rest of the way if you want, just don't do anything to her. I'll answer your questions true."

"Hmm. Forgive my skepticism. What assurance can you give of your honesty?"

"You just threatened to skin my little girl alive in front of me! What more assurance could you need? Ask me your fucking questions! Just leave my family out of it! Please!"

"As you wish." He gestured to another of his men. "Tell them to sit on their horses for the moment." To Rukhmire, he said, "Your family will know nothing of this, so long as you keep your word. Let us begin again. What is Pisaqar doing in the Valley of the Kings?"

Senanmuht faced the other boat as it rowed closer. The oarsmen were off their pace, sloppy from fatigue. They had journeyed all the way from Memphis, after all, and Senanmuht more than suspected that his cousin had kept them at the gunwales the entire way.

Indeed, Khaemon looked every bit as frayed as Senanmuht felt. The fat nobleman paced the pavilion set on the back of his boat. Clearly he was worried, for it wasn't often that Khaemon troubled himself to move at all.

"Hail, dear cousin!" Senanmuht's deceptively light greeting carried across the water. He waved jauntily before returning to clasping his hands tightly behind his back.

Khaemon returned the wave. "Fond greetings to you, Senanmuht! Too long have we been parted!"

"I intended it to be longer still," he said under his breath. He cared nothing that the servants and eunuchs had likely heard. They said nothing. Their discretion could be counted on. Unlike Khaemon's. It was on account of their yapping that he had been forced off Pisaqar's scent, obliged to deal with this ludicrous distraction instead.

He turned to his boatmaster. "Draw up beside them. I do not trust their oarsmen not to sink us by mistake."

The boatmaster bowed and turned to his duties. The banks of oars swayed and fell immediately into the rhythm set by a beating drum.

In no time at all, the two sleek craft were lashed hull-to-hull in the middle of the river. A plank bridged the gap between them. Standing at its end, Senanmuht beckoned to his cousin.

"Come aboard, Khaemon. My servants have laid a feast to sate you after your long voyage."

Khaemon looked askance at the gangplank laid between the joined hulls, its narrowness quite at odds with his own considerable breadth. He chortled anxiously. "My deck is far more spacious. I would be glad to host instead, should you be gracious enough to—"

"I insist," Senanmuht interrupted. To his lack of surprise, several of Khaemon's servants whispered behind their hands. His own menials kept their peace, as *should* have been the way of things.

Realizing at last that no amount of pleasantries could rescue him, Khaemon had to comply. With the help of his gossiping servants, he waddled across the gangplank, his jowls quivering with each miniature step, his little hands bunched in his robe. He was sweating profusely by the time he stumbled onto Senanmuht's deck. He'd traveled all of five cubits.

Greedily, he snatched the goblet from an approaching servant and gulped down the wine.

"Forgive my thirst, cousin," he said between hard breaths. "I missed such good vintage. My own supply has run short."

I wonder why.

"Of course," Senanmuht said smoothly. He indicated his pavilion, where the table had been set—as promised—with pickled fish, onion bread, sugared dates, and naturally, more wine.

He watched his cousin gorge himself for a while, quietly amazed that the man had any appetite left. Surely he was aware of the circumstances under which he'd been called to the capital. His exhausted rowers, who watched them over their own weevily loaves of bread, had carried him south speedily enough. The importance of this meeting couldn't have been plainer. Yet Khaemon seemed in little mood to talk. He opened his mouth only to cram it with food and drink.

It was left to Senanmuht to begin their business. "Cousin. I have heard the most troubling rumors."

"Rumors?" Khaemon wiped his face with a cloth a servant girl held out to him. "I fear I have little notion of our conversation topic."

"I am no fool, Khaemon. Do not treat me as such. You know as well as I do who has drunk all your fine wine."

"It is no small matter, playing host for such a long time," Khaemon admitted sorrowfully.

"Self-pity does you little credit. Spare us both. Tell me what you've done. I require your honesty, cousin. Too much is at stake for you to keep playing at intrigue."

Khaemon was incredulous. "Dear Senanmuht! Fifty Assyrian swords, I kept beneath my roof. You cannot call such a number *play*!"

"And yet you behave like a child! How could you imagine you could hide away a whole company of foreign soldiers? Their horses, even! People see these things, Khaemon! They talk!"

Khaemon had gone from red to white. "My hand was forced. The Assyrian captain—Ashurizkadain, he is called—he demanded my hospitality."

"Then you should have rejected him! Your blunderings are known as far as Memphis! You have put our entire house at stake!"

"He threatened to reveal us," squealed his cousin.

Senanmuht scoffed at that. "To whom?"

"I don't know! He would have found a way! This Ashurizkadain, he does not make idle threats. I watched him... I..." Khaemon covered his eyes with a quivering hand. "He claimed he had proof enough to force the pharaoh's hand against us."

Senanmuht sat back, appalled at his own blood's stupidity. "Khaemon. You cannot have believed that Assyria would dispense with a crucial ally on a whim."

"You did not meet this Ashurizkadain. He does not threaten," Khaemon reiterated, "he makes promises."

"And in keeping them, he would squander a decade of cooperation between Assyria and Sais. To what end? Sennacherib cannot mean to conquer Egypt with a mere fifty men."

"The Assyrians didn't come to break the peace. They seek vengeance against one man. You know him well, cousin. He's the same one who hobbled you and killed our uncles." The table protested as Khaemon leaned on it, watching him with the fervency of one who thought he'd behaved rightly and couldn't understand why anyone would dare think otherwise. "It's true, cousin, we must wait some years longer before Egypt is given to us. But look to the meantime! Sennacherib's wishes have aligned with ours once again. We can finally be rid of that self-righteous mercenary. And at so little cost!"

Senanmuht chuckled hollowly. "So little."

"Yes! All that Ashurizkadain sought from us was shelter and information. Now he has both. He is gone from beneath my roof. The small danger has passed. And imagine! Soon, Pisaqar's wrinkled hide will be flapping from a column in Nineveh. What delicious justice that will be!"

And suddenly, all became clear to Senanmuht. The slaughtered soldiers in the Sinai, the horsemen on the Delta, the collapsed tavern in Memphis. All this time, he had been certain that Pisaqar was bent on *isfet*, seeking to undo the Divine Order that had betrayed him. "It was never you," he whispered.

"What did you say?"

He thought of the missive from the vault of Osiris. Two Kushite priests had visited there—to make offerings for the man they'd lost in Jerusalem, he'd felt certain before. But he had been mistaken.

Assyrian schemes had already met Saite ambition. The two factions had sealed their pact with the promise of gold. That of a long-dead pharaoh, to be precise.

And now, for no obvious reason, Pisaqar was in Thebes. No, not *in* the city. Across the river. With his Assyrian hunters homing in on his scent.

"Cousin?"

Senanmuht was jolted out of his thoughts. He understood what he needed to do. But first, he would need to conclude this sordid business.

"I apologize, Khaemon. You've given me much to consider. Of course, I was wrong to worry." He looked to a servant, who scurried forward with a fresh jug balanced in his hands. "The danger is past, and Pisaqar will soon be dead."

"Butchered," smiled Khaemon. He licked his lips as the perspiring servant filled his goblet to the rim.

"Indeed. Let us drink to it." Senanmuht reached for his wine, but Khaemon was well into the act of guzzling his down. He thumped the empty goblet on the table. He belched and dabbed at his mouth. He paused. Quizzically, he looked at his napkin, the cloth stained so oddly with two different shades of bright red. He burped again, this time with a little spatter of blood.

He looked to Senanmuht with huge eyes. They'd already taken on a glassy sheen. "Senanmuht. What...?" His pupils rolled upward. He slid off his chair, knocking a bowl from the table as he toppled. He wallowed on the deck amid the spilled dates, his fingers curled, his limbs convulsing, foaming pink at the mouth.

"I am sorry, beloved Khaemon," Senanmuht said sincerely. He watched as his cousin lay dying, hearing but not acknowledging the screams of Khaemon's servants as his oarsmen hopped the gap and started with their knives. "It's not that you acted wrongly. But the *timing*." He shook his head. "If we are to free Egypt from the Kushite usurpers, we must lay our plans with exceeding care. Not jump every time the Assyrians tug the leash. I am afraid that Taharqa's cursed peace has changed everything. We must start anew."

He stood up, wiping his hands, though he hadn't touched food or drink. He knelt at Khaemon's side, and just as the man breathed his last, whispered into his ear, "We Saites will rule Egypt in the end. I swear before the gods. Tell them that when you meet them."

His loyal servants watched him expectantly from decks awash with blood. All was quiet except for the river lapping on the joined hulls.

"Deal with them as traitors," he commanded. "Dump the bodies in the shallows for the crocodiles to find. Leave my cousin where he lies." He regarded the fat corpse sadly, knowing full well that poor Khaemon would never glimpse the afterlife. Taharqa would demand proof that the treachery had been smashed. After that, Khaemon's body would suffer the fate of all ranking traitors: to be dismembered and burnt, scouring the afterlife of his *ka*'s presence. A fate worse than death.

But Sais would endure.

THE FULL FLAME IN FRONT OF THEM

"THE GUARDIAN IS gone."

Yesbokhe's news brought the work to a halt. The Desert Mice looked at their panting scout, their alarm deepening as the implications of the news unfolded in their minds.

Pisaqar gave them no time to linger. "Draw her out," he commanded, pointing to the star shaft. As they hastened to obey, he told Yesbokhe, "See to his family. Return immediately if anything seems amiss." The scout vanished into the darkness with his sandals flapping.

That their endeavors would go unnoticed had only ever been a faint possibility, but Pisaqar had hoped that by winning the valley's guardian to his side, he could at least expect to plunder the tomb at some leisure. Indeed, Yesbokhe had gone to Rukhmire's hut three times in as many days, and each time the guardian had been dutifully sitting at his post. The last time he had been seen was at sunset. Meaning that sometime in the night, Rukhmire had left.

Pisaqar scanned the early morning darkness. Ra's chariot would come soon, heralding a bloody day.

Nibamon came up beside him. "He could have run off. Maybe he had second thoughts," he posited in a surge of misplaced optimism.

"That would have been a foolish choice. Rukhmire is no fool."

The foreman nodded glumly. Rukhmire would have understood that condemning the Desert Mice would invite them to do the same for him. "He didn't leave by choice, then. Could it be Taharqa?"

"I do not know."

"The priests?" Nibamon touched his face reflexively.

"I do not know."

"What do we do?"

"There is no time to carry all this down to the valley. We must take what we can and flee."

Presently, Amani emerged from the hole, clinging to the rope. The Mice tugged her free and stood her up, dusting off her clothes as she coughed.

The captain pointed to the heap of treasure. "Put it all back. Then seal the shaft."

With pained expressions, the mercenaries set about the task. They poured antiquities into the opening by the armful. Tariq audibly groaned as he emptied out a sack of rubies. A pile of golden plates followed, which promptly got stuck, obliging Qorobar to shunt them free using an ornate elephant tusk. Back to the burial chamber the pharaoh's treasure went, at such length and volume that Pisaqar wouldn't have been overly surprised if Ramesses woke and roared for quiet.

When it was done, they rebuilt the cairn above the star shaft and piled it over with as much loose dirt and rock as they could gather. Dejectedly, the sweating group tramped down the hill into the Valley of the Kings.

Nawidemaq was sitting on the cart, humming to his bull and rummaging with minimal interest through the artifacts they'd gathered so far. He sprang up at the group's approach. "Danger?" he called.

"Yes. Make ready to move," Pisaqar answered. As the medicine man set about yoking the Apis, the rest squeezed into the alcove of the decoy tomb.

Their kit was in the first tunnel where they'd left it. Lit by dancing torchlight and under the empty stares of the hieroglyph figures on the walls, the Desert Mice prepared for battle.

For Pisaqar, Ramesses' burial chamber had yielded a useful upgrade: a coat of bronze scales. The scales were finely made, as befitted a pharaoh, with ridges running down the center of each to keep them from jostling out of alignment. Many centuries had rotted away the original threads, but Senet had sewn them back together in the Assyrian style using Kalab's armor as a model. The long sleeves rustled reassuringly as Pisaqar slid into the coat. Silently, he thanked the woman for her gift and sent Isis a prayer on her behalf.

Kalab came over and helped cinch his belt and arm straps until the armor lay snug against the thick linen shirt beneath. Pisaqar returned the favor. Kalab's scales were of Assyrian manufacture: ovular, remarkably uniform in size, of rougher make than Pisaqar's—signs of mass production. He supplemented the short sleeves with hard leather bracers. He wore a funnel-shaped Assyrian helmet and offered a spare to Pisaqar, which he declined. If his warriors were destined to fight today, they would do so better with the unmistakable sight of their leader in their midst.

"Then perhaps you'll accept this," Kalab said, his voice catching as he held out a khopesh in both hands. Pisaqar recognized Ermun's weapon from its wire-wound grip. He took it gently, tested the balance, and found the blade end heavy. Less a sword than an axe, he was reminded—but surely an advantage against a man with a shield. And the weight alone meant that even a cut to an armored neck would kill.

Kalab stepped back, nodding approvingly. "He'd have wanted you to wield it."

Pisaqar smiled. He had never been much for personal swords. To him, weapons were meant as tools, and anything beyond seemed an expression of vanity. But here, he would make an exception. "For Ermun." For good measure, he tucked a long dagger into his belt.

The others were finishing their own preparations. Eleazar had kept the Assyrian panoply to which he was accustomed: padded blue tunic, blackened scales, iron sword, and a round cedarwood shield. Tariq had encased his breast in hardened leather bands. He wore a stabbing sword at his waist and a longbow slung across his back. Amani carried her ever-sharp blackstone dagger as well as her sling, with which she was an undisputed artist. Qorobar had liberated a stunning axe head from the tomb, plated in electrum that glowed a foreboding crimson in the torchlight. He'd hafted it to a metal-cored grip of his own commission, since an ordinary haft couldn't have matched his strength and size. A richly decorated golden collar covered his shoulders and upper breast, the only protection he'd troubled to wear. Likely he'd meant the piece to accentuate his enormity rather than offer much defense. And Nibamon—the poor fellow knew nothing of war—had tried to don Ermun's old armor. The vest visibly strained to encompass his pot belly. Someone had wisely given him a spear and wicker shield: the ideal kit for an amateur.

Soon, Yesbokhe had slid into the tunnel. He shook his head sadly; Senet and the children were gone, too. He went to comfort Nibamon, his prized longbow in hand. From horn to horn, it was very nearly as tall as he was. None but he and Qorobar could have hoped to draw the string fully. He'd filled his quiver with Ramesses' arrows, though he'd meticulously re-fletched them to his own exacting standards.

Reedy-limbed Nawidemaq followed him down, his holy staff bouncing against the ladder rungs. His war preparations amounted to squatting, unrolling a clean cloth, and praying over a metal shard of unknown provenance. Over his mutterings, one could hear the white bull braying near the entrance.

The Desert Mice gathered around their medicine man. Kalab raised a chant to Amun, which drifted eerily down the tomb and came echoing back, multiplying upon itself. They listened to the holy men pray, adding silent entreaties of their own.

"It's going to be a hard day," Qorobar grumbled. Their collective silence passed for affirmation.

Pisaqar surveyed his mismatched band, each ready to fight and die for the other. There were no wet eyes to be seen. A hard day indeed.

"Let us face it together."

As Nawidemaq folded his prayer cloth away, Pisaqar cast one last look down the tunnel into the tomb that had very nearly become his own. Somewhere in that hideous dark, he imagined the sight of unearthly fire—and silhouetted against it, an inhumanly thin form, its pointed ears grazing the hieroglyphs on the ceiling, its clawed fingers atwitch, its eyes glowing with baleful fire of their own. For but a flicker of an instant, the thing locked gazes with Pisaqar. And now, as he had before, the captain could only flee from death's clutches, exchanging one doom for another.

"Together," he repeated, turning away.

THE FALLING RAIN

YESBOKHE DIDN'T LIKE the look of the heights. This bothered him, because the rocky crags had given him no tangible reason to suspect ill of them. Not on the three other trips they'd made during the evening, not on this one. The heights stood tranquil in the morning sun, soundless and still.

By contrast, the trundling cart raised an awful clamor. Its overladen axle squealed while its studded wheels clattered on the rough trail. The other mercenaries were straining at the tailgate or pushing hard on the spokes, themselves burdened down with packs of treasure. Yesbokhe pitied his flagging friends—Amani especially. The poor girl had spent many days in that burial chamber, with no opportunity to rest once they'd pulled her out. But still, she craned her head alertly toward the heights.

Pisaqar had made the correct decision when he'd ordered them to abandon the venture. Rukhmire had gone. Senet, too, and the children. No one knew exactly when or why, not even Nibamon. The foreman was sick with worry. As far as anyone could fathom, there were only two explanations for the family's disappearance: they'd left, or they'd been taken. Neither possibility boded well.

So the captain had given his command: it was time to go home. Amani had been hauled free, the star shaft covered up, the tomb entrance concealed. Once they made it to the river, they were to pack their loot onto Pepy's boat and sail south as fast as the winds would carry them.

Yesbokhe set the pace for the cart, his bow nocked, his gaze roving along the quiet crags high above. Behind him, the bull bayed—almost at the same time that a small stone bounced, unbidden, from the top of the valley. Yesbokhe's grip on his bow tightened. He raised the weapon, scanning the hills. He sniffed. There was a new scent tinging the still air, one he couldn't quite place. One that didn't belong.

His sense of foreboding swelled into menace.

"Trouble, Yesbokhe?" called Pisaqar.

He held his arrow nocked and traced its point along the heights.

The motion was all that saved him.

Something came hurtling out of the sun and slammed into his bow. The weapon spun from his hand, simultaneously folded in twain, then exploded into splinters under the strain of its heavy bowstring. The scout stumbled back. His bow hand was numb and bleeding. His faithful longbow lay shattered at his feet.

"Arrows!" he cried, not that there was any need. Shafts were whistling through the air all around the group, plunging into the towering cargo, snapping on the rocky ground. Seasoned veterans, the Desert Mice scattered, dumping their packs as they ran. Eleazar retained enough soldierly instinct to grab a cringing Nibamon and drag him into cover behind the cart, which visibly shuddered beneath the impacts of many arrows.

Pisaqar was the first to realize what was happening. "They aim for the bull! Protect him!" No sooner had he spoken than an arrow sank deep into the poor animal's shoulder. It convulsed, baying.

Yesbokhe sprinted through the hail of arrows and skidded behind the cart. He climbed the tailgate, started to sift through the baskets of priceless oddities. Ushabti and scarabs and gold tubules scattered on the ground before Nibamon's and Eleazar's wide eyes.

"What are you doing?"

Even in peril, words eluded him. Rather than try to explain, he kept hurling things out of his way. At the bottom of the cargo bed, he found what he'd been looking for. He pried out a shield—much more decorative than practical—and tossed it to Eleazar. "The bull! Go!"

Eleazar caught it. He swung over the side of the cart and rushed to the thrashing bull's side, angling the shield upward. The thought occurred to Yesbokhe that none of them had given the Israelite much credit for bravery. Nor Nibamon. The potbellied foreman knew nothing of combat, but he reached for the next shield all the same, with no mind paid to his own trembling. Amani came up, her useless sling tucked into her rope belt, and grabbed two more—one for her, and one for Nawidemaq, who was covering the white Apis's head with his own body.

With no more shields left, Yesbokhe found a weapon for himself: one of Ramesses' bows, a masterpiece of ivory and cedar and sinew, with horns of shining bronze. It rebelled as he tried to string it with one of his spares from Jerusalem, as if sensing that he was mating it with a thing of Assyrian manufacture. Finally, the weapon bent to his will and allowed itself to be strung. Then Yesbokhe rushed out to even the fight.

The barrage continued unabated. Arrows were making a pincushion of the cart. Surely the assailants would have succeeded in killing the bull if not for the shields now arrayed before it. But the enemy archers were well concealed in the morning shadows, and the Kushites' marksmanship counted for nothing against targets they could not see.

"Make for the canyon!" Pisaqar yelled. He pointed to the black canyon mouth. The medicine man jabbered encouragement to his bull and the cart lurched into motion. But Yesbokhe understood that the distance was too great, the ambush too well laid. His friends wouldn't make it there alive.

He scurried up to the half-buried tomb alcove where Pisaqar and Tariq had taken cover, harried the whole way by shrieking arrows. They stood and loosed arrows of their own, apparently at random.

"Keep shooting!" he told them. They stared at him, open-mouthed, as he rushed past and went up the slope at a sprint, his blue-stained leopard-skin cloak flying.

"Amun protect you, Yesbokhe," called the captain as he strung his next arrow.

Yesbokhe scaled the hill without losing pace. At first, arrows thudded into the dirt around his searing legs, but they soon abated. As he reached the crest and looked back, he saw why. Pisaqar had ordered the Desert Mice into a tight cluster around the cart, a target too tempting for the enemy to pass up. He was buying Yesbokhe time to act. The cart provided bare cover for Pisaqar, Tariq, Qorobar, and Kalab, and the shield wall protecting the bull could only hold for a time.

Yesbokhe ran along the rocky hillcrest, seeking targets. The sun was out of his eyes now, and at last, he could resolve the shapes of men kneeling amid the rocks. Men wearing blue tunics and funnel helmets. He realized with a chilling shock that he'd seen those recurve bows before—on the banks of the Delta outside Sena, and before that, at Jerusalem.

"Assyrians!" He made the hissed word into an oath.

There was no time to ponder the revelation. He hauled on his empty bowstring to test its draw, found it light. The wind was south and east, toward the enemy. That would speed his arrow's flight, as would the bone-dry air of the valley.

He nocked an arrow, laid its point on an Assyrian's heart. Took a deep breath. Drew the string to his ear. Lifted his aim. Released string and breath, both at once. The arrow arced across the heights. With a high-pitched cry, the Assyrian collapsed, the arrow rammed to its fletchings in his groin.

Yesbokhe cursed himself for a dolt as he drew a fresh arrow. His bow had been made for a taller man.

He accounted for the shallow draw with his next shot. This time he managed to score a clean piercing through a second Assyrian's lungs. A good kill.

He was just lining up another shot when the enemy remembered him. Their return arrows spanked off the rocks. One whizzed past his left ear. His arrows jostled in their quiver as it shaved through them. The burst of feathers haloing his head told him that he'd just been deprived of several arrows.

He kept moving, pausing only to loose his bow. His enemies reminded him that though they were no artists, they were professionals. They did not make his work easy. Whenever he slowed, they anticipated him and ducked out of sight. Their return shots came in disciplined volleys that forced him to shrink into cover. Four archers, he counted. A chance shot took one Assyrian in the eye as he peered from his hiding place. The remaining three ought to have cut their losses and retreated. Reasonable men would have. Instead, these Assyrians showed what unreasonable men could do.

Stubbornly, they held their ground against the one-man onslaught. Their volleys came at a frenzied rate. Yesbokhe curled into a divot while the shafts whistled overhead. When the flow abated, he stood to resume his advance. An Assyrian arrow smashed into the crook of his arm and nailed his elbow to his side. He gasped, more surprised than hurt—although the upwelling of pain in his side told him that his troubles had barely begun. His bow fell from his numbing fingers. He sank to the ground atop it, his whole left side a mass of crawling agony. Through shimmering eyes, he saw blood gathering in the crease where his arm and his side had joined.

He'd always thought that when the moment came, he'd come up with something profound to say. That he'd at last find the words. But really, all he could think of was how much dying fucking hurt.

He heard an almighty bellow, an ululation that seemed to fill the gap between the hills. Its source: Qorobar. The hulking man had climbed the opposite slope, axe in hand, only to find the canyon blocking the way to his quarry. But against his berserk wrath, it posed little obstacle. He launched across the gap. His feet found the steep wall opposite. He nearly lost his balance on it, but instead he clambered and scuffed his way upward by sheer force of will. He went vaulting over the lip with his great axe raised and his bloodshot eyes fixed murderously on the nest of Assyrian archers. Their collective shriek matched his own until he silenced them, one at a time. He made gory chunks of them all and kicked their hewn remains down the hill, leaving blood spattered trails beneath the ledge where they'd perched.

Yesbokhe looked on with detached interest until a fit of coughing overwhelmed him. The convulsions were agony. It felt as if the arrow point was drilling deeper into his lung with every shudder. The harder he tried to stifle the coughing, the more violent they became. A black ring constricted the edges of his vision. It swelled until, at last, he fell into blissful unconsciousness. There, Kasaqa found him.

"There you are, my quiet husband. Oh, you look dreadful."

"I fell," he said. "But look. I brought you a present." He looked around for the irtyu fabric. He was certain he'd left it nearby.

"Another one? Yesbokhe, please. I wish only for you. You won't leave me again, will you?"

"It's here somewhere."

"I've been alone for so long. I beg you."

"Yes, I promise. But wait until you see it. Such a lovely blue."

Kasaqa smiled ruefully. "You do promise?"

"Forever," he swore.

She reached for him. "Yesbokhe."

"I'm here."

"Yesbokhe."

"Yesbokhe!"

He woke unwillingly to find Pisaqar at his side, shaking him. The captain inspected his wound, his face writ with concern. "The injury is not very bad. It is one of those bleeders." His vise grip on Yesbokhe's upper arm belied the flippant words. "Kalab! Come quickly!"

"She likes bright colors," he rasped. His throat was terribly dry.

"What?" The captain frowned at him. "Who does?"

"Kasaqa. Bring her something bright."

Pisaqar patted his cheek. "I will, my friend. Here." He opened a waterskin and held it to Yesbokhe's mouth.

He drank gratefully. The water brought some measure of clarity. "Did they get anyone else?"

Pisaqar squeezed the wound. "No. You saved us all, my friend. Kalab!"

"They are Assyrians. The same ones from Sena."

Pisaqar absorbed the news. "Then Taharqa was never after us. It was Assyria all along." He shut his eyes. "Rukhmire. Senet. The children. Amun have mercy."

They'd just finished loading Yesbokhe's pallid form onto the cart when Tariq raised the alarm. "Hooves behind us! Among the tombs!"

Pisaqar swore to himself as the first horses rounded the bend. Two men sat on each mount, one wielding a bow, the other holding both shield and reins. The Assyrians made no pretense of their identity any longer. They openly displayed their blue tunics and blackened copper armor. They wanted the Kushites to know who had come for them. That this would be a fight to the finish.

So be it, Pisaqar decided. If he was destined to die today, he was going to make his enemy's task as arduous as possible.

"Qorobar!"

The big man peeked over the lip of the canyon. Steam from the massacred archers' corpses haloed his head. "I'm here, Captain!"

"Hinder their path! Use whatever you can find!" He turned to Eleazar and Nibamon. "Can you use a bow?"

They shook their heads. Pisaqar passed them each a bow regardless. The wood still glistened with the blood of their former owners. "Tariq, teach them."

Yesbokhe gasped with pain as he propped himself sitting. "No, I will."

"Very well. Nawidemaq, get the cart moving."

The medicine man patted his bull, whose shoulder oozed bright red. "Forgive me, my friend." He hauled on its lead, and with a groan, the animal lurched forward. Nibamon and Eleazar jogged behind the bouncing cart, fumbling with their bows under Yesbokhe's hurried instructions. Meanwhile, behind them, an Assyrian corpse careened to the canyon floor and landed with a splat. Stones large and small thudded down around it amid showers of gravel. It wasn't much, but then, it didn't take much to give a horse second thoughts about its footing.

The Assyrians were content to keep their distance, at least for the moment. The twisting canyon soon blocked the line of waiting cavalry from view.

As the cart rumbled past Rukhmire's deserted hut, Qorobar slid down the slope to rejoin them. "Bad news," he informed Pisaqar. "More cavalry to either side. Two groups of five horses, give or take. And the same number behind us in the valley. There's two men riding each horse."

"How far are the new groups?"

"Just outside our range and holding. Scared of our arrows, I reckon."

"I fear otherwise," said Pisaqar, just as Tariq came up to them.

"What's the plan?" he asked in earnest.

It was in moments like these that the weight of leadership rested heaviest. The Assyrians had left him but one course. What lay at its end was at best uncertain—except that he would need to spend more lives to get there. Some of those eyes staring at him, full of tension and hope, would never look upon another dawn. Nothing he did would change what was about to happen. All he could do was lead them in false confidence and pray the gods were good.

"Pisaqar?"

"They want us alive, these Assyrians. They would have killed us already if they meant to. They have the numbers for it. They wish to scatter us in panic. We will be easier to capture if we run away. We must stay together no matter what they do. The plan is the same as before: we make for the river. Drive back any horses that come near. Conserve what arrows you can."

Yesbokhe said, "The Assyrians shoot quickly. They do not trouble to save arrows."

"Then I can gather up the enemy arrows that land nearby," Amani volunteered. "I don't have the strength to draw a longbow regardless."

"Good," said the captain. "We will need every spare shot for our escape. Once the enemy realizes he cannot take us, he will try to kill us instead."

Heads nodded. Tariq asked, "Do we dump the load, to speed up the cart?"

Pisaqar looked at the bull. It plodded along steadily, scarcely seeming to notice its wounds. "Nawidemaq, how does the animal fare?"

"Mushtun, mover of mountains, imbues my friend with mighty strength," Nawidemaq chittered confidently.

"To the river, then. Bows at the ready."

As they rattled down the gentle slope, the Assyrians followed. The rearguard drew out of the canyon at a walk, their surefooted warhorses untroubled by the obstacles Qorobar had hurled into their path. On either side, palls of stirred dust announced the approach of the Assyrian wings. Bronze helmets and armor shone in the morning sun.

"They got themselves all polished up just for us," said Tariq with a forced laugh. "Isn't that just fucking touching?"

The Assyrian riders stooped to allow their archers their shots. Bows sprang. Arrows arced into the air, their points catching the morning light as they gained height. The hissing shafts plummeted into the rocky earth with sharp *crack*s.

Nibamon peeked over the side of the cart as Amani sprinted out to grab the fallen arrows. "Those didn't even come close!"

"Those were their ranging shots," Pisaqar told him.

"We should shoot back!"

"Save your arrows. You as well, Eleazar." He raised his voice. "Mice, shots from the breast."

His men obeyed at once. Their return arrows sailed toward the enemy, wriggling like fish. They fell well short, a fact Nibamon observed with no shortage of oaths. He fell silent in horror as the Assyrian riders kicked their horses in closer, the archers seated behind them already stringing their next volleys. Another enemy salvo came over, this time straddling the cart.

Pisaqar rose from his crouch. "Now from the ear! The group on the left! Take them!" He nocked his own arrow and drew in tandem with his Kushite brothers, the Israelite and Egyptian scrambling to do the same. The longbows clattered in unison. This time their arrows didn't waggle. They sped straight and true, plunging into the thicket of unsuspecting Assyrian cavalry. A horse convulsed and fell, throwing its riders to the dirt where they lay twisting in agony. Those remaining, realizing they'd been fooled, hauled the reins and retreated to a safer distance. The Desert Mice loosed again at the other groups in turn. They succeeded in dropping another horse and sticking several riders through. The others were obliged to fall back.

"A clever ruse," the Israelite said.

"Good soldiers, these Assyrians. They will not let their confidence get the best of them a second time." Pisaqar watched a wounded horse thrash on the hard ground. Its struggles only succeeding in driving the pair of stuck arrows deeper into its ribs. He could hear its awful squeals even from this great distance. The nearby horsemen made no effort to end the poor creature's suffering. Assyrians spared no thought for such things. Pisaqar's sole comfort was knowing he had taken at least two enemy bows out of the fight.

Half a league onward, the glittering curve of the Nile beckoned. The Assyrians quickly made it clear that they intended to fight the Kushites for every cubit. "Pick your shots!" Pisaqar urged as the cavalry squadrons closed in once more. They advanced in bursts, pushing forward, then wheeling around and falling back again. When flights of arrows came the Assyrians' way, they weaved madly. They reminded Pisaqar of ants who'd caught the scent of fruit, scurrying to and fro across a tabletop. Even the sound of their arrows in flight had an insect-like quality. They buzzed in ever nearer as the Assyrians haltingly closed the distance. Just as their slain archers had done at the valley mouth, they aimed for Nawidemaq's bull.

Amani hampered their efforts. Darting and leaping, she deftly caught Assyrian arrows on one of Ramesses' ornate shields, which gonged under each impact. Between salvoes, she scurried into the open, plucked arrows from the dirt, and gave them to her brothers. Then they returned them to the enemy at speed.

Pisaqar directed their aim. Whenever a group of horsemen wandered too close, they were punished with a burst of arrows. More often than not, the enemy shield bearers ably blocked in the midst of steering their mounts. Then they would stoop to allow their archers to shoot back. Had the stakes not been everything, their consummate skill would have been admirable. Only occasionally did an arrow get past their guard to fell archer or rider. Pisaqar and his men were all fine archers, but Yesbokhe's mastery of the bow had no equal, and was sorely missed. Without his sure aim, the milling cavalry thinned only slightly.

The distance to the river shrank to a quarter league. Pisaqar's right hand grew numb from firing dozens of arrows. His callused palms cracked open, and the butts of the arrows he loosed were greased with blood. In his three decades of war, he'd never seen so many arrows unleashed in so short a time to such small effect. The arrows Amani handed him were dulled and frayed from reuse. They wavered in flight and fell well short.

Yesbokhe regained consciousness and gave away arrows he found amid the treasure hoard. Each was its own work of art. Letting them fly was painful; the bowstring had begun to cut into Pisaqar's joints. But the new arrows immediately proved their worth. Flying far and fast, they slew another pair of horses and several men besides. The Assyrians ceased shooting and retreated to a safe distance.

"They're giving up!" Tariq cheered.

"More like they're out of arrows," said Qorobar, showcasing his empty quiver.

Pisaqar was dismayed to find that the other Mice were little better off. "Six bows and ten arrows between us," he said after they'd finished counting. "If they choose to push us at the riverbank, we cannot repel them."

Kalab eyed their precious cargo. "We can leave the treasure behind. It isn't worth our lives."

"Ermun would have been proud to hear you say that, Kalab. If we must discard it, we will."

The cavalry kept their distance as the mercenaries closed in on the Nile. The cart rolled onto the black silt deposited by the receded waters. Ahead, propped on the shore amid the young reeds, sat their boat, its deck piled high with carefully bundled treasure they'd already ferried down. They whooped joyfully.

"Pepy! Wake up, you fat old stud!" hollered Tariq.

Pepy-Nakht waddled out of his cabin. He waved his arms from the prow. With the climbing sun behind him, only the boatmaster's smile was visible. His eyes were hidden in shadow.

Pisaqar called, "Ready the boat, Pepy! We must leave now!"

Pepy didn't react to them. He merely kept on waving. Tariq's grin slowly dropped away. "What's he doing?"

Which was when Pisaqar saw that the boatmaster's eyes weren't in silhouette at all. They were gone. Gouged out. The bloody trails running down his cheeks touched the corners of a mouth formed into a pained grimace.

"A trap!"

Men rose from the gunwales, men with shields and spears. Shoving the listless boatmaster onto the deck, they splashed down in the shallows and formed a line, their movements quick and efficient. These were drilled soldiers—and not all of them wore Assyrian scales. Half the score of men had on kilts, their hair in neat black coifs, with scarabs worn prominently at their throats.

"It seems the proud Assyrians have hired mercenaries of their own," Pisaqar observed sourly.

"Bloody *traitors*." Qorobar spat on the ground.

The sound of hoofbeats heralded the arrival of enemy cavalry. The horsemen closed into a semicircle. They dismounted, drawing their short swords. It appeared they'd indeed used up all their arrows—a lone advantage in a lopsided fight. The enemy had forty blades against the Mice's eight.

The Kushites put their backs up against the cart, facing outward as the enemy began tightening the noose. The acolyte murmured a prayer to Sekhmet. The redhead and the thief squeezed hands. The medicine man laid a kiss above the Apis's eye, his bag of holies sealed. The Israelite raised his chin, baring his neck to Yahweh or Ashur or both. The scout lay insensate—a rare mercy for a warrior, to die sleeping. The foreman guzzled down a jug of warm beer. The big man weighed his axe in his hands.

Looking to Pisaqar, he said, "If Osiris doesn't let me through, tell Pakheme…" His voice broke.

Pisaqar reached out and gripped his wrist. "We will all meet him together."

A new voice rose, its sonorous tone spiced with foreign vowels. "Your Desert Mice have made a good account of themselves, Pisaqar of Kush." The man stood behind his spearmen, cleverly shielding himself from any chance shot from his vengeful prey. He'd affected black iron scales, a crimson cape, and a meticulously squared beard.

Amani called, "Is this where you make us a generous offer? Get fucked!"

The Assyrian captain stood unperturbed until the chorus of taunts had subsided. "I am Ashurizkadain the Flayer. King Sennacherib has commissioned me to make him a gift of your skins. The manner in which I strip them from your bodies, I leave to you, Pisaqar. Surrender, and I shall grant you easy deaths. Give battle, and I shall flay you alive."

The Mice sagged as the last hope of escape was denied them. Pisaqar stilled a fresh outburst from Amani. "Is that what you did to Rukhmire? His family?"

"The guardsman has perished. If you give me reason to punish his kin, I shall do as Ashur wills."

Nibamon moaned in anguish.

Pisaqar drew his sword. The whispers of metal on leather announced that the others had done the same. The enemy soldiers moved forward a step, but a bark from Ashurizkadain stopped their advance. Pisaqar ignored them all. He rested his forehead against the flat of the blade. "Amun, guide my hand," he murmured.

Ashurizkadain cocked his head. "Is that to be all? Would you not even attempt to bargain for all these lives in your keeping?"

"I have nothing to offer that you will not simply take," declared Pisaqar. "You have made your intention plain. Mine is to fight you to the last."

The Flayer's face lit with an expansive smile. "Then die knowing this: when you go scraping before your pallorous god of death, you will be raw, and red, and weeping. Your ebon skins shall adorn—"

An arrow whistled past Pisaqar's ear. Ashurizkadain's eyes went round. He began to duck, but fortunately for him, the soldier guarding him was quick with his shield. The arrow was deflected. Rather than sink into the Flayer's throat, it glanced off his helmet, shattering on impact. Flying splinters scored his cheek. He flinched, clutching the bleeding scratches.

"Man needed to shut up," Yesbokhe said with an ashen grin. His bow slipped from his hand, and he sank amid his torn bandages, never to stand again.

The enemy soldiers raised a cry, but the Kushites were already charging. Pisaqar made directly for Ashurizkadain, leading with his sword. The enemy shields shivered as the last Kushite arrows *thunk*ed into them, the powerful close-range shots breaking their planks. Even as Tariq and Qorobar tossed away their bows, Amani's sling stones caterwauled into the fraying line, breaking teeth and pulping eyeballs. The line of spear tips was wavering as Pisaqar closed the remaining distance. An Assyrian with a red-feathered dart protruding from his neck sluggishly raised his spear to impale him, but Kalab's sweeping khopesh yanked its point aside, enabling Pisaqar to twirl along its shaft and hack the man down with a collar stroke. The Assyrian folded in a spray of bright arterial blood.

Pisaqar launched over the thrashing body into the thick of the enemy line. Bowing low, he chopped into the back of a Saite mercenary's knee and finished the howling man with a thrust through the ribs. The man beyond got his shield around to block the follow-up, but only succeeded in leaving an opening for Qorobar. The berserker's axe clove into his skull. Qorobar took the convulsing man by the neck and hurled him, with one arm, onto an Assyrian sword. Before the soldier could pry his weapon free, Qorobar opened his ribcage to the sun, all the while shrieking like a condemned soul. The Assyrians and Saites nearby drew back in instinctive terror.

Pisaqar felt an impact on his back and spun around. Tariq rolled at his feet, pummeling an Assyrian kidney bare-fisted. Amani darted in from someplace and slit the enemy's throat with her blackstone dagger. She grabbed the fallen man's sword and flung it, spinning point over pommel, at a pair of charging cavalrymen, who had to scurry to avoid being slashed. Nawidemaq promptly broke one's elbow using his staff before killing him with a swift blow to the base of the skull. As the other tried to back away, Nibamon slew him with a golden sword, and sloppily. Beyond them, Eleazar chopped the great white bull out of its harness. The beast erupted into motion, stampeding the enemies who'd ringed the cart, horns goring, hooves stamping and kicking. The Assyrians weren't lacking in bravery. They stood in the path of the onslaught, closing ranks around the bull even as its rampage made pulped cadavers of their brethren. The beast was soon kneeling on its forelegs, crosshatched with bleeding slices. Only Eleazar, fending at them with a scavenged spear, prevented them from felling the bull for good.

Pisaqar found that his own string of fights had carried him into the shallows. A bald Assyrian hacked at him, and the silt tugged at his sandals as he twisted to deflect the repeated blows. He started to back up, but the Nile betrayed him and sent him splashing amid the broken reeds. He attempted to push himself back up, but his arm sank elbow-deep in the soft riverbed. The enemy moved to finish him, only for the mischievous river to make a fool of him in turn, causing him to lose his footing and fall. Pisaqar wallowed on top of him while he lay prone, grabbed a fistful of one ear, and forced the man's head beneath the muddy water. The Assyrian struggled fiercely, but Pisaqar spotted the knife at the man's belt. He fumbled it from its sheath and drove it into the back of his neck, again and again until the water turned from brown to red and the struggling ceased.

"Ashurizkadain!" he roared. The shallows roiled with the ferocious struggle. The corpses of the enemy spearmen bobbed where they'd been slain. Pisaqar couldn't see the Assyrian captain among them. Nor was there any sign of him in the teeming ranks of enemy cavalrymen now sprinting for the riverbank.

With a sickened heart, Pisaqar saw an Assyrian junior officer plunge a spear into Eleazar's side, driving him to his knees. The Israelite snarled, his teeth glistening red. With a supreme effort, snapped the head off the spear, leaving it embedded in his guts. The Assyrian dropped the broken haft but crumpled as Eleazar's sword punched through his ribs. Eleazar swayed where he knelt. His last shuddering act was to slap his blade against the bull's flank. Thus freed, the loyal Apis tottered toward its remaining friends, bleeding profusely. Eleazar fell on his face behind it, still clutching his sword.

The bull joined the Kushites in the shallows. Its hide glistened with sticky blood. The Desert Mice were little better off. Qorobar was a frightful sight, his cheek laid open, his smashed molars clearly visible. Tariq's sword arm hung limp, cut to the bone. Kalab, the finest warrior among them, had lost his khopesh and was covered in bleeding cuts. Amani swayed on her feet, gripping a deep gash across her right shoulder blade. Nawidemaq had lost all the fingers of his left hand, evidently by the same blow that had chopped his holy staff in two. Nibamon, miraculously, was unharmed. His eyes had the crazed look of a cornered animal.

Ashurizkadain appeared on the edge of the river. "Hold!" he ordered his much-diminished force. "See how they bleed! Allow them to weaken first!"

"What's he saying?" slurred Tariq.

"He wants to let us succumb to our wounds," Pisaqar said. He cast a look at the boat, where poor blind Pepy rolled about in confused agony. The Kushites could attempt to run, but he knew the Assyrians would cut them down the moment they attempted to scale the gunwales.

His Mice seemed to shrink as they reached the same conclusion. "Damn, but we came close," said Kalab.

"When I go to the next world," Pisaqar told them all, "I will face Osiris's trials with a light heart. It is an honor to meet my end at your sides."

They lifted their weapons and steeled themselves for their final charge. The Assyrians prepared to meet them.

If Ashurizkadain had saved a last taunt for the occasion, his words were lost in the blast of war horns.

From the desert brightness hurtled a wave of chariots—dozens of them packed into a dense mass of blues and golds, pulled by teams of handsome Dongolan purebreds. The air reverberated with the rattling of studded wheels and the joined thunder of hundreds of hooves—and just audible above it, the keening of Kushite arrows. The clustered Assyrians made an easy target for the first volley.

"Spread yourselves!" bellowed Ashurizkadain as the arrow barrage hammered into his ranks, sending many of his men toppling. The survivors scrambled to obey his orders, hunched over with their heads turned aside as if striding into a gale. But in truth, they merely faced a choice of deaths. The wall of chariots kept on sweeping straight toward their fragmented line.

Pisaqar recoiled as an arrow hissed into the water between his legs. There were so many arrows flying that the river fairly boiled with stray shots. They would die for certain if they lingered. "Aboard the boat!"

Sluggish from their wounds, the Desert Mice did their best to hurry. Pisaqar climbed the side first, ripping out fistfuls of reeds in his haste. He dropped over the railing and trod on poor Pepy-Nakht, who raised his hands and whimpered. "Help us, Pepy!" he shouted as he hauled the eyeless boatmaster to a seated position. Pepy managed to get his feet under himself and joined Pisaqar at the railing. Bending over it, they dragged the panting Mice out of the water. Nawidemaq set down the ramp for the bull and hauled on the wounded animal's lead line until it had clomped aboard. Tariq quickly set about slashing the anchor lines. The rest of them grabbed poles and stabbed them into the river. With much pushing and prying, the boat haltingly slid off the riverbed and drifted into deeper water. Amani climbed the mast to drop the sail. It billowed as it caught the wind.

Meanwhile, the chariots did their grisly work. The Assyrians were trained soldiers, but with all their arrows spent and spears broken, there was little they could do but prolong their own slaughter. They sheltered from the rain of arrows behind half-ruined shields. They hurled the detritus of battle toward the enemy, but made no impression whatsoever on the onrushing war machines, which, having spent their arrows, plunged into their line. The doomed Assyrians faced death in stoic silence, spoiled somewhat by the terrorized Saite mercenaries, who moaned in terror as the chariots fell upon them. Hooves mashed their bodies into the soft earth. Wheels rolled through the carnage, pink entrails dangling from their spokes. The cruel procession murdered its way through them. What few Assyrians managed to escape the massacre tried wading into the open water, only to be stuck through by gusts of javelins. Their corpses sank into the foaming water, weighed down by their armor.

Tariq dragged himself to the railing, where he joined Pisaqar in watching the chariots wheel around the scarlet shore.

Presently, the chariot archers hopped down and began slashing the throats of the wounded, the first of the ignoble rites that followed every battle. They'd begin looting the bodies before long.

"Revenge for what they did to the men at Eltekeh," Tariq said grimly.

"These Assyrians likely fought in that battle," agreed Pisaqar. "They deserve it well enough."

Qorobar came up, a thick bandage of honeyed lint pressed to his face. "They'll be counting the right hands, soon." He left unspoken the implication that the charioteers would take Yesbokhe's and Eleazar's hands as well, mistaking them for enemy corpses to add to their awful tally. Another fight abandoned, more friends left behind to be casually mutilated and discarded.

Pisaqar swallowed his bitterness. "We will make sacrifices in their names," he swore. Tariq and Qorobar nodded, their expressions glum.

"But why did the chariots come?" asked Tariq. "Who sent them to our rescue?"

Pisaqar turned his eyes away from the slaughter and looked upriver. The southerly breeze coaxed them south, toward what he was certain would be an unwelcome answer.

"Look what I've found!" called Kalab. Pisaqar ran to the stern, where the heavily bandaged acolyte was leaning over the railing.

"By Amun, can we not be rid of you?" he groaned.

Ashurizkadain clung to the reed hull with clawed fingers. He gazed up at his would-be prey with burning eyes.

Pisaqar curled his lip. "An honorable leader would have died with his men. Instead, this one slinks away when no one is looking."

Kalab gave Pisaqar a quizzical look and raised his pole. "Should I shove the miserable shit off?"

The Assyrian leered. "Pull me up, Pisaqar of Kush. I promise I will be a good guest."

"It's a bad idea, making a house pet of a serpent," warned Kalab.

Pisaqar shut his eyes and shook his head. "An unarmed man asks for mercy." He reached over. "Come up, Assyrian. You will not be harmed, much as you have earned it."

Ashurizkadain took his hand. Pisaqar fully expected to lose it to a concealed blade, but the beaten man allowed himself to be rescued without a fuss. He flopped on the deck, dripping and breathing hard. Amani quickly bound his wrists with rough movements as the others gathered around, boring into their enemy with hateful stares.

He met their gazes with studied indifference. "How unjust, that such a rabble has weaseled its way to victory."

"Twice," sneered Tariq. "Twice we've done that, don't forget. We fucked you over at Jerusalem, too."

"Indeed," Ashurizkadain said amiably.

"What was your intent?" inquired Pisaqar. "I suppose you meant to wait in the water until nightfall, and then slit our throats while we slept."

He shrugged as best he could, bound as he was from wrist to elbow. "Is that so different from what you did outside Jerusalem? That is why I was sent. To deliver my king's justice. Your ends would have been fittingly ironic, given the crime. Alas."

"And what of your own crimes?"

"Which crimes?"

"You posed as Egyptian soldiers. A lie. You invaded Egypt in violation of our kings' treaty. An oath forsworn. You killed innocents. Murder. Those are merely the crimes I know of! Surely you have committed far worse."

Another shrug. "Doing a king's bidding is the precise opposite of sin. But suppose I err. Would you not be guilty of the same accusations you level at me? We are both mercenaries, in a way. Our kings entrust us with tasks that would leave their names sullied. It is true, I have broken the peace with Egypt. But you have done the same in Libya, and Lydia, and even Judah, before your Pharaoh Shabaku saw fit to take King Hezekiah as an ally. You have sinned in your pharaoh's name and called it duty. Deny it if you like, but you know we are quite the same. If I am a criminal, then so are you.

"And for what this truth is worth, those innocents—the guard's family? They live. I have kept them in a little farmhouse upriver, among a copse of five trees. It has a blue door. They might still live if you find them soon."

"Your liar's grin says otherwise."

"I care not what you think of me. I smile because I know one day they, too, will be servants of Assyria. You have seen it, Pisaqar. Corruption. Stagnancy. Grift. You know in your heart that Egypt's best days are long gone, never to return. Your victory in Judah merely delays what is to come. Assyria will rule Egypt in the end. Be certain of it."

Pisaqar inclined his head. "Perhaps. Perhaps not. Mostly, I grow weary of listening to you talk. Qorobar, gag him. This way I can consider his fate in blessed silence."

Nawidemaq suggested, "Make Marduk a gift of Assyrian flesh."

"Turn him into a eunuch first," added Amani.

"No." Pisaqar watched Qorobar cinch a rope tight between the captive's teeth. He squatted in front of him. "I will not harm a prisoner. That is the difference between you and me, Flayer. Mere decency."

Tariq touched his shoulder. Pointing over the railing, he said, "There's a chariot following us on the shore."

Pisaqar's last small hope of escape sank. Feeling tired and ill, he loped to the railing. Just as Tariq had said, a chariot trundled along just beyond the line of reeds, an enormous machine pulled by four long-limbed white geldings. In its golden cab towered a bare-chested man with deep ebon skin, a leopard-skin cloak, a golden skull cap, and a pleated kilt.

General Taharqa lifted his hand in greeting. "Hail, Pisaqar! Come ashore, my old friend! We have matters to discuss!"

The Mice stared at the general in dead silence, broken only by the swish of waves and their captive's muffled laughter.

"Well, that's it then," Kalab muttered. "After all that trouble. Stakes up the asses for everybody."

Taharqa must have noted the mood, but didn't comment on it. "Pisaqar, I have boats waiting for you upriver. Come now, let us not trouble ourselves with such nonsense. Let us settle this here, man to man. Neither you nor your men will come to harm." He seemed to squint, adding, "Nor the girl."

Pisaqar called, "Do you swear on it?"

"I swear, on my undying *ka*!"

Pisaqar told the Mice, "To the oars. Bring us ashore."

"He's broken his word before," said Kalab. "This all happened because of him."

"I know. But you heard him. If we go up the Nile, his boats will kill us all."

"What if he's lying about that too?" speculated Amani.

"This is our only choice. We go ashore," Pisaqar said firmly.

With a whisper of reeds and a heavy lurch, the hull bit the riverbed. By then, more chariots had closed in, still spattered with Assyrian blood. Only Taharqa's remained pristine. The general waited on the dry shore as Pisaqar waded to him. Pisaqar's bones ached from hours of battle, but he kept his head high. Only as he reached his old student did he fall to his knees.

"General Taharqa," he said to the Nile's silt. Taharqa had affected soldier's sandals in abrupt contrast to his emerald necklace and golden armbands. Appealing to the common man while overawing him—clever, but vulgar.

"There is no need to kneel before me, Teacher." Taharqa gently lifted him by the elbows, generosity personified. He frowned as he looked over Pisaqar's shoulder. "I see you've taken a prisoner."

Soldiers had already climbed aboard the boat. They busied themselves disarming the Desert Mice, politely and firmly. Swords, daggers, bows, and Qorobar's axe clattered on the deck. The mercenaries sat against the railings in impotent rage as they were stripped of their hard-won finery. Precious metals and stones they'd hidden about themselves were found and pocketed with unvarnished glee. Ashurizkadain, ostentatiously foreign, was separated from the other prisoners and shoved down the gangplank by a burly Kushite. He tumbled unceremoniously into the river. He emerged spraying muddy water through his gag.

"Ashurizkadain the Flayer," said Pisaqar. "Sennacherib dispatched him to fetch our skins."

Taharqa chuckled. "Senanmuht has made me quite aware." He studied Ashurizkadain with casual contempt as the Assyrian captain struggled in the brown shallows. "How vile. Telqo, see to him."

The Kushite hopped down and planted a foot between the Flayer's shoulders as he fought to rise. Ashurizkadain vanished beneath the river. His kicking feet thrashed the surface while the Kushite calmly pressed him into the silt.

"I doubt Sennacherib will miss a man he sent on such a suicidal mission," Taharqa said without a hint of care, and as Pisaqar watched Ashurizkadain's movements slow, he couldn't find a reason to disagree.

Qorobar, though, was not finished. "General," he called from the deck, "let me be the one to end him! We have business to finish, him and me."

Taharqa considered this, then nodded to his man. Ashurizkadain came back up sputtering as the soldier released him. Whatever relief he might have felt did not last long. Qorobar, his bonds cut, landed beside him, axe in hand. He took a handful of the Flayer's collar guard and dragged him out of the river, trudging methodically toward a lone palm tree further down the bank.

Pisaqar watched his true enemy go with some small measure of pity. It was true, what Taharqa had said: Ashurizkadain's king had sent the man uncaringly to his death. But the captain more than suspected that Taharqa hadn't expected *him* to return from the Assyrian lines outside Jerusalem, either.

We were both tools, he thought. *We were the same, only not for the reasons you thought.*

"Tell me how you came to rob Ramesses' tomb," said Taharqa, the small matter already forgotten.

He did as he was commanded. The general listened with growing astonishment as his old teacher delivered the tale. As Pisaqar regaled him, the fruits of his labors were hauled bit by bit from the cargo hold to be stacked on the river's edge, the pharaoh's treasure gleaming in the sunlight it had never been intended to witness.

"A stunning achievement," Taharqa commented once the tale had drawn to a close.

"I lost several friends seeing it through." Pisaqar barely bothered to conceal his anger. He knew Taharqa wasn't unloading the treasure merely to gawk at it. Once again, the Desert Mice were about to be cheated.

Taharqa at least put on a show of remorse. "A tragedy for which you have my deepest sympathy. Much must be sacrificed in the name of Egypt. It's with that same aim—"

Pisaqar gritted his teeth so hard they creaked.

"—that I must lay claim to this wealth. I'm sure you understand."

"I am afraid I do not. What will you do with it all, Taharqa? Does it go to Assyria as further tribute? You seem keen to satisfy King Sennacherib with gold."

"You wound me, Teacher." Taharqa clutched his breast as if physically struck. "As you've spent much sweat and blood prying this treasure from the ground, I at least owe you the truth. None of this will find its way to the royal treasury."

It was Pisaqar's turn to be astonished. "You would claim all this for yourself?"

"No! Understand Egypt's predicament. We hobble ourselves with tribute to Assyria, an enormous debt that Shabaku must pass to the nobility and the priesthood. You know yourself how fractious these people are under even the best of circumstances. Imagine the state of affairs after just a few years of heavy taxation. It will take a steady hand to prevent Egypt from dissolving into the factionalism we've spent our lives quelling. A strong hand. Shabaku is ailing, not long for this life. His son, Shebitku, is but a callow youth. He is not one to follow."

Pisaqar at last understood. "And then there is you."

"Taharqa, victor of Jerusalem, favorite servant of Pharaoh Shabaku. With this treasure, I will have vast wealth to back the fame and influence I've already won. This gift you have given me will serve to pacify Egypt. When Assyria breaks the peace, we will stand against them as one nation."

There was no humor in Pisaqar's smile. "Led by the strong, steady hand of Pharaoh Taharqa."

"Is it not a worthy cause?" Taharqa challenged, his tone carrying just enough of an edge to make clear the threat it bore. Pisaqar paused. He considered that perhaps he had taught young Taharqa a little too well. Such ambition—he should have seen where it would lead.

To Egypt's salvation. Or its servitude.

All that was certain was that the wheels of history were grinding on. If he chose to lie in their path, he would be crushed asunder. As would the ones he loved.

He bowed his head. He hated how much of a relief it was to submit. "Egypt will always be a worthy cause, Taharqa. Do with the treasure as you will."

Taharqa visibly relaxed. "I knew you would see reason."

"I have only one boon to ask of you."

Taharqa wiped his expression clean. "I will hear it."

"My Desert Mice served you well at Jerusalem. For reasons I know were beyond your control, we finished the campaign without seeing payment. This venture was my attempt to see the debt put right. They labored long and hard. I ask a mere pittance for them in return."

"Ah, Pisaqar," sighed Taharqa with a pitying smile, "you were ever the best and most selfless of Egypt's servants. I regret that you have passed these most admirable of traits to your student. My eyes must remain fixed on the greater goal. And thus, it is with boundless regret that I must deny your request. I hope your people will be able to comfort themselves knowing they've been granted their lives, despite committing what you know to be a capital offense. Do you agree?"

Pisaqar bowed his head once more. He understood, comprehensively now, how badly he had failed the earnest boy Taharqa had once been. The knowledge would have disappointed him, had it not been so unsurprising.

"I agree, and I understand. It was my duty to ask. I do have some last counsel to offer."

Taharqa hoisted his brows. "Oh?"

"It regards the Kingdom of Judah. We agree that Assyria will one day return, whether under King Sennacherib or a successor. I suggest that in such an event, the Assyrians must first march south—through Judah. In which case, it would be best that they face a strong, united kingdom there. I suggest that some of this wealth," he gestured to the vast pile, "find its way to King Hezekiah in Jerusalem."

After a long pause, Taharqa nodded. "Your counsel is most prudent. And appreciated."

Where sympathy had failed to win, naked cynicism had succeeded. Pisaqar could at least content himself knowing that Eleazar's goal was fulfilled. Judah could never withstand a full-fledged Assyrian invasion, he knew. But they were at least owed the chance to resist.

"I have a request of my own, before I allow you to leave," the general said after a stretching pause.

"Of course."

Taharqa took a purposeful step forward, crowding him. His smile was cold. "Show me the tomb."

The tree was a small one, its trunk barely taller than Qorobar and two palms wide. It had a bit of a lean, which wasn't ideal. There would be better ones further down the bank, but this one would have to serve. Besides, the axe man was too tired to march any further. And the Assyrian would just keep struggling the whole way.

He tipped the self-styled Flayer off his shoulder and deposited him on the ground with a hollow thud. Something cracked. The Assyrian squawked through his gag. It occurred to Qorobar that the wretch might try to scurry off. Just to be sure, he flipped the man over, knelt on his sternum, grabbed a nearby stone, and set about breaking his knees. Again, the miserable bastard wallowed about and made all sorts of noise, and the thing took longer than it ought.

"Quit mewling or I'll do your elbows too," Qorobar rumbled.

With tremendous effort, the Assyrian got his breathing under control. He tried to say something.

Against his better judgment, the axe man ripped his gag out. "There. Careful with your words. I'd rather this be a short conversation, and gods know you're terrible at those."

"You wish to kill me," wheezed Ashurizkadain. He bared his throat invitingly. "Be done with it. Spare us further difficulty."

"It's no trouble," Qorobar said agreeably. He hefted his axe, but to the Assyrian's disappointment, he turned his back and walked over to the tree instead. Then he got to chopping. Stringy bark flew, and his axe soon bit into green wood.

Though Ashurizkadain did as he was told and kept quiet, Qorobar sensed his growing dread. He likely knew exactly what was about to happen to him. There was some satisfaction in the knowledge—less than he might've felt a month ago, before he'd glimpsed the land of Duat, but still. This was a debt that needed paying. A balance to be redressed.

Between huffing blows, he said to his watchful prisoner, "You mentioned ... you were going ... to skin us."

"As was my duty," Ashurizkadain said, his mellifluous voice taut with hurt and fear. "I would have done this thing cleanly, had your captain permitted."

"After you killed us, you mean to say."

"Yes."

"Mind your head." With a squeal of young wood, the tree twisted around and fell. Its branches rustled as the top half landed, leaving Qorobar to face a stump about navel high. That would do nicely. He set about clearing the leafy top away. Once the area was tidy, he took his axe again and started hewing at the top of the stump with oblique chops, lopping off chunks of soft, yellowish wood.

Pausing for breath, he regarded his prisoner. "It that what you did with Pakheme?"

The Assyrian met his gaze. Though his mouth grimaced, there was no hint of his agony in his calm black eyes. "Ah. The one you left at Jerusalem."

The big man nodded once.

"He was days perished by the time he was given to me. But indeed. His skin graces my king's court."

Qorobar closed his eyes. He had known, even as he howled at the barred city gate, that the Assyrians would mistreat Pakheme's body. Now he knew for certainty. The hard truth burned. But still, not as much as it might have, before he'd seen his love's face again. Though Pakheme's mortal flesh was defiled, his *ka* had still made it to Osiris's throne and beyond. In the end, that was what truly mattered.

And yet the debt remained.

He turned back to carving the stump. By now, it had taken on a dull point. "Maybe it will cheer you up to think about that, in coming days."

Judging by Ashurizkadain's silence, he knew exactly what the choice of words meant.

Deeming the job done, Qorobar dusted his hands and approached the Assyrian, who'd turned very pale. He hoisted the Flayer off the ground. The man screamed. His broken legs dangled as Qorobar held him up, staring into his eyes.

"It's going to take some time for you to go," he informed him. "In case I hadn't made that plain."

"As Ashur wills," panted the Assyrian.

Qorobar cocked his head. "Isn't that your name? Ashurizkadain. Must mean something."

"It means, 'Ashur punishes the wicked.'"

"Ah." Qorobar nodded. "Well then."

Ashurizkadain landed belly first on the stake with a moist crunch.

EPILOGUE

NAWIDEMAQ SQUATTED ATOP the ruined wall of the gatehouse, taking great interest in the flies crawling over his hand. One of the gods had seen fit to claim his fingers in the previous week's battle. Another god—or perhaps the same one—had sent this swarm to feast on the pus leaking through his bandage. All part of some plan, he had no doubt, for the gods were ever laying their schemes, each trying to outdo the next in a mischievous game they'd been playing since the creation of time.

He considered that one of these flies might ride the wind to Thebes, where she might land in a priest's stew, making him ill enough to misinterpret a supplicant's dream, thus setting that crucial person's life on a new course and upending the board. Such were the games the gods played—of grandiose schemes hatched and foiled across the breadth of eternity.

Of course, this was mere speculation on his part. The business of the gods was not truly his to know. He was only a mortal.

But he did see the detritus of their cosmic rivalries in the faces of Taharqa's men as they rode their chariots past Set-Ma'at. Hopes dashed, efforts squandered. They all looked crestfallen. And damp.

He wondered how many of their comrades had drowned trying to swim through that flooded tunnel. Likely more than a few, for several of the chariots held but a single rider. Their fruitless swims had left most of the rest sodden. And empty handed, every last one of them. The torchless procession spoke of many hours grasping through the inky dark, only to emerge, shivering, into Set's cool night. Or Ereshkigal's, if the question were put to the Babylonians.

Taharqa looked bitterest of all. He swung his gargantuan chariot into the shadow of the gatehouse and reined in the horses so quickly that the war machine skidded sideways to a halt. The would-be pharaoh very nearly ended his vast ambitions smeared across a mud-brick wall. The gods had evidently decreed otherwise.

With a near murderous expression, the general nodded to Pisaqar's bow, permitting the captain to step down. No sooner had Pisaqar done this than Taharqa pitilessly lashed at his horse team. His fury sent them out into the sloping desert at a hot gallop.

Pisaqar watched his former student vanish into the night, his own expression concealed in shadow. When he looked up at Nawidemaq, though, he was smiling again. "Well, they fell for it."

Nawidemaq scattered the flies. His bare feet thudded the sand. "I prayed for your success. Damu claimed my pus as payment."

Pisaqar accepted this claim imperturbably. It was one of the reasons Nawidemaq liked him. "Your efforts are always well appreciated, my friend. How fares the bull, our own Apis?" They began to stroll down the dim street. Up ahead, notes of boisterous song rose from amid the smoke of a cookfire.

"His wounds bind. He must sleep for some days."

"Sleep does sound wonderful," agreed Pisaqar. "A fortnight of rest for everyone, I think. A chance for our wounds and our hearts to heal. Besides, Taharqa might well have second thoughts about leaving us so quickly."

In the corner house, the glowing window was momentarily blocked as someone peeked out. “He’s back,” said Tariq’s muffled voice.

The door swung open, and the mercenaries spilled into the dusk to greet their captain, all covered in honeyed lint bandages and with cups of beer in their hands, for its healing properties were well known to all. Of course, no amount of beer would bring back Pepy-Nakht’s sight. But the boatmaster, hobbling along with a hand on Qorobar’s shoulder, could at least content himself knowing he would be fabulously rich for his trouble. So would Senet and her children, whom Ashurizkadain had left unharmed, if only as a last taunt. Nibamon stayed in the doorway beside his grieving sister. Nawidemaq was certain that whatever path the foreman chose for himself, he would make Rukhmire’s family a part of it.

The Kushites gathered around Pisaqar with tentative smiles. “Let’s have it, then,” said Qorobar, wincing with every word as the stitches yanked his torn cheek.

“Taharqa lost five men in the flooded tunnel,” said Pisaqar. “In the end, one got through. He found precisely what I said he would: an empty sarcophagus. That was enough. They have all gone.”

Amani asked, “How’d Taharqa take it? Bastard must have been *livid*.” She smirked at the thought.

“He did what great men do when the world fails to bend their way. He raged.”

Kalab nodded in satisfaction. “He’ll have more rude surprises in store. Ramesses already had his way with us. That curse will follow our dear general now. He might get the double crown someday, but it’ll get smacked right off his head. He’ll live to watch all his accomplishments crumble. Then he’ll die forgotten. He’ll be denied the immortality he wants most.”

The redhead looked at the acolyte sideways. “That’s awfully grim of you, Kalab.”

"You should have heard the way Ramesses said it. It was dire stuff."

"So," said Qorobar, "the general just ends up the same way as us. No one will remember him. Or Yesbokhe. Or Eleazar. Or Rukhmire. Or Ermun." He paused. "Or Pakheme. That doesn't sound like justice to me."

Nawidemaq clicked his tongue. "We are little pieces. The gods move us. We do not decide where."

There was a lengthy pause, which it fell to Pisaqar to finally break. "Nawidemaq alone has learned the lesson the Valley of the Kings ought to have taught us all. Think of it, my friends. Many pharaohs spent centuries picking the limestone here in search of immortality. They devoted their entire lives to the preparation, and the lives of countless others. Men to dig their tombs. Men to embalm their corpses. Men to pray at their temples. They molded an entire civilization to fulfill the rituals of death. See where their efforts led." He indicated the abandoned shells around them. "Ruin and decay. Their treasure is all gone. Their bodies have been smashed. For all their precautions, their sole reward was to share in the same oblivion as the toiling people they ruled.

"It is the inescapable lot of every man and woman to die and be forgotten. Let us not obsess over the things we cannot change. Before we die, let us live first. That is the gift of our departed friends: the surpassingly rare chance to live well."

He sniffed the air. "Is that roasted lamb I smell, Kalab?"

The acolyte grinned. "I traded an emerald for a little jar of salt."

"These priests and their culinary delights," sighed Tariq, following them toward the house and the wafting scent of seasoned meat. Amani slunk up to him and draped his arm around her shoulders.

"We might take him on as a cook, once we open that place," she suggested. "If he's anywhere near as good as Ermun was."

Qorobar lumbered after them. "You'll need a big fellow to guard the door, I reckon. Nibamon, you ever thought about brewing beer instead of just guzzling it all the time?"

"It can't be too complicated. Though I'd rather do the second thing," admitted Nibamon as the Kushites filed past him into Senet's house.

The woman frowned at her little brother. "Where's all this supposed to happen, now?"

"As far from this damned place as humanly possible."

That satisfied her.

"It's settled, then," cried Tariq. "On to Kush! Together!"

Nawidemaq spared a glance for the undying stars, and fancied that he felt the innumerable gods gazing back down on him in turn. Already, he was thinking of all the delectable southern plants he could introduce to his bull. No more mouthfuls of thorns or stabbing Assyrian blades. A life of peace and plenty. Their Apis had earned it. They all had.

Then he looked west, to the purpled sky surmounting the black peaks, beneath which the remainder of the Robber Pharaoh's hoard lay. Perhaps when they were finished with it, they would honor their fallen friends with a royal burial.

The medicine man smiled to himself. Ah, such plans! He wondered which of the fickle gods would seek to meddle in them first. Schemes dreamt up and foiled—such was the way of things. What could a mortal do but seek some enjoyment in the calm waters between the swirling eddies?

Pisaqar lingered at the door, waiting on him. Inside, the others had already begun to sing. "Nawidemaq? Will you not leave the gods be for just a few moments? Come feast with your friends."

"The gods will wait," he said, moving toward the door. "Never for too long."

THE END

ABOUT THE AUTHOR

THOMAS KRUG LIVES outside Philadelphia with his wife and two sons. He studied newswriting at the University of Scranton, and saw service in Afghanistan as a U.S. Army officer.